The
Wanderers

" we are not human beings
on a spiritual journey
– we are spiritual beings
on a human journey "

The
Wanderers

Naomi Gladish Smith

CHRYSALIS BOOKS
WEST CHESTER, PENNSYLVANIA

Library of Congress Cataloging-in-Publication Data
Smith, Naomi Gladish
The Wanderers / Naomi Gladish Smith

p. cm.
ISBN-13: 978-0-87785-322-0
1. Future life—Fiction. 2. Hell—Fiction. 3. Heaven–Fiction. I. Title.
PS3619.M5923W36 2007
813'.6—dc22
2006035203

Edited by Mary Lou Bertucci
Design by Karen Connor
Set in Minion by Karen Connor

Printed in the United States of America.

Chrysalis Books is an imprint of the Swedenborg Foundation, Inc.
For more information, contact:

Chrysalis Books
Swedenborg Foundation Publishers
320 N. Church Street
West Chester, Pennsylvania 19380
(610) 430-3222
Or
www.swedenborg.com

Cover Photograph: Seth Goldfarb/Getty Images

Again—to my family

But also to all the scribblers, past and present, whose works have delighted, inspired, and sustained me.

☾

· CAST OF CHARACTERS ·

Maggie Stevens
> A 20-year old former world-class gymnast,
> attempting a comeback in Frankfurt, Germany

Kate Douglas
> A middle-aged academic on sabbatical in Europe
> with her husband

Frank Chambers
> An ex-cop from Chicago, now at a Swiss cancer
> clinic

Patrick Riley
> A church organist, getting treatment at the same
> Swiss clinic

Marjorie Harrison
> A Midwestern socialite on a European tour

Sven and Clare
> A young couple (ages 19 and 16) running away
> from an American army base in Germany

Ryan James
> A traveler biking through Europe

The
Wanderers

1

I'm too old for this, Maggie thought. She looked over at the beam where Jacquie was performing an aerial cartwheel/back hand-spring. *That's how old you should be in this business, thirteen and counting, not twenty and trying for a comeback.* Maggie gave an appreciative nod as Jacquie nailed a full-twisting dismount and landed perfectly.

She braced her shoulders: *Don't think about Jacquie. Don't think of anything but the beam. Don't think of anything but getting through this practice.* Maggie stood still, breathed deep, rose to her toes and sprinted, arms and legs pumping. She felt good—scared, but good. Hardly aware of her bad ankle. But when she pushed off into the round-off, Maggie felt the adrenalin rush boost her a shade too high. She landed hard and her right foot slipped off the spring-board.

Don't try to pull out. Go through with it. Try to compensate and stretch into the back flip. Reach for the beam—lean to the left. Please, let me feel the beam. Let me push off and twist.

One hand brushed the beam. It did not find purchase. There was only blinding pain.

(

Maggie opened her eyes. Tubes were everywhere. A fat, white plastic one and thin, winding ones, red or clear, spread across her chest and up into the air like giant spider legs. Next to them hung bags of clear liquid, of yellow liquid, of red liquid. She felt no pain.

The beam. She'd pushed off too high into the round-off and missed the beam. She was in a hospital.

Where's Mom? No, she's in the States. Rose didn't have the money to hop on a plane and come to Germany. Besides, Mom wasn't in her life nowadays.

A doctor came into her field of vision, a nurse at his side. He leaned over her, then jerked upright and shouted something at the nurse as he pounded Maggie's chest. Maggie tried to raise a hand in protest, but her hand didn't move. She tried to lift her head. Nothing. It was like being enclosed in a giant cocoon that absorbed every straining attempt to push against it. She cried out, but no sound emerged.

The light exploded. No sound, just a flash of unbearable brilliance. Then, nothing.

℄

Kate Douglas looked into the valley below, then closed her eyes against a sudden swirl of vertigo. She shifted her position on the sun-warmed terra-cotta parapet, arching her shoulders and breathing deep against the pressure in her chest. She turned to look back at the hill-town church, hoping to see her husband picking his way over the slanted cobblestones. Another part of her, however, hoped Howard wouldn't emerge from the cool darkness of the little church until this heaviness in her chest eased, as it had the other times. This was not the way she'd intended to spend the last month of their joint sabbaticals. They'd gambled that the trip through Italy and Germany wouldn't exacerbate Howard's condition, and for the most part it hadn't. Ironically, what had happened were these increasingly alarming episodes. No, no, not alarming, just inconvenient.

There he was. Kate watched Howard's sandy-red head lower as he concentrated on maneuvering his canes over the uneven stones. Kate began to call out to him, but instead gasped as a sharp pain caught at her sternum. She sat absolutely still until the pain flickered, dwindled, and vanished.

Ah, yes, just a momentary stitch. Needn't worry Howard.

Kate forced a smile, grasped the carved stone of the balustrade, and pushed herself upright. She took one, then two unsteady steps before the hammer-pain split her chest.

((

"Come on, babe! We gotta get out of here before the storm gets any worse." The tow-headed boy shouldered his backpack and held the door open. The girl, just as blond and even younger than the boy, nodded. She tucked the blanket about the sleeping baby in the middle of the double bed and quickly pulled her motorcycle helmet over her stringy hair.

"You're sure Frau Blore'll get here before she wakes up?" said the boy.

The girl's milky complexion blushed a mottled pink. "Yes," she said, "sure." She ducked beneath his arm into the darkened hall, but then turned and came back to stand above the bed. She leaned to touch the curved fingers of the sleeping child.

"Careful," the boy said softly, "you'll wake her."

"She just ate; she's not going to wake up."

A lightning flash filled the room, followed immediately by a crack of thunder. The baby pursed pouted lips, flexed a tiny hand. Her eyes fluttered but did not open.

"Maybe we shouldn't take the bike on the Autobahn, not in weather like this," the girl whispered.

"Look, you want to go or not?" the boy said. "You're the one who's scared we'll wind up back on base with me in the brig."

"No, I want to go."

The girl buckled the helmet's chin strap. With one last look at the baby on the bed, she turned and headed blindly toward the patch of dark where the stairs angled down three floors to the street.

Another flash of lightning lit the room; a rolling smash of thunder shook the air. The boy reached the bed in three silent steps and stood a long moment over the still-sleeping baby. He backed away, closed the bedroom door gently, testing the knob to make certain it was locked, and hurried after the girl.

((

The white-clad doctor closed the chart with a snap. "I'm fairly certain Mr. Riley's not going to last the night," she said to the nurse. "Has he family here?"

"He hasn't had visitors since he came to the clinic," the nurse replied. "But that's not unusual for Americans. I'll check the chart for numbers to contact." She relaxed the stiff stance she'd assumed at the doctor's entrance and touched the blue-blotched arm resting on the white sheet. "He's one of the nice ones," she said softly. "No grumbling, no complaints, always a smile, even when the treatments didn't help."

"They come here too late and expect miracles." The doctor's pager beeped; she seemed relieved at the interruption. "That will be the patient in 374," she said, glancing at it. "Different diagnosis, but another American who waited to come to us until he'd tried everything else." She gave an impatient twitch of her shoulders. "I'm afraid he's another one who may not be with us tomorrow."

2

Maggie blinked at the early morning sunlight that streamed in the window. Where was she? Oh, yes. She'd fallen from the beam during practice. She was in a hospital, but not in ICU. She didn't think they had windows in ICU.

The tubes were gone! And no whooshing vacuum-cleaner sound. Maybe things weren't as bad as she'd thought. Cautiously, Maggie tried to lift her hand. Yes! It rose slightly. She gritted her teeth and concentrated on her foot, the one that had slipped from the springboard. It moved—Maggie was sure of it. She tried again, and this time she saw the blanket wiggle. She sank back and closed her eyes. Tears of relief crept from the corners of Maggie's closed eyes and fell to wet the pillow beneath her head.

⟪

Across the hall, Kate Douglas felt the sunshine touch her face, heard a gentle coo outside the window—a mourning dove?—but did not open her eyes. The cinnamon fragrance of petunias and the sweetness of wisteria induced her to look out from between slitted eyelids. As when she'd awakened before, there was no pain, no clutch at her chest. How marvelous! Her hand sought the space on the bed beside her. *Howard.* Kate turned from the sunlight, her lower lip caught in her teeth. No. She wouldn't think of Howard. Not now.

She remembered the words she's heard during her first awakening, a message so gently given it might not have been spoken aloud: "Don't worry, child. It will be well with you."

And she, middle-aged Kate Douglas, had felt like a comforted child, had known without a doubt that indeed all would be well. She'd rested, then dressed and gone to explore the hospital where she'd met other newcomers like herself. It really was all so wonderful. If it weren't for Howard . . . .

"It will be well."

Kate heard the words again, and again it was almost, but not quite, as though they had been spoken aloud.

Okay. She'd go with it. Trust the voice.

Kate smelled the rich aroma of coffee and sat up.

"Have a good sleep?" The red-headed nurse put a tray with a pot, cup, and saucer on the bedside table.

"Wonderful."

"You'll leave us soon," the nurse said, smiling at Kate. "The ones who accept what has happened as readily as you usually do."

"I was wondering about that. The people I've met here had been traveling, and they all seem to think they're still in Europe."

"It's not unusual." The nurse picked up the soft coverlet from the floor and put it back on the bed. "At first, most people think they're still on earth. And that's all right. They'll realize what's happened when they're ready."

((

Maggie Stevens woke to an early morning sun that seemed in much the same position as when she'd awakened before. Had she catnapped through a whole day?

Who cared? She could move! Maggie stretched, arched her back, and pushed luxuriously against the end of the hospital bed. She rolled over, propped herself with her good hand, and sat up. She was light-headed and a little weak, but otherwise she felt marvelous. She slid to the edge of the bed and put a foot on the tiled floor, braced for pain, but she felt only a vague stiffness. She stretched her arms high and flexed her legs.

"You've decided to wake up this time. How do you feel?" The nurse wasn't much older than Maggie. The white uniform she wore reminded Maggie she wasn't in the States, that this wasn't an American hospital where nurses wore vari-colored smocks or scrubs.

Maggie realized the nurse was waiting for a reply to her question. How *did* she feel? She slipped the other foot to the floor and stood up, holding the bed rail for balance. What was this? Ever since she'd begun serious gymnastics training again, she hadn't been able to get out of bed in the morning without wincing. Medication was the only thing that allowed her to ignore those hairline fractures in her ankle. She rotated her foot. Not a twinge. *Wow!* The time in bed must have given the garden-variety injuries a chance to heal too.

Her left hand crept up to her neck; she turned her head gingerly. "For a while there I thought I was paralyzed," she said.

"Fortunately, it was only temporary."

"Has my coach been here?" Stupid question—of course, Jerry must have come to the hospital.

"He came to see you often. While you were unconscious."

Maggie had a vague recollection—or had it been a dream?—of Jerry sitting by her bed.

"And my mom? Has my mother been here yet?" Rose *must* have come. In spite of the money, in spite of everything.

The nurse hesitated.

Maggie watched her. "She came, didn't she? And now she's gone home again." Maggie's shoulders slumped. "Did she stay long enough to know I'm all right?"

"She knows you'll be fine."

Sure! Just like her! If Rose had been assured Maggie was about to awaken, why couldn't she have waited a few more days? Maggie lifted her chin. "When can I get out of here?"

"Soon. But for now, how about breakfast? You can have it here, or if you'd like, you can have it in the recreation room down the hall." The nurse slipped a flowered cotton dressing gown from a hanger in the closet. "Would you like your robe?"

Maggie took the flowered wrap. It was one she'd thrown into her suitcase at the last minute in case the Munich hotel where the team was staying turned out to have communal bathrooms instead of the promised *en suite* variety. Jerry must have brought it to the hospital, she thought, touched. He must have been scared witless by the accident, probably felt guilty about telling her she could compete even after the ankle broke down again. Maggie grimaced. Nah, more than likely he'd been thoroughly ticked off, scared that if she were seriously injured some of the parents of his other elite gymnasts would take their daughters from him.

She pulled the flowered robe about her and went into the hallway. The tiled floor felt cool to her bare feet. She took an experimental step, then another. Suddenly, more than anything Maggie wanted to walk, to run, to slide. She rose on her toes as if she were starting a floor exercise, then broke into a gliding run, her heels barely touching the tiles. It felt so wonderful to move, to control her body. She'd always healed quickly, but this was incredible!

Maggie heard the murmur of voices, the twang of a guitar, and smelled the aroma of coffee even before she reached the recreation room. She paused at the opened double doors and took a quick breath. What was it besides coffee? Toast? Bagels? Maggie's stomach gave a protesting spasm, her mouth watered. Of course, even if it *was* bagels she couldn't eat them. Well, maybe just one. After all, she was convalescing. Even Jerry would admit she'd have to eat enough to get her strength back.

The room looked more like a country-club lobby than a recreation room, the floor carpeted with oriental rugs, one wall filled from floor to ceiling with shelves of books. Two men and a woman sat in comfortable chairs placed in front of a big screen T.V. None of them seemed to be watching the golf tournament on the television. The woman held a coffee mug in one hand and an open book in the other, and the men, one large and one slight, both with a pale, wasted air of sickness, seemed more interested in their breakfast than the golf. A beautifully dressed, sharp-faced woman sitting at a rococo writing desk looked up at Maggie's entrance, an abrupt movement that made the wattles of the woman's neck shake like stringy rubber bands. Her cool eyes dismissed Maggie, and she returned her attention to the papers before her. In a corner of the room, two teenagers sat close together at a card table, their blond heads almost touching. Maggie couldn't help a twinge of distaste as she noted the bulges that strained at the girl's black leather pants and jacket. Too much apple strudel there, not enough self-control.

The guitar player, hawk-nosed, twentyish, and tanned, glanced up from where he was sitting on an oversized ottoman, one leg drawn up over the other knee. His fingers pressed against the guitar's strings, stilling them. "Hey! You the gymnast?" His voice sort of reminded Maggie of plucked strings too, deep and resonant. A singer, maybe? He placed the guitar on the carpet.

Maggie ducked her head and murmured an assent. It shouldn't make such a difference—being recognized again. But after three years away from the circuit, from the interest of the media and the fans' admiration, she had to admit it felt good. "Maggie Stevens," she said.

"Ryan James." There it was, that fascinating resonance. He rose and came forward, holding out a hand and Maggie noted that his hair was not short and slicked back as she'd first thought, but tied back in a neat ponytail.

"One of the nurses told me you were here with the U. S. team," he said. "'Fraid I didn't recognize the name, but that doesn't mean anything because I don't know much about gymnastics."

"You're American."

"We all are." His nod included the others in the room. "Have you heard that we're going to some kind of rehab place?" He continued without waiting for her to answer, "Don't know why *I* need rehab. I haven't felt this good in months. As soon as I find where they've got my ten-speed, I'm off." The toaster clicked, and he turned to it. "That's my bagel. Want it? I can fix another."

"Just coffee, thanks," Maggie said automatically. Then she swallowed and said, "Well, maybe I'll have half." She tried not to seem too eager as she accepted the plate. She bit into the toasted bagel. Heaven. She watched Ryan spread his half with cream cheese.

"What are you in for?" she said, and then laughed. The sound surprised her. She didn't usually laugh out loud. Maybe it was simply being on her feet again after the scare of waking up to all those tubes—that and munching on a bagel and talking to a friendly American.

Ryan grinned. "Me? Nothing spectacular like your fall, just an asthma attack. It must have been a bad one, because I passed out while I was biking. They tell me a guy saw me in a ditch and brought me here. So far I haven't been able to find out if he brought my bike to the hospital too or if he left it for the police to pick up."

Maggie started at a whimpering cry that came from the table in the corner where the teenage couple huddled. The pudgy girl looked up, then ducked her head again. Of course, everyone had heard the stifled sob; and of course, all pretended they hadn't.

Ryan leaned toward Maggie. "They came in together," he said, his voice low. "I hear their motorcycle flipped on the Autobahn.

Seems they have a baby somewhere. Been trying to find out where it is ever since the accident."

"Those kids have a baby?" Maggie gave a surreptitious glance in their direction. The boy's wispy, blotchy chin was half-way between unshaven and bearded. Tears spilled from the girl's pale blue eyes and ran down on either side of her wide nose, the tip of which was a bright, raw red. The girl's pasty white complexion was mottled with pale pink splotches and teenage acne. She could have been fifteen, sixteen; he was older, but not much.

"Got some things here for a Maggie Stevens." A large woman in a navy-blue uniform stood at the hallway entrance. She had a beeper at her ample waist and carried Maggie's suitcase and a plastic bag.

Maggie stared. An American security guard with a genuine country drawl? Had they imported her for the hospital's American patients? Either that or they'd all been spirited back to Kentucky. "That's me," she said. "I'm Maggie Stevens."

"How do? I'm Connie. My, but you're a bitty little thing. Don't come up to more'n my shoulder, do you?" The guard approached, smiling genially.

Maggie ignored the comment. Despite years of hearing remarks like this, it took an effort. What did they expect? Gymnasts are *supposed* to be small.

The guard looked past her to the assembled group. "I was sent to tell all you good folks to get on out to the front entrance," she said. "A van will be there to take you to the Guesthaus—that's what they call the rehab center. You people who've already packed will find your things out at the van, but the rest of you had best pack up now." She turned back to Maggie. "You too, honey." She indicated one of the side doors. "Since you got your suitcase here, you may's well use the restroom over there to change into your clothes."

Maggie picked up the suitcase and plastic bag. They were going to let her go this soon? Hey, if someone had made a mistake, she wasn't about to call attention to it.

When she returned, the guard was still in the recreation room. She was standing beside the teenagers' card table, talking to the blond girl.

"I can't go," the girl said. Her lower lip trembled. "Not 'til I can phone about Essie."

The boy got up and stood behind her, his hand on her leather-clad shoulder. "You heard her," he said to the guard. "We're not going. There's this woman, Frau Blore, who's taking care of our baby; we've been trying to call her to check if Essie's okay, but we haven't been able to get through, and we can't go see her ourselves 'cause our cycle's not fixed yet." He glowered. "So I guess we're not going anywhere in your van, lady. Not 'til we get some answers."

Maggie expected Connie to reassure them, but the guard simply looked at them, her expression an odd mixture of firmness and compassion. "Like I said, van's out front. You two better be on it like the rest."

"I don't want to go," the girl bleated. Her head drooped, stringy, blond hair falling forward to shield her face.

The boy glared at the guard; his jaw twitched.

"Time you two left," Connie said to him, her voice gentle. "You just might find you like it where you're goin'." She gave a nod that included the whole group and left.

Ryan slung his guitar over his shoulder. "Coming?" he gestured to Maggie.

She hesitated. Did she want to go? Why had she been in such a hurry to leave? She felt a sudden rush of kinship with the sniffling girl. This might be a hospital, but it seemed like a safe, comfortable sort of place.

Galvanized by the guard's exit, the people in front of the T.V. had risen from their chairs. The old woman at the desk rose, looking for the first time uncertain, as though she too would like to stay in this comfortable sanctuary. Then she lifted her wattled chin and marched out to the hall, stopping on her way to pick up the remote and click off the T.V., quite as though this were her own living room. The slight young man on crutches followed. His close-cropped head, his gaunt face, skin stretched across the fine bones, looked like a Halloween skull. The older, taller man who accompanied him seemed in a way as diminished as his companion, though he gave the impression of having once been quite large, even hulking. Now the brown-plaid sports jacket hung on him. These two, Maggie noted, seemed far more ill than the rest of the group. Matter of fact, she thought with a slight jolt, everyone else seemed remarkably healthy for hospital patients.

The middle-aged woman who had been reading went to where the young couple huddled at the table. "I'm Kate Douglas," she said to them, and leaning over, she quietly murmured something to the girl. The girl lifted her head, and for a moment, it seemed she would respond. But then the momentary light flickered from her pale blue eyes, and she thrust out her lip and lowered her head, the greasy, blond hair again falling to hide her face. The woman gave a shrug, patted the girl's shoulder, and walked toward the hallway.

As she passed, Maggie couldn't resist whispering, "What did you say to her?"

"Hi, Maggie; I'm Kate," the woman said, holding out a hand. "I told her what I've been told. That everything will be all right. I said it wasn't any use trying to stay here if it has been decided it's time for us to move on. I'm sure there's nothing we can do to stop the process." She smiled and walked past Maggie into the hall.

"Coming?" The easy, low-voiced question came again from Ryan James.

Maggie looked at him. "I'm not sure. I thought so, but things . . . things are moving so fast. I guess I wonder why they're allowing us to leave so soon."

"These days hospitals kick you out before you've come out of the anesthetic. Anyway, are you complaining?" Ryan hitched his guitar case higher on his shoulder.

"No, of course not." Maggie's grip tightened on her suitcase. "Look, I'll see you at the van, but right now there's something I want to ask about." She ran into the hall and hurried down the corridor to where the woman called Kate stood by a bank of elevators.

"Mind if I ask you something?" Maggie said. She realized she was breathing hard.

"Go right ahead, but perhaps you'd better put down that suitcase first."

Maggie eased the suitcase to the carpet and rubbed a damp hand against her jeans. Why was she was sweating? "Maybe I *am* a little bit shaky," she said. "Look, what you said back there . . ." she hesitated, "something about a process we aren't able to stop? What process?"

Kate Douglas gave Maggie a steady, appraising look. "I wouldn't have thought I'd be the one to tell you," she said slowly. "I mean, I just got here myself. But if you're asking questions, you must be ready for some answers." She paused, as though debating whether she should continue. "We're all in the process of discovering that we're no longer on earth," she said at last.

"Say what?" Maggie gave a little laugh. She put her hand on the wall to bolster her suddenly precarious balance.

"Yes, it's true," said Kate Douglas. "We died. You did, I did. All of us."

Kate was just in time to catch Maggie as she slumped to the floor.

3

Kate Douglas took cream-colored linen slacks from a hanger and placed them in the suitcase. Poor little Maggie Stevens. Kate should have let someone else tell the girl, should have kept her stupid mouth shut. She leaned over to reach for a pair of tan leather shoes on the closet floor, half expecting to feel a stabbing pain in her chest when she straightened. But, of course, there was none. Kate breathed deep. Her lungs filled with glorious air, inflating effortlessly. It was wonderful; everything here was wonderful.

Except for Howard.

A wistful tenderness swept over Kate, and this time she couldn't help but let herself feel it. She ached to be with Howard. Howard, whom she had supported through the years, who in turn had supported her during her swift, surprising illness with amazing strength and resilience. He'd stayed with her, held her through those last hours. He had begged her to live, but then—informed by the boy-faced physician that there was no hope—he had let her go, held her hand until the pulse fluttered and failed.

An indistinct image appeared before the half-opened doors of the closet. It became clearer; Kate's hand went to her throat as she recognized the figure of her husband. Howard was sitting on the bed in an unfamiliar hotel room, his head cradled in his hands, his canes propped against the nightstand. Kate reached out in an involuntary movement. "Oh, my dear, who is there to help you now? If only I could. . . ." She drew back her hands and held them, clasped against her chest. "Don't grieve, love," she whispered.

15

Howard's shoulders slumped; his head remained lowered.

"It's going to be all right," Kate said, the words as much for herself as for him. "Please believe me."

Howard raised his head. His red-rimmed eyes narrowed and fixed upon the ceiling light as though he were listening. Kate saw Howard's eyes lose their haunted look, felt his sorrow lighten, as though he sensed her presence. In that moment Kate knew that whatever had happened or was to come, the tie between them remained firm, enduring.

"It's all right," she repeated softly. Howard remained seated a few moments and then gave a sigh that came from deep in his chest, reached for his canes, and began to make his slow, painful way to the bathroom.

"Howard," Kate said, her voice thick with longing. But the image had already faded. Then it was gone. Kate stood before the closet, pensive but comforted. She didn't know exactly what had just occurred; she was only sure that for one brief moment she and Howard had been together, that each had found solace.

                                          ❨

Patrick Riley gave a last glance at the mirror and patted the silk tie he'd knotted about his neck. He still looked like hell but, unless it was his imagination, the shrunken, taut facial muscles had loosened a bit. He lifted his thin shoulders, pleased to see in the shrug a hint of his former insouciance. Was that weird Swiss diet finally doing some good, or was there something more mysterious going on in this hospital? Not that he was complaining. Take these crutches. He picked them up and adjusted them beneath his arms. He didn't really need crutches anymore; the leg hadn't buckled since he'd first gotten out of bed the other morning. Still, it felt comfortable to have them as back-up.

Patrick stood on one foot and, balancing on his crutches, stretched out the other, the bad leg. No problem. He headed for the door. As long as he continued feeling as good as he had the past couple of days, he'd just enjoy it and not question how it all had come about. He wasn't about to rock the boat by asking questions. Smile a lot and keep a watchful eye on things. It had worked pretty well in the past.

Patrick hesitated at the door next to his but passed it without knocking. Let Frank come out to the van on his own. Not that Chambers wasn't a great guy. Frank Chambers's steadfastness in the face of his illness had been an upper for everyone else at the clinic. And it had been flattering that Frank hadn't rejected Patrick's tentative attempts at small talk, but the comment about being straight that the big guy seemed to feel necessary to drop casually into their last conversation rankled. Did Frank think Patrick was waiting to make a pass? Really. Patrick smoothed his close-cropped, nearly hairless head. A good forty if he was a day and as scrawny as a stray cat after months of chemo, Frank Chambers should be so lucky.

((

Frank Chambers heard footsteps and the thump of crutches in the hallway outside his door, heard them halt and pass on. *Good.* It wasn't that he didn't like Patrick, but it was difficult to ignore the looks they got from the rest of the group when they entered the recreation room—and left it—together. Not that he wasn't broadminded. On the force and in his personal life, he accepted others as they were, educated or not, savvy or out in left field, gay or straight. Still, the covert looks this morning bothered him. And it annoyed him that they had. Must be the cancer. He, who had never given a damn about anyone's opinion, had become much too sensitive to the reactions of others during this miserable illness.

Frank snapped the suitcase shut. He wasn't about to start paying attention to what other people thought at this late date.

Frank shrugged a raincoat over his jacket. He was always cold these days, though he had to admit he'd felt warmer here than he had in a long while. Frank glanced at the bony wrists that protruded from his worn sleeves. Once he would have filled the coat; now, despite the fact that he was wearing a jacket, the London Fog hung in limp folds. *Don't go there. At least you're alive. At least you're feeling pretty good.* He reached for his suitcase.

((

Marjorie Harrison tapped the polished fruitwood desk as she waited for security to come get her bags. She noted that one of the two diamond rings on her right hand stayed in place instead of slipping to the side so that she had to twist it upright as she constantly had to do these days. Her fingers actually seemed plumper, less—she hesitated but then let the thought emerge—less claw-like. Must be the new diet. The food at the hospital seemed to agree with her. Breakfast in the recreation room had been excellent, and more importantly, her delicate stomach hadn't rebelled. In fact, it had not made a whisper of protest. It was annoying to have to eat with a group of strangers, of course, and now to have to travel with them, but until this recalcitrant memory of hers stopped playing tricks she'd have to put up with it. Marjorie touched the sparse hair the latest hairdresser cut and waved so that it would cover her high forehead.

What exactly had happened the other day? Yesterday? She'd been in the airport lounge, waiting for her flight from Frankfurt to Lucerne. The unexpected two-day stay at the hospital had been annoying, but the doctors had assured her that she was quite fit to travel, ready to rejoin the group in Lucerne. She remembered her name being paged, remembered quickly pushing to her feet at the realization that her flight was leaving. (Had she fallen asleep?) What then? She could remember nothing until she awakened in this hospital that at first seemed similar, but was, she soon realized, quite different from the one in Frankfurt.

Marjorie smoothed her crisp linen jacket. Why was she back in a hospital? There was nothing wrong with her now. She hadn't felt this good in years. Too bad they hadn't been able to contact her group in Lucerne yet, and she was stuck with these people, none of whom she knew, none of whom—except perhaps for that Douglas woman—seemed at all her sort. Ah, well, these were simply bothersome things a traveler sometimes had to put up with. Fortunately if you were Marjorie Harrison, you didn't have to do so often.

There was a knock on the door, and a uniformed security guard entered.

Marjorie glanced at her watch. "Don't stand there smiling, young man. I tip for service, not for smiles." She gestured to a pile of luggage lined against the wall. "The bags are over there."

The guard looked at them and shook his head. "I'm sorry, Mrs. Harrison," he said, "but there won't be room in the van for all these. Would you like to select one to take with you? We'll send along the rest when you've reached your destination."

Marjorie Harrison drew herself up, raised a penciled eyebrow. "One suitcase? One?" Outrage frosted her words. "Let me tell you, young man, I don't travel without my baggage." She caught herself and made a tsk'ing noise. "Why am I arguing with you? You take yourself off and find the manager. Tell him I want to speak with him. *Now.*"

"Yes, ma'am."

"And I don't want to be fobbed off with a phone call. You tell him I want him here—within the next five minutes."

The guard didn't seem at all bothered by Marjorie's waspishness. "Yes, ma'am," he repeated. "I'm sure he'll be right up."

☾

The gentle motion of the van woke Maggie. She eased upright, wincing at a slight stiffness in her neck. It felt like the times when she'd been little, driving in the gray dawn with Mom to the arena for her gymnastic sessions. *Mom.* The thought of Rose brought with it the usual jumble of anger, guilt, and love. Maggie shifted from the perilous issue of Rose.

Where were they headed? Maybe the old woman had the right idea. Throw a tantrum and demand to stay at the hospital. They'd let her stay without a murmur when the old gal had flatly stated she wasn't moving until she found a way to get to where she wanted to go with any and all luggage she wanted to take with her. What was this Guesthaus? Some kind of psychiatric center? Or was Kate Douglas the only nut case among them? Maggie looked across the aisle at the leather-clad Clare who sat next to her glowering boyfriend, tears trickling down her cheeks. They hadn't let those two stay, no matter how much the girl kept up the waterworks. The plump blond saw Maggie watching her and, dabbing at her eyes, looked away. Sven darted a frowning glance at Maggie and put a protective arm about Clare's quivering shoulders.

Maggie's jaw tightened. Sure. They were all dead. Guess nobody had told the pudgy blond and her boyfriend that they were about to exchange the black leather for white robes and a harp. The van passed a tidy-looking farmhouse where four cows gathered in the shade of a freshly painted barn. An absolutely normal, everyday scene. Maggie gave a snort. *Right. This is heaven.*

19

The skinny guy sitting next to the older man pointed out the window. "Look! Here we are," he said.

Maggie saw what had caught his attention. Just around the bend in the road were several low-lying, white-brick buildings clustered about a large, glass-fronted structure. A discreet sign announcing "The Guesthaus" stood in the middle of a landscaped mound beside the driveway that led past great trees and manicured lawns and gardens. Maggie relaxed. No fences or gates. Surely a psychiatric facility would have fences and gates.

The van was met at the turn-around of the main lodge by a smiling, official-looking group of men and women. As each of the passengers stepped from the van, one of the welcoming committee came forward to receive him or her with a handshake and greeting.

Maggie shivered as a curly-headed girl came toward her, hand outstretched. Did everyone smile around here? All the time?

"Hi, I'm Val Shellenberg," the girl said. "Glad to have you with us." She picked up Maggie's suitcase and gestured toward one of the pebbled paths.

The name was vaguely familiar, but Maggie couldn't remember where she'd heard it. "Maggie Stevens," she said. She followed the girl. Wasn't anyone else bothered by the fact that they were being carted off separately to who-knew-where? Would she see any of her fellow passengers again? Did she care? "Hey," she called to the girl's retreating back. "Hey, wait up!"

The girl turned around, her look politely questioning.

"Before we go anywhere, I want to ask you something. Just to set the record straight." Maggie took a deep breath. "Are we dead?"

Val looked at her intently.

"One of the people I came with on the van, a woman, told me we were," Maggie rushed on. "I mean I thought she was nuts, but then I remembered—I was paralyzed, with tubes and machines all over the place. Then when I woke up this morning, I felt great. Hopped out of bed and started running around like I hadn't even sprained an ankle." Maggie looked down at her clenched hands and scowled. "So what's the story? Am I . . . are we dead?"

Val's lips twitched. "Doesn't look like it, does it?" At Maggie's glare, she gave an apologetic grin. "You're no longer on earth, if that's what you mean," she said lightly.

Maggie took a quick, short breath. It hurt her chest. "I guess that's exactly what I mean." She put a hand to her head, suddenly dizzy.

Val dropped the suitcase and guided Maggie to the wooden bench by the path. "Oh, I'm sorry. I should have put it better, but I thought if you were asking questions, it meant you were ready to hear the answers. That's how it usually goes." She held her fingers lightly on Maggie's wrist. "Your heart's going like a trip-hammer. Better sit down."

"Why should I?" Maggie straightened and tried to breathe normally. "If you've got all this right, it's not like I could have a heart attack and die."

Val grinned. "At least your sense of humor's intact."

Maggie held up her hands and flexed her fingers. These were *her* hands, not the hands of some spirit. There was the scar on her left thumb, a blemish so old she couldn't remember how she'd gotten it; there was the crooked little finger on her right hand, a souvenir of the time she'd fallen from the parallel bars when she was twelve. She swallowed. "Look," she said to Val, "If we're not on earth, where are we? Is this heaven?"

"No. It's not heaven."

"You're trying to tell me this is *hell*?"

Val giggled. "No," she said, suppressing a smile, "It's not hell. It's a place between heaven and hell."

"A place between heaven and hell." Maggie said it experimentally. She shook her head. *No!* She shook her head again. *I must be hallucinating. Must be.* Maybe she was dreaming this whole thing. Was she really in ICU somewhere in Germany? Was she really lying in a hospital bed attached to tubes and bags? If she closed her eyes and opened them again, would she look down to see a still body under a white hospital sheet?

"Easy, Maggie, easy." Val's gentle voice broke through Maggie's terror, edged it away.

Maggie breathed in a fragrant current of air, looked at the spring-green grass at her feet, at the delicate white flowerlets on the bush beside her. No. She wasn't in a hospital bed—she was here, wherever that was. And, astonishingly, it was okay. So she was some place between heaven and hell? She wasn't at all sure she believed in heaven, but she knew darn well she didn't believe in hell. Did any-one, except for T.V. evangelists? The last of the horror left her, and Maggie felt her heart slow, her pulse return to normal.

"How about I show you to your room?" Val said.

Maggie cast a sidelong look at the dark-skinned girl. Hadn't she read a newspaper article about a Val Shellenberg? It had been some time ago, months, maybe even a year. Maggie stiffened, remem-bering. Val Shellenberg was one of the newest of the young tennis phenoms who'd come from abroad to work at one of the U.S. tennis academies. The teenage Dutch/Nigerian girl had been killed in a boating accident just before she was to have gone to England to play in her first Wimbledon.

Maggie took in the girl's smoothly muscled form. The tennis prodigy had been fifteen, but the woman beside her seemed in her early twenties, just about Maggie's age. It didn't compute.

"Anything the matter?" Val asked.

Maggie clamped her teeth together. "No," she said. "Why should there be anything the matter?" It was only when she tasted blood that Maggie realized she'd bitten the inside of her cheek. Her tongue sought the wound. "Look, if you don't mind, I think I'll take you up on that offer and go to my room."

⟨

Kate followed the rotund maitre d' to a table by the reflecting pool. A great willow arched over the brick-walled entryway near the table, its drooping branches shading the linen tablecloth. She nodded her thanks as she slipped into the chair the maitre d' held for her. A vague unease swept her as she looked about. This "Guesthaus" seemed more like a prestigious hotel than a rehabilitation facility, the courtyard with its waiters and maitre d' more like a first-class restaurant than an institutional dining area. Would she be expected to pay for all this? Surely money had no place in this world. Or did it? On leaving the hospital, when she'd been told that there would be no bill, she'd accepted that assurance gratefully. But this place with its luxurious rooms and service, this might be something different. Perhaps Marjorie Harrison had chosen the wiser course. Not that any possible lack of funds would have entered Marjorie Harrison's mind, but the old woman's hissy fit and ensuing decision not to accompany the group had ensured her of the continued comfort and safe haven of the hospital.

Kate frowned. Would there be any American dollars, any Euros, or credit cards in the purse she'd left in the room? Why hadn't she thought to look? Did it matter? She gave a wry grin at the thought of asking the maitre d' if they accepted credit cards here. Don't worry about it. Remember the voices, go with the flow.

But when the young, pink-cheeked waiter appeared with the menu, Kate couldn't help checking for prices. There were none, just a list of selections.

"This is all quite lovely," she said, "not like an institution at all."

Her young waiter looked pleased. "We try for a relaxing atmosphere, Dr. Douglas. We feel it can be as helpful to regaining one's health as medicines and exercise," he said.

So he knew her name. "I'm sure it is, but it seems rather..." Kate searched for a word, "upscale for a health facility. And I'd really like to know more about, well, how your guests are charged for the services."

"Oh, you don't need to consider payment here at the Guesthaus, and when you go elsewhere, arrangements can be made," the waiter said quickly.

"I see. Thank you." She frowned, considering the unspoken nuances of his statement. "Then we *will* be expected to pay for things when we leave here?" she asked.

"Please, don't be concerned," he said, distressed. "You'll be given any information you need ... when it's appropriate. Your only responsibility right now is to get well, and mine is to see that you enjoy yourself while you're doing it." The last, though it sounded like a memorized spiel, was said with wide-eyed sincerity.

"You're part of the health-care staff?"

"I'm in training," he said with a bashful smile.

"In training for what?"

He hesitated. "I'm learning about food, about providing surroundings that enhance nourishment learning to be part of the welcoming team." He raised his pencil and cocked his head in what he obviously hoped was a business-like manner. "And now, may I suggest today's special, quail salad with pine nuts?"

Kate studied him. He could have been one of her freshman composition students; push him just a bit, and he'd come up with more information. But then she took in his anxious smile, his mild, expectant eyes. "Sounds great," she said.

She watched him leave and sat back in her chair, forcing herself to relax. Exactly where were they? When she'd awakened in the hospital, she'd realized almost immediately what had happened. Before, in that other hospital, she had known she was dying. And at the end, she had accepted it, had wanted to go. And she had gone, quite suddenly. First there had been a feeling of release, then the enormously loving presence that had enveloped her, a feeling of safety, of being cared for. She had slept and then awakened as though from a much-needed nap, refreshed and without pain. She, who had never given much thought to what or whether heaven was, had immediately assumed that this was it—heaven. But though there had been nothing really concrete to disabuse her of the idea, since being informed that they were coming to this rehab center, she hadn't been so sure. When she'd first awakened, she had assumed she would at last discover what was behind all the myths and stories of heaven she'd vaguely wondered about but never really studied. It wasn't, after all, her area of expertise.

But *was* this heaven? It was lovely. There were the flowers and constant sunshine, her every want attended to almost before she had a chance to think of it. But there seemed something . . . something temporary about it all.

Kate speared a forkful of salad and looked at Maggie and the guitar player with the ponytail at the table nearer the pool. They were talking animatedly, the girl gesturing with her water glass. Had either of them accepted the fact that they were in a different place, or what, perhaps in a different continuum than they'd inhabited before? Ah, well, she knew enough now to let others come to the realization of what had happened in their own time. Why had it all seemed so normal, so natural to her: to wake up in a place that was like Germany but that she'd known immediately wasn't?

Howard and she had enjoyed Germany, loved it almost as much as Italy. *Howard.* Kate's hand went to her chest in an attempt to allay the piercing pain, a pain that had nothing to do with a heart attack. She crushed her napkin, tossed it on the table, and got up. She lifted her chin and walked across the courtyard, her head high. She didn't know where she was going, only that she had to be alone.

When she got beyond the stone arches of the patio, her shallow breathing deepened and slowed. She paused at the vista that opened to a distant, wooded grove and gazed at the scene, soothed and quieted. It was all right. She was all right. She'd just take things one at a time. Kate stepped onto the dirt path that led toward the cool, inviting oasis of trees. Her sandals kicked up puffs of dust as she walked on through a wild, tangled meadow completely unlike the rest of the facility's clipped grounds and cultivated gardens. Her cream-colored slacks brushed weeds that grew on either side of the path, tall plants with purple flowerlets at the top of their rangy stems. A faint, pleasantly spicy odor scented the warm air.

Kate slowed her pace as she reached the trees, but did not stop, not even when she saw the inviting stone bench set beneath a towering beech tree. Instead, she walked on more slowly still, passing from shade to sunshine into shade again.

Was this really some sort of way-station? She'd felt so safe and welcome in the hospital; why did she feel wary now? She had so many questions. At the hospital, she hadn't felt the need to ask many questions, but the few she'd asked had received gentle, forthright answers that she'd known in a deep, visceral way to be true. Here it was different. Here, people seemed more hesitant—at least, her young waiter had given ambiguous replies to some of her questions.

Kate suddenly realized she was walking on a springy carpet of soft needles beneath a canopy of tall pines and that there was no evidence of the dirt path she'd been following. She turned and hurried back the way she had come and drew a quick, sharp breath of relief as she came upon the well-trodden path. She scolded herself for her frisson of fear. After all, it wasn't a very large woods; it would be difficult to get lost in something that was more a copse than a forest.

A murmur of conversation stopped Kate before she reached the clearing where she'd passed the great beech tree. Through the undergrowth, she saw Sven and Clare on the stone bench beneath the beech. Sven had his arm around Clare. She leaned against him, her blond head nestled on his leather jacket.

"If I could know how she is," Clare said, snuffling into a tissue. "If I could just know she's all right."

Sven tightened his embrace and murmured something into her hair.

Kate lifted her hand to cough and let them know she was there, but the nanosecond before she did she saw another person. Ryan James was watching the couple from across the clearing where he stood in the shadow of a clump of cedar bushes.

Perhaps sensing Kate's observation, Ryan looked up. He raised a hand in greeting and stepped into the clearing. "Hey there, folks," he said. "Everybody seems to have the same idea—get some exercise after lunch."

Sven scowled and grunted something unintelligible.

Unfazed, Ryan grinned and thrust his hands in his back pockets. "Oh, oh," he said, glancing down the pathway, "looks like they've sent out the troops to bring us back."

The man who entered the clearing wore a blue denim uniform. "Dr. Faber would like to extend an invitation to you all for the orientation meeting," he announced pleasantly. "It will begin as soon as everyone assembles, so if you will follow me, I'll show you to the auditorium where the meeting will be held."

Kate joined the group in the circle of sunlight. "No one mentioned a meeting," she said. "I wouldn't have gone off like this if I'd known we were expected to meet somewhere."

"No problem." The guard included her in his smile as he inclined his head, gave a little bow, and headed back to the compound.

The little group obediently filed out of the woods after him, walking single file along the path across the meadow, Ryan first, followed by Sven who reached back to hold Clare's hand like a guilty teenager caught on a sneak date; and finally Kate Douglas, bemused, intrigued, and slightly apprehensive, brought up the rear.

4

The crowd. Maggie stood at the threshold of the auditorium. Where had all these people come from? There were easily three-or four-hundred people in the seats in front of her. Surely the few low buildings of this rehabilitation center would not be sufficient to house them? Maggie looked about, trying to quell a rising stab of panic. She couldn't see anyone she knew, not Val Shellenberg, none of the group from the hospital. No, wait, there was Ryan James standing on the lower stairs, looking uncharacteristically hesitant.

Maggie hurried down, pausing only long enough to take a program offered her by a uniformed usher.

Ryan saw her coming and grinned. He seemed as glad to have met up with Maggie as she was to see him. "How about this place? I'd say everyone here looks pretty healthy for a convention of rehab patients, don't you think?"

"It does look like some kind of convention." She glanced at the program. "They're calling it a 'convocation.'"

Ryan bent his dark head over hers to scan the program. "I see a Dr. Faber is doing a welcoming thing," he said, "and some guy called Taylor is going to present an overview."

Maggie craned her neck. "See anyone from our group?"

"Kate Douglas was right behind me with Clare and Sven when I walked in," Ryan said, turning around. "There they are."

"And look, there's the guy with the crutches," Maggie said, nodding to Patrick Riley, who stood midway down the auditorium, surrounded by a small island of empty seats. He was looking at Kate who at that moment caught his hesitant invitation and headed in his direction, Sven and Clare in tow. Without discussing it, Maggie and Ryan made their way to join them. As Maggie slid into a seat next to Ryan, she noticed that Patrick Riley had left a vacant seat between Kate and him. Saving it for the older guy? Or did he want to be near but not part of the group?

She settled back, wishing whatever was about to happen would hurry up and get going. But maybe she was the only one anxious to start. Many of the people around them seemed quite happy to sit and chat while they waited for the convocation to begin.

Four people filed onto the stage to sit in the chairs arranged at the front. The lights in the auditorium dimmed, and the audience grew quiet. Or perhaps the auditorium lights only seemed to dim because the light that filled the stage suddenly appeared so much brighter.

As one of the men approached the podium, Frank Chambers came down the aisle. He may or may not have seen the empty seat next to Patrick Riley, but he slipped into the one next to Maggie. "Glad I saw you people," he whispered.

"Welcome, my friends," said the slim, silver-haired man at the podium. "I am Dr. Faber. To both those of you staying with us at the Guesthaus and those who are merely stopping on your way elsewhere, may I say we most sincerely appreciate that you are here with us today."

He scanned the crowd before him. "By now most of you are well aware that you have left the natural world and are in the spiritual world." He paused to let the low murmur that greeted this announcement sweep the auditorium.

Maggie felt her throat constrict. She could feel Ryan tense beside her, see shock reflected in the sudden movements of Clare and Sven in the row in front of them. But the whispered murmurs ceased almost as quickly as they had begun. Many were quietly nodding to themselves, as though Faber had stated the obvious.

"I know there are those among you who may have some trouble understanding this," Dr. Faber continued. "Perhaps you will want to stay to speak with others, either in the audience or those of us on stage, after our presentation. In any case, each of you will attend to as much of this program as you are interested in and can absorb.

Whatever you miss today will be presented again in another mode when you wish to know more."

Maggie looked at the white-knuckled hands clutching the arms of her chair. She stared at the little finger on her right hand and for a moment forgot about the man on the stage. She flexed her hand. The little finger was straight, as straight as the one beside it. She quickly inspected the palm of her left hand. There was no scar at the base of her thumb. Maggie felt a prickle at the back of her neck.

Ryan James had been staring straight ahead at Faber, but at Maggie's sudden intake of breath, he reached over and placed his hand on hers. Maggie felt a rush of gratitude. Right now she needed someone to hold on to. His fingers laced with hers, and she realized that perhaps Ryan needed reassurance too. The fact that he wanted human contact as much as she did made Maggie feel stronger, a little less frightened.

Dr. Faber introduced the woman seated in the chair next to his as Taylor, the director of Guesthaus, who would present the overview.

The audience clapped politely, but before the woman could begin, there was a sudden commotion in the back of the auditorium. Everyone looked around to see what looked like the beginnings of a brawl between an usher and a disheveled, middle-aged man who was trying to push his way down the auditorium steps.

"Are you all just going to sit here and listen to this?" the man yelled as he twisted in the usher's grip. "The man's insane. This stuff, the lights, the tunnel, it's simply oxygen deprivation—endorphins. You can't make me believe—" He succeeded in freeing himself from the usher, but before he'd gone more than a step, a uniformed guard appeared beside the usher. He placed a hand on the back of the charging man's neck. It was a mere touch, but the man stopped in his tracks. He looked about dazed, his agitation gone. He eyed the guard warily, then tossed his head in a gesture that was more petulant than belligerent. "Okay, okay. Let's not get our shorts in a knot." The security guard waited patiently while the man straightened his tie and tugged at his rumpled suit jacket.

"Shall we go somewhere quieter, sir?" Only those near them heard the security guard's murmur, but his meaning was apparent to all. The man gave a last, annoyed glance around the auditorium, then shrugged, and followed the guard from the hall.

The woman on the stage, who had been standing calmly during the interruption, made an infinitesimal adjustment to the gray material of her sleeves and instantly everyone's attention again focused on her. "Some of you will be here for the time it takes you to discover your home," she said, her light voice musical, rhythmic. "I'm afraid we can't give you directions to help you find your home because we ourselves don't know exactly where it is you wish to be. Others of you will elect to move on, and to those I ask that you not be distressed if the places you stay are not quite what you thought they'd be. Learn what you can from your experiences. In each place you will have the opportunity to find out about yourself, about what it is you really want."

Maggie, still stunned by Faber's earlier announcement, had stopped listening. She stared at the lovely woman on stage without really seeing her. She felt as though her brain couldn't take in one more new concept than those with which it already had been bombarded. How could the woman down there on the stage mouth meaningless phrases about discovering their "home"?

Home. Where *was* home? For the past months, it had been the gym where she worked under Jerry's constant but welcome supervision. For a long time before that, it had been a room in a high-rise she'd shared with another washed-up gymnast. It sure wasn't with Mom. Not since Maggie had found out about her, not since she'd left gymnastics.

And if she was really in some "spiritual" world, that meant she couldn't talk to Mom. Ever. The breath caught in Maggie's throat. Even after she'd left the circuit, Rose had made sure Maggie knew she was there in the background, available if needed. And lately they'd begun exchanging phone calls, Maggie asking for medical records, Rose calling to tell of a new job or another change of address. In the back of her mind, Maggie had always known it was only a matter of time before they made up. She'd almost called the night the team had left for Germany. But she hadn't. And now, if Faber was telling the truth, she wouldn't have another chance.

Here she was, listening to this Dr. Faber telling them they'd "left the natural world." Where had they left it? Somewhere two stars over, in the middle of the second galaxy on the right? Maggie squeezed her eyes, closing them on tears she would not allow to fall.

❦

Kate Douglas stirred, clasping her hands together as the final speaker—a clergyman? priest? therapist?—invited those who wished to do so to join him in prayer, suggesting that each person say whatever invocation he or she generally used. *What about those of us who don't pray regularly enough to have one we "generally" use,* Kate thought ruefully. But she knelt with the rest and bowed her head and, without really intending to do so, found herself reciting the words of the twenty-third psalm into her entwined fingers. Kate felt the tension leave her shoulders and arms, felt a lightness and a gentle peace settle over her as she surrendered to the comfort of the ancient words. Gradually, she became aware of murmuring a few rows behind, and from those in the seats ahead. The hair on her arms prickled. It seemed that everyone who was praying was quietly saying the same psalm—and in English! Surely not every person in this diverse audience would, when invited to pray, recite the twenty-third psalm instead of a formal prayer, and certainly not in English. Kate stole a look about her. In the next chair, Clare was staring ahead, slack-mouthed, weeping. No news there; the girl seemed to spend most of her time weeping. No, wait. Kate shot another look at Clare and realized she wasn't crying. She seemed in shock, as though she'd absorbed a body punch that had knocked the wind out of her. Had the news that they were no longer on earth caused that look? There was more than just shock in that pudgy face, there was panic ...and something else...despair? *The baby.* There had been a baby. Kate looked away. That frightened-fawn look was one she was all too familiar with. She'd had to help steer many a panicky young student who had suddenly found she'd lost her compass. Perhaps she should talk to Clare, help the girl accept this new world.

A few seats away, Maggie Stevens looked near tears too. Ryan James knelt beside Maggie, his sharp, angular face disclosing nothing. Kate raised her head to look at the people further down the sloping rows. Some appeared absorbed in contemplation, some apparently had paid no attention to the call to prayer and were looking about unabashedly. A few interrupted their reflections to dart startled glances around. Had they heard their spoken prayers repeated too, Kate wondered? Belatedly, she realized the murmur she'd heard before was indistinct now, its cadences no longer those of the twenty-third psalm.

Kate realized that the speakers had risen, and with them, the rest of the audience. She stood up, annoyed with herself and a bit ashamed of her inattention. *Shows my experience with prayer!* Given the chance to think of spiritual things, she'd promptly been sidetracked into watching everyone else. She glanced around. What was supposed to happen now?

Many in the audience seemed to share her uncertainty. Some headed for the doors at the back of the hall, some stood in groups of twos and threes, taking advantage of Dr. Faber's invitation to question each other.

Kate edged toward one of the groups, but at that moment Maggie called to her. Kate saw that the rest of the group from the hospital was heading toward the exit. She hesitated, then turned and hurried after them.

((

Dr. Faber watched the milling crowd of people as the auditorium slowly emptied. "How much do you think they heard . . . or understood?" he asked the director.

"As much as each was able," Taylor said.

"Looks as though quite a few are taking my suggestion to talk to other new arrivals about what they've encountered so far." Faber pulled aside the curtain for a better view. "Except for this morning's group from the hospital." He frowned. "I'd say they need more help in acclimating than most."

Taylor nodded. "But it's not up to us, of course. However they decide to experience their time here, what needs to be uncovered will be. We can only protect them while they're with us and offer whatever guidance they are willing to accept when they move on."

"Of course." Faber repeated, momentarily chastened. He fiddled with a gold cufflink. "Have you heard anything about my transfer?"

Taylor smiled at him and gently touched his shoulder. "You know it's not up to me, Emil. But I have heard good things about your work here. You're coming along nicely; try not to rush things."

Faber did not press it. "Not that I don't enjoy it here," he said. "It's just that—"

"I know," Taylor said. "To quote Dorothy, 'There's no place like home.'"

"Right." Dr. Faber flashed Taylor a smile and returned his attention to the departing crowd. "About this group from the hospital. What do you think I should do with them?"

"Let them go," she said promptly. "They're not the type to get a lot from a closed community like this. It might be better if they became wanderers."

"That can be dangerous," Faber objected.

Taylor's wry glance stopped him before he could say more.

"Sorry, that was silly of me," Faber said hastily. "You might think I was a newcomer myself."

"You're doing well," Taylor repeated easily. "It's all right to be concerned, but I wouldn't worry about the group. Being a wanderer can be a marvelous experience." She turned from Faber; an instant later a brilliant light flickered and was gone. Faber showed no surprise when his eyes adjusted to the empty space where Taylor had been standing.

Had Taylor seen what he had, he wondered, the dark shadow about one of the hospital group? Should he have mentioned it? Surely Taylor must have seen it too; her vision was much more acute than his. Still, it bothered him. He had seen that kind of floating shadow just once before, when as a wanderer himself he had encountered the Nephilim.

Dr. Faber buttoned his suit jacket as though suddenly chilled. He returned to his study of the people leaving the auditorium.

5

"So that was the big orientation meeting?" Ryan James signaled the waiter to replenish the pitcher of beer at the center of their table. "I gotta say I expected more."

"More than being told we're dead?" Frank Chambers looked at him levelly. "It was enough to get my attention."

"Did you believe him, Frank? D'you think it's true, what he said?" Patrick Riley asked. His expression begged Chambers to reassure him that it wasn't.

The big man shrugged. "What's our choice? It's obvious we're not in that Swiss clinic anymore; do you want to believe we're in some mental institution where the head man is more psychotic than the inmates?"

"It wouldn't be any worse than believing we're some place between heaven and hell. Listen, Frank, can't you do some investigating, pull a few strings, get some information on Dr. Faber and the rest of these people?"

Ryan James studied Frank, suddenly alert. "Why would he be able to pull strings? Who are you, Frank?"

Chambers merely gave a half-smile, but Patrick answered eagerly. "He was a Chicago police detective."

"*Was* is the operative word," Frank said. "Haven't worked for the better part of a year. Been on sick leave."

"If Faber's right, there wouldn't be much call for your line of work here, you think?" Ryan said to him.

"Don't expect so," Chambers agreed easily.

"I can't believe we're sitting here talking about being dead," Maggie said, looking around the table. She took a large pretzel from the bowl in the center of the table, then looked at the hand holding the pretzel, the right hand with its perfectly formed little finger. She spread her fingers, letting the pretzel fall onto the white tablecloth, and put both hands into her lap.

"What I can't believe is that we're sitting around drinking beer in the hereafter," Ryan said. He considered. "But come to think of it, things here seem pretty logical, and what's more logical than for a Guesthaus to have a beer garden on the premises?"

"Whatever they call it, this is supposed to be a rehab center," Frank said, "and I've never heard of a rehab facility that allowed drinking." He took a sip from his ornamented stein. "Not that I'm complaining."

Patrick refused to be side-tracked. "I still think there's a possibility someone's trying to pull a fast one. Maybe we're being brain-washed." He looked from one to the other. "I think we ought to stick together. How about it?"

"Her, too?" Ryan pointed to where Kate Douglas sat by herself beneath the grape arbor at the far end of the garden, seemingly absorbed in her thoughts.

"All of us," Patrick said. "Even Sven and Clare, if they want to."

"Has anyone seen them since the meeting?" Maggie asked, looking around. "Clare looked like the night of the living dead." Her hand went to her mouth, but her eyes danced. "Sorry about that."

Frank Chambers grinned. He felt for his shirt pocket, a gesture that indicated he might be searching for a cigarette pack. "The girl's reaction to being here seems a little excessive. But then, maybe she's traumatized."

"Welcome to the club," Patrick said under his breath.

"They took off as soon as the doors were opened," Ryan said, "Clare was full bore into her waterworks mode again. Sven probably figured he better go somewhere and wring her out."

It was heartless but so apt Maggie couldn't help but smile. It was difficult to feel sympathy for the pudgy, white-faced girl. Maggie picked up the pretzel that she'd dropped. Hardly any calories in pretzels.

"I see you find each other's company congenial."

The only one at the table who wasn't startled at Dr. Faber's appearance beside the table was Frank Chambers, who had been watching his approach. "What can we do for you?" Frank said.

"Your group seems to be exceptionally compatible," said Faber, "and on reviewing your records, I see that you really seem to need very little in the way of restorative measures, at least those that our facility is equipped to give you."

Ryan James lounged back in his chair, stretching out his long legs before him. "You got a pretty nice place here for some 'r and r.'"

Faber inclined his head in a graceful acceptance of this praise of the Guesthaus, but indicated Patrick Riley with an upraised palm and said, "Ah, yes, but it seems Patrick here already feels strong enough to leave his crutches in the auditorium, and this young lady," he turned toward Maggie, "fairly dances from place to place instead of walking. In fact, you all seem quite healthy and eager to, as they say, get on with the program." Faber smiled, as though pleased to have come up with the phrase. "But perhaps more than that, your group seems to want to . . . ah . . . scout things out, see things for yourselves."

"We just get here and already you want to toss us out?" Ryan said, a ripple of amusement in his voice.

"Not at all," Faber answered with bland good humor. "Should you choose to stay we would be happy to accommodate you. But if you decide you would like to move on, we want you to feel free to do so." He took an envelope from the inner pocket of his tweed jacket and added, "although we do recommend that you stay together." He removed a sheaf of laminated plastic cards from the envelope and spread them on the table.

Maggie leaned closer and saw that each had a gold seal and a picture on it that shifted as she looked at it—some kind of hologram.

"These are yours if you decide to continue your journey as wanderers," Faber was saying. "You may each pick up your card at my office."

"Wanderers?" Patrick said uneasily.

Faber permitted himself another small smile. "Just a term we use to designate a certain type of newly arrived." He gathered the cards and returned them to the envelope. "These credentials will allow you to stay at most hotels or inns and restaurants, and to purchase any food or clothing you may need. As I say, should you wish to take advantage of the offer, please come to the office either today or tomorrow morning." He gave an amiable nod and moved off.

"Wanderers." Ryan enunciated the word carefully as he watched Faber advance on Kate Douglas's table. "Can anyone think of any reason we shouldn't take off and see this 'spiritual world'? All those in favor of vacating the Guesthaus and seeing what's out there, say 'aye.'" He raised his hand.

The silence that followed this demand did not seem to indicate refusal on the part of the others, for though no one raised a hand, Maggie, Patrick, and Frank looked at each other in questioning uncertainty.

"Why d'you suppose we've been invited to become a roving band of pre-paid travelers?" Patrick asked. "Sounds weird to me."

"The whole set-up's weird, when you think about it," countered Ryan, "but I'd rather be on my own than be expected to take part in whatever rehab stuff they've cooked up for us. I vote we give the Guesthaus a pass and go off on our own."

Patrick grinned. "This isn't Chicago; you've already voted once."

Ryan flicked the slender man a glance but turned to Maggie instead of replying. "Faber's done giving Kate his spiel. Come on, let's see how she feels about going." He headed toward the table under the grape arbor.

Maggie followed, moving perhaps more deliberately than she would have before Farber's comment about her dancing rather than walking. But by the time she got half way across the patio, she had regained her buoyant step, muscled legs and feet moving in a gait that was almost a skip.

Ryan leaned on Kate's table, hands splayed flat on the red-and-white checked cloth. A smile softened the intensity of his hawk-like face. "So, did Faber tell you he's tossing us out of here?" he said.

"No," Kate said, puzzled. "He said *you* wanted to leave and suggested that I talk to you about it."

Ryan exchanged a look with Maggie. "That old fraud!"

"You mean it wasn't your idea?"

"He trotted up to our table and announced that, since we seem to be so compatible, we should consider becoming what he calls 'wanderers' and go off to explore together. He even arranged for us to become card-carrying members."

Patrick had come up behind them. "I'm not sure I like the idea of those cards," he said hesitantly.

Kate looked at him. "Why ever not?"

"It could be a good way for them to keep track of us."

"What if they do?" Kate shrugged. "Look, we're strangers here; we need all the help we can get. Anyway, if we get into trouble, I'd just as soon someone knows where we are. We've been offered a chance to travel with what amounts to free room and board; why not accept it?"

"So you're definitely for this," said Ryan.

"I must admit I have a yen to take off and see what this world is like." Kate looked past them. She was looking at the grape arbor, but she seemed to be thinking of something far removed from the Guesthaus garden. Then she gave a small shake of her head and brought her attention back to the people before her. "And to tell you the truth, I don't feel totally relaxed here, haven't really since we came."

"Me neither," said Patrick. "It's not like it was at the hospital."

"Really? I was more than ready to leave the safe and friendly confines of that hospital," said Ryan. "And if we gotta travel together, this group wouldn't be bad to hang around with." He smiled at Maggie. "We have Maggie, who's an elite gymnast, and you, Kate— from what I hear, you're something special in the academic world." He glanced at the table where Frank Chambers sat staring into his beer stein. "There's Frank, who seems to have been something important in the police department—"

"Frank claims he was just a regular detective for the CPD," Patrick put in. "As for me . . ." he lifted a shoulder, "I'm just a church organist who does an occasional concert on the side."

Ryan held up his hand in mock surrender. "Hold it! I just realized this means we have Sven and the weeping Clare too."

"They don't seem to have much in common with the rest of us," said Maggie. "Maybe they got into the group by accident."

"I don't think there are 'accidents' here," Kate murmured. She tossed her napkin on the table. "But I think Ryan has a point. We might as well head out and see what this world is like. And since Dr. Faber suggests we stick together, I say we should—*all* of us from the hospital." She looked at Maggie and then at Patrick. "How about it?"

"Sure," said Maggie.

Patrick was slower to respond, but then gave an affirmative, "I guess so."

Ryan gave a quick nod. "Okay, let's go and ask Chambers. If he says yes, I'll find the weeping Clare and her blond boyfriend and see if they want to come along. And if they do, we'll consider it a go, and we can pick up those cards and see what, if anything, Faber has arranged for transportation."

(

It felt early, but the sun stood high above the manicured lawns of the Guesthaus. Kate closed her eyes and stretched her neck to the gentle warmth of its rays as she waited at the curb by the van. She could feel the lump of the map Dr. Faber had given her through the soft leather of her shoulder bag. Odd that Faber should have chosen her to be navigator. Howard had been the map reader during their travels, sitting beside her during the long drives through various states, through England, Europe.

Howard. A sharp pain seared her chest. *Howard, where are you?* An image appeared in her mind, and immediately the pain lessened. She saw Howard bent over his desk in his study, his familiar face grave, the deep laugh lines about his eyes now cavernous folds of flesh. He put down his pen and massaged his withered legs, something he did only when he was in great pain and thought he was alone.

"Love, oh, my sweet love," Kate said softly.

Howard stared absently at the map on the wall beside the bookcase, the map Kate had given him two Christmases ago. She'd traced their travels on it with a magic marker. A look of peace stole over Howard's tired face. He smiled.

He was thinking of her. Kate knew it as surely as if he'd spoken. "Yes," she whispered. "Yes, I'm with you."

Howard leaned back in his chair for a few moments and closed his eyes. Then he picked up his pen and began writing again. The image faded. Kate took a deep breath. *Thank you.* She touched her face, her fingers brushing a tear. Did the others have experiences like this?

Where *were* the others, anyway?

As if in response to her thought, Maggie appeared on the path from the main building. "Hey," she called out to Kate. She skipped across the flagstones as though playing hopscotch. "I can't believe I slept like that. I'm not late, am I?"

"No, of course you're not late. I'm the first one here." Kate attempted a smile. "I had a wonderful sleep too. After getting my card, I thought I'd go to my room and lie down for a couple of minutes and the next thing I knew it was morning." She looked around. "If the others aren't here soon, we'd better go ask at the office."

As if on cue, Patrick Riley and Frank Chambers appeared, walking across the lawn. Ryan James sauntered behind them, his guitar case slung over his shoulder, suitcase in hand. "Everybody here except our teenagers?" he asked as he came within range of the rest.

"There was some trouble about their release forms," Frank Chambers said. "I saw them waiting outside of Dr. Faber's office a few minutes ago."

"Don't tell me, let me guess. Clare was crying."

Chambers ignored him. "Sven said they wanted some assurance they'd get their motorcycle before they'd be willing to sign any forms. Apparently Faber said the cycle would be shipped to them. They were just waiting to get the appropriate papers signed, so the kids should be here shortly." He looked up and saw the couple come out of the building, Clare crowding next to Sven, walking stiffly, as though her joints hurt. "Here they are. I just hope Faber remembered to send the van keys with Sven."

"I looked in the van," said Kate. "The keys are in the ignition."

Ryan snorted. "Now there's a piece of incompetence for you. Leaving keys in a standing, unlocked vehicle." He leaned toward Maggie and murmured, "Hey, get that; they've ditched the leather outfits."

Maggie looked. They had indeed. Sven, in jeans and a plaid shirt, seemed much less threatening than he'd been in black leather, and Clare, though she was stuffed into jeans that seemed at least a size too small and was staring straight ahead like a zombie, looked better than Maggie had yet seen her. Perhaps it was the wheat-colored hair that hung to her shoulders like yellow silk. Yes, praise be! Clare had washed her hair!

"Okay, let's see if this thing starts," Ryan said, getting into the van.

"You're driving?" Chambers asked.

"Why not?"

Frank Chambers looked at Ryan James, a glimmer of amusement flicking across his face. He seemed larger than he had yesterday, more substantial. He reached across Ryan, took the key from
the ignition, and stepped back on the sidewalk. "Seems this is our
first chance to manage our affairs as a group. Let's do it democrati-
cally. Who'd like to drive?"

Ryan had stiffened at Chambers's action, but now he looked
inquiringly at the rest and slowly raised his hand, his black eyes
dancing. "Me?"

The laughter from Kate and Maggie that met the mock-humble
question broke the momentary tension. Even Sven and Patrick
grinned. Frank Chambers shrugged and smiled with the rest as he
tossed the keys back to Ryan.

Ryan caught them and started the engine. "If we're going to be
a democracy, I vote we get out of here. Any objection?"

There was none. Patrick helped Frank arrange suitcases in the
luggage rack on the van's roof as Kate took the seat behind Ryan
and pulled the map from her purse. Maggie sat behind Kate, and
then Frank took the seat across the narrow aisle from Kate, and
Patrick the one behind him across from Maggie. Sven and Clare
came aboard last, making their way to the triple-seated bench that
stretched across the back of the van.

"We were late because . . . because Clare and me had to get some
stuff straightened out," Sven muttered as he stuffed his duffle bag
under the bench. Clare stared out the window and said nothing.

Now that the moment of leaving was on them, everyone
seemed in a hurry to get away. Ryan gunned the motor and the van
sped past the low brick wall and onto the highway.

((

"It looks sort of like Pennsylvania." Maggie leaned forward to
peer at the map Kate Douglas was studying. "Where are we? We've
been driving for forever. How long do you think it will take us to get
to this Eastlight place?"

"It looks as though there's a range of hills between Eastlight
and the Guesthaus, but there's no indication of distances, so I've
absolutely no idea how far it is," Kate said. "Does it really matter? Dr.
Faber suggested it as a destination, but he didn't say we had to get
there on any particular schedule, just to enjoy our travels."

"I'd say Oak Creek Canyon in Arizona rather than Pennsylvania," said Patrick. "Look at that gorge on the left." His voice sharpened, and he pointed ahead. "If that map says we're supposed to go over some hills, I'd hate to see what they consider mountains around here."

"Where did *those* come from?" Frank asked, looking out the windshield. "Maybe we should revise our plans for being in Eastlight for lunch."

"Look, there's snow on top," Maggie said.

"Snow! More like glaciers." Ryan brought the van to a stop at a turnout by the side of the road. "I'm ready to take a break," he said. He got out of the van and stretched as he surveyed the mountains in the distance. "Getting over those babies may be more than this van can take." He chewed his lip thoughtfully. "And I was missing having my bike! Y'know, I was looking straight ahead as I was driving, and I swear there weren't any mountains a few minutes ago. Do you suppose they're some kind of mirage?"

"I don't know, but Frank's right about not making Eastlight by lunch," Patrick said after a moment. "Does that map of yours show a town anywhere in between where we could stop?" he asked Kate.

But before Kate could consult the map there was a shout from the van. They turned to see Sven wrestling what looked like an enormous hamper out the narrow van door.

"Hey, look what I found under the back bench," he called to them.

"What is it?"

"I think it's food," Sven said. "I was getting Clare's bag out for her and there it was."

Ryan helped him maneuver the hamper onto a large, flat rock by the edge of the drop-off. Together they opened the wicker top.

"Sandwiches," said Ryan. "Bless Dr. Faber's pointed little head."

"There's steam coming from the round crock there." Frank sniffed appreciatively. "It smells like some sort of pot pie," he said. "Can't believe it; haven't had pot pie since I was a kid. And is that wine I see tucked in over there?" He pulled out a bottle. "Fruit juice." He checked the other bottles. "I guess wine was too much to hope for ... looks like it's all fruit juice." He twisted off the top of the bottle he was holding and reached for the stack of plastic glasses. "At least it's cold."

Sven had already handed a sandwich to Clare and unwrapped one himself. He took a bite. "Chicken salad," he said, his mouth full. Frank carefully lifted out the ceramic pot and placed it on a flat rock. He took a few plates from the hamper and handed two of them to Kate and Maggie. "Want to try the pot pie, Maggie, Ms. Douglas, or it's Dr. Douglas, isn't it?"

"Kate," Kate responded, accepting the plate and flicking it with her fingernail. "Funny, this isn't plastic, but it's not china either—perfect for a picnic, but different from anything I've seen."

"A lot of things are different here, not real different, just a little," Maggie said.

"Just enough to remind you that, as someone said a while back, it's not Kansas anymore?" Patrick had remained at the rear of the group, but now that the rest had helped themselves he came to take a sandwich from the basket and squat on one of the flat rocks near the edge of the overlook. For the next half hour, they enjoyed the bounty tucked into the hamper. Besides sandwiches and the hot casserole, they found a steaming chowder, chilled fresh fruits, and cheeses. Conversation ranged from appreciative comments on the food to desultory remarks on the scenery. Not one of the group mentioned their questionable journey to some place called Eastlight or discussed the fact that, if Dr. Faber was to be believed, the rugged country they were traveling through was some sort of way station between heaven and hell.

At last Kate stood up, brushed off her slacks, and joined Patrick, who had begun to collect the plates and put them back into the hamper. "Where's Maggie?" she asked casually.

"She went off beyond that outcropping," he said.

Frank Chambers frowned. "Perhaps we should have some rules. I think the first should be that no one should go off by themselves."

"Herself," Kate murmured as she tucked her napkin into the hamper. "I'll go get her."

But at that moment, Maggie appeared from behind the rock and walked toward them, pale but composed. "Why is everyone looking at me?" she said, looking at the circle of inquiring faces.

"Frank thinks we shouldn't go off alone," Patrick offered.

Maggie shrugged. "Look, when nature calls I'm not about to bring a bodyguard with me."

"She's right. Anyway, what do we have to be afraid of in a place—"
Kate caught herself, "—in a world like this?"

"If you're not disturbed at being told we're someplace where
everyone's dead, okay, but I don't mind telling you I'm having some
major problems with it." Chambers's depreciating words were
amused, but then he sobered. "I repeat: I'd advise people not to wander off alone."

Kate looked at him. Though the big man's voice was steady and
he seemed as imperturbable as ever, Chambers's eyes belied his
tone. "No, I'm not frightened," she said slowly. "Does this world or
anyone in it look dead? Has anyone we've met been anything less
than friendly and caring? More often than not since I awakened, I've
been aware of a peaceful presence nearby." Her gaze traveled to
those around her. "Haven't any of you felt it?"

"Yeah, sort of." To everyone's surprise, it was Sven who spoke.
He looked abashed. "Haven't slept in a comfortable bed this many
nights in a row since I was a kid. Say nothing of having some really
good food around any time we want it." He looked out from beneath
the shaggy blond hair, his eyes half-mocking. "But then maybe what
I've mostly felt more'n any 'peaceful presence' is a full belly."

Clare stared up at him. "You didn't tell me. I haven't felt anything like that."

"You haven't been able to eat since we came, 'cept just a little,"
Sven said. His finger brushed a strand of corn-yellow hair from her
face. "Haven't been able to sleep much neither."

Clare looked away. "I don't think I'll ever—" she broke off and
for a moment it looked as though she was going to cry. But she took
a ragged breath and then pressed her lips together in a thin line.
Brushing Sven's arm in a quick gesture, she ran to the van and
climbed in. Sven followed her, covering the ground in long, sham-
bling steps.

The rest exchanged glances, shrugged, and straggled toward the
van, except for Patrick Riley, who went to edge of the gorge and
stood looking into it, his hand shading his eyes.

Frank Chambers looked back. "What is it?" he called to Patrick.

"There, downstream in the trees. Looks like a building. And
there's another . . . and another." Patrick leaned forward.

"One more step, and you'll be needing those crutches again."
Chambers walked back. "You're right." He turned and called to the

45

others, "There's a town down there." He frowned, looking into the valley. "How could we have missed it?"

"We were all looking out over the mountains; nobody looked right down, I guess," said Patrick.

The others had come back. Kate stood, the unfurled map in her hand. "Yes, here it is," she said. Right here."

"Why didn't you tell us there was a town nearby?" Frank asked.

Kate rolled up the map. "I guess I missed it." Then she added, "Either that or it wasn't on the map when I looked at it before."

6

The town turned out to be further away than it looked. By the time Ryan James negotiated the steeply winding road to the half-hidden buildings at the gorge's bottom, the group's picnic lunch was only a pleasant memory. The sun's rays did not reach into the deepest parts of the gorge, and mist chilled the evening air. The trees growing along the rock-bordered stream that ran through the valley were sparsely leaved, and what had seemed like verdant grass when they'd viewed it from the ridge turned out to be dried, yellowish-green weeds.

Ryan gripped the wheel as the van lurched over a deep groove in the rutted dirt road. "Does anyone know why we came down here instead of going over the mountains?" he muttered.

They passed a ramshackle barn and deserted farmhouse and rounded a bend where the dirt road became a dirt street lined with wooden houses and empty two-story shops.

"Looks like a ghost town," said Patrick, with no attempt at humor.

Frank, Ryan, and Kate turned like a rehearsed chorus to look at Patrick. After a beat, Maggie did too. Patrick gave a sheepish grin and ducked his head.

"I don't like this," Clare whimpered. "I don't want to stay here anyway; I want to get somewhere where we can . . . can phone someone," she ended hopelessly.

The others exchanged glances, but no one remarked on the impossibility of this.

"Gas indicator's almost on empty," Ryan announced. "We're going to have to stay long enough to fill the tank anyway."

"There's a gas station." Kate pointed to a corner where a rusting pump crowned with a red-and-white cloverleaf emblem stood in front of a building whose dirt-flecked windows obscured whatever was inside it. A few of the wooden building's boards had come loose, and the building itself leaned precariously to the right, but attached to the rear like an after-thought was a large, low, fairly new-looking structure.

"Haven't seen that kind of gas pump outside of old flicks," said Patrick. He shifted in his seat. "This whole place looks like something out of a '30's movie."

Frank Chambers was already out of his seat and at the door.

"He shouldn't go alone," Kate murmured.

"Hang on, Chambers," Ryan said, sliding from the driver's seat. "If you're going to check out the natives, you'd better have somebody ride shotgun."

Chambers didn't seem especially enthusiastic about Ryan's offer, but he didn't object. The two strode across the cracked concrete pavement to the station, pushed open the unpainted door, and entered.

Those in the van waited silently as flies buzzed the windows, attacking the glass like kamikaze pilots. "What's taking them so long?" Maggie said finally. "Either they have gas or they don't."

At that moment, the station door opened, and a man bounded out, followed by Frank and Ryan. The man in the lead was handsome in a theatrical sort of way. Dark, sculpted hair fell smoothly to the collar of his white satin shirt, a scarlet embroidered vest hugged his chest, and slim black trousers encased muscular legs.

"Olay!" Patrick said softly. "Bring on the bulls."

The man stepped onto the van's running board and ducked inside. He gave a little bow to the ladies, his hand to his chest. "I am Oliver Wendell Garcia," he said.

"Oh, surely not," murmured Kate.

"Papa was a great admirer of the jurist," he bowed again, in Kate's direction this time. "If you all would like to join us for some refreshments, we would be delighted," Garcia continued smoothly. "Unfortunately there is no gas in this pump, but we have sent a messenger to the next town to see if they have some."

"Mr. Garcia's people are staying here," Frank said from behind.

"His *people*?" Patrick raised an eyebrow.

Garcia had stepped back onto the pavement and now extended his arm in an invitation. Those aboard the van exchanged glances, shrugged, and clambered onto the cement.

"Since it looks as though we're here for the foreseeable . . ." Chambers said, then stopped and gave a lopsided grin. "Uh, since we're here until we can get some gas, we all might as well go inside."

"I don't want to go in there." Clare's whisper was barely audible.

Oliver Wendell Garcia's dark eyes narrowed as he inspected Clare, then Sven, but his smile remained in place. "Of course! It is as the senorita wishes. However, if the rest of you care to accompany me, I think you will enjoy the addition we have fixed in the rear as a temporary camp." For a moment, Kate thought he was going to pirouette, but Garcia merely waved a graceful hand above his head and turned to lead the way inside. Sven put an encouraging hand on Clare's back, and after a tiny hesitation she went with the rest.

The station was nondescript and dusty, the glass case beside the cash register empty of any merchandise. Garcia went behind the counter and opened an inner door, holding it wide to a blast of flamenco music that reverberated about them. Maggie gasped and took an involuntary step back, pitching herself into Ryan James's chest. "Wow, what's that?" she said.

Ryan steadied Maggie, let his hand stay resting lightly on her shoulder. "Yeah, wow!" he said. "That's some kind of dancin' music. And someone in there knows how to play a pretty mean guitar."

Garcia stood aside. He grandly gestured them into a room awash with colors, noise, and motion, a room where music pulsed through the smoky air and around the dancers who filled a circular dance floor. The women were in colorful woven skirts and low-cut silk blouses, while the men wore spangled vests and replicas of Garcia's tight black pants. Waitresses weaved among tables scattered at the sides, round trays held high above their heads.

"The '30's motif continues," Patrick murmured. "A speakeasy? A Spanish one?"

The look Garcia gave Patrick was not amused. Although Patrick Riley and he were about the same height, Garcia lifted his chin as though looking down at the younger man. "When my people stop to rest from their travels, they like to make music, to dance, and sing.

It is the way of the Romany," he added with an odd sort of dignity. He led the way to two battered, tilting card tables and gestured an invitation for them to take seats. "We are happy to extend to you our hospitality," he said, and left them to cross the dance floor. He slid adroitly through the dancers, exchanging greetings with some, touching a shoulder of another, playfully flicking a twirling skirt out of his way, until he'd crossed to the other side of the room.

Frank and Kate seated themselves at one of the tables, and after a moment of awkward hesitation, Patrick joined them. Ryan and Maggie sat at the other, and Sven placed two lopsided metal seats for himself and Clare against the wall a short distance away.

"What's with the 'Romany' bit?" Maggie asked.

Ryan raised his palms with a shrug, but Kate answered from the next table. "Romany are gypsies. Our gentleman friend is saying his people are gypsies."

"You're kidding," Maggie stared at her. "When we came in, I thought we'd walked into some kind of costume party."

"If it's a costume party, then everyone decided to come as the same thing," said Kate.

A scarlet-skirted woman came toward them with a tray on which was a pitcher of what looked like wine and several tall glasses. As she placed these on Kate's table, droplets spilled from the frosted pitcher onto her ruffled black satin blouse. "Damn," she said, gingerly dabbing at it with the hem of her outer skirt, a gesture that showed a second, multi-colored skirt beneath it. "Oh, well, it'll dry." She smiled at them. "This is our special sangria—with Oliver's compliments. You can pour yourselves starters, and I'll bring another pitcher in a minute."

"Thank you and thank Mr. Garcia for us," said Frank. "Is there any chance of our ordering something to eat?"

"This is a camp, not a restaurant," the woman said with some asperity. Then she gave them a quick smile. "I guess we could see that you get something to eat."

"That's generous of you," said Kate. "We feel somewhat as though we've intruded on your party. By the way, I'm Kate Douglas."

"I'm Bella," the woman said. "Party?" She looked around the room. "This isn't really a party. We spend most of our evenings like this."

"You people have these supper-time bashes all the time? Hey, can I come live with you?" Ryan seemed only half kidding.

"That's not a bad idea; we can use more men." Bella swished her skirts at him and gave a laughing smile that included them all. "Actually, if any of you would like to come with us, you'd be welcome." Her glance returned to Ryan. "As I said, we can always use men, especially good-looking ones. Now help yourselves to the sangria. Enjoy. Munchies are on the way. In the meantime, feel free to join the dancing." She gave the men an exaggerated wink and flounced off.

"Well, that's sexuality in the raw," Kate said dryly.

"Come on, you know she was kidding." But Ryan looked pleased at Bella's flattery, and even Patrick sat a little straighter in his battered chair.

Kate snorted and passed Patrick the pitcher of sangria. She noted the young man's face had lost its cadaver-like gauntness. If not handsome, Patrick was certainly presentable. He poured the sangria into a glass and took a sip. "Umm," he said, and took another long swallow. "If the food is up to the drinks, I just may vote we take the lady up on her offer."

"First we'd have to find out if they can play any other kind of music—not that this Spanish stuff is all bad." Ryan held out a hand to Maggie. "Want to show the natives a couple of steps?"

Maggie was out of her chair before he'd finished. "I've hardly been able to keep my feet still since we came in," she said.

The rest of the van's passengers watched the couple walk to the tiny dance floor and, after a moment of surveying their competition, join the heel-clicking dancers.

"She's good," Frank said. "But I guess it's not surprising."

"What's surprising is that our bus driver is better," Kate observed. And he was. Ryan James stood erect and snapped his fingers, his neatly caught pony tail flicking as he expertly spun his partner about.

"All he needs is a flower in his teeth." Patrick dismissed him and studied Chambers. "You've been pretty quiet, Frank."

Frank grunted.

Undeterred, Patrick pressed on. "You've been thinking of something. What is it? Something about this group doesn't jibe with what you know of gypsies?"

Frank considered his glass of sangria. "They seem more like some Hollywood version of what gypsies should be than the ones I've seen blow through town, but there's something else about this whole set up that feels a little too familiar."

"Such as?"

"I don't know whether or not they're really gypsies, but you can lay money on the fact that they're hustlers. The air around here reeks of petty larceny."

"How can you say that?" Kate said.

"Open mouth. Put together vowels, consonants, that kind of thing." Chambers's grim face relaxed as he smiled at Kate. "I don't know how I know. I guess it's mostly years of watching people say one thing and mean something completely different."

"What do you think we should do?" Patrick asked him.

"For starters, watch our wallets," Chambers replied.

One of Garcia's followers, a short, dark man with a mustache, sidled up to their table. "Greetings," he said with a poor imitation of Garcia's regal bow. He nodded at the dance floor. "Your friends are excellent dancers. I hope the rest of you might also be persuaded to join us on the dance floor?"

They were saved from answering by the arrival of Bella with the second pitcher of sangria, Oliver Wendell Garcia close behind her. Responding to a sharp glance from Garcia, the mustachioed man made another hasty bow and scuttled off.

"Good news, my friends," said Garcia. "One of my men has returned from the next town, and they do indeed have a working gas pump. Tomorrow morning we will take you there."

"Mighty kind of you," Frank Chambers said. "But if your man has already driven there and back it must be just up the road. Any reason we can't go there tonight?"

"Ah, my friend, are you in such a hurry to desert us? Surely you have nothing so pressing that you can't enjoy our hospitality for the evening." Garcia seemed genuinely distressed.

"I don't mind staying," Patrick chimed in. "I've had enough of that van for a while." He looked around the large room. "But where would we sleep?"

"You're right," Garcia smote his temple. "My friends and I simply put down sleeping bags, but I should have thought that you

people would like a little more . . . conventional arrangements. I'll
see that rooms are made available." He left them before anyone
could object.

Bella watched him glide through the throng with an indulgent
smile. "Don't worry; Oliver's a wonder at making arrangements."

"What gypsy tribe do you belong to?" Frank asked Bella.

She shot him an amused glance. "Oliver gave you the Romany
bit?"

"Then he's not really a gypsy?"

"Oliver is whatever he wants to be."

Chambers considered the enigmatic statement. "So what was
Oliver before he became a gypsy?" he said.

"A stockbroker. And a good one. But I must say he makes an
even better Romany."

"A stockbroker!" Kate stared at the departing Garcia.

"He had a condo on Lake Shore Drive and a summer home in
New Buffalo by the time he was twenty-eight," Bella told them. "And
a Porsche. If we hadn't been in the middle of a five-car crash on the
Outer Drive, he'd have bought his second."

"So why does he go around dressed up like a gypsy?" said Patrick.

"He *is* a gypsy," Bella reminded him, annoyance sharpening her
voice. "Now, if you'll excuse me, I have to go check on the goulash."

"Goulash," Patrick said, renewing his glass from the second
pitcher. "Figures. At least it's better than munch—" He stopped, his
mouth open.

"What?" Kate followed his gaze and put down her glass. "Oh,
my."

A woman half-way across the room was making her way along
the edge of the crowded dance floor. The tray she carried on which
three beer glasses rested precariously was not held high like those of
the other waitresses, but out in front of her, as though to use as a
shield against the milling bodies. But it was not the awkwardly held
tray that had caught Patrick's, and now Kate's, attention; it was the
woman's glaring, hawk-like gaze.

"Is that who I think it is?" Patrick breathed the question.

"Couldn't be." Kate shook her head. "She's too young, not a
spring chicken, but still too young. And anyway, Marjorie Harrison
couldn't be blackmailed into wearing a get-up like that."

The woman had gained their side of the room and smacked down her tray on a nearby table in front of two men in baseball caps, splashing beer as she did so. She ignored the men's startled oaths and advanced to the table where Kate, Frank, and Patrick sat staring. "What, may I ask, are you doing here?" she said.

"Mrs. Harrison?" Kate struggled to keep both the shock and the amusement from her voice. "Is that you?"

"Who else would it be?" Marjorie Harrison looked down at her spangled skirt. "Oh, yes, these abominable clothes. Not what I'd have chosen, but I'm trying to fit in here." Suddenly she looked not only older, almost as old as she had at the hospital, but vulnerable. Then she lifted her chin. "How did you people get here? Why did you come?"

"More to the point, how did you come to be here?" Kate asked gently.

Marjorie Harrison looked confused. She accepted the chair Frank pulled over from Ryan and Maggie's empty table, and sat down. She brushed back dark-brown hair from her eyes, hair that had been steel-gray in the hospital. "I'm not sure," she said uncertainly. "I remember worrying about some business problems I hadn't been able to deal with before I left on this trip. There had been some trouble with my portfolio. My stockbroker died in a car crash just before I left for Europe, and apparently some things had been handled in. . . " she paused, "in an unorthodox manner. I tried to reach his office from the hospital and couldn't, so naturally I was annoyed. Perhaps I became somewhat upset."

"As well you might," Patrick said with a concern that was belied by the glint of amusement in his eyes.

"They said if I wasn't happy with them, perhaps I would like to come here, and suddenly I was in this terrible town, surrounded by these . . . these gypsies."

"It must have been a shock," Kate commiserated. "They're . . . ah . . . unique, aren't they?"

"Dreadful." Marjorie shuddered. "Simply dreadful."

"Why don't you leave?" Frank Chambers asked with interest.

"Because I want to find out what happened to my stocks," she snapped, "because my broker is here."

"Garcia?" he asked. "Oliver Wendell Garcia?"

"Yes, apparently the papers got it all wrong. He must have survived the crash. But I find he's quite different from the person I thought he was. He always seemed so capable, so ready to do whatever I needed done. But I can't get the man to hold still long enough to listen to me, to give me the answers I'm entitled to. And then he has got these people doing everything he says, even to the point of dressing as though they're at a costume party and pretending they're gypsies. Well, he may have them completely fooled, but not me." But she gave an uneasy glance about her. "I shouldn't sit here too long; these people of his get angry if I don't help with the work."

Kate looked at her, nonplused. "Why should you work? Why do you care what they think?"

"Dr. Douglas, I think we should dance." Frank Chambers cut into her questioning.

Kate looked at him as though he'd lost his mind. "Even in my salad days, I didn't do anything more adventurous than a fox trot; this is flamenco."

"And I can't even fox trot," Chambers said, rising to his feet. "I want to get our two dancers back with us without drawing any more attention than I have to," he added quietly.

Marjorie Harrison looked at Chambers, something oddly like hope in her eyes, but she said nothing.

"What's the matter?" Patrick's eyebrows shot up.

"Forget the sangria, and go tell Clare and Sven to come sit here with us," Chambers told him. "I want us out of here in the next ten minutes. I don't know what they have planned, but everything I hear makes me realize something's in the wind." He motioned Kate to go before him. "Garcia's too anxious to have us stay." And with that he lumbered after her to the dance floor.

Patrick looked unconvinced but hurriedly swallowed the last of his sangria and went to speak with Sven and Clare. Marjorie Harrison, left alone at the table, nervously drummed her fingers on the scarred wood and darted anxious glances around the room.

Frank's head bobbed above the milling, heel-clicking dancers. He was almost in time to the music as he maneuvered Kate toward Ryan and Maggie. When he reached them, he lowered his head and whispered to Ryan. Ryan gave a surprised nod, and Frank stopped any pretence at dancing. He led Kate off the dance floor, followed by a bewildered Ryan and a wide-eyed Maggie Stevens.

Frank did not sit down when he reached the table where Patrick, Sven, and Clare now sat with Marjorie Harrison. "Okay, everyone, follow me," he said. He paused a moment to address Marjorie Harrison who was sitting quite still, her hooded eyes gazing at her clasped hands on the stained table. "Mrs. Harrison?"

She hesitated only a moment before she rose from her chair. "I'm coming with you. Staying here isn't worth it, stocks or no."

"Right, then." Chambers jabbed a finger at Sven. "You bring up the rear, and if anyone tries to interfere, deck him."

"What's going on?" Ryan protested.

Chambers had already turned to go. "Shut up and move," he snapped and led them toward the door.

A shout came the other side of the room. "Look out! They're leaving!"

Most of the dancers stopped uncertainly, though the amplified guitar music continued. Three men separated themselves from the crowd on the dance floor. They ran toward the escaping group but came to a skidding stop as Sven grabbed a chair and, moving backwards, held it above his head. Ryan grabbed another chair and stepped next to Sven, jabbing its legs in short thrusts at the oncoming men.

Clare stared at Sven, frozen in place, until Maggie grabbed the girl's hand and pulled her along. They sprinted through the store with the others, skittering out the door Frank Chambers held open and on through the chill night air.

"They want your van," Marjorie Harrison called out, a tremor cracking her brayed words. "They only have a decrepit bus of their own." She lunged ahead of the rest into the van, desperate to reach safety. In her haste, the sleeve of her voluminous blouse caught on a seat back, and the shiny material ripped with a sound like a yanked zipper. Marjorie merely pulled the torn cloth about her arm and scurried to the back seat where she huddled, looking like a fierce, ravaged bird of prey.

Ryan charged up to the van. "Sven's back there holding the door shut," he panted. "We'd better be ready to go when he makes his move."

"This is all a great mistake." Garcia's affronted voice came from the darkness in front of the van.

Ryan swore. "How did he get out here?"

"Probably left while we were all doing our Jose Greco impressions. Get in and turn on the lights," Chambers ordered.

Ryan leaped for the driver's seat and pushed a knob. Light flooded the area, showing Garcia and three other men six feet in front of the van. Garcia held up his hand to shield his eyes. "Please. How can you think we would harm you?"

"Maybe you would and maybe you wouldn't, but we're not staying around to find out." Frank took something from beneath the driver's seat and handed it to Ryan. "I'm going to get Sven," he said under his breath. He stepped onto the parking lot and called back to Ryan, "Stand by the door and if anyone tries to get in the van, use that pipe wrench on them."

For a moment there was only the sound of Frank Chambers's crunching tread on the gravel and Garcia's loud whispers as he consulted his men. Before Chambers had taken more than a dozen steps, the station door burst open and Sven came running out, followed by the milling figures of a dozen men spilling from the building.

"Don't let them get away with the van!" Garcia called to the reinforcements. He signaled the men with him to charge, but Frank and Sven had already swung onboard and slammed the door shut.

"Let's get out of here," Chambers barked.

The van jolted forward, scattering Garcia and his black-clad men before it. Those who could looked back, and in the light that poured from the open doorway, saw Garcia shake a raised fist at the departing van. As the group of gypsies dwindled in the distance, however, they saw Garcia lower his hand, and placing it over his breast, give a last, low, ironic bow.

There was silence as they picked up speed. No one spoke for the time it took to rumble out of town and follow the road into a countryside lit only by a waning moon.

Ryan James glanced over his shoulder at Frank Chambers and nodding at the flashlight on the dashboard, asked, "*What* pipe wrench?"

"They often have a tool kit under the driver's seat," Chambers replied. "Unfortunately, the only thing I found was that flashlight. In any case, it seemed like a good thing to say at the time."

7

"Thanks for getting us out of there, Frank," Kate said, her voice slightly unsteady. "But next time you decide to dance a flamenco, do me a favor and try not to stamp your feet quite so vigorously."

"Got you a couple of times, did I? Sorry about that," said Chambers. "As for thanks—without Sven's and Ryan's rear-guard action, we'd never have gotten away." The van lurched, and Frank reached out to steady himself. He shot a glance to the rear seat where Mrs. Harrison sat, squeezed in with Sven and Clare. "Thanks for the heads-up you gave about them wanting our van, Mrs. Harrison, but it would have been helpful if you'd told us earlier."

Marjorie Harrison ducked her head in what seemed like confusion. When she looked up, however, the old woman glared at Frank. "How was I to know they would try to attack you? I knew they wanted the van, but I certainly didn't think they'd use violence. Oliver might be a lot of things—he's as likely as the next to cut a few corners—but he has never resorted to violence," she hesitated, "—that I know of." She became absorbed in repositioning the rings on her long fingers.

"Do you think Garcia was telling the truth about us getting gas in the next town?" The question came from Maggie.

"I can pretty much guarantee that Garcia wasn't telling the truth about anything," Frank replied. "I'm not sure if there *is* a next town. People like Garcia make a game of lying; they lie even when they don't have to."

Ryan looked over at Chambers, a nonchalant hand on the wheel. "You can tell this after less than half an hour with a person?"

"I knew after five minutes with him. When did Garcia tell us the truth?" Frank ticked off on his fingers. "They have no transportation, so he lied about sending someone to the next town. He lied about—" he was interrupted by the sound of vomiting. He pushed away from his seat.

"Patrick's sick," Kate said sharply. "Stop the van."

Ryan James swore, pulled onto the soft shoulder of the road, and opened the door. Chambers helped the hunched, retching Patrick from the van, and the rest tumbled out after them, taking deep breaths of the clean night air.

"Who's going to clean up that mess?" Marjorie Harrison's voice was thick with disgust.

"I will," said Kate, though she sounded none too happy about it. "Does anyone have anything I can use?"

Maggie rummaged in her canvas bag and pulled out a cotton tee shirt. "I know I should offer to help," she said, handing it to Kate, "but if I tried to go back in there, you'd end up with even more of a problem. Just toss it when you're done."

Kate swabbed up as much as she could and poured a bottle of soda water she found in the picnic basket over the floor and Patrick's seat. Even so the reek of vomit hung in the air. Kate switched on the key in the ignition, opened the windows, turned off the engine and escaped into the sweet night air.

"What do you think's the matter with him?" Maggie asked as Kate poured another bottle of soda water over her hands.

Kate looked to where Chambers stood over the still-retching young man. "I don't know, but I'd put my money on the sangria."

"But we all drank it, at least everyone except Sven and Clare," said Ryan from where he stood conspicuously upwind of Chambers and Patrick, "and, of course, Mrs. Harrison" he added, gesturing to the old woman who stood even farther away than the rest.

"Kate's right," said Chambers. "I'd guess the bad stuff wasn't in the first pitcher, which was probably just to get us slightly oiled. Anyone besides Patrick have a glass from the second pitcher?"

All shook their heads.

"Sure, Garcia wasn't going to hurt us," Maggie said, her voice tight. Then, as Patrick bent over, wracked by another spasm of vomiting, she whispered, "Do you think he's going to be all right?"

"At least there's not much chance he'll die," said Ryan.

"Been there, done that," Maggie murmured. "Y'know, that's something else that's been bothering me." She swallowed and turned to Kate. "If we're all like, I mean, if we've died, how could something like this happen? Aren't we supposed to be protected or something? Where are the angels?"

"We're not in heaven, remember?" Kate said quietly. "And not in hell, either, though from our experience back there, I'd guess we may well be somewhere in the vicinity." She handed Patrick yet another bottle of soda water.

"Where'd all that come from?" Ryan asked, gesturing to the bottle.

"The picnic basket." Kate shrugged. "I know, there wasn't any soda water in it when we looked before, but then Patrick's seat wasn't an easy-to-swab-off naugahyde before either."

"Interesting." Frank helped Patrick to his feet. "Come on, Mrs. Harrison," he called out, "time we got going again."

Marjorie stalked onto the van, clutching her rent garments about her. The rest followed Frank and Patrick, taking their seats in a now-fresh-smelling vehicle.

"My seat isn't naugahyde," Ryan murmured as he slid behind the wheel.

"Patrick's isn't either, at least not anymore," Frank said grimly. "None of the seats is."

"Do you really think we're headed for hell?" Clare said in a small voice.

"No," Kate told her. "At least, I don't think so. For one thing, remember how Dr. Faber encouraged us to become wanderers? How he helped us when we decided to go together? He doesn't seem to be the kind of person who would happily send us off on a trip that would take us straight to hell."

"What about it, Frank?" Ryan looked at Chambers. "As an expert on human nature, do you agree with Dr. Kate's analysis?"

Chambers answered the question seriously. "Faber seemed genuine," he said slowly. "Matter of fact, I thought he seemed pretty much your standard bureaucrat, though as Kate says, more helpful than most. No, I don't think he'd hand us those cards with a smile and send us off to hell." Frank was silent. "As for the rest of this, I gotta say it's beyond me," he said after a moment. "I can tell you how bad guys usually act, and I figure I can spot a scam in this world as good as I could in . . ." he paused, "in the other. But as for where we are or what we can expect to meet up with, I know just as much as the rest of you."

"So what was the point of sending us off in the first place?" Ryan said. "What *is* this wanderer business?"

"Perhaps we're supposed to check out this new world, travel around and see what it's like?" Kate looked at the others.

"Why? What is it we're supposed to find out?" Ryan persisted.

"How should I know?" Kate said. "As Frank says, your guess is as good as mine."

((

For the rest of the night, Patrick Riley slept, exhausted. Although the sleep of the rest of the passengers was fitful, the sweet night air that flowed through the opened windows lulled the van's occupants into a series of contented dozes. True to Frank's prediction, the "next town" Garcia had promised did not materialize.

Dawn came, first crimson lightening the sky, then rosy pink. The van's passengers roused themselves, yawning and looking about surreptitiously, checking to see whether the others were still asleep.

Ryan James rubbed his neck and looked back at them, his dark eyes dull with fatigue. "I guess I oughta have someone take over for a while." He pulled over onto a grassy stretch beside the road.

"What about the gas?" Chambers stood up, ready to take Ryan's place behind the wheel. "I thought we were almost on empty when we stopped at Garcia's."

Ryan nodded to the gauge. "We're still almost on empty."

"You think the fuel gauge is broken?"

"Could be," Ryan's voice was laconic.

"Care to tell us what you mean?" Patrick pulled himself upright, his voice weak but determined.

Ryan James shot Patrick an enigmatic look and edged past Frank to take the seat in front of Patrick that Frank Chambers had vacated. "I don't know how many gallons the tank holds, but one thing I know for sure is that a van this size doesn't have one big enough for it to cover rough terrain all day and most of the night without running dry."

Everyone took this in. "How many miles have we gone?" Frank peered at the gauge. "Oh, oh, odometer's not working either." He looked back at Ryan. "Was it working yesterday?"

"Y'know, that's another interesting thing," Ryan said. "Fact is, I can't remember. Don't recall even looking at any of the gauges— except the fuel indicator—and I'm not in the habit of driving for hours without checking my gauges."

"Don't worry about it," Kate said calmly. At the others' stares, she continued evenly, "I think we only notice what we either need to or want to. Or maybe a better way of putting it would be that we notice only what we're ready to do something about. I think we'll find we have exactly enough gas to get where we want to go." She gave a slight smile. "Wherever that is."

"And how did you come by this fascinating information?" Ryan asked her. It was said with more than a trace of sarcasm, though the smile he gave her was as charming as his rakishly cocked eyebrow.

"Look at it logically, and it simply makes sense," Kate said without rancor. "This is a different world or continuum or whatever you want to call it; and though many things seem similar, it stands to reason that they're not going to be the same. For one thing, this world seems to have a different time and space than the one we came from." She paused a moment and added thoughtfully, "I wouldn't be surprised to find there *isn't* time or space here."

"I don't understand what you're talking about," Marjorie Harrison sat up stiffly, blinking herself awake. "What's all this about time and space?"

Ryan answered her, his tone unexpectedly mild. "Dr. Douglas is just fooling around." He grinned. "You might say the professor is having an acute attack of Philosophy 101. I hear it's something that hits teachers from time to time."

"Oh, brother, I may do a Patrick," Kate said.

"'Do a Patrick.' That's a heck of a way to be labeled," Patrick commented. He held his head gingerly. "I swear all I had was two glasses of that lousy wine cooler—well, maybe three."

"Frank thinks it was a glass from the second pitcher that had your number," said Ryan. He slid back on his seat and closed his eyes. "Don't wake me up unless you see a place where I can get a cup of coffee and some breakfast."

Sven looked wistful at the mention of food. "Wish we could have stayed for that supper those people said they'd bring us," he said. "Or was that part all a lie too?"

"I think that waitress Bella was the one person in that place who seemed to have some acquaintance with the truth," said Frank. "If she said there was supper for us, she'd have delivered."

Ryan opened an eye. "Maybe she's honest, but she certainly could have had better taste in men. A stockbroker, for Pete's sake! What I'd like to know is—"

"Watch out!" Kate shrieked.

The van swerved off the road and onto the narrow strip overlooking the valley. Those on the left side of the van gave a collective gasp and flinched away from the sheer drop outside their window.

Fighting the wheel, Frank brought the vehicle back onto the road. "Damned van steers like a ten-ton truck."

Ryan craned to look down and paled. "What happened, Frank?"

"Sorry. Should have been paying more attention to the road," Chambers muttered.

"I guess so." Ryan looked over the drop again. "You'd think they'd have guard rails on a road like this, for God's sake."

"For our sake, but surely not for God's," Kate said under her breath.

At that moment, the van rounded the bend, and they saw an inn. It was perched on an outcropping that jutted over the valley below, an ancient stone building that looked as though it had grown out of the rock. There were no people at the tables and chairs on the patio, but a white-aproned waiter could be seen moving about inside.

"How 'bout some food?" Sven grunted.

"Y'know, right now I feel like I could use food more than sleep," Ryan said, surprised.

"We might as well see if these wanderers's cards work." Frank pulled into the parking lot without waiting for further discussion.

The paneled dining room wasn't quite empty. A couple at the table next to the window were being served by a pale, thin waiter who struggled to hold aloft a large tray on which plates of food and steaming cups of coffee teetered perilously. The tray wobbled and bobbed until the waiter got it onto the stand beside the table, but it came precariously near the oblivious couple in its final approach.

The waiter who came to greet the group was as ostentatiously efficient as the waiter across the room seemed inept. He fingered an inch of immaculate white shirt that showed beneath a tailored coat sleeve and inclined his head in polite inquiry. "May I help you?" he asked. "We have a nice table over here that will accommodate your group." He led the way to a large table set for eight.

"I can't believe I'm hungry," said Ryan, picking up a menu, "but I am. Man, those smells coming from the kitchen must be eggs and hash browns." He grinned at Maggie. "Maybe this *is* heaven."

Maggie examined her menu. "I think I'll have half a bagel with light cream cheese," she murmured. "And coffee. Black coffee." She shrugged at Ryan's look. "I have to be careful; if I'm not, I balloon up like a blimp." She caught sight of Clare's scarlet face. "What I meant was, I mean, it's what happens to me when—"

Clare hung her head. "I didn't used to be this way," she murmured. "But after the baby—" A stricken look swept away her embarrassment. Two large tears coursed down her cheeks.

"Oh, for goodness sakes, girl, you're not going to start caterwauling again, are you?" Marjorie Harrison waved a be-ringed hand at the waiter who had seated them. "A pot of Earl Grey tea. And bring two cups. It's what this child needs," she said, indicating Clare.

"I don't like tea," said Clare.

Mrs. Harrison dismissed this. "Tea's good for everyone." Somehow the older woman had managed to hide the billowing sleeves of her blouse in the brown wool blanket she'd twisted about her shoulders like a cape. Seated at the table so that one could not see the voluminous gypsy skirts beneath it, she looked almost like the woman they'd first seen at the hospital. Now she turned back to the waiter. "I'd like you to bring our tea now, please, before you take any more orders. And some honey for the girl. Heaven knows she needs the energy." Any indication of unease had vanished from Marjorie Harrison's angular features.

The waiter scanned the rest of the table and seeing no objection, bowed and left. Sven scowled at Marjorie, seeming undecided whether to be furious or grateful for her interest in Clare. The rest looked at the old woman with a mixture of dismay and amused interest.

"Is there any particular reason why you couldn't wait for the rest of us to give our orders before you sent our waiter off?" Ryan asked her.

"People in large groups take forever to decide what they want," Marjorie said complacently. "I might as well have my tea while the rest of you hem and haw." She placed a napkin in her lap with meticulous precision, ignoring the looks her comment provoked from her fellow diners.

"This seems like a very nice place," Kate said into the brief silence. "Matter of fact, everything has looked pretty good since we've come into the mountains. Certainly, I've seen nothing as shabby as the town where Garcia and his people stayed."

"Maybe we ought to stay away from valleys," Patrick said thoughtfully.

Frank shook his head. "As wanderers, we've been given pretty much carte blanche to go where we want. I don't think we should start shying away from places simply because of one bad experience."

Their waiter came to the table carrying a delicately flowered china teapot and cups. Behind him were two servers with huge round trays of covered dishes. The waiter presented their tea to Marjorie Harrison and Clare and then took a coffee pot from one of the trays and poured coffee for the rest. One of the servers uncovered a plate of poached eggs on toast and placed it before Kate Douglas, while the other gave Maggie her half bagel with cream cheese.

When the waiter put an omelet in front of Patrick and a plate of eggs and bacon before Frank, Chambers said it for the rest. "How did you know what to bring?"

"Is there anything wrong?" the waiter asked. "Did we miss something? Or perhaps someone changed his or her mind?"

"My friend just wants to know how you knew what the rest of us wanted," said Ryan. "You have microphones around?"

"Is it some sort of telepathy?" Patrick asked.

"In a manner of speaking," the waiter said.

"You mean you know what we're thinking?" Patrick looked stunned.

"Only if you wish it, sir," the waiter said. "You see, you were each thinking of a particular food. And you were all so anxious to eat, we didn't want to make you wait any longer than necessary. But then you're newcomers, aren't you? I should have taken your orders in the manner to which you're accustomed. I'm afraid I've been remiss." He gave his subordinates a look that dared them to agree with him.

Ryan looked at the plate of eggs and hash browns before him. "You forgot the fresh fru—" He stopped as a platter of pineapple, mango, bananas, oranges and grapefruit was placed beside his eggs and bacon. "Okay, I don't care how you do it; it's a nice trick," he said. "You know if there's a gas station near here?" he asked the attentive head waiter. "We seem to be doing okay without filling up," he said to the rest of the group, "but I'd feel better if we covered all bases."

"Since we're so far from the nearest town, we have our own pump," the waiter assured him. "If you'll pull around back, I'll see the tank is filled while you enjoy your meal."

Ryan looked at the others. "You've gotta admit the service here is pretty good."

"It's more than good," said Frank. "It's excellent. Give my compliments to the management."

"The Management will be pleased." The waiter bowed. "By the way, if you have a picnic basket you'd like us to fill before you leave, just give it to the kitchen staff when you bring your van around back for gas." He left, his assistants at his heels.

"My, oh, my." Kate took a bite of poached eggs, then sipped her coffee and closed her eyes in contentment. "What have we done to deserve all this?" she murmured.

"Maybe we got all the answers right on our questionnaires," Patrick quipped.

"What questionnaires?" Ryan said it, but there was the same query in the faces of the others.

Patrick looked around, suddenly alert. "The form Faber had us fill out at the Guesthaus before we left. Eight pages. And some of those questions were pretty personal."

"I filled one out, too," Frank Chambers said slowly.

"I didn't fill out any form," Ryan said. "Did any of you guys?" The rest shook their heads. "Guess you two were the lucky ones. Eight pages, huh?" He gave them an appraising look. "Maybe they felt they needed to know more about you two."

A sudden wariness flitted across Frank Chambers's face, then vanished, leaving his expression unreadable. "Maybe so," he said brusquely. He looked about the room as though interested in the decoration, but suddenly he squinted, his attention caught by the thin waiter who was now clearing the table at the window. The muscles in Frank's cheek tightened; he examined the pale man a long moment.

"You know that guy, Frank?" Patrick said, alert.

The big man took his time about replying. "No," he said at last. "For a moment I thought I did, but I guess he just seems familiar." He returned his attention to his meal.

They ate silently, the only sounds being clinks of silverware against china and an occasional satisfied sigh. Clare sipped her honeyed tea, at first reluctantly and then with appreciation. When a server brought her a plate of pancakes, the pale girl dug into them. She looked up, her cheeks full, and saw Maggie watching her.

She flushed bright red. "Would you like some?" she said hesitantly. "They gave me two stacks, and I haven't touched that one."

"No, thank you." Maggie licked her finger and picked up the remaining crumbs of her bagel from her plate.

"I'm not going to eat them, really," the girl said.

"Well, maybe one." Maggie reached out and put two of the pancakes on the plate that had held the bagel. "I'll do laps."

Frank abruptly pushed away from the table. "Okay, people, everyone ready to roll? I'll gas the van and take the picnic basket to the kitchen."

"Pit stop first," Kate Douglas said firmly.

Ryan tossed his napkin on the table and watched Kate head toward the illuminated restroom sign. "Y'know, that's interesting. I sort of thought that stuff wouldn't apply here, that we'd have put it behind us, as it were."

"Nicely put," Patrick observed. "But when you think of it, it's logical. We still eat, therefore we still ... uh ... defecate."

"That's disgusting," Maggie shot at him as she got up to follow Kate.

Patrick grinned unrepentantly.

"I don't know what you're talking about, young man," Marjorie Harrison said, rising majestically from her chair, "but you don't surprise or shock me, if that's your purpose; it's what I've come to expect from young people these days. Come, Clare." She pulled the brown blanket more securely about her shoulders and stalked off toward the ladies' room, a docile Clare behind her.

Sven frowned at their retreating backs but said nothing.

Kate Douglas returned just as Frank Chambers walked in from the rear of the restaurant, the picnic basket in his hand.

"I have this nasty feeling we're eventually going to be sent a bill for all this," Patrick said as Chambers heaved the basket onto the table.

"Everybody here?" Frank cast a cursory glance at the group.

"Maggie's not back yet," said Kate. "You go on ahead; I'll get her."

Maggie was standing before the mirror, combing her hair when Kate reentered the ladies' room. The girl's cheeks were flushed, and she avoided Kate's eyes as she hurriedly splashed water on her face. "Bad hair day. I must have slept on it wrong."

"You're not going to be competing any time soon, you know," Kate said gently. "There's no reason to do this."

Maggie stiffened. "Do what?"

"You don't have to watch what you eat, at least not the way you did when you were competing."

"I'm not!" Maggie jerked a paper towel from the dispenser. "Look, I'm just not feeling good."

"If you were Pinocchio, your nose would be growing."

"Who do you think you are?" Maggie flashed at her. "You're not my mother."

Neither spoke for a long moment. Then Maggie's face crumpled. "I don't want to do this. Eat and then throw up. I thought maybe I wouldn't need to here."

Kate reached out a hand but stopped short of touching the girl. "Perhaps you could work on it?"

Maggie drew herself up. "You think I don't try? You think I want to be like this?" She dabbed at her face. "Come on, we'd better get back. They probably think we fell in."

"I've never had children, but I've advised a lot of students and I can usually come up with something that helps the situation." Kate's eyes met Maggie's in the mirror. "If you want to talk—"

"Except for a few phone calls, Mom and I haven't talked for about three years now." Maggie flicked a tongue over her lipstick. "Last time we talked face to face I called her a whore and told her I never wanted to see her again."

Kate searched for something to say but then simply put a light hand on the girl's shoulder. Maggie ignored the gesture, took a deep breath, and marched past Kate out of the rest room, her small frame erect.

Kate glanced at the mirror. "Good going, Kate," she said to her reflection. "Maybe you're not always as helpful as you think." Then, examining the woman in the mirror, she forgot about Maggie. The Kate staring back at her had the smooth skin and clear eyes of a woman much younger than Kate's fifty-four years. Kate touched the curl of brown hair that swept from her forehead. A curl that was no longer threaded with gray. *Interesting.* She turned and headed for the door. *Very interesting.*

8

All day they drove through crisp, clean air, bright with sunshine. After a picnic lunch that rivaled the one the Guesthaus had provided, Ryan James took over the driving once again.

The winding road dipped to a tree line of pine and spruce, then rose to snow-covered rock that towered to meet blue sky. Occasionally they saw small towns in distant valleys set beside meandering streams and surrounded by patchwork fields like toy villages in a child's playroom.

"Switzerland. I knew that's where we were headed," Marjorie Harrison informed Clare, her voice complacent.

The girl peeked across Sven at the old woman and nodded uncertainly, then glanced at Sven. He shrugged as though it was all the same to him if Marjorie Harrison was determined to deny any evidence that they had entered a new world.

"Gstaad was always a favorite of mine," Mrs. Harrison continued. "Rudolph told me I would have been a marvelous skier if I'd wanted to take the time."

"By any chance did this Rudolph have a red nose?" Patrick asked. But his face was sober as he leaned forward to murmur to Frank Chambers's solid back, "Sure does look like our late, unlamented clinic might be somewhere up ahead, doesn't it?"

Frank indicated he'd heard by a slight shrug. He looked at Kate, who was refolding the map she'd been studying. "Have we passed anything you recognize?" he asked her.

"I think I've got the road we're on," Kate said, "but one of the problems is that there are no boundaries and no distances." She looked worried. "And there's another thing. This seems to have changed since I last looked at it."

All heads turned toward her.

"You're saying the map has changed?" said Frank, clearly jolted.

"I can't find the Guesthaus, and I know I saw it near the bottom of the map when we took off yesterday. And then the valley where we met Garcia—it isn't there any more."

"What do you suppose it means?" Clare asked, a catch in her voice.

Kate's eyes were troubled. "I think it means we can't go back to where we've been."

"I wouldn't particularly want to," said Patrick. "The Guesthaus had great rooms and the service was fine, but it felt too much like a summer camp for problem grown-ups. And as for Garcia and his gypsies, I can't say that I'd be too broken up if we never see them again."

"But what if we come to a place we like, someplace we feel we fit in?" Kate asked. "If we leave and go on, does it mean we can't return?"

Ryan licked his lips, staring out the windshield. Then he gave an annoyed shake of his head. "Let's see what's ahead before we panic."

"I'm not in the habit of panicking," Kate told him, her voice cool.

"What does it show ahead of us?" Maggie asked. "These mountains seem to go on forever, and we haven't gone through a town all day." Then her eyes grew big. "Look over there!"

As though her statement had evoked it, a town appeared before them. Bigger than a village but not quite a city, it spilled down the mountain into a valley split by rushing waters that gleamed silver in the afternoon sun. Church spires rose above the trees in almost every street, streets that were lined with houses and small shops. Here and there they could see an onion-shaped tower of what could have been a mosque. Within minutes they were on the outskirts of the town, driving alongside other cars and an occasional bus in a steady stream of unhurried traffic. They passed couples walking dogs on the sidewalks, gardeners tending flower beds in front of tidy houses, and as they neared the center of town, a group of uniformed musicians carrying instruments, apparently headed for a white bandstand in a pocket-sized square of park.

"Why do they have all these churches here? Is this Eastlight, do you suppose?" Maggie asked softly.

Kate considered. "Too small for the place Dr. Faber told us about."

"Any idea where we should go?" Ryan James asked as he pulled up to a stoplight.

"Find a hotel and check in," Frank Chambers said. "After last night, we all need a decent sleep." He peered through his window and pointed to an old-fashioned building at the end of the block ahead. "There's one." Ornate lettering on the sign hanging out over second-floor windows announced the Hotel Crusader. Beneath the lettering were three stars. "Pull up in front, and I'll go see whether they have room for us." Chambers was out of his seatbelt and at the door before Ryan had cut the van out of traffic and brought it alongside the sidewalk.

"If the guy at the desk is dressed up like a gypsy, don't bother to ask about vacancies," Patrick called after him.

Chambers was gone only moments before reappearing with a bellman to help with their bags and a valet to park the van.

"Y'know, we should be exhausted," Maggie said as they trooped into the hotel, "but I'm not really tired and nobody else looks all that bushed."

"I haven't had this much energy since I was nine," said Patrick. "Maybe it's the mountain air, or maybe they put something in those lunches everyone's packing for us. Whatever it is, I'm not about to knock it."

"Find out where we are?" Ryan asked Frank as they piled into the lobby.

Frank nodded to the dapper clerk at the ornately carved reception desk. "This gentleman says the town's called Presbe."

The desk clerk twisted the guest register around so that Chambers could sign it. "The rest of you needn't sign." He beamed at them. "But if I could have your wanderers's cards for a moment?"

The group found their cards and gave them to the clerk who slipped them through a scanning machine before returning them. "Presbe welcomes you," the clerk said with a formal bow. "We always enjoy having wanderers. This is a small hotel, however, and we have a limited number of rooms available, so I was delighted that Mr. Chambers said some of you wouldn't mind doubling up."

"*I* mind," Marjorie Harrison said in glacial tones.

"Then you shall certainly have a room to yourself," the clerk assured her. He took in the brown blanket Marjorie Harrison wore flicked across her shoulders with the insouciance of a matador's cape. "Should madam wish, I can have a dressmaker bring some, ah, appropriate garments to madam's room."

Marjorie favored the clerk with a wintry smile. "Madam wishes."

"Very well." He turned to the rest. "I've put you all on the second floor, so if you'll take the elevator over there, the bellman will meet you and show you to your rooms."

"Just shows what a person can do with enough chutzpah," Ryan muttered to Maggie.

The bellman disappeared with his suitcase-laden trolley down a dark hallway and left the group to stare dubiously at the wrought-iron cage of an elevator secured with what looked like ancient pulleys.

"Will that thing hold all of us?" Maggie asked anxiously.

Patrick eyed the fragile gears. "I'd say the only question is how far from the basement will it be when it falls apart?"

"Not to worry about the elevator: it's really in excellent condition. It appears a trifle, ah, old-fashioned in order to fit with the hotel's decor," the desk clerk said. "Oh, and I forgot to mention, if anyone wishes to attend evening services, there are schedules here at the desk, and I would be happy to give directions to any of our churches."

Several of the group at the elevator exchanged puzzled glances, but all crowded onto the creaking elevator without taking him up on his offer. By the time they arrived at the second floor, the bellman was waiting for them.

"Next time I vote we check out the freight elevator," Patrick murmured.

"If you'll come this way." The bellman escorted Mrs. Harrison to the first room in the hallway where he opened the door and handed her a key. He nodded to the door of the next room and handed Kate Douglas another key. "That one is yours, ma'am. The manager thought you might like a room to yourself also."

Marjorie Harrison didn't seem particularly happy that someone other than she had been afforded a private room, but made no comment as she shut the door firmly after her.

With Kate deposited in her room, the bellman placed Maggie's and Clare's suitcases in the next room and stood aside to let the girls enter. Sven began to protest but stopped at a commanding gesture from Frank Chambers. Though Sven managed to swallow whatever he'd been about to say and followed the doorman and Frank to a room down the hall, his look made clear what he thought of the rooming assignments. And when the bellman indicated that the next room was for Ryan and Patrick, neither was unable to conceal his dismay at having to room together.

All four men stood in the hallway until the bellman took his trolley off to the freight elevator, then quietly converged.

Sven's jaw thrust out; he included all three men with his belligerent scowl. "Clare and I are together." It was a statement of fact.

"Let's not make waves," Chambers said easily. "They're providing us rooms; maybe we should let them call the shots about who goes where."

Sven did not look convinced.

"Besides, is there any particular reason why we should rearrange things for your convenience?" Ryan James leaned against the wall, his guitar slung over his shoulder. Though the position was nonchalant, the hand jammed into his jeans pocket twitched against the stretched material. "The rest of us may not be too excited about the rooming assignments either, but we're not putting up a stink. No offense," he added, glancing at Patrick.

Patrick's thin face tightened, but he said nothing.

The door to Maggie and Clare's room opened, and Maggie came into the hallway, Clare tagging behind her. "The rooms are small, but they're really cute and thank goodness the bathrooms are *en suite*," Maggie said. She stopped. "What's the matter?"

"Sven has some idea about changing the room arrangements," said Frank Chambers. "Frankly, I don't suppose it matters all that much whether Clare moves in with him or not. The only thing I'm concerned with is having a decent dinner and getting some rest."

Kate Douglas's door opened. "Problems?" she asked as she surveyed the crowded corridor.

When Frank explained, Kate gave an exasperated cluck and took charge. "Any objection to my sharing your room instead of Clare?" she asked Maggie. "And I'm sure Frank doesn't mind rooming alone." At Maggie's acquiescent shrug, Kate handed her key to Sven. Sven muttered something that could have been "Thank you" and headed for Maggie's room to get Clare's bag.

Kate watched him go, a faint smile on her face. "Now I don't know about the rest of you," she continued, "but in spite of that wonderful breakfast and more than adequate lunch, I'm hungry. The information booklet in my room says there's a French restaurant on one side of the hotel and an Italian ristorante on the other."

The debate on French versus Italian was quickly decided in favor of Italian. There was no discussion about separating; all seemed to take it for granted that the group would stay together.

"Okay, troops," Frank said as they headed for their respective rooms, "let's meet in the downstairs lobby as soon as we've showered and freshened up."

Kate, who had gone back to get her suitcase, paused at Maggie's door. "What about Marjorie?" she asked.

"Let the old bat starve." Patrick said, without rancor.

"They must have room service here," said Frank.

"Oh, yes, I hadn't thought of that. They had a menu in the information packet," Kate said. "There you go. Marjorie can always order something if she's hungry." Chambers smiled briefly at Kate and closed his door.

(

"Thanks for giving me first shot at the shower, Maggie." Kate tossed a robe over her arm and selected a small plastic bag from the open suitcase on the bed. "I promise I'll be out in a flash."

Maggie watched Kate as she went into the bathroom. She didn't relish sharing a room with this sharp-eyed, observant woman; but, of course, when Kate had asked if she would object to their rooming together, Maggie had to consent. Would Kate tell the others about the food problem? Probably not, but still—

Maggie squatted in a deep knee bend, then rose, stretching first one leg and then the other. Squatted again, two, three. Soon she'd have to find a place where she could work out. Nothing to do with the food bit; it was just something she had to do. Especially now, feeling the way she did, with no low-grade aches, no stabbing pain in her ankle, not even when she'd forgotten about it this morning and taken an exuberant leap from the van's top step to the sidewalk. She looked up at the sound of the bathroom door opening.

Kate emerged, toweling her hair. "Sorry I took so long. It felt so good standing in that marvelous hot water I forgot about my promise to hurry."

Maggie stared at her. "But you just went in!"

Kate frowned. "I was lollygagging in the shower so long I was worried about becoming a prune as well as using up all the hot water."

"You couldn't have been in that bathroom more than a couple of minutes," Maggie said firmly. She paused. "You think it's your no-time-or-space idea?" she asked.

Kate pulled a comb through her wet curls. "I wouldn't be surprised," she said. "Interesting, isn't it?"

"What does it mean?" Maggie asked. "That we can do whatever we want without affecting what other people are doing? I mean, could I, like, go shopping right now or check out the town and still come back and meet the rest of you guys in the lobby in time to go to dinner?"

"I don't know." Kate smiled. "As I said, it's interesting. Perhaps the only reason we're even thinking about time at all is because we've just arrived. There it is again, 'just arrived.' Maybe our preoccupation with time will gradually become less and less of a consideration." Her look was thoughtful. "Have you noticed that, although we've spent two days riding in that van, no one complained about being bored? Everyone, even Marjorie Harrison, seems content to ride a while, stop for lunch, then ride some more until we stop for the night."

"It hasn't seemed like two whole days, has it?" Maggie said. "When we're in the van, I spend my time thinking all sorts of things, like things that happened long ago, things I thought I'd forgotten; and then I look out the window and all of a sudden it's time to stop somewhere." She gave Kate a sideways look from beneath her long lashes. "Is there anyone special you miss? I mean, anyone from . . . back there."

Kate glanced away. When she finally spoke, Maggie had to strain to hear her.

"My husband," Kate said. The whisper was an ache of longing. "I miss him terribly." She cleared her throat and continued, attempting to speak matter of factly, "No, to be honest, I shouldn't say I miss Howard all the time. Most of the time I'm just too involved with what's happening here to think about him consciously. But he's always with me, always there at the back of my mind. And sometimes," Kate stopped and looked down at her hands. "Sometimes I do see him." She looked at Maggie, her gaze level. "I don't know if he sees me, but I think he knows I'm with him. Make that, I *know* he knows I'm with him."

Maggie laced her hands together. "Do you think I could 'see' someone if . . . if I wanted to?"

"I don't know. Whom do you miss, Maggie?" Kate said gently.

"My mom." Maggie busied herself slipping her bathrobe from a hanger in the closet and taking fresh underwear from the dresser drawer.

"You wish you hadn't said what you did?"

Maggie nodded. "I've felt bad about that ever since. And now I can't tell her. Ever." Maggie looked at Kate, her eyes filling with angry tears. "But it was wrong, what she did. She made like it was all for me, but it wasn't. And you can't tell me it was."

Kate waited.

"She was sleeping with him all the time, ever since I was thirteen." Maggie spat out the words. "She said he told her he was going to have to let me go, that I wasn't quite good enough, not to become an elite gymnast. She said she slept with him so he'd keep training me."

"Your coach?"

Maggie nodded.

"This is the one who was helping with your comeback?"

"Jerry?" Maggie snorted. "Not Jerry. Jerry took me on because he knew he'd get a lot of press if I made it back. Coach is the guy I trained with since I was nine, ever since we left Mrs. Hollings." Maggie bit her lip. "I never knew. I thought Coach gave me extra instruction because he liked me." Her eyes were desolate. "I didn't know, but it turns out just about everyone else did. Sometimes the other moms said things about how easy it was for my mom to pay the gym bills, but I still didn't get it. Not 'til the day someone came right out and told me." Maggie cracked her knuckles. "I went and asked Mom why she didn't just turn tricks to get the money."

"What did your mother say?"

"I didn't wait around to hear. Later on, when she tried to tell me it all began because of Coach saying he had to let me go, it just made it worse." Maggie went to the window and looked down at the darkening street. "She quit seeing him. When I left off competing, she went back home and never saw him again. But I didn't know about that part 'til later."

"And now you want to 'see' her?"

"I'd like to tell her I'm all right." Maggie turned and with one fluid movement ran across the room. She stopped at the bathroom door, her hand on the knob. "Sometimes I want it more than anything," she said softly, "but then, I don't. Look, I have to go take a shower. You just go on without me."

Kate nodded. "Sure. Go get cleaned up, and we'll test this time/relativity thing. I'll tell them you'll be along in a minute, and we'll see what happens." But when Maggie went into the bathroom, Kate stood looking at the closed door for a long moment, her eyes troubled.

((

"So who's missing?" Frank Chambers stood in the center of the hotel lobby's blue-and-green patterned carpet.

"Our motorcycle lovebirds," said Patrick. "Probably too busy gettin' it on to think about dinner."

Frank raised an eyebrow. "There's sex here? Don't know why it should surprise me, but I guess I just hadn't considered the possibility."

"You must have a *lot* on your mind," Patrick commented. Then he saw Kate's expression. "Sorry about that, Dr. Douglas; I swear I'll try to clean up my act."

"It's Kate; and I'd appreciate it if you would, Patrick."

"Where's Maggie?" Frank said, looking around.

"Here I am," Maggie called out from the carpeted staircase where she took the last two steps with a lithe skip, her hand resting lightly on the ornately carved banister. "Didn't Kate tell you I'd just be a minute?" She gave Kate a little grin and then looked past her and said, "Hi, Clare. Hi, Sven."

The young couple got off the elevator looking flushed, as though they, not Maggie, had taken the stairs. Observing that they were the objects of the group's attention, Clare slipped her hand into Sven's and moved closer to him.

"My apologies folks," Patrick said solemnly. "Looks like they remembered us."

"That's enough, Patrick." Frank headed for the door. "Come on, let's get something to eat."

The sidewalks were crowded with clusters of people who seemed intent on getting wherever it was they were going. The proprietor of the Italian restaurant greeted them warmly and showed them to a large corner table where their food was brought almost as soon as it was ordered. Diners sat at nearly all the other tables, but before the group had begun to eat their entrees, the restaurant began to empty and within minutes they had the place to themselves.

"Where's everyone going?" Ryan asked a passing waitress.

She stopped obligingly, her dish-laden tray balanced before her. "To services, of course."

Ryan mulled this over. "Church services?" he said.

The young woman nodded.

"*All* these people are going to church?"

"Sure."

The group around the table exchanged glances. Frank Chambers cleared his throat. "We noticed when we came into town that you have a lot of churches here. Are they mainly of one denomination?"

"Oh, no. Matter of fact, we have just about every brand you could think of. It's sort of the town specialty." The young woman waited patiently. "Is there anything more you'd like to know?"

"Building churches is the town's specialty?" Frank asked her.

"Not the buildings. It's what goes on inside. Praising God. That's why it's called Presbe."

Chambers frowned. "What has 'Presbe' got to do with—"

"Presbe," Ryan muttered, "as in 'Praise Be.'" At their looks of astonishment, he gave an impatient shrug. "Anyone with half a brain could figure it out," he snapped.

Maggie looked at him in surprise. It was so unlike the smiling musician whose company she'd come to enjoy, but then Ryan had been doing the lion's share of the driving—he deserved to be cut some slack.

"I suppose you're in a hurry to have us done so you can go to services too?" Frank asked the waitress.

"Oh, no, enjoy your dinner. Take as long as you wish. I don't live here, you see. I don't have to go to services." And with that she gave a friendly nod and headed for the kitchen.

No one at the table made more than commonplace observations as they ate their dinners. Kate put down her fork, and at the same moment Maggie pushed away her plate. Sven and Patrick ate impassively, but neither Clare nor Ryan seemed to have much appetite.

Frank Chambers placed his napkin on the cloth. "Shall we?" he said, rising. "I think we should go back to the hotel and discuss this. Looks like everyone's almost finished anyway."

"Discuss what?" Clare asked, bewildered.

"What the waitress said a while back, babe," Sven told her gently. "That everyone here goes to church but that *she* doesn't have to because she doesn't live here."

When the proprietor left the table after returning their wanderers's cards, Patrick put his in his jeans pocket and said, "Look, so far no one's forced us to do anything we don't want to. I'm betting we can leave when and if we want. You guys can go back to the hotel if you want, but I think I'll check out some of these churches."

He grinned at the incredulity on their faces. "Think about it. With this many churches, there's bound to be some awesome music."

Frank gave him a long look. "I'm not sure I'd be so anxious to go exploring without first finding out more about this place," he said. But he didn't pursue it.

The streets were virtually empty when they left the restaurant, but for a lone man who cast a startled glance at the group and scurried by. Frank Chambers drew Patrick aside. "There's something strange about this place. You sure you don't want to come back with us?"

But at that moment the doors of a white-columned church across the street opened, and the sound of a Bach cantata drifted through the evening air. Patrick's lips parted, his eyes shone. "See you back at the hotel," he said, darting across the road.

Frank did not call him back, but watched Patrick bound up the broad church steps. He turned to the rest of the group. "Before anyone else takes off alone, let's see if we can get some information about this place." When they got to the hotel, he strode ahead of them to the registration desk.

The clerk looked up. "May I help you?" he said politely.

"My friends and I would like to find out more about this town," Chambers told him. "It seems that just about everyone here is going to church this evening. Is there something special going on?"

"Nothing in particular."

"You mean everyone just decided to go get some religion this evening?"

"Everyone who lives here," the clerk said amiably.

"Do they have services every night?"

"Yes indeed, and every morning."

"And everyone goes to them."

"Oh, yes."

Frank and Kate exchanged glances.

"Some of the people we saw didn't look all that happy about it," Ryan said to the clerk. "You're telling me they *want* to spend all that time in church?"

"At first they do." The clerk smiled slightly. "You see there are a great many people who, when they learn that they've come to the spiritual world, assume that they will find blissful happiness in eternal worship. Presbe was founded by such people."

Maggie shook her head in disbelief. "I can't believe they don't do anything but go to church."

"Presbe's citizens can spend part of their days doing whatever they wish," he assured her. "They have their afternoons off."

"So they're forced to go to church twice a day?"

"I didn't say that." The clerk made a steeple of his fingers. "As I said, most enjoy it—especially at first. From what I hear, Presbe has some absolutely marvelous services. But they soon find going to church can get pretty boring if that's all you do."

Kate chuckled. She couldn't help herself. She cleared her throat and said, "But you don't go to the services?"

"Not in Presbe," he said with an enigmatic smile.

"Why don't these people get up and leave if they find it so onerous?" Kate asked him.

The desk clerk busied himself with the ledger before him. "They do. Eventually."

"Why 'eventually'?" Kate persisted.

"Well, you see, most folks who come here have spent a good deal of their lives on earth being good, church-going people. When they come to this town with its churches and nearly continuous worship, they feel they've found their heart's desire. They haven't, of course. Some just take longer than others to admit it."

Ryan looked at his companions. "I don't know about anyone else, but I haven't spent a lot of my time in churches—at least not in the past fifteen years anyway—so I guess I'm immune," he said.

"Me, too," said Maggie. The others nodded.

"I thought that might be the case," the clerk said. "Besides, wanderers are apt to be rather different than the general run of people we get here."

"You said 'of course' they hadn't found their heart's desire," Kate prodded him. "Why 'of course'?"

"Because no one can be happy unless he or she spends a great deal of time being useful."

Kate repressed the thought that the desk clerk sounded rather like one of her more pedantic colleagues addressing a freshman class. "What about the lovely music we heard?" she said. "Weren't those musicians doing something useful?"

The clerk's smile broadened. He regarded Kate as though Dr. Douglas was not only a pupil, but one who had surprised him by coming up with a correct answer. "They are indeed. Those who provide the music for these services, however, are not residents of Presbe."

"If they don't live here, where *do* they live?"

"Elsewhere." The clerk said it as though 'Elsewhere' were a place like Spokane or Toledo. And although his beaming smile remained in place, it was obvious that he considered the question-and-answer session at an end.

"Thanks. Guess it's time we got some shut-eye," Frank said, heading for the elevators. "Anyone who'd like to come to my room and discuss travel plans before turning in is welcome," he added. His tone was casual and unemphatic, but the van's passengers were not in any doubt that they were being ordered to the detective's room for a conference.

❲

"Nice room," Ryan said, looking around Chambers' room. He sprawled in one of the deep, upholstered chairs. "Think we'll have any trouble getting out of Presbe?"

"Depends. Right now the person I'm worried about is Patrick. Apparently you don't walk into one of these churches and then walk right out."

"I vote we leave town as soon as we can. With or without Patrick," Ryan said mildly. He looked at the others. "Hey, nobody asked him to go into that church. In fact, Frank warned him."

"We're in this together," Kate said. She turned to Frank. "So what do you think we should do?" she asked him.

"Plan to leave early tomorrow morning and hope Patrick shows up for breakfast."

"Why wouldn't he?" Ryan asked. "The guy downstairs didn't say anything about services lasting all night."

"I'm wondering if they get you to sign a town roll or join the church or do something that obligates you to return," Frank said.

The discussion lasted a while longer until Kate noticed Maggie slumped in her chair and Clare rubbing her eyes like a sleepy child. "We can't do anything about Patrick tonight," she said, "or anything else, for that matter. I vote we go to bed and see what happens in the morning."

The group broke up, Frank securing a promise from Ryan to notify him when Patrick returned.

"If you're that concerned, I'll tell him to come knock on your door," Ryan said with a shrug. His gaze lit on Maggie sitting with half-closed eyes and his expression softened. "Come on, Maggie," he said, pulling her to her feet. "Hope you don't read in bed," he said to Kate. "This kid shouldn't be kept up any longer than necessary."

Kate pursed her lips, amused, but said only, "I'll try to bear it in mind."

9

Frank Chambers woke to the melodious sound of chiming bells and to bright sun streaming in the diamond-paned windows of his hotel room. He threw back the covers and bounded from the bed, his feet hitting the floor with a satisfying thump. Man, he felt good! Hadn't done much springing out of bed for the past months. Frank strode to the window and cranked it open, wincing at the amplified sounds. He breathed the crisp morning air and contemplated the snow-crested mountains surrounding the town. So this was Presbe.

A vague feeling of disquiet edged into his sense of well-being. There it was again—the feeling that had dogged him since yesterday's breakfast stop. He hadn't let himself dwell on it during the van ride, but now it returned to intrude on today's sunny morning, persistent as a pebble in a shoe. That shaft of unease he'd experienced watching the pale waiter serve the couple at the window. What was it about the thin, stooped figure that had caught his attention? Frank automatically flipped through a mental rolodex of criminals past and present, reviewing a litany of thieves, murderers, and pervs. No go. Frank smacked the window crank. *Give it a rest.* Why should he care? He wasn't a cop any longer; what could he do if he came across bad guys here anyway? If there *were* bad guys in a town full of churches.

Church. *Patrick!* Frank's head snapped up. Where was Patrick? Chambers scanned the scurrying crowds below. Was Patrick Riley among them? Frank cranked the window closed, pulled on the clothes he'd left by the bed, and padded down the hall to Ryan's room.

Only after Chambers's polite rapping became a sharp knock did Ryan James answer the door, his lank hair unfastened from its pony-tail, flowing about his shoulders, his piercing dark eyes sunken. Frank reminded himself that Ryan had been doing most of the driving since they'd left the Guesthaus; probably his lingering exhaustion was delayed reaction to being at the wheel for so long.

"He hasn't come back," Ryan said before Chambers could ask. He stepped aside to let Frank in.

The detective looked around, slid open the closet door, checked the bathroom. "Where's his stuff?" he demanded.

Ryan looked puzzled. "What stuff?"

"Suitcase, toiletries." Then Chambers opened the drawers of the bureau, one after another. All but two were empty. "This all yours?"

Ryan frowned. "Yeah."

"Were Patrick's things gone when you came in last night?"

"How should I know? I didn't have any reason to look for his clothes or check the other drawers."

Chambers headed for the door. "Get the rest of the group together and have the van packed and ready to go. I'm going to see if I can find him."

"Where you going?"

"To the church he went to last night, for starters."

"What do we do if you don't come back?" Ryan called after him. But Frank Chambers was already down the hallway, choosing to ignore the question.

((

Yesterday's clerk had been replaced by a smartly dressed, thirty-ish woman who gave a friendly greeting to each of the travelers as they appeared in the lobby.

"I purposefully did not leave a wake-up call. I was up late choosing the best from a rather complete line of designer wear brought to my room," Marjorie Harrison said as she joined them. "I hadn't expected a hotel of this quality to be able to extend such services," she added, her face relaxing into a pleased half-smile. Then she looked about her sharply. "But while I must admit I enjoyed having my breakfast brought to my room, I'd like to know who took the liberty of ordering it."

"My fault, Marjorie," Kate said. "I didn't want to wake you and just announce that we've decided to leave this morning, so I asked to have a tray sent up to you."

The desk clerk's eyebrows went up at this. "You're leaving?" she said. "You didn't mention that." She hurried out from behind the massive registration desk. "You mustn't leave Presbe without having a tour and seeing its churches. Everybody does. Wanderers aren't required to attend the services, if that's what's bothering you."

"It's not that," Kate assured her. "We just decided we'd like to get an early start and go on to Eastlight."

The woman looked startled. "You're going to Eastlight? All of you?"

"All of us," Kate said firmly. "We're waiting for someone in our group who didn't make it home last night. Mr. Chambers is out looking for him."

"Ah, yes, Mr. Riley," said the desk clerk. "I think Mr. Chambers has found him."

Before anyone of the group could react to this statement, the door to the street opened and Frank Chambers walked into the lobby followed by Patrick Riley.

"Where were you?" Kate snapped.

Patrick glanced at her. "You not only sound an awful lot like my mom, but that ticked-off pose with the hands on the hips even makes you look like her. And believe me, it's more scary than you can imagine." But Patrick didn't look scared. He smiled at Kate, his tired expression oddly peaceful.

"Where *were* you?" she insisted.

"Spent the night talking with the church organist." The lopsided grin wavered and then vanished. "Can't tell you the times I've said something like that and meant something entirely different. But that's exactly what Paul and I did. Talk. Mostly about music."

"Paul?"

"He's someone I knew . . . back when we were on earth. A great musician. We didn't do that much together socially, but he was always someone I could talk to. Still can."

"We thought you might have been . . ." Kate glanced at the woman who had gone back behind the desk, "detained."

Patrick's nod indicated that he understood. "Uh, uh. Because I was with Paul everything was cool. Besides, wanderers aren't as apt to become residents of Presbe as the others who land here." Before Kate could ask anything more, Patrick turned to Ryan James. "What's this I hear about my things being gone?"

"Hey, I didn't know anything about it until Frank came in this morning." Ryan adjusted the strap of the guitar case about his shoulder. "Near as I can figure, someone must have taken your stuff last night while we were at dinner."

The desk clerk coughed politely. Her blue eyes were troubled as she surveyed the group. "The bellman has informed me he found this in the alley behind the hotel." She slid a suitcase from behind the desk and onto the carpet's edge. "The clothes were scattered about," she explained, "so the bellman gathered them and put them back in the suitcase."

Patrick stifled an exclamation. He dropped to his knees beside the torn, gouged suitcase and opened the lid cautiously. To those near enough to see, it looked as though it was filled with a jumble of rags. Patrick lifted an unattached sleeve, half a shirt, ripped from tail to collar, a broken tooth brush. "Haven't seen anything like this since I was invited by some of my good buddies at the university to leave our rooming house," he said softly. "They didn't leave one piece whole, did they?"

"Maybe someone wasn't too pleased to have you checking out Presbe's churches," Frank said.

"I doubt that it's anything to do with that," the desk clerk interjected.

Frank's head swiveled in her direction. "You know who did this?" The question was whiplash swift. The group stared at Chambers. This was a different Frank Chambers, one used to questioning people not eager to give him answers.

The clerk, however, did not so much as blink. "No, I don't," she said calmly, "but there's nothing to fear from anyone connected with the hotel or the churches. The authorities have been informed about this. They're the ones you'll want to talk to."

"By the authorities, you mean the police?" said Frank.

"You could call them that."

"I have no intention of waiting around while the police make nuisances of themselves." It was Marjorie Harrison.

Frank ignored the old woman and turned to Patrick. "We should probably stick around and make a report, but it's your call. What do you want to do?"

Patrick was staring at the remains of his wardrobe. He looked up at Frank's question. "I vote we leave—now," he said quietly. "I don't think I want to stay here."

"Don't blame you," said Ryan. "I wouldn't either." He pulled the guitar from his shoulder and rested it against a chair. "But y'know, while the rest of you load the van, I think I'll go take a look around the alley." He handed the van's key to Frank Chambers and headed for rear hallway. "Just want to check things out."

Chambers made a movement as though to stop him, then shrugged. "Guess he feels bad about sleeping through and not noticing you hadn't come back," he said to Patrick, "but I don't know what he thinks he's going to find out there."

"We don't encourage people to wander the alleys in Presbe," the desk clerk said, distressed. "I'm sure the bellman picked up everything that was to be found." She seemed about to say more, but busied herself with her ledger instead.

"I'll check on him if he doesn't get back in a couple of minutes," said Frank. "Right now we might as well get the bags on the van." He picked up Kate's suitcase and motioned to Sven and Patrick. "We can get these out in a couple of trips."

"What's Patrick going to do for clothes?" Maggie asked when they came back for the last of the suitcases. "Shouldn't we see if there's someplace where he can get some?"

Frank shook his head. "We'll take off now, get Patrick some clothes later." He looked at his watch, or rather the place on his wrist where it would have been if he'd had one. "I'm going to get Ryan."

But before Frank did more than start down the hallway, the door at the far end opened, and Ryan James staggered into view. Ryan weaved down the corridor, one hand against the wall, the other held awkwardly against his chest.

Frank hurried to him, half lifting the young man along the hall and into the lobby. He eased him onto the carpet. "Steady there! Let's take a look." Frank inspected Ryan's face. "That eye's going to close, and they got your jaw and the side of your face pretty good. Can you move your arm?"

"I think it's broken," Ryan gasped.

Frank felt the arm, gingerly at first, then gently turned it. "No, it's not. Not if you can let me do this."

Ryan pulled himself to a sitting position. "My back," he groaned.

Frank leaned over to look, his face grim as he lifted the shirt from Ryan's back. "There's a slash near the shoulder blade," he said. He wiped away the blood with a handkerchief the desk clerk held out to him. "You're lucky," he said. "Looks as though this is the only place they got you."

"I sure don't feel lucky." Ryan accepted Frank's help and got to his feet. He felt his jaw; his eyes hardened. "Didn't give any warning, just came at me."

"How many?"

"Three, four." He winced. "Appeared out of nowhere and started pounding me. With all the black leather they were wearing, they could have been buddies of Sven. Talked about as much as he does too." Ryan moved his arm gingerly. "Anyhow, I managed to break away, and soon as they saw I got the back door open, they took off."

Frank looked at the desk clerk who had returned to her position behind the registration desk. "Any suggestions?" he asked her.

"You seem to be handling things quite well. I've called an ambulance; it should be here shortly."

"What about your unfriendly citizens in the alley?"

"I've already informed the authorities about them. They will have been picked up by now."

Chambers eyed her. "Fast work."

"Yes, isn't it?"

"You wouldn't think this sort of thing would happen in a town like this, would you? A town of churches?" he mused.

"I said that we don't encourage people to go in the alleys," the clerk replied, an edge to her voice. "At least not in the mornings."

Ryan had been looking from one to the other. He straightened, trying to contain a grimace. "Everyone's in church in the morning, right? Stop me if I'm wrong, but could it be that one of the reasons they go is because bad things can happen to you if you're not attending services?"

"We try to see that no one comes to harm, but it isn't only churchgoers who come to Presbe. There's your group, for instance."

"I beg your pardon, but I certainly am a church attendee." Marjorie Harrison gave the desk clerk a glacial look. "And a very regular one, I might add. I haven't felt the need to attend any of your churches here, but why should I? If I need to attend services, I'll wait and go to my own church in Wilmette. Visiting other churches just encourages people to ask for donations, and I give quite heavily to mine, thank you very much."

"Yes, of course you do," the desk clerk said with the ghost of a smile. She cocked her head. "Here's the ambulance."

"I don't hear anything," said Maggie. She looked at Ryan. "If you don't think you're too badly hurt, I think I'd like to leave as soon as possible," she said in a small voice.

Ryan James touched his bruised face and tentatively stretched his injured arm. "Me, too."

In any event, the paramedics, who washed and bandaged Ryan's shoulder and checked his face and arm, agreed that there was no need for him to accompany them to the hospital, not if he didn't want to.

"Sorry about your taking a beating just because you tried to find out what happened to my things," Patrick said stiffly as they filed out to the van. Although he didn't add that he hadn't asked Ryan to perform this act of charity, it was implicit in his demeanor and his tone.

Frank got into the driver's seat and started the engine. "By the way, did you find anything before those guys jumped you?" he asked Ryan.

"Didn't have a chance to do more than look around the dumpster," Ryan said.

"They have garbage here?" Maggie said, surprised.

"Guess so, or maybe it was a recycling bin." Ryan felt the gauze bandage on his shoulder. "I'm glad we're leaving this place. Frankly, I wouldn't trust the people around here if they went to church 24/7." He didn't seem about to elaborate, but at Frank's questioning look, he said, "At the end of the alley, there was this couple, well-dressed, like they were on their way to church. They just stood there when I was jumped—had to have seen what was happening—but they didn't do anything, just stood there watching and then scuttled away." He buttoned the clean shirt Maggie handed him.

"Unfortunately, you're describing the behavior of over sixty percent of bystanders who witness a violent crime," Frank said, steering the van onto the deserted street.

As they approached the edge of town, bells began to peal. Church doors opened, and people streamed out of the buildings into the sunshine. Congregants raced down the broad steps of a splendidly ornate church opposite the stoplight at which the van had halted, and though the light had changed from red to green, continued to dash across the street.

"Looks like school's out and no one can wait to start the afternoon's fun and frolic," said Patrick.

A plump, white-haired man wearing a gray suit and black shirt with a clerical collar, moving more slowly, trailed the first wave of parishioners. He paused at the door of the van and peered in, then tapped at the glass.

Patrick glanced at Frank and, at the detective's nod, opened the door.

"Have you room for one more?" the cleric asked, beaming.

"No." It was Marjorie Harrison. She looked at the rest. "It's crowded enough as it is."

Patrick ignored her. "Where are you going?" he asked the old gentleman.

The cleric peered at him uncertainly. "I have a room in a house just a few blocks down," he said, "but if I'm inconveniencing anyone—"

"Of course not," Kate said. "We'd be happy to give you a ride." She looked directly at Marjorie Harrison, daring her to object.

Mrs. Harrison gave a little expulsion of breath and pressed her lips together. The rest made various noises of assent, and the elderly cleric got in, heaving into the seat Patrick had vacated.

"Well, isn't this nice of you?" the old man said. "Peter Cadmium here, lately of Charleston, now of this wonderful town of Presbe. Fine service back there. A bit long for some I noticed, but then maybe I'm old-fashioned; I like them long."

"You've just arrived in Presbe?" Kate said.

"This morning," he smiled at her. "A few days ago—that is, I think it was a few days ago—I awoke in my little home on Charlotte Street feeling fit and hearty (can't tell you how long it's been since I've felt fit, let alone hearty), only to discover that I wasn't in Charleston after all, but in this wonderful world. You could have knocked me over with a feather!

"When I asked about where I could find a church, I was directed to Presbe. My goodness, what a town! Charleston has its fair share of churches, as you may know, but Presbe … well, you're here, you must have seen for yourselves. And so hospitable! I was quite overcome to find a space reserved for me in the church back there." Cadmium's cheeks reddened, and the wattage of his beaming smile increased. "In the front pew, no less." He whipped out a snowy handkerchief and blew his nose in emotion. "And to top it off, I've just been informed I'm to preach tomorrow. So you can see why I'm anxious to get back to my room. I must work on my sermon."

"And won't the flock be happy to discover you admire lengthy sermons?" Patrick murmured.

"Oh, I'll try not to go on too long," Cadmium said. "I don't want to bore people. Especially my first time on chancel." He started, pointing to one of the brick cottages ahead. "Oh, there it is. My wee lodging house."

Frank pulled over and Patrick opened the door, but it took a while before Peter Cadmium finished his many thanks and expressions of good will.

"Any bets about who gives out first, Cadmium or his congregation?" Patrick said as the van swung back into traffic.

"I think he was nice," Maggie said.

"He's older than most of the people we've seen in Presbe, did you notice?" said Ryan. "Mostly they seem to be young or youngish middle-aged."

"That's why I knew he'd just come," Kate observed obliquely.

Maggie, sitting beside Kate, saw Kate's glance flicker to Marjorie Harrison. Maggie frowned. The old woman did look good. Mrs. Harrison looked more than good, Maggie decided on closer inspection: she seemed to have dropped a good ten years since the morning they'd met at the hospital. "Are we all getting younger?" she asked Kate quietly.

"You're about the same," Kate said. "And if Sven and Clare got any younger, they'd be in diapers, but the rest of us seem to be backpedaling." She spread out her hands and inspected them. "I first realized it when I noticed the backs of my hands," she said. "I couldn't believe it—my skin is supple and smooth and those ugly liver spots are gone."

"There goes the last church; we made it out of town," Frank Chambers announced. "I don't know about the rest of you, but I can't say I'm unhappy to see the last of Presbe."

"I know I voted to leave, but I've been thinking—except for the thing with my clothes, it wasn't a bad place," Patrick said.

"You *liked* Presbe?" Frank turned to stare at Patrick, and the van veered toward the side of the road and skidded onto the gravel. Chambers fought the wheel and swerved the van back onto the road. "Sorry." He gave an abashed grin. "In my old squad-car days my partner used to do all the driving."

"Bet he had it written into his contract," Ryan muttered.

"To answer your question, Frank, yes, I liked Presbe," Patrick said. "At least I didn't dislike it. It's been a while since I've had a chance to hear music like that. Besides, I'd like a chance to see Paul again. A lot of things sort of fell into place last night when we were talking."

"Paul's gay?" Ryan asked casually.

It took an obvious effort, but when Patrick spoke it was without inflection. "No, he's straight, always has been."

"No offense, but I've heard that a lot of male organists are gay. And it just crossed my mind that maybe the person who trashed your clothes was someone who was jealous of you talking to this guy Paul."

"Whoever did that to my clothes had no connection with Paul," Patrick said flatly.

"Weren't you scared last night, Patrick?" Maggie said quickly. "You knew people who go to services in Presbe aren't allowed to leave town."

The smile Patrick gave Maggie was genuine. "Not really. I knew nothing terrible could happen when I was around music, especially music like that."

"If that's what it takes, I wish I'd had my guitar with me in the alley." Ryan James held a hand against the bandage on his shoulder as he gingerly attempted to get into a more comfortable position. "I'm sure I could have dredged up a hymn from my repertoire."

"I wasn't listening to hymns," Patrick said shortly. Then he flushed. "What I mean is, Paul was playing mostly Bach and Mozart at the service. Later on—this is the fantastic part—he knocked my socks off with some absolutely marvelous stuff, music I'd never heard before."

Ryan raised an eyebrow. "So?"

"Believe me, if those pieces had been composed anywhere in Europe or North America or South America, for that matter, chances are I'd have known them."

"Good stuff, huh?" Maggie said encouragingly.

"As good as the Bach and Mozart. Maybe surpassing them." The authority in Patrick's voice left no doubt that the music had been exceptional. "And I hear it gets even better."

"The music?"

Patrick nodded. Then his shoulders slumped. "Not that I have much chance of getting to hear it. Unless…unless—" he paused and fell silent, becoming engrossed in the countryside outside his window.

Maggie looked at him, wide eyed. He was talking about a place he didn't think he had much of a chance of getting to. He was talking about heaven. She stared out her own window. What about her? What were her chances? What had she done or not done during her twenty years of living that might qualify her for heaven? Maggie curled her hands about her knees and slowly exhaled.

The picture that formed, a scene of dark colors superimposed on the rushing countryside, looked as though it was just beyond the glass. Behind the glass, a figure sat in a shadowy booth with cracked naugahyde cushions. It was Rose. Maggie's mother sat gazing into the short, squat glass on the table before her. A tear trickled down Rose's cheek and fell into the amber liquid, and Maggie knew beyond a doubt that her mother was thinking of her. Why at a bar? Couldn't Rose have been thinking of her somewhere else, like in a church while she was praying, for Pete's sake? Maggie didn't recognize the man opposite her mother, but then she saw the tape recorder and note pad and realized he was a journalist. What was the jerk thinking of, interviewing Rose in a bar? Two drinks and Rose would be slurring her words, three and she'd be telling him the same story in seven different versions. Maggie couldn't hear what they were saying, but she knew Rose was telling the reporter about the accident, about what a great gymnast Maggie had been, and about how she'd been on the verge of a comeback. Rose wiped her eyes and sighed. When she began to speak again, Maggie knew as certainly as if she'd been able to read Rose's lips that now her mother was talking, not about Maggie, but of Rose Stevens's many struggles and hard life. Maggie groaned. *Oh, Mom, you're not still doing the I-gave up-everything-so-Maggie-could-succeed bit.*

It was as though Rose had heard her. She stopped speaking and dabbed at her eyes with a crumpled tissue.

"I shouldn't be talkin' about my troubles," Maggie heard her mother say. "Things weren't easy for Maggie either. There were a lot of things I shoulda done different." Rose paused. "We had some rough times between us for a while there, but lately she'd begun to call now and then. I think maybe she wanted—" Rose bit her lip; another tear fell.

"I was going to call after the trip to Germany, Mom," Maggie said softly. "I was going to say let's meet and see if we can manage not to bite each other's head off."

"I think she was planning to call me when she got back," said Rose. "I think maybe she wanted to get together."

Impulsively, Maggie reached out to touch the window; but as her finger grazed the glass, the dark picture faded, and Maggie was looking at a waterfall rushing down the granite mountainside. Maggie looked about her, shaken. Patrick was gazing out his window, bemused, while at the wheel Frank Chambers seemed deep in thought; and though Maggie was certain Kate wasn't asleep, Kate sat with her eyes closed. Everything was normal. She was here. Rose was there. Maggie eased her shoulders against the cushioned seat. But Rose knew. Surely, somehow, she knew Maggie had forgiven her.

((

Mountains and alpine meadows gave way to forests that became aspen groves, then rolling countryside and woods of what seemed to be maple and oak and other trees that seemed vaguely familiar but not readily identifiable. As the air grew warm, the van's passengers opened windows to the breeze.

"My, look out there," said Marjorie Harrison. "We've left Switzerland, and we're back in Germany, somewhere in the Black Forest region, I'd guess."

Ryan shifted his bandaged shoulder into a more comfortable position. "You mean you still think—" He stopped and tried another tack. "Y'know Presbe, the town we just came from? Didn't it seem strange to you that everyone spoke English there? Wouldn't you think that if we were in Switzerland, you'd hear at least some people speaking German or French?"

A shade of confusion crossed Marjorie Harrison's face, and her eyes widened. "Everyone speaks English these days." But it was more a question than a statement.

"Let it alone, Ryan," said Kate.

Marjorie looked from Ryan to Kate. Then she gave a ladylike sniff and appeared to put the matter from her mind. She turned to Clare. "We'll have to get you some clothes when we stop to replenish Mr. Riley's wardrobe," she said.

Clare looked down at the jacket that stretched over the bulge of her plump waist. It was tight, but perhaps not quite as tight as it had been.

"We'll have to decide—" Mrs. Harrison went on, now in full bore, "in this weather, an understated cotton, I think. An A-line, if we can find one."

"I don't wear dresses," Clare objected.

"Time you started doing so." Mrs. Harrison opened her capacious purse and took out a small black book. "My dressmaker gave me the names of some reliable places in Germany, but I don't suppose they will do us any good if we stay out in the countryside. As soon as we get to a sizeable town, however, I'll call the nearest address and see if something can't be done."

For a moment Clare looked intrigued. Then she slouched in her seat and shook her head. "Don't bother. I don't care about clothes," she said.

Sven touched her cheek. "Since when don't you care about threads, babe? Anyway, if you want something to wear, I'll get it for you next town we come to." He lowered his voice. "Dressmakers! The old bat thinks she knows everything."

Marjorie Harrison may not have heard him, but Kate Douglas did. "Oh, I don't think it's going to be a problem finding clothes," Kate said. And when Sven looked at her, blond eyebrows raised, she continued, "Remember Mr. Cadmium waking up in what he thought was Charleston? I think there's a good chance when Mrs. Harrison phones she'll find a 'little dressmaker' who will be only too happy to help her."

"Well, of course," Marjorie snapped. "I don't understand why everyone's making such a fuss about things. While I'm certainly not used to traveling by this peculiar method of transportation, I've no intention of letting it disturb me." She looked about the van and included the rest of the passengers in her lecture. "You people seem not to have done much foreign travel," she said. "It's the mark of a seasoned traveler to take the unexpected with composure. I can assure you that, though I'm not accustomed to traveling in this make-shift way, I can put up with it. And if I can, surely the rest of you can make do."

Her listeners looked at her and then at each other. No one responded to this little lecture; apparently the thought of Marjorie Harrison's putting up with anything, let alone with composure, left them speechless.

With a rueful gleam in his black eyes, Ryan James finally said, "You're right, Mrs. H. Don't know why I got so uptight about being beaten up and knifed. As a seasoned traveler, I should have put it all down as having an interesting experience."

"How's the shoulder, by the way?" Frank roused himself to ask.

Ryan moved his arm. Then he raised it above his head and swung it down. "That's funny," he said, a trace of uneasiness in his voice. "There's no pain, no pain at all." He unbuttoned his shirt. "Take a look at my back, will you, Maggie?"

She leaned across to lift a corner of the bandage covering his wound. "The cut's still there, but it's almost healed," she said slowly. "No scab, just new, red skin." She smoothed the bandage back in place. "And your face is hardly swollen, y'know. That big bruise on your chin is almost gone."

Ryan felt his jaw gingerly. "I always healed fast, but this is crazy." Then he grinned. "Or not."

Marjorie Harrison listened with unfeigned interest. "If you're feeling better, perhaps you should take over the driving, young man," she said, adding with uncharacteristic tact, "I'm sure Mr. Chambers is tired by now."

"Ryan may be feeling better, but I doubt that he's in any shape to drive yet." Kate turned to Sven. "Sven, why don't you check out our picnic basket and see what's in it?"

"Didn't we pretty much finish yesterday's lunch?" Patrick said. But he looked on with interest as Sven hauled the basket from beneath the rear seat and lifted the top.

"Not the usual display of lunch-time goodies," Patrick reported to the rest, "but there's fruit juice and bagels, some Danish and cheese and crackers and a thermos."

Sven twisted off the cap and sniffed appreciatively. "Coffee," he said.

"What do you know that the rest of us don't?" Patrick asked Kate.

She shrugged. "So far we've been provided with food whenever we've needed it; I just had the feeling there would be something in the basket."

"Well, I take this as an indication we ought to stop for a mid-morning snack. How about it, Frank? Want to take a break?"

Frank blinked and relaxed his grip on the wheel. "Stop? Oh, I don't think so. Let's give it half an hour more, put some distance between us and Presbe." Not waiting for further comments, he returned to his musings.

Why had he and Patrick been the only ones asked to fill out a questionnaire? When he'd been asked to fill it out, he hadn't thought twice about it. Filling out forms had been a way of life on the police force. Frank tried to remember exactly what he'd answered. He'd put down the usual stuff, "divorced" next to marital status, "retired" next to employment, and "none" next to children.

But, of course, that last wasn't quite right.

Frank's jaw tightened. Was Ben here? Somewhere nearby? Would he be the same? Frank swallowed hard. No, he didn't want to think about that. Maybe in a while. Not right now. Think of something else.

Marge. She'd been a laughing, fun-filled girl when he'd married her, but by the time they'd parted he could hardly remember how she looked when she smiled. Most of that had been because of Ben, of course. She hadn't slept for months after the day Ben toddled off. Frank hadn't either. They didn't talk. Frank wasn't even sure whether Marge had been aware that he too was awake. When he wasn't on the late shifts he'd requested, they lay side by side throughout the long nights, each careful to keep to his or her side of the bed, their bodies not touching.

Marge seemed happy enough now. Married to a dentist with two kids, she'd made the adjustment of becoming a stepmother without missing a beat. Maybe it was easier to care for someone else's kids than have more of her own. She'd told Frank that after being married to a cop, anything was easy.

Don't think of Marge.

Frank looked at the reflection in the rearview mirror. Most of this bunch he'd gotten himself hooked up with seemed okay. Marjorie Harrison could have been the prototype for every rich, domineering North Shore woman Frank had ever had the misfortune to come across; but Kate Douglas was a nice enough woman. Smart, too, though the appraising, sardonic look she sometimes gave her listener before speaking left him feeling ill at ease. Made him feel like a rookie cop hauled on the carpet, matter of fact. And Maggie Stevens was a cute kid, world-class gymnast or not, a cute kid who thought no one but Kate had noticed her problem with food.

Then the teenagers. Sven and Clare were hiding something, of course. The girl was settling down, but every now and again whatever it was surfaced, and water works erupted. Something to do with the baby. Was it something that had been done *to* the baby? By her, not Sven, he guessed. Over the years, Frank had grown adept at spotting a guilty conscience, and Clare had one, but not Sven. He was concerned only with anything that bothered Clare.

Ryan James. Frank glanced at the image of the young man's hawk-nosed profile. Why had Ryan gone out to check the alley? Even though they were fellow musicians, Ryan had made no effort to hide the fact that he wasn't happy about rooming with Patrick. The reconnaissance of the alley had been a macho gesture, Frank decided. And it had almost gotten the kid killed.

Frank suppressed a snort. Guess not. You didn't get killed here. But obviously they had something like police here; the woman at the hotel had talked of "the authorities." What would it be like to be a policeman in this place? No murders to photograph and detail. You'd never have to tell a mother that her child had stopped a bullet, never have to console a widow. Never have to get a confession from a bad guy and find out that maybe—. Frank shook himself. *Don't go there.* What was he doing, anyway? Thinking of applying for a job?

You could be lulled into thinking stuff like that here. In spite of the odd things that happened, like a knife wound healing in an hour or food appearing when you wanted it, a lot of things here were amazingly like the world they'd left. Perhaps that helped to explain how quickly they'd all accepted the fact of this new life, this different world. All except Marjorie Harrison, of course. The old woman would deny the sky was blue if she'd already decided it was pink.

The roar of engines brought him back to the present. He grabbed the wheel and twisted the van to the side of the road as a line of motorcycles screamed past. The van bumped and shuddered over a small mound, scattering a shower of stones before it stopped. "Damn!" he gasped. "Those cycles came out of nowhere."

"Did you get a look at that Heritage Springer? And that other one looked like a '15 Harley." Sven's comment was tinged with awe. "Couldn't be though. No one would actually ride one of those."

"Did you see the guy in front?" Patrick said, peering at the dust that was all that was left of the motorcyclists, "looked like some kind of road warrior with the red bandana and the beard hanging down to that pot belly."

Ryan scanned the road ahead, his lips tight.

Frank Chambers watched him with interest. He started the engine and brought the van back onto the road. "You recognize them, Ryan?" he said, his voice casual.

Ryan James's eyes narrowed.

"Were those the guys who beat you up back in Presbe?" Frank persisted, glancing from the road to the image of Ryan in the rear-view mirror.

Ryan looked as though he was about to deny it, but then he gave an infinitesimal nod. "Guess they could be."

"In that case I say we forget our mid-morning snack and get to the nearest town as fast possible." Chambers gunned the motor, pressing the gas pedal to the floor, and the van took off down the macadam road, a rocket released from its launching pad.

10

"There's a town! And look, there's the ocean!"

"Those pastel-painted houses and all the palm trees! Looks like we're in the Caribbean," said Ryan.

"The Mediterranean, you mean," Marjorie Harrison said.

"Of course," Ryan gave the old woman an easy grin. "And I won't even ask how we got from the Black Forest to the Mediterranean."

Chambers surveyed the immaculate, palm-lined streets. "See the big white building up ahead by the water? The one with all the red-tiled roofs? Looks like a hotel; let's try it."

"Could be the second cousin of the Marriott in Palm Desert," Patrick said, squinting at the drive that wound through gardens and waterfalls. "We're going first-class."

Frank drove between stone pillars and down the driveway to the front of the main building where they were waved to a parking space.

"I don't think we should sign anything until we're sure what it entails," Kate murmured as they walked into the lobby.

"I second that," said Ryan, adding, "like anyone with half a brain would."

"Welcome to Bucknall." The lavender-suited receptionist took their wanderers's cards and spread them on the counter before her. "We have some individual suites available," she said, consulting her ledger book, "but we're a trifle overbooked at the moment, so could we ask a few of you to double up?"

"I shall need a room to myself," Marjorie Harrison announced.

"I'd like one if it's available," Ryan said quickly.

Sven put his arm about Clare. "And we're together," he said firmly.

The clerk looked at them. "Are you?" she said gently. But she made a notation in her book without further comment.

"Maggie and I can share a room," said Kate, raising an eyebrow at Maggie.

"That leaves you and me, Patrick," Frank said easily, "and I'm fine with it if you are."

Patrick gave Frank a grateful look and nodded.

"Well, that's it then." The desk clerk looked up, smiling. "And which banquet will you be signing up for this evening?"

Ryan glanced around at their little group. "Why do we have to sign up for anything?" he asked.

"It's customary here at Bucknall to attend the banquets and the entertainments afterwards. We can reserve a table for you at this hotel or at any one of the others in town," she explained. "Each banquet features a different kind of entertainment, so you just have to decide which one you'd like to see."

"What kind of entertainment?" asked Patrick

"We're having a musical comedy tonight here at the hotel," the receptionist said, "and, let's see, there's a ballet scheduled after the banquet at the Monte Carlo, or if you prefer, you can hear a program of classical music at the Savoy."

"I'll take the Savoy," Patrick said promptly.

"I'd rather see the musical," said Maggie.

"We stay together, remember?" said Frank. "Should we take a vote and find out what the majority wants?"

"I don't care what the majority wants. I don't know how much longer I'm going to be able to hear really good music, and I'm not wasting my time on musical comedies." Patrick's tone and expression were uncharacteristically uncompromising.

Frank gave an exasperated grunt. He turned to the receptionist. "If we sign up now, can we change our minds later?"

"Switch to another banquet? Certainly. And of course, you'll be able to see one of the other programs tomorrow night."

"Could we opt out of going to anything tomorrow, or maybe choose to leave tonight before the program's ended?" Kate asked.

"Oh, that's not usually done." The receptionist studied her and then said, "But you're wanderers, aren't you? Let me check and see.

Exceptions are sometimes made for wanderers." She went to the rear of the desk, picked up the phone, and carried on a murmured conversation. When she returned she said, "I've been told that since you've made the request before signing, it will be all right."

"Thank you, Kate," Frank murmured. "Fine," he said to the receptionist, "but we have some things to discuss before we can tell you which banquets we'd like to attend." Frank glanced at the plastic card she'd given him. "Okay, Patrick's and my room is 204," he said to his companions. "Let's have a meeting in—" he looked at his wrist and then quickly put his hand at his side, "in however long it takes you to unpack and get there," he amended.

((

"So your watch is gone too?" Patrick asked as they began to unpack. "I can't remember putting mine on this morning, but then I can't remember not putting it on either."

Frank nodded grimly. "Either there's someone in our group who's a better pick-pocket than anyone I've ever run across at home, or it's gone because, well, because we don't need watches here."

A few minutes later there was a knock at the door of room 204, and Patrick opened it to Sven and Clare, who were followed by Ryan, Maggie, and Kate.

"Should I get Marjorie?" Kate asked Frank.

"When we came upstairs, she said that she was going to rest and that she didn't feel the need to come to a meeting," he said. "However, while she hasn't decided whether or not to dine in her room, if she *does* attend a banquet, it will be the one at this hotel."

"That's our Marjorie," said Kate.

"You were right about reading the fine print before we sign anything, Kate," Ryan commented from his seat in his straight-backed chair beside the desk. "Some of those folks in Presbe were getting pretty tired of attending church services, but they sure were having a hard time leaving." He frowned. "I'd feel better if I knew what these towns we keep coming to are all about."

Kate was standing by the sliding glass doors opened to a balcony that overlooked sunlit waters. "It's obvious," she said, twitching the gossamer draperies impatiently. "Think about it. What kind of ideas do most people have about heaven or a life after death?"

They looked at her and then each other.

"Angels with wings and harps?" Bright red crept across Clare's pale face when she realized the rest were looking at her in astonishment. "My grandma had a picture in her bedroom," she said quickly. "It was a picture of angels with big wings going up and down a staircase—" Her voice trailed off.

"The people I hung out with didn't talk about heaven or anything like that," Maggie said. Then she added with a trace of uneasiness, "But then, I've never really thought about it. Didn't have time."

"But some people have pretty definite ideas," Kate said. "The man at the hotel in Presbe said the town was founded by people who thought being in heaven meant worshiping at church services all the time."

"So people who go there get just what they've imagined heaven would be like," Patrick said slowly, "church every day, almost all day."

Kate nodded. "And at first, as the hotel clerk told us, they think it's wonderful. But many we saw seemed to be in the process of finding out it isn't nearly as wonderful as they thought it would be. Some of them heading for church looked as though they'd rather be going to the dentist."

"Wait a minute," Sven looked at her. "You're saying going to church is a bad thing?"

"No, no, our waitress said she went to services, but not in Presbe, remember? I think Presbe exists because if someone's convinced going to church is all heaven consists of, he or she has to come to realize there's more to it than that."

"Sort of like aversion therapy?" said Patrick.

"It's possible, isn't it? And I'm sure there are a lot of people who think heaven consists of sitting around eating great food and watching first-class shows."

"Bucknall is just another place people imagine heaven would be like?" said Ryan.

Kate gave a small shrug. "What do you think?"

"I think if you're right there are a couple of heavens I'd rather be checking out than Bucknall." Ryan gave her a Groucho Marx leer and flicked an imaginary cigar. "Like I wouldn't mind one of those ones with the horiis, or whatever those babes are called."

Then he caught Maggie's expression. "Just kidding," he said, flashing her a smile.

"I'd like to visit that one myself," said Kate, amused. "Give those girls a short lesson in assertiveness training."

Frank raised a hand. "All right, folks, how about we get back to tonight's plans? We seem to have been given a pass to take part in these banquets on a temporary basis, so let's figure out which one we're going to. Like Maggie, I'd just as soon stay here, but it's probably a good plan not to have anyone go out alone, and since Patrick's set on the classical program, is there someone who'd like to go along with him and get some culture?"

"Not me." Ryan had been leaning back in his chair; now he straightened. "Damned if I'm going to sit through hours of classical stuff just because Patrick won't go along with the rest of us." He turned to Patrick. "Anyway, I'm surprised you didn't opt for the ballet."

Patrick moved from where he leaned against the wall to the center of the room. "I'm not asking anyone to go with me," he said, "Matter of fact, I'd rather be alone. You all feel free to do whatever you want."

"Yeah, and when you don't come back until morning, we have to go looking for you again and possibly end up with someone getting beaten."

"That's enough." Frank's cool words carried an edge. "It's your choice, Patrick. I suggest you pick up your wanderer's card from the reception desk and take it with you—just in case." He glanced at the rest. "Looks like the rest of us want to stay here." He gave an approving nod at the affirmative murmur. "Okay, Patrick, I think we should go downstairs and do some shopping at one of those stores off the lobby. You need to pretty much re-outfit yourself and something tells me my outfit isn't going to hack it for a banquet."

"Do you think I could do some shopping too?" Maggie asked, brightening. "Just go down and pick out a dress for tonight?"

Frank smiled at her. "Go for it. I'll bet they have something that has your name on it."

((

Evening stars studded a dusky sky as Kate came down to join the banquet attendees on the terrace outside the lobby. She stood looking over a crowd of what seemed to be a couple hundred people gathered on the great stone terrace. Africans in caftans mingled with men and women in dinner dress. Indian women in shimmering saris listened attentively to couples with Palm Beach tans. White-jacketed waiters wove among them all, proffering trays of drinks and platters of shrimp puffs and caviar with lemon and wafers.

Patrick appeared beside her. "Mind if I join you before I head off to my banquet?" He took a wine glass from the tray of a passing waiter.

"Of course not." Kate smiled at him. "My, don't you look nice."

Patrick flushed with pleasure. "They had a pretty good selection in the hotel shop, and in my size too. Wait 'til you see Frank; they got him to take a dinner jacket." He looked over her shoulder. "Here he comes now."

Frank Chambers came up to them looking sheepish. "They told me tonight would be formal," he said.

"Frank, you could be wearing white tie and tails, and no one would take you for anything but one of Chicago's finest. Sorry, I should have said one of Chicago's finest *detectives*."

Frank didn't lose his good-humored smile. "Since a detective is one step above a patrolman, and not a big step, I wouldn't worry about it."

But Patrick wasn't listening; he was looking at Frank's wrist. "You're wearing your watch!"

Frank's jaw tightened. "Yeah, found it on my dresser."

"It just appeared?"

Chambers looked down at his wrist, his eyes hooded. "Yeah," he said again. "It was my Dad's. I've worn it for years. Maybe since it's something I'm so used to wearing, it, or rather one like it, was returned to me."

"What do you mean, 'one like it'?"

"My watch is somewhere in Switzerland, remember?" Chambers said, lifting an eyebrow. "Either buried with me or swept together with the rest of my stuff waiting for someone to dispose of it."

They stood silently, Frank engrossed in his thoughts, Patrick contemplating his wine, Kate looking at the moonlit waters.

A waiter gliding by paused before them and Kate took a fluted glass from his tray. "If you'll excuse me, I think I'll take a walk before we sit down for dinner." She smiled at the men and turned away quickly, but not quickly enough to hide the pain in her eyes.

"Is something the matter?" Frank said, concerned.

Patrick shrugged. "Probably. We're all going through periods of being on edge. Could be she didn't need a reminder that the body she knew is rotting away somewhere." He took a long swallow of wine.

"Well, it's a fact." Frank said. "I've spent my life facing facts, not about to start ducking 'em now." But the look he gave Kate's disappearing figure was troubled.

(

Kate put her untasted drink on the edge of the parapet and walked slowly down the stone steps. Heedless of the damage to her gold strapped sandals, she wandered across the sand to where wavelets gently lapped the shore. She walked on until she could no longer hear the chatter and the music, walked until the muscles in her legs began to ache. Finally, she stopped and looked out over the dark water. She took a long shuddering breath. "I won't cry," she whispered. She flung her head back and repeated defiantly to the myriad stars above her, "I will not cry!"

But she did. She buried her face in her hands and cried as she had not since she was a child, cried until she collapsed onto the wet sand, a sobbing, huddled mass of grief. At last her sobs lessened, and she became aware of a warmth about her shoulders. It felt as though someone had placed a feather-weight blanket over her misery. The tight knot in her stomach loosened. Still, she did not lift her head. She remained crouched in the sand, her fists pressed against her eyes.

The vision came without warning. Howard was sitting awkwardly on the grass beside a flat, inscribed stone, his canes on the ground beside him. Kate caught her breath as she saw that his familiar face was streaked with tears. Howard, who except for that last day at the hospital, never cried, Howard, the man whose sole expression of anguish throughout seven surgeries and a host of personal and professional disappointments had been an occasional snort of disgust, Howard dropped his head into his hands and sobbed.

"Oh, darling," Kate cried. She caught herself. "Dear love," she whispered urgently, "you've got to know that I'm not there beneath that stone. I'm here, I'm here, and I'm all right."

Howard looked up, then off into the distance, appearing to strain to hear something.

"Don't grieve too much," Kate said softly. "Get on with your life, my love. Finish the Milan paper—now while all the research is fresh. I can't help to edit this one, but Andy will help if you ask him." Kate took a deep breath and leaned close to the bright vision. "We'll be together when it's time," she said. "I know it."

Howard Douglas sat quietly. The sadness in his eyes lessened. He brushed his cheeks and fumbled for his canes. Kate found herself reaching out to help him and for just an instant, a heart-stopping instant, she felt the familiar, sharp angle of his thin elbow as he steadied himself. The image faded and the picture before her vanished, but not before Kate's husband turned abruptly and looked behind him. And for that micro-second, as she looked into Howard's eyes and saw his wondering, answering smile, Kate felt a joy so sharp it was akin to pain.

（

"Kate, I was looking for you! Come on!" Maggie waved to Kate from the top of the stairs. "You should have come to the store with Clare and me," she said, pirouetting so that her gauzy peach dress swirled and eddied about her. "See what I got?"

Kate put a hand against her cheek, hoping the darkness hid her ravaged face. She glanced down at the long skirt that swept her gold sandals. Made of some uncrushable fabric with gold and tan figures on a brown background, it had been an essential part of her travel wardrobe for years, but its fashion quotient was, she knew, distinctly lacking.

Kate brushed away the remnants of sand and realized the skirt had already dried. "Your dress is absolutely gorgeous, Maggie," she said. "I should have made the effort to get something new. This old thing has been to more faculty gatherings than I like to think about."

Maggie looked at her sharply. "Kate, what's happened?"

Kate felt herself flush. "It . . . it's hard to explain. Do I look terrible?"

"Terrible? You're *glowing*," Maggie said. "You look as though you've won an Olympic gold or something. And that outfit may not be new, but it sure fits in all the right places."

Kate touched her waist with an uncertain hand. The skirt did fit well, the top too. Kate's hand smoothed a slim hip, her flat stomach. *Slim? Flat?* She hadn't had a figure like this since she was a teenager. She felt a momentary pang, wishing Howard could see her. Then a small smile curved her lips as she realized that, God willing, he would, he would indeed. *Thank You. Thanks for whatever it was that happened back there on the beach. And please*—Please what? What did she really want ... more than anything? *Please, let me learn what it is I need to learn so that Howard and I can be together.*

"There's the dinner gong," Maggie was saying. She took Kate's arm. "They have name cards at the table. I'm sitting on one side of Ryan, and you're on the other."

"Lucky us," said Kate. But she allowed herself to be drawn across the flagstones to the table where the others were sitting.

If a round table could be said to have a head, it was where Marjorie Harrison sat. She inclined her beautifully coiffed head toward Ryan James, listening to the attentive young man, who was dressed in a golf shirt and jacket and clean, pressed chinos. She looked up at Kate and Maggie's arrival and said approvingly, "I'm glad to see you've dressed for dinner," her gaze flicked to her companion's attire and then to Sven's denim shirt, "unlike some others who have no idea of the niceties of civilized behavior."

Not a whit discomposed, Ryan James grinned at her. "I'm wearing a jacket. What do you want?"

Kate took in the dark hair, drawn smoothly back into a gleaming, neatly tied pony tail, the navy blue jacket that fit him perfectly. Ryan James did look good. Frank Chambers began to rise from his chair, but Ryan was there before him and, much to Kate's surprise, pulled out chairs to seat both women. Evidently Ryan James had more of the "niceties of civilized behavior" than Marjorie Harrison gave him credit for. Kate looked across the table, and for the first time noticed Clare. Kate winced. Whatever had made Clare choose that dress? Its low-cut neckline emphasized a broad expanse of mottled chest and its unbecoming shade of red emphasized the pallid chalkiness of the girl's complexion.

Frank Chambers leaned toward Kate. "All hell broke loose when Marjorie came down and learned Clare had gone out and bought that dress without her," he said under his breath. "Seems Madame had arranged for a dressmaker to come to the hotel with some clothes. Clare was ready to go take her new one off and jump into the dressmaker's, but Sven told Marjorie to stuff it."

"Sven should have kept his mouth shut," Kate said. "That dress is a disaster."

"Looks okay to me, but the Harrison agrees with you. Unfortunately, she said so to the poor kid." Frank looked down at the tablecloth and fumbled with his fork. "By the way, I'm sorry about what I said back there. It was way out of line. I thought I'd really upset you," he glanced up, "but I guess I didn't." His tone invited her to comment, but at that moment the string quartet finished the Dvorak piece they were playing and, amid polite applause, put away their instruments, leaving the raised platform to arriving members of an orchestra.

General conversation resumed as the orchestra began playing muted background music, and waiters appeared with a clear soup in which swirled wisps of herbs.

Kate took a sip and gave an appreciative nod. "My father used to say that you could tell a kitchen by its soup and its salad. If this consommé is any indication, the rest of the meal will be outstanding."

The others were too busy making short work of the first course to reply, but when they were served small plates of artichoke salad, Maggie took a bite and said, "I don't know what the rest of you think, but I'd say the salad is as spectacular as the soup." She took another mouthful, then hesitated and put down her fork. She picked up her water glass and took a long drink of sparkling water. She looked down at her salad, then gave her shoulders a slight shake and leaned forward to listen to what Ryan James was saying. For the rest of the evening, Maggie ate sparingly. She finished her asparagus but not the Beef Wellington, and when the dessert tray came, cut the Napoleon she chose from it in half. She did not, however, excuse herself from the table at any time during the meal, something that did not escape Kate's attention, though Kate was careful not to appear to notice.

During a leisurely dessert and coffee, everyone at the table seemed relaxed and content. Even Marjorie Harrison declared a grudging amnesty about Clare's dress. "Oh, stop sitting there like a wilting anemone, Clare," she snapped. "Come to my room tomorrow morning, and we'll see if the dressmaker left anything that will make you look less like an over-ripe tomato."

Clare accepted this thorny olive branch with such painful eagerness that Sven, although he glowered at Mrs. Harrison, answered the pleading in Clare's eyes and swallowed whatever he'd been about to growl.

The orchestra swung into a brassy overture, a medley of tunes that seemed familiar, yet not quite recognizable, and the assembled guests shifted expectantly in their seats as the terrace darkened and brilliant lights flooded the flagstone area just in front of the lobby doors, now hung with deep-crimson velvet draperies. Two brilliantly painted actors dressed in costumes of ancient Greece entered from improvised wings constructed of more velvet draperies.

"*How'd you make it home after the banquet last night, Lysander?*" said the taller actor.

"*Didn't make it home. Woke up with my arms around the wine amphore,*" said the second.

"*You're sure it was an amphore and not Khryseis?*" The tall one gave a toothy grin and at a note from the orchestra's clarinetist, sang in a well-modulated baritone:

> "*Khryseis, now she's a girl that you want to*
> *Have your arms about—guess we all do!*
> *But we can't have you mooning about, like this*
> *Spend your drachmas on her pretty pout, like this . . .*"

(

"Not too bad, but I've certainly seen better," Marjorie said above the applause as the flood lights illuminating the stage blinked off and those on the terrace brightened. "I must say it wasn't up to the food."

"I thought it was wonderful," Maggie said. "The dancing was great, and I loved the songs."

"I have to agree with Marjorie," Kate said. "I didn't assume it would be up to a Broadway production, but I must admit I expected something a little more sophisticated for this crowd. That plot was a take off of every farce from *A School for Scandal* to *A Funny Thing Happened on the Way to the Forum*. And I think I recognized lines from both."

"This isn't heaven, remember?" Frank Chambers murmured to her, sotto voce.

"I hope not," Kate said with some asperity. "As a matter of fact, sitting through a millennium of second-rate musicals might be a good definition of hell."

Frank stared at her in surprise and then let out a shout of laughter. "You're quite a woman, Kate," he said, shaking his head. "How would you rather have spent the evening?"

"I think I should have gone with Patrick," she said. "But if his program was as second-rate as this one—"

"You're making it mighty difficult to confess that I enjoyed tonight's play, beginning to end," Chambers said with a wry smile.

"You did?" Kate said. Then she caught herself and grimaced. "Academics tend to be rather intolerant—in case you hadn't noticed." Then she said quickly, "You don't have to be a drama critic to get my vote as the most valuable member of this odd little group of ours, Frank. I'm glad you're with us. By the way, speaking of our group, what do you think about Bucknall? Should we leave tomorrow, or stay here awhile?"

"I'm not sure. My gut feeling is we should go on to Eastlight, but I can't tell you why. I haven't the slightest idea what's special about Eastlight or what we'll do once we get there." He glanced at their empty table. "Whatever we find there, I don't see how the food could get much better than what we had tonight."

"It *was* excellent. I noticed we all dug into the coq au vin as though we hadn't had any breakfast or lunch."

Frank frowned. "Coq au what?"

"Chicken."

"I know from chicken, professor. I had a New York Strip. Best I've ever eaten."

Kate stared at him. "What else did you have?"

"Baked potato, succotash." He paused, pensive. "Haven't had succotash like that since I was a kid."

"Succotash?"

"Lima beans and corn cooked with milk and butter; Mom used to make it."

"Well, well. Isn't that interesting. I wonder what Maggie and Marjorie and all the rest had."

"Am I missing something?" Frank said.

"I certainly didn't realize you were having New York Strip with succotash or whatever. I saw us all being served what I was eating: coq au vin after a really superb quail salad."

Frank's eyebrows raised. "That *is* interesting. I guess we all got what we thought was about the best food we could imagine."

"And because we assumed it would be high on everyone else's list too, that's what we saw them being served."

Frank shook his head. "You'd think we'd be used to this sort of stuff by now, but it still surprises me."

"Me, too."

"Y'know, it's funny, but I don't seem to miss anything from my life—the one before we came here, I mean. I guess we've been too busy learning about this place and having new experiences."

A shade of sadness crossed Kate's face. She stood up. "Yes, well, it's been quite a day. I think I'll go back to my room and get some rest."

Frank stood with her. "I guess I'll mosey off too. I just hope Patrick decides to call it a night before too long. One thing I wanted to ask, Kate, have you figured out why this place is called Bucknall?"

Kate came from somewhere far away and attempted to look interested. "Yes," she said, "Matter of fact, I have."

"Care to share?"

"It's a slurring of 'Bacchanal.' At least, that's what I think."

"I'm not about to bet against you, Dr. Douglas," said Frank.

Kate smiled and said goodnight. She did not see the look on Frank Chambers's face as she left, or notice that he stood on the stone terrace, watching until her slim figure disappeared in the fading evening light.

11

At the sound of the key in the door, Frank Chambers jerked awake. He scrambled from the chair in which he'd been dozing. "So how's the concert-goer?" The growled question couldn't quite hide his relief.

"It wasn't bad—for a bunch of amateurs." Patrick walked to the couch, sprawled on it, and kicked off his shoes. "That's what these entertainments are, you know. Tone-deaf people who've wanted to sing all their lives, pianists who figured if they'd ever had the time to practice they'd be wowing 'em in Carnegie Hall."

Chambers's eyebrow went up. "So that's it. I suppose ours were actors in local rep companies who've always dreamed of making it on Broadway? Come to think of it, from what Kate said, and I guess she ought to know, the playwright was probably some guy who wrote advertising copy because he couldn't sell his plays."

Patrick grinned. "Seems to be a great place for folks playing out their fantasies. Evidently if they really want to do something, they're able to—to a certain extent. But I'm happy to say there's still a big difference between a professional and an amateur, at least here in Bucknall. None of tonight's musicians is anywhere near Paul's league—" he paused and then added, his tone oddly wistful, "or mine." He tossed a restless arm over the back of the couch. "The food was great, though; how about yours?"

"Mine was fine, and everyone else seemed to like theirs too. Even Ryan stopped charming the ladies, including our Marjorie by the way, long enough to scarf down dinner."

"Slimeball." But Patrick said it with little rancor, his mind obviously elsewhere.

Chambers studied Patrick and said casually, "So you think most folks in Bucknall are here for the eating and drinking and won't complain about the entertainment as long as the gourmet stuff keeps on appearing?" When Patrick didn't respond, Frank sat down on one of the twin beds and said with a sigh, "All right, friend, shoot. I'm tired, but I know I'm not getting to bed until you tell me what's on your mind."

Patrick did not look up, but at last he mumbled, "I don't think I'm going to make it, Frank. Back in Presbe, when I was talking to Paul, he told me a lot about it."

Chambers had to strain to hear this last word. "It?"

"Heaven."

"What'd he say?"

Patrick looked at him. "You know angels are married there?"

Frank felt a pang of something he did not even acknowledge. "No, but thinking about it, I guess it doesn't surprise me. If we're talking about versions of eternal bliss, I'm not exactly sure what mine is, but I know I'd want to share it with someone." Frank paused, vaguely surprised, and realized he hadn't known that he felt this until the moment he heard himself say it.

"Paul knew about me back when we were on earth, of course." Patrick swallowed. "It never made any difference to him—I mean, we always respected each other." Patrick's chin went up. "And when I met him in Presbe it was all right. He wasn't judging me or anything, but I guess he just wanted me to know about how things were in, in heaven . . . like it was something for me to think about. That's what we're here for, to think about what we are, what we've been, where we want to go."

Chambers waited.

"And I have been doing a lot of thinking," Patrick continued, his voice low. "About my life. First and always, there was the music, of course. My music is the best of me, the best I had to offer," he looked up at Frank, "and my best was really good. But the rest? I've tried to be kind, but was I always? Not a chance. Been thinking about my life . . . some of the people I've hurt, some of the ones who hurt me." He ducked his head and fell silent.

Chambers cleared his throat. "I don't know a lot about this stuff, Patrick. All I know is I'd say you've been given pretty many lousy things to deal with in your life, but I haven't heard you complain. Saw it at the clinic. You didn't moan or whine, just took what came and made the best of it. That counts for something with me; I'd guess it counts with the One who brought us here." Frank looked away, embarrassed. He got up and clapped the younger man roughly on the shoulder. "My advice for now is to get some sleep, okay? Maybe you don't need it, but I sure could use some."

Patrick brushed a hand through his short hair. "Thanks," he said. "An advice columnist you're not, Frank, but thanks."

When Chambers turned out the light between the beds, Patrick pulled the light down comforter to his chin and stared into the darkness. *Where is Brian now?* Did he ever think of Patrick or had he erased any memory of their time together from his present life ? Brian had always been good at that. An insubstantial shadow appeared by the foot of the bed. Patrick sucked in an inaudible breath, but couldn't help his next thought. The ghost of Christmas past? Or not. That had been a jolly Father Christmas sort of apparition, hadn't it? And this, the picture was clearer now, this was a slim guy in a suit, a guy with wavy brown hair. This was Brian. Patrick squeezed his eyes shut and opened them. Brian was still there.

He was standing in his usual listening position, hands in his pockets, chin on his chest, his eyes focused on something just to the left of the man before him. Although Brian wasn't looking directly at the speaker, there was a flattering air of attentiveness about his listening pose that seemed to draw the raconteur closer, make his gestures more flamboyant. Patrick sympathized. He knew the feeling, the desire to hold in thrall the absorbed listener that Brian appeared to be, giving the story more emphasis than it deserved. How long would it take before the man realized that Brian listened only to himself, that most probably he was contemplating his next hot project and who he was going to pitch it to? Or not even that. He was probably wondering what their hostess was going to serve for dinner.

Patrick lay rigid, his fists clenched. He wanted to smack the back of that bowed head, to demolish the wavy hair's careful elegance. He took a deep breath. *No!* Brian couldn't help being what he was. Life might well take care of that serene detachment, that indifference to anyone else's concerns. Did he want Brian to endure what he, Patrick, had? No. Patrick's head shifted on the pillow in a slight, negative movement. He wouldn't wish that on anyone. But there were other things that might give Bryan the opportunity to reflect, he hoped, before it was too late. The figures of the two men were less distinct now. Patrick watched them fade until there was only a shimmer against the dark at the foot of the bed, then nothing. He rolled over, punched his pillow, and scrunched it beneath his head, puzzled at the sudden lightness that swept him. What was it? Relief. That was it. Relief that he was no longer at the mercy of Brian's caprices, that he really didn't care what Brian was doing or who was trying to hold his attention. Patrick slept.

((

The vote was six to two with one abstention in favor of remaining in Bucknall at least one more day. Sven informed the group at the breakfast table on the terrace that he couldn't care less what they did or where they went as long as Clare and he continued being able to camp out in rooms like the ones they'd been given in Presbe and now here in Bucknall. It almost, he said, made up for the loss of his Husqvarna. He held out a hand for Clare, and together they left the table.

Kate watched them go. The girl no longer wept, but her eyes were shadowed, and from time to time Kate caught an expression of deep sadness when the girl thought no one, especially Sven, was looking.

"I have some things to attend to," said Frank as he tossed his napkin on the table. "See you later."

"Me, too," said Patrick. He rose and crossed the terrace in the direction opposite to that Chambers had taken.

"I didn't care which way the rest of you voted, "Marjorie Harrison said, "I'd already decided I'm not going to get on that van and go tearing about the countryside. Not today and quite possibly not ever."

"Tell us how you really feel, Marjorie." Kate rose from the table. "Since we've decided to stay, I'm going for a swim. How about it, Maggie? Want to come?"

Maggie shook her head. "Thanks, no. I'm going to work out in the gym."

Kate looked at her, surprised, but then said, "I hadn't thought about it, but in a place like this—yes, of course, there'd be a spa and a work-out room."

Maggie grinned. "I'm not going to any spa, Kate. They have a gym here that has all the equipment I need and then some. I talked to the guy who manages it, and when he found out who I was, he said I could reserve it for as long as I wanted this morning."

"Good for you. Do a few round-offs for me."

But when Kate strolled off Maggie made no move to leave the nearly empty terrace. She turned to Ryan James, shading her eyes against the morning sun. "Patrick and you were the only ones to vote to leave today. How come?"

"I don't claim to have Patrick's great musical sensitivity, but I'm enough of a musician to not particularly enjoy the idea of having to sit through any more second-rate performances."

"But that's not the real reason."

For a moment Ryan looked almost annoyed, but then he gave her one of his quick smiles. "No, I guess that's not all there is to it."

"Tell me."

He studied his empty plate a moment and then looked at her, his dark eyes warm. "To tell you the truth, I just enjoy traveling. Don't particularly like staying in one place, never have. That's one reason I liked the idea of us being wanderers when they first brought it up. And then later, when I got the chance to talk to you, to know you—" He stopped and covered her hand with his. "Well, it's made traveling all that much better. I guess it all comes down to the fact that I like the idea of gearin' up the old van and headin' on out."

Maggie flushed, but did not remove her hand. "If it wasn't for the fantastic gym they have here, I wouldn't mind taking off either, but it's been so long since I've had a chance to work out—" She was stopped by the sound of china smashing against the terrace flag-stones.

"I won't stay!" a woman shrieked. "I won't stay another day! You can't make me!"

At the far side of the terrace, an enormous woman swept a hand over the table before her and sent another plate flying to the flagstones. Then, placing her huge, dimpled elbows on the table, the woman put her frizzed head into her hands and burst into tears. Her waiter, who had dodged the last plate's flight with an agile hop, signaled toward the lobby, and an instant later a young woman in an aqua uniform appeared. She sped down the stairs, nodding to the waiter who picked up the pieces of china and fled. The attendant crouched beside the sobbing woman, patting her shoulder, and murmuring into the wild mass of tangled hair. The woman's sobs quieted. She wiped her eyes with the sleeve of her shapeless, tent-like dress, but twisted in her chair and turned her back on the still-kneeling attendant, refusing to be comforted.

"What'd you suppose happened there?" Maggie whispered to Ryan.

"They wouldn't bring her a third Danish custard?"

Maggie's lips twitched. "Stop it," she said. She resolutely tore her gaze from the tableau across the terrace and stood. "Look, Ryan, I gotta go. They've reserved the gym for me."

"Can I come watch?"

Maggie hesitated. "This is going to be a working session," she said uncertainly. "I haven't had a work-out in so long I'm going to need to really concentrate."

Ryan gave an easy shrug. "Hey, no problem. I'm going to the beach later on. Come for a swim when you're done?"

"You've got it," Maggie said, grateful he'd understood.

Ryan headed for the lobby, making a circuit of the terrace that left as much room as possible between him and the table where the fat woman sat, her head again in her hands.

Maggie, not able to bring herself to such pointed avoidance as Ryan's route, took a more direct course that passed close to the woman's table. Although Maggie averted her eyes, she could not resist a furtive glance as she passed, and to her horror, at that moment the woman looked up.

"Go ahead," the woman said bitterly. "Look your fill, honey. Enjoy."

Maggie's cheeks flamed as though she'd been smacked. "I'm sorry," she stammered. "I wasn't . . . I didn't mean—"

The woman gave a shuddering sigh. "How long?" she said to the attendant, and when the younger woman shrugged, the large woman turned back to Maggie. "Do *you* have any idea how long this is going to go on?"

"Sorry, I don't know what you're talking about." Maggie had taken a couple of hesitant steps away, but as she attempted to resume her passage, the woman thrust out a massive hand to halt her.

"Look at you," the woman said. "Such a tiny, skinny little thing. Were you always like this?"

Maggie's chin went up. "I'm a gymnast."

"So? I'm a cook. Or I was. Now I can't seem to remember anything, not even my favorite recipes. Can't work in the kitchen and sample my Boef á la Chartreuse, my Raspberry Chocolat Mousse." Tears welled in the deep-set eyes. "All I can do is eat other people's cooking, and even if it's not that good, I can't ... I can't stop."

"I'm sorry," Maggie said again.

"Let's go up to your room, Blanche," the attendant coaxed her.

But Blanche dismissed the suggestion with a flick of her head. Suddenly her hand snaked out and closed around Maggie's arm. Maggie gave a sharp intake of breath that was part fear, part revulsion.

"Look at all the rest of the people around here." Blanche waved her other hand at the now empty terrace. "Everybody in this place is thin, even if they eat like pigs, but every time I eat nowadays I seem to put on more pounds. They look at me as though ... as though I'm some sort of freak."

"I have to go. I have an appointment." Maggie tried to twist away. "Besides, I can't help you; I'm new here."

Blanche did not let go of Maggie's arm. "I'm not," she said, gloomily. "I've been here a long time. At first, I actually lost weight. Got so I looked almost like everybody else. Would you believe it, I could eat anything I wanted and still lose weight. It was heaven."

Maggie looked at her, startled. "That's *not* my idea of heaven," she said abruptly. "I don't want that."

Blanche eyed her. "No?"

"Please—" Maggie felt faint. She tried again to twist her arm from Blanche's grip.

"Let her go, Blanche," the attendant said quietly. And when Blanche did not immediately respond, she put a gentle hand on the fat woman's shoulder.

Blanche quickly released Maggie's arm. "All right, all right. See you around," she said to Maggie. "And sooner or later . . . well, you'll see."

"No, I won't!" Maggie massaged her arm. "I'm a wanderer. I don't have to stay here." She gave the attendant an anxious look that begged her to agree, but the young woman was busy assisting Blanche from her chair. It took a grunting effort, but finally the huge woman heaved herself from her chair and stood. Maggie looked at them. Could she possibly end up like the huge woman? *Never. Never. Never.*

Blanche pulled away from the attendant. "I don't need your help," she growled, and waddled off, head high. Though the attendant gave a deep sigh, she let Blanche go.

Maggie bit her lower lip. "She's unhappy here. Why do you make her stay? Why can't she leave if she wants to?"

"Oh, she can," the attendant assured her. "Sooner or later she'll realize it. Right now, in spite of what she says, she really doesn't want to leave all this wonderful food."

Maggie stared at her. How much did this uniformed young woman know? Did she know about—. Maggie squelched the thought. "If you get what you really want here in Bucknall, why can't Blanche remember her recipes?"

The attendant hesitated, as though she was considering to what extent she should answer. "Blanche loves to cook, but for herself," she said finally. "There was a time she loved to cook for other people, too; I don't know how much of that desire remains with her—that's not my job—but I do know if her own needs and appetites are all she really cares about, Blanche will never be very happy. The reason she can't remember how to cook is because the total focus of her love of cooking became herself."

Maggie stared at her. "Who are you?"

"Susan." The attendant held out her hand. "And you're Maggie, right?"

"No, I mean, who *are* you?" Maggie repeated.

"Oh, I see. I'm a student at the Res Medio School, at least until recently. Right now I'm on the work part of a student/work program."

"Doing what?"

"Helping people like Blanche."

"It doesn't look like she's getting much help."

Susan smiled and said, "She's getting more help than she knows. It's not always as bad as it was this morning. Blanche may have a lot to work through, but the very fact that she's been here so long means she's got something to work with." A buzz sounded, and Susan glanced at the beeper at her waist. "I have to go," she said. "Nice to have met you, Maggie; it's always fun to talk to a wanderer." And with that she left, pony tail bouncing as she bounded up the terrace steps.

Maggie headed for the gym. It was ridiculous. She wasn't anything like Blanche. She didn't even like cooking. Scrambled eggs was about it for her culinary knowledge. Sure, she might have some problems with food. There had been nights when she'd taken a half gallon of ice cream from the freezer and ended up with an empty carton. But there had always been a reason. She'd had things on her mind.

She would never end up like Blanche. Maggie placed a hand on her queasy mid-section. She hadn't felt this way for a couple of days. It was Blanche's fault, all that food, the way she looked. She had to find a lady's room before she went to the gym. No, she wouldn't even think of that. She'd go to the gym and warm up and do her routines.

If she could still remember her routines.

"Please, God," she whispered, "let me be able to do my routines."

((

Everyone except Patrick, who said he was going to risk attending a performance of *Don Giovanni*, stayed at the hotel and saw another musical comedy. The dinner before the musical was, as expected, superb, and to their surprise the play wasn't half bad.

"Either the cast is getting better, or my critical faculties have been dulled by all this marvelous food," said Kate.

Ryan pushed away his dessert plate. "If this keeps up, maybe I'll change my mind and vote with Mrs. Harrison to stay here a while."

"No, please," Maggie said sharply. When the rest looked at her in surprise, Maggie's chin went up in the familiar gesture of defiance. "I think we should leave," she said.

"I thought you liked it here. Your session in the gym didn't turn out to be all you thought it would?" Ryan said, puzzled.

"It was great, maybe too great. I couldn't miss," Maggie said. "But I think we've spent enough time here. We're wanderers. We should get our cards back and move on."

Frank Chambers was immediately alert. "Have you heard anything that makes you suspect the cards will be taken away if we stay in any one place too long?"

Maggie wouldn't be drawn in. "I just think we should leave."

"I think she's right," Ryan said, smiling at Maggie. "Glad you like the idea of traveling, too." He got up. "But I must admit I'll miss the beach as much as this food. Come for one last walk with me, Maggie?"

Maggie's look of discomfort disappeared. She slipped off her shoes and ran ahead of him, speeding down the terrace steps to the sandy beach, her light steps almost a dance.

Clare looked after her wistfully. Sven saw her expression, and his arm, negligently draped over her shoulder, tightened about her. "Want to go for a walk, babe?"

A rare smile lit Clare's face. "Yeah, I'd like that," she said softly. She stood, brushing the skirt of the simple black cotton dress Marjorie Harrison had ordered the hotel's seamstress to adjust so that it slid smoothly over the slight bulges. Marjorie had also bought the girl a red jacket that completed the outfit and hid whatever the dress did not.

"I told her she could wear red if she wanted," Marjorie Harrison said to Kate, "just has to be the proper shade." Marjorie raised her voice. "Remember to hold in your stomach, Clare. No one needs to be reminded you've just had a baby."

Clare's head jerked back as if she'd been slapped. She tore her hand away from Sven's, ran a few steps, then came back to snatch the room key from his pocket, and dashed off toward the hotel.

"You old—" Sven snarled at Marjorie Harrison. He took a menacing step toward the old woman, but than gave a disgusted grunt, and strode after Clare.

"The girl has to face reality," Marjorie Harrison said, her voice faltering. "Can't pretend it didn't happen."

"Marjorie, how could you?" Kate said quietly. "That was cruel, gratuitously cruel."

"What nonsense! Maybe she'll shed a few tears, but she'll be right as rain tomorrow morning."

"Shed a few tears! You saw her face. How could you ignore causing such pain? How can you act as though it's perfectly all right?" Kate stood. "I'm going to see if there's anything I can do to help the girl."

"What a to-do about nothing," Marjorie grumbled. But she looked down at her ringed fingers, unwilling to meet anyone's eyes and plainly discomfited.

☾

Kate stood outside the third-floor room. She steeled herself a moment and then knocked on the door. Someone had to try to help the girl. Although Sven obviously loved Clare, he didn't seem to know what to do when she was hurt, other than to rage at the world. Not a particularly effective method of handling the situation.

"Who is it?" The barked question came from the other side of the closed door.

"Kate Douglas. May I come in?"

The door opened a scant few inches, and Sven's glowering face appeared. "She doesn't want to see anybody."

"No, I imagine not. But perhaps she'd feel better if she did. Don't you think it might help if someone talks to her?"

He thought a moment and then opened the door wider. "Okay," he said grudgingly, "but if I let you go in there and she starts getting upset, you leave her be."

Kate strode past him into the suite's small sitting room. Clare was nowhere to be seen.

Sven stood twisting a hand over the knuckles of his other fist. "Lately it's been better, not like at first when she cried all the time. I thought that's what would happen now—she'd cry, and I'd hold her and she'd be better, but she's not crying. She just sits in there and won't let me near her. It's worse than if she just cried."

"She's in the bedroom?" Kate nodded at the closed door.

"Yeah."

The first thing Kate saw as she entered the darkened room was an expanse of mirrored wall that reflected dark, polished furniture and a great canopy-hung bed. Kate blinked, awestruck. The place looked like someone's idea of a nineteenth-century bawdy house in the old West (had Sven seen something like this on T.V.?). Then she saw Clare. The girl was sitting on a loveseat by the window, staring out at the star-lit sky.

"Clare?" Kate said softly.

The girl gave no sign of having heard her. Kate perched on the chair opposite the pink velvet loveseat and reached out to put a hand on Clare's unresisting arm. "Maybe it would help to talk about it," she said.

"About what?" Clare said, listlessly.

"The baby."

A flicker of pain swept across Clare's face.

"It's natural that you miss your baby," Kate said. "But if we've learned anything since we've come here, it's that the life we lived in the world isn't the only one we're destined to have. It's not the only one your baby is destined to have; eventually she'll be here, too."

Clare shuddered, as though a chill wind blew across her shoulders. She didn't look away from the darkness beyond the window. "I didn't want her," she said at last. "Not before she came, not after."

Kate was silent.

"Seemed like she was always crying. And my mom would hardly ever take care of her, said she was my responsibility. Besides, Mom was at work at the PX most of the time. So there I was at home with the baby. It was a pain to have to take her everywhere, so sometimes … sometimes I just didn't. And when I'd get home, she'd be crying."

Kate held her breath. Barely moving her lips, she asked, "Where was Sven?"

"He was in the brig the whole time I was carrying her and some after. On account of me being sixteen. He really liked us having a baby though, said we'd get married and bring her up. But when he got out, my mom and dad wouldn't even let me see him. And when Sven and I decided to run away and we realized how hard it would be to take her—" Clare stopped and held a hand to her mouth.

"Sven wanted you to leave the baby?" Kate tried to keep the rising dismay from her voice.

"Oh, he wanted to take her. I was the one who said we couldn't travel with her. He hadn't been around, didn't know what it was like with Essie, always having to feed her, change her."

Kate noted that, for the first time since they'd been talking, Clare had said her baby's name. Kate took a breath and held it. She was, after all, a teacher. She'd heard a good many similar stories from weeping students. Mustn't overreact. "I'm sure your parents took good care of her when you left."

"We didn't leave her at home, remember? She was with us. Sven really loved having her with us—at least 'til the weather turned bad and he saw how hard it would be to keep her while we were on the move. So we decided to tell Mom she had to take Essie for a while— just until we could arrange to come get her without anyone finding out."

"That's right, you left her with a Frau Somebody, didn't you? Well, I'm sure this woman will have contacted your mother by now and Essie is safe with her."

"That's just it," Clare said, her voice sinking to a whisper. "I told Sven it was all right, that I had it all arranged. But I didn't."

Kate gave a sharp intake of breath. "What?"

"I was scared to call Mom, scared she'd say 'No,' so I thought we'd leave Essie, and I'd have Frau Blore call and Mom would *have* to come get Essie. But when I asked Frau Blore about if she'd call Mom and take care of Essie 'til she came, she just said she was too busy." Clare struggled to get the words out. "I didn't tell Sven; I said everything was okay. So we left Essie asleep on the bed. I figured Frau Blore would come in and take care of things. I meant to leave a note with my mom's name and phone number in Essie's blanket, but I couldn't write it without Sven seeing."

Kate edged back in her chair, shrinking from the girl in an almost imperceptible movement.

Clare, intent on her story, didn't seem to notice. "I was going to call Mom the first place we stopped and tell her where Essie was; I was going to call Frau Blore, too." Clare darted a glance at Kate and then looked down at her hands. "But it was raining and the Auto-bahn was slick, and then that car swerved into us—"

"You left your baby," Kate said slowly. "You just left her on the bed in a hotel room."

"Frau Blore must have found her, don't you think? She would have found her when she went in to make the beds and clean the room, don't you think?" Tears choked the blond girl's pleading voice. "You think she did?"

Something inside Kate seemed to tear apart. She and Howard had adjusted, had built a complete and satisfying life without children, but there had been all those years at the beginning of their marriage, years of trying to have a baby and not being able to. And this kid before her had left her baby like a sack of dirty laundry.

Fury swept Kate, thickened her throat so she could hardly speak. "You stupid, stupid girl!" She spat out the words. "You thoughtless, selfish, stupid girl!" Her breath came in short gasps. She wanted to slap that milk-white face. She wanted to kick the round body bulging with baby-fat, to smash a fist into that pudgy nose.

Kate realized she had risen to her feet, that she was standing above Clare, her hands balled into fists. Clare cringed against the back of the pink velvet loveseat.

Kate backed away, then turned and stumbled toward the door.

"You think maybe they put Essie's picture in the paper and Mom saw it?" Clare whimpered at her back. "That's what I've been telling myself," she said, stifling a sob. "That must have been what happened."

Kate couldn't trust herself to speak. She closed the bedroom door quietly. She hardly noticed Sven, waiting anxiously in the middle of the room.

"Is she better? Did she say anything?"

Kate stared at him. He didn't know. More than anything she wanted to tell him. She wanted to tell this hulking boy that his precious Clare had left their child in a hotel bedroom to hunger and thirst, to cry alone. Kate clamped her lips tight on the words at the tip of her tongue, words that begged to be spoken. It was all she could do to bite down on her rage and stagger past him out into the hallway. She slammed the door behind her.

Marjorie Harrison stood in the corridor a few doors away, a key in her hand.

"How's the girl?" said Marjorie. "I suppose you spent the better part of the time telling each other what a horrible person I am?"

Kate took a shaky breath. "No, Marjorie. As a matter of fact, we didn't mention your name."

"I like Clare, you know." It seemed to take some effort for the old woman to make the admission. "I really didn't mean to cause her pain."

Kate stared at her. So Marjorie Harrison did not want to cause Clare pain. What a laugh. Because a few moments ago inflicting pain on the sniffling blond girl was something Kate could have done quite easily. Back there in the bedroom, Kate had had to stop herself from physically attacking Clare. She still wanted to. Kate Douglas lowered her head and walked past Marjorie Harrison without speaking.

℃

Kate let herself into her room, shut the door, and leaned against it. What had happened to Essie? How long had the baby whimpered, then wailed for food, for comfort? How long had it been before someone had found her? Had Frau Blore found the baby in time, picked her up, and held her? Was there anyone to hold her now? Kate's chest hurt. She stood erect, her arms crossed against her breast as though to comfort an invisible little body. She forced herself to lower her arms, to breath deeply.

This was what had haunted Clare since she'd awakened in the hospital. This was the source of the girl's unending tears.

A shudder swept Kate as she realized that even having heard Clare's story, even knowing it and seeing her agony, she felt no compassion for the girl. Only a cold rage.

Sickened, she covered her face with her hands. "*Please, please,*" she prayed, "*take away this anger. Help me understand.*" It was a small, inadequate prayer, but there came an immediate easing of the tension in her chest, and the dark rage retreated a small distance. "*Please, help me,*" she said again. The anger loosened its hold and retreated further. Kate took a deep breath. "*Thank You,*" she whispered.

12

"Everybody here?" Frank Chambers counted heads and frowned. "Where's Mrs. Harrison? Don't tell me she's going to make good on her threat to stay here?"

"No such luck." Sven nodded morosely toward the elevators. Marjorie Harrison marched off, followed by a bellman pushing a luggage rack.

"What the—" Frank said, staring at the two hanging bags and three large suitcases on the rack.

"I refuse to travel without an adequate wardrobe," Mrs. Harrison said as she sailed through the lobby, bellman in tow. "If I'm going to traipse along with you in that horrible van, at least I'm going to have some decent clothes. Here, be careful with those," she admonished the bellman. "And you can give me that one; I want to take it with me in the van."

"She was told if she stayed she'd have to give up her wanderer's card," Ryan James said in explanation.

Frank Chambers's eyebrows went up. "So Maggie was right." He looked at Ryan with interest. "How did you find out about the wanderers's cards?"

"Happened to be near the registration desk when the lady found out she couldn't remain a wanderer without wandering," Ryan said. "Marjorie threw a tantrum that would have made Mt. St. Helen's look like a seismic burp—not that it cut any ice with the guy at the desk."

"So wanderers have to keep moving," Frank said thoughtfully.

"I asked about that," said Ryan. "No, we don't. The guy at the desk said we can spend as much time as we like in most places we visit. It's only resorts like Presbe and Bucknall where we're asked to make a decision about staying or leaving."

"Did he give you a clue as to just what makes Presbe and Bucknall your non-standard type places?" Frank asked him.

"Said something about these places being, what was it . . . oh, right—he called them 'imaginary heavens'." Ryan suppressed a smile. "Sounds a little like a kid's bedtime story, doesn't it?"

"No, it sounds sort of like what Kate was talking about," said Frank.

"Well, regardless, I left Mrs. Harrison still raising a stink and went up to pack."

"Speaking of packing, she is *not* taking all that luggage along." Frank picked up Kate's suitcase with his free hand and headed outside. Kate fell into step with him, and the rest of the group drifted across the lobby after them.

"At least we know we don't have to stay on the road if we don't want to," Chambers said to Kate. Then he looked at her. "Anything the matter?" he said.

She shrugged, but didn't answer.

"Don't tell me you're unhappy about leaving Bucknall's fancy eats and entertainments?"

"No," Kate said. "I'm glad to be going." She looked at Clare and Sven who had gone to stand by the rear of the van, a little apart from the rest of the group.

Frank followed her gaze. "Oh. She didn't just shed a few tears, go to sleep, and wake up 'right as rain,' did she? Matter of fact, looks as though the kid didn't get much sleep at all."

Kate Douglas bit her lip.

"Y'know, I'm glad you took control of the situation yesterday evening and went upstairs. The girl needed comfort, and besides, I can't tell you how good it was to hear you tell the old biddy off." Chambers did not see Kate's stricken look, for his attention had been caught by the sight of Marjorie Harrison, who was instructing the bellman to place her luggage in the van, despite objections from Ryan, Maggie, and Sven. Frank lengthened his stride and joined the disputants.

Kate watched him remonstrate with Mrs. Harrison, and then, unable to stop herself, reluctantly shifted her attention to Clare, who was standing alone at the rear of the van. Kate took a breath and walked toward her. Clare flinched as she saw Kate approach, and before Kate could say anything, ducked her head and scuttled toward the group at the van's door, moving through the crowd to climb into the van.

Kate followed slowly. "How is she?" she said to Sven.

Sven's eyes were somber. "She was really bad after you left," he said quietly. "Just sat there. Wouldn't say anything. And she didn't sleep. Every single time I woke up she was just sittin' there, looking out the window."

"I'm sorry," said Kate. "I shouldn't have—"

"Hey, it's not your fault. At least you tried to help her—not like that Harrison witch. I should have thanked you last night; I wanted to but you left so fast—"

"Oh, please." Kate raised a hand to fend off his praise. Her heart ached at the desolation in the boy's face. Obviously, Clare had said nothing to Sven. Kate knew she should admit that she'd only made things worse, but how could she tell him about last night without divulging Clare's secret? Another realization smote Kate. There had been no anger in the flickering glance the girl had given Kate before fleeing to the van, only a dull pain. The realization that Clare had accepted Kate's murderous rage as justly deserved twisted like a knife in Kate's gut.

"She hasn't had an easy time, y'know," Sven was saying, his voice low. "Her stepdad hated me from the moment he knew about Clare and me. Wouldn't let me near her."

Kate closed her eyes.

"I think that's one reason she feels so bad about Essie. Knowing her stepdad is so strict and all. Still, her mom will be there, and she'll like having Essie now that Clare's gone, don't you think?" He swallowed hard. "Look, do you think you could try to talk to Clare again? I know you tried before, but—"

Kate straightened her shoulders. "Yes, Sven," she said. "I think maybe I should." And before she could tell herself any of the hundred reasons she shouldn't be doing it, Kate found herself walking past Frank and Marjorie and the mountain of luggage, found herself climbing into the van and going to Clare, who sat huddled in the back seat.

"Any bets on who's going to win the luggage war?" Kate asked.

Clare did not meet Kate's eyes, but she obediently looked out at the disputing parties.

"I'm sorry," Kate said gently, "I had no right to judge you." She perched on the edge of the seat beside the girl.

For a moment Clare was silent. Then she shook her head. "When I let myself think about what you said, I saw how awful what I did to Essie was. It's probably even worse than what I let myself think." She swallowed a sob. "And there's nothing I can do. It would help if I knew how she was doing. I keep on thinking about her and wondering—"

"Clare." Kate placed a hand on the girl's arm. "Have you tried asking about her?"

Clare stared at her. "What do you mean?"

"Praying. Asking the Lord about her."

For a moment Clare looked hopeful; then her shoulders slumped. "What should I say? I don't even know how to pray."

Kate looked about. Who was there who could talk to the girl? Who was there in this patchwork group who could teach this child to pray? "I don't know much about it myself," she said finally, "but I'd say now's as good a time as any to talk to God and ask for help. Try it. Just tell him how you feel and ask him to help you."

"Doesn't he already know? I mean if he's God, he's got to know about me and Essie." Clare caught her breath, clearly appalled at the thought.

"Yes, of course, he knows. That's not the point. The point is for you to admit what you've done and tell him how sorry you are and ask for help."

"Would it change things?" Clare said, a glimmer of hope in her eyes.

"For Essie? I don't know; I don't think so." Kate saw the light in the girl's eyes dim and said quickly, "But it might change things for you. It did for me." Kate got up and placed a light hand on the girl's shoulder. "Try it," she said again. "As I say, I'm not much good at praying, but when I tried it a little bit ago, it helped. It helped a lot."

Clare looked uncertain. "Okay," she said, "but—" She looked down at her lap and mumbled something Kate couldn't quite hear.

"Pardon?" Kate said.

"Doesn't God hate me for what I did?" Clare whispered.

"Oh, Clare," The words stuck in Kate's throat.

"Okay, folks," Frank Chambers called out from the front of the van, "the Great Baggage Question has been resolved and we're moving out. Kate, get out that map of yours and make a stab at finding a way out of town, will you?"

"Right," Kate said. But before she went to her seat, Kate leaned over Clare's bowed head and whispered, "God doesn't hate you, Clare. He loves you. That much I'm sure of. He loves us. He brought us here and provided us with this new life, didn't he?" Kate took her seat in a daze, vaguely astonished at what she'd just said. How could she know—and she knew it as certainly as if she'd heard it proclaimed aloud—that the Lord loved poor Clare? That the all-powerful, all-seeing love that enfolded the abandoned little Essie also enveloped Essie's miserable, misguided young mother? Kate's grip on the map tightened. And that meant he loved Kate too, despite what she'd allowed herself to say and feel last night. Another, utterly foreign thought burst upon her. Though God might love her, had her burst of savage, unreasoning hatred saddened him? Kate shivered, suddenly desolate.

Ryan James gunned the motor, and the van sped down the long palm-lined drive, past the wrought-iron gates and out to the broad street that curved around the bay. Several smartly dressed walkers stopped to look at the van. One stuck out a thumb in a hitch-hiking sign, but after a hasty glance at the guard shack by the gates, he grinned and gave a "just-kidding" gesture.

"There's one guy who's decided he has had enough high-class food and fun," Ryan noted. "I wonder what it takes to get out of Bucknall?"

Frank Chambers grunted. "Be thankful you don't have to stay and find out."

"You got that right." Maggie Stevens craned her neck to look at a block of Moorish buildings, its mosaic facade glinting in the morning sun. "It's a pretty town, though. Is this the hotel where you were last night, Patrick?"

"No, that's the Monte Carlo," he said. "The Savoy is in the other direction."

A companionable quiet settled over the wanderers as they left town by the coastal road. Following Kate's map-reading, they passed secluded beaches fringed with palm trees and an occasional village where dogs sunned themselves in the central squares. The people in the squares glanced at the van without curiosity, though some waved a friendly greeting.

They were almost through a tiny village beside a quiet inlet when Maggie saw the children. "Oh, look, kids!" she called out.

"Hey, it's our first sighting of rugrats." Patrick surveyed the group of brown-skinned children playing in a shaded garden beside the road. A small boy looked up at the van and waved.

"Could be any place in the Caribbean," said Ryan.

"Uh, uh. Mexico," Patrick countered.

Before anyone else could give an opinion, the van swerved.

"What the—" Ryan jammed on the brakes, and the van skidded to an abrupt stop.

A man stood inches from the front of the van, his right hand raised, seemingly unaware that stepping in front of the van might have posed any possible danger to himself. Dark skinned and of medium height, he wore a khaki uniform and an expression of calm good humor. Though his gesture was one of command, he looked up at them like a welcoming host greeting guests to his home.

Ryan opened the door, and the officer stepped into the van and smiled at them all. "Clare Barnes?" he said, his warm brown gaze going to the back seat.

Frank Chambers was the first to find his voice. "What's the trouble, officer?"

"No trouble. None at all. But I'd like to talk to Ms. Barnes." Everyone in the van knew without question that there was nothing to fear from this man. Even Sven, who had protectively half-risen from his seat at the man's announcement, paused uncertainly.

"I'm Clare Barnes," Clare said in a small voice.

The officer searched her face, his smile tinged with something that might have been sadness. "Would you step off the van?" he said gently. "We can talk in my office." He gestured to a neat thatched house by the roadside, its walls open to the sun and breeze.

"That place wasn't there before," Ryan muttered.

"Before what?" the officer said pleasantly.

Ryan looked as though he'd like to say something but instead merely shook his head. Clare went to the front of the van, moving in a daze. Ducking her head, she accepted the officer's hand and stepped onto the road.

The van's passengers watched them enter the thatched house, saw the officer seat Clare, and take his chair on the opposite side of a large desk.

"You were right, Ryan," Frank Chambers murmured. "That place wasn't there a couple of moments ago."

The interview, if that's what it was, was over before anyone, even Mrs. Harrison, had time to become restive. The officer escorted Clare back to the van and handed her up the steps. Her eyes downcast, her face a pasty white, Clare moved to her seat beside Sven at the back of the van.

"You folks have a nice trip," the officer said. His expression was pleasant, but several of the van's passengers moved uneasily under the scrutiny of those searching eyes. He flicked a finger to his cap and backed off the van, motioning Ryan to drive on.

"Who was he, Clare?" Ryan's question had an odd urgency.

"Rafael? He's an angel." Clare was staring out the back window where the children had gathered about the slim officer. A woman in a brightly colored dress standing next to him held out a plate of cookies to the clamoring cluster. "Rafael said those kids have just come," she said quietly. "He said something about a mudslide covering their village."

Everyone turned to look out the back window. Just before the van followed the road's curve out of sight, they saw Rafael say something to the woman, saw her startled glance toward the van and the involuntarily motion of her protective hand as she reached out to shield the small heads about her.

"This guy Rafael said he was an angel?" Ryan said.

"No." Clare curled at the far end of the seat. "I just knew."

"Of all the ridiculous notions," Marjorie Harrison grumbled. She stared defensively at the other passengers, daring anyone to contradict her.

"How did you know he was an angel?" Patrick asked gently.

Clare's lower lip quivered. "I ... I don't want to talk about it."

"You heard her. Butt out," Sven said. But he leaned closer to Clare and said quietly, "What did that guy say, babe?"

"It wasn't what he said." Clare looked over at Kate and swallowed. "Y'know what you said I should do?" she said to Kate. "Well,

I did, and, and I guess it worked. Rafael told me if I wanted I could see . . . could see what I wanted to." Clare's blue eyes were haunted. "I didn't know it would be so bad," she whispered. Tears welled in her eyes, but she brushed them away. "I'm tired," she announced. "Real tired." She closed her eyes, and within minutes she was asleep. Or appeared to be.

"What was that all about?" said Ryan.

No one answered him.

"What I want to know is what the officer said to the woman taking care of the children back there," said Patrick. "And I'd give a lot to know why she looked at us like that."

"Like what?" asked Ryan. They had reached a straight stretch of road, and he increased the speed.

"Like she smelled something bad."

No one, it seemed, had anything to say to that.

((

Frank Chambers peered out the window at the barren country-side. "Doesn't seem too promising out there, but I'd say we'd better start looking for a place to stay."

"Yeah, looks like we've got a couple of hours until dusk," Patrick said. "Remember how it was at the hospital? Hadn't thought about it until now, but it never seemed to get dark there."

Maggie looked struck. "You're right. And the sun always seemed to be in pretty much the same place."

Ryan yawned, a negligent hand on the wheel, the other hanging to the floor at his side. "Well, it does get dark here, and Frank's right—we haven't passed a town for the last few hours; we'd better be on the lookout for a place to stop." He looked over his shoulder at Kate. "How about that map of yours? Show anything that might help us?"

"There's a section here called the Desert Wastes," she said, examining the map. "And I'm afraid we're in the middle of it."

"Why doesn't that surprise me?" Frank murmured.

"Hey, look at that!" Ryan straightened in his seat. Just ahead, a bus was pulled off to the side of the road. It was tan like their van, but the resemblance ended with its color. The sides of the bus were pocked with dents, its rear bumper tilted and dragged on the road, and a grimy rag was draped over the raised hood like a distress flag.

"I don't think we should stop," said Patrick, his eyes narrowed.

But Ryan had already pulled up behind the decrepit vehicle and cut the engine.

"Olá!" came the cry from the bus as several bodies leapt from it and came running back to the van.

"I don't believe this!" Ryan reached for the key, but before he could turn it in the ignition, the door was wrenched open, and Oliver Wendell Garcia hopped into the van.

Garcia favored them with a deep bow and flung out a welcoming arm in greeting. Oblivious of the overpowering stench that accompanied him and caused the nearest passengers to suck in their breath, Garcia gave them a glinting smile. "How wonderful to see you good people again!"

He still wore his gypsy costume, but the scarlet embroidered vest was torn, and his black trousers bagged at the knees. The once-sculpted hair now hung in greasy strands over a satin shirt that was no longer white but gray and spotted with food. "You appear like rain on the desert, like manna before the starving," Garcia continued. He began to edge forward, making a discreet motion to the men behind him.

"That's far enough, Garcia." Frank Chambers was on his feet, his considerable bulk between Garcia and the rest. "Why don't you get off, and we'll be on our way."

"My friend, you don't intend to leave without stopping to give assistance! As you can see, we are having a few small troubles with our bus, and unfortunately, none of us is experienced in the care and servicing of vehicles." Garcia managed to look both reproachful and beguiling at the same time. Then, studying the large presence before him, he dropped the posturing and said abruptly, "If you can help us get the damn thing moving, we'd be grateful. Look, the women have dinner cooking over the campfire; we'll even feed you."

"If Sven comes with me to keep an eye on them, I don't mind taking a look," Ryan said to Chambers.

Frank considered. "Okay. If you want. I'll stay here and make sure none of them gets on the van."

Garcia drew himself up and looked from Frank to Ryan. "What do you insinuate?"

"That even on your best day every one of you guys would steal us blind," Frank said.

Ryan got out of the driver's seat. "Come on, Sven, let's go."

Garcia seemed torn between wanting to challenge the calumny and being unwilling to jeopardize the possibility of getting his bus repaired. The bus won. The gypsy/stockbroker backed off the van and signaled his followers to make way for the two men.

Maggie made a face. "What an awful smell!"

"And it's getting hot," Kate said, brushing the hair from her forehead.

Although the van had no air-conditioning, it had been quite cool while they were traveling; but now they'd stopped, the dry, burning air of the desert filled the van. Dirt rose in little spirals of dust devils beside the road and filtered through the open door and windows, clogging the hairs of their nostrils and settling on their teeth.

"There's Bella with the other women," said Maggie. "It looks like they're making some sort of drink. Hey, that's ice they're taking from the cooler. Can't we go outside?" she asked Frank.

"You're going to ask them for a drink?" Patrick stared at her. "You forget about the sangria the lady gave us last time?"

"Sure, there was something in the second pitcher, but how do we know she was the one who put it in? Anyway, I just want to get out and walk around. And I have no intention of drinking anything unless I see them drinking it too." She looked up at Frank. "Please?"

He turned to Kate. "What do you think? I don't trust these guys any further than I can throw them, but the women don't seem threatening and it *is* hot in here."

Kate fanned herself. "And getting worse by the minute. As long as it's daylight and everyone sticks together, it's probably all right."

Frank nodded to Patrick. "Okay, you go with the women and keep an eye on things. I should go check out how Sven and Ryan are doing. I'll lock the van and take the keys with me."

"I don't particularly like the idea of parading around a hot, dirty gypsy camp," Marjorie Harrison said, looking oddly hesitant. "But I don't want to pass up the opportunity to demand that Garcia tell me about my stocks. He has never given me any satisfactory answers, and I intend to know the reason why."

The rest of the passengers looked at each other as though hoping someone would step forward to explain to Mrs. Harrison just how inconsequential any manipulations of her stock portfolio were now.

At last Kate said, "I don't know whether Garcia will talk to you about your stocks, Marjorie; but it's much too hot to sit here and swelter, so come on out with the rest of us." She held out a hand to help Marjorie out of her seat. "In any case, you'll feel better if you get out and stretch your legs."

Marjorie Harrison frowned, but before she could voice an objection Kate took her arm. "If I were you, I'd stay next to Frank when you go talk to Garcia," she said. "You don't want to give him or his men any ideas about taking you hostage."

Marjorie Harrison's eyes widened just a fraction. "I'm well able to take care of myself," she said stiffly. But there was no heart in the comment.

The group with Garcia was definitely smaller than the one that had been in the room behind the gas station. Only about ten men gathered around Frank, Sven, Ryan, and the bus. Ryan, who had taken off his t-shirt and wrapped it about his hand, poked his head beneath the raised hood and unscrewed the radiator cap. Even fewer women were congregated beneath a scrawny, leafless tree, the only vegetation in the area larger than the dusty stick-dry puffs of bushes that dotted the desert. The women hovered about a rickety card table. One poured what looked like iced tea into pitchers, three sliced and buttered bread, and Bella stirred whatever was cooking in the large pot on the nearby campfire.

No one took much notice of Clare, Kate, and Maggie, but several of the women cast looks from beneath lowered lids at Patrick, who stood a little apart and watched the scene, hands in his pockets.

Bella looked up, as though just noticing the group from the van. Her clothes were in as unsavory a condition as Oliver Wendell Garcia's, her blouse spotted and sweat-stained, the brightly colored skirt dingy with dust. She straightened, holding her back, then put her hands on her hips with a hint of her old swagger. "So we gotta feed you? And can you tell me why we should share our food? By the looks of you, I'd say so far no one's had to look too hard for meals." The change in Bella's face was more striking than the depredations to her attire. Her expression was haunted, her hollowed eye sockets bruises in her thin face.

"Y'know, I have a hunch there might be a cooler full of food on our van," Kate said. "Why don't I take a look and see what I can find?"

"Hey, that's right, we haven't looked in it lately," Maggie said. "It's usually there under the back seat."

"'Usually?' What does she mean?" Bella frowned at Kate.

"It's sort of like the goose with the golden egg," Kate said. And then at Bella's look of incomprehension, she explained, "Whenever we're hungry, we look in the hamper and find food."

Bella studied Kate. "You don't say?"

"Oh, but I do. Why don't we both go take a look?" said Kate.

"It's pretty heavy," Maggie said, "you'd better have Patrick help you."

Kate gave a slight, negative shake of her head. "No, let him stay here with you. I'll get the key from Frank, and he can help Bella and me." At Maggie's hesitation, Kate said carefully, "It'll be all right, Maggie."

Kate walked across the hard-packed earth toward the men, Bella falling into step with her. "What makes you people so special?" Bella said to Kate. "I mean, how come you get to travel all over the place in that nice van of yours that always seems to have plenty of gas for wherever you want to go? And you even get food without having to scavenge."

"You scavenge for food?" Kate asked. Then she caught herself, not quite sure she wanted to go there. "We're wanderers," she said. "I don't know why, but we're allowed to go wherever we want." She hesitated. "No, make that, we go wherever the van takes us. I think we're supposed to check things out for ourselves, find out what things are like here and at the same time find out what *we're* like." She paused, surprised to hear herself say it. "Yes, that's it," she said slowly. "We're supposed to find out what we're really like."

Bella gave a snort. "How sweet. And just what have you found out? That you're a one-hundred percent wonderful person?"

Kate stood still. "What's happened, Bella? You were so different when we saw you at the dance. You were funny and smart and completely clear-eyed about that crazy Garcia, even though anyone could see how much you loved him. Now you're bitter. You seem . . . hopeless."

"Hopeless?" Bella looked away. "What's there to hope for? That things will go back to the way they were? That Ollie will come to his senses? That the next time we find a cache of tequila and have a party, he won't give me to his second in command?"

"Oh, Bella." Pity rose in Kate's throat like bile.

Bella shrugged off her sympathy. "I was too drunk to care. We all were. It's really only when I saw you people get off the van and prance around all clean and neat and well fed that I remembered what it was like—" She stopped and gave a short laugh. "Look, let's go get that food, okay?"

Frank wasn't happy about leaving the men, but at Kate's insistence he accompanied them to the van and brought out a mammoth hamper from beneath the rear seat. "Why didn't we think to look for this earlier and stop for the usual picnic?" he asked, grunting beneath its weight.

"Because it was important that we stop here?" Kate said. When Frank looked at her in surprise, she shook her head and said, "Just thinking aloud. Has Ryan found out what's wrong with the bus?"

"He thinks so. Says he's almost done."

"Good. We don't have all that much daylight left, and I have a feeling we don't want to be here after dark. Frank, I think we should share the food and be on our way," Kate said, her tone suddenly urgent. "Take the basket to Maggie and have her distribute the food to the women, will you? I want to talk to Bella."

Chambers looked at her. Then he gave a quick nod and carried the hamper to the campfire.

Kate waited until he was out of earshot. "Come with us, Bella," she said quietly.

Bella stared at her.

"This is your chance to leave. You know where this group is headed, Bella. You've seen what's happening to these people; they're living like a bunch of animals."

Bella looked away. Only the small pulse beating at the base of her throat betrayed her. "You're wanderers. Wanderers have cards that identify them."

"Come with us, and we'll see what happens. I bet you'll be provided with a card, but if not, when we reach the next town, we'll find a place where you can be safe." Who was she to promise Bella something that might well be impossible? Kate fought down her uneasiness. There had to be a reason they'd stopped here; surely it must be to give this desperate woman a chance to escape.

"I can't leave. I love him." The words were barely audible.

"How can you love someone who gives you to his friend?"

"Oh, I hated him then." Bella wrapped her arms protectively about her chest. She looked as though she was standing in a chill wind rather than in a scorching desert. "I ran away the next morning, headed off on the nearest road out of camp. But Ollie came and found me and swore he'd never do it again. We haven't had a good time of it since then. When some of the group left, they stole us blind; took just about everything of value we had. He needs me."

Kate swallowed an impulse to swear. "You want to stay here? Look around. This camp of Ollie's doesn't just smell of dirt and decay, it reeks of suspicion and envy and malice."

"I know," Bella said, her voice low. "I know it better than you."

"Then come away," Kate pleaded. "I don't know much about this world, but I'm learning. I think you'll be protected—if you ask for it, if it's what you truly want."

"Ask?"

"Pray." Kate fought down her embarrassment at the word. "Look, I'm not one to talk. I've never been very good at praying, but you could try. It might help."

Bella's lips curved in a slight, patronizing smile. "Right."

"Haven't you the slightest clue, Bella?" Kate's embarrassment vanished. "You aren't in Chicago, you know. How do you think these hampers appear, and we're given gas for the van? Who do you think runs things around here?"

"You're telling me that there's not only a God, but that he's concerned with baskets of food and filling gas tanks? I thought he had a universe to run. Not that he's doing that great a job if it's the same God who dumped three inches of rain on the Outer Drive when Ollie and I were trying to make Arlington."

Kate ignored the sarcasm. "The same. Only we're a step closer to him here. Or at least we're in the process of finding out whether we are or not."

Bella seemed uncertain. "You're talking about heaven and hell, aren't you?" She looked over at the bus where the men were standing about relaxed and laughing now that Ryan had closed the hood of the bus and was wiping his hands on his filthy t-shirt. Mrs. Harrison was talking rapidly, her hands gesturing in the air, but Garcia seemed oblivious to her harangue. Then, as though aware of their scrutiny, Garcia turned in their direction. Seeing Kate and Bella, he swept them a smooth bow and came toward them. A momentary flash of sorrow crossed Bella's face. "I know Ollie," she said, her voice low. "He has never prayed to anyone or anything, and he never will."

"We're talking about *you*," Kate snapped. "*You* can pray! And you can come with us. It's your choice."

Garcia halted to confer with one of his followers, and Frank came back from the campfire, the empty hamper in his hand. Maggie and Clare tagged close behind, with Patrick bringing up the rear.

"You might want to go back with the other women," Frank said to Bella. He handed Patrick the hamper and motioned him into the van. "From what they told me, you stand a better chance of getting a decent share of this food if you get to it before the men realize it's there. Oh, there you are, Mrs. Harrison. Get in the van, will you?" He watched the rest clamber in after her. "I'll go get Ryan and Sven."

Kate ducked her head out the window. "What's wrong, Frank?"

"I've been considering what you said, and I think you're right. Didn't you notice? The sun's going down."

13

The sun had dipped low on the horizon and ominous clouds blanketed the eastern sky. A breeze sprang up, not a cooling breeze but one that felt as though it came through the doors of an open blast furnace.

Kate stepped out of the van and placed an urgent hand on Bella's arm. "Bella, you have to decide," she whispered, ignoring the malodorous stench as she leaned close. "You have to decide *now*."

Frank Chambers had gone back to the men surrounding the bus. Kate saw him give a quick nod to Sven and Ryan and flick a thumb toward the van.

Garcia, who was standing to one side speaking with one of his compatriots, looked over and saw Frank's gesture. He muttered something to the man and turned toward the van. "Surely you are not leaving us!" he called out gaily to Kate. "Bella, haven't you told her of our plans to entertain them?"

"We have to get to the next town before nightfall," Kate said as Garcia came near. "Was Ryan able to fix the bus?"

"It looks as though he did, and we're most grateful." Garcia's appreciative smile changed into an expression of concern. "But you don't want to travel these roads after dark; they can be dangerous. Besides, we couldn't think of letting you go without showing you our thanks."

Out of the corner of her eye, Kate saw Frank approach, Sven and Ryan behind him. The rest of Garcia's men had fanned out. Kate stepped back into the van, at the same time pointing in the direction of the campfire. "Oh, my goodness, look at that!"

In the instant that Garcia turned toward the women clustered by the campfire, Kate grasped Bella's arm. "Come on," she whispered fiercely.

"I can't." Bella pulled away.

"Hold onto her, Bella," Garcia commanded crisply. But his attention had already shifted to the cadre advancing on the van. "Take them!" he ordered his men.

Knives appeared, snatched from the depths of dirty, billowing shirts as the eight men converged on Frank, Ryan, and Sven. The encircled three drew close together. Ryan took a wrench from the wadded t-shirt he was still carrying, Sven slipped a length of metal pipe from his sleeve, and Frank Chambers opened his jacket and pulled from his belt a short, thick branch. Holding the cudgel aloft, he looked about him, daring anyone to come nearer.

The slight man with a wispy mustache who had been standing with Garcia made the first move. He took a gliding step toward Frank, then veered and darted toward Sven. He feinted to the right, thrusting his knife at Sven. Sven parried the blow with his pipe and sent the knife skittering to the ground, but did not see and was unable to avoid an attack from the man behind him. Sven gave a sharp, surprised cry and reached a hand awkwardly behind his back.

Frank gave a snarl and smashed his cudgel at Sven's attacker. The man howled in pain, holding his arm. He tried to scrabble for his fallen knife, but Frank snatched it from the sand and at the same time landed another swinging blow, this time to the man's head. The man fell, poleaxed, and did not move.

The three wanderers backed toward the van, Frank with the knife in one hand, his stick in the other. Sven, though gasping in pain, still managed to hold the pipe before him like a sword, and Ryan swung his wrench in a wide arc with each step. The next moments were blurred. Those inside the van saw the ersatz gypsies retreat, saw Garcia dancing up and down, shouting at his men's ineffectiveness. Having regained a knife and perhaps stung by his leader's taunts, Garcia's lieutenant tried again. A moment later Sven's pipe connected in a cracking blow, and the man clutched his shoulder in pain. By the time Ryan and Frank reached the van, most of Garcia's men had slunk away.

"They're going to get away again!" Garcia screamed. "Throw your knives at them! Throw them!"

The three remaining seemed befuddled by the order, but one man obeyed, hurling his knife at Ryan James. Ryan ducked, deflecting the blade with his t-shirt-wrapped arm. "Get Sven inside the van," he panted to Frank.

But Frank had already hoisted Sven up the step and into the van. Now he pulled Ryan after him. "Here's the key," he said. "Fasten seatbelts, everyone," he called out. "We're out of here!" He leaned a massive shoulder against the van's door, holding it closed against Garcia's frantic attempts to wrench it open.

As the van pulled onto the road, Kate twisted in her seat to look out the back window. She paid no attention to the furious Garcia or the assorted wounded who sat or lay on the desert sand. She looked only at the slim woman who stood watching the van, arms wrapped about her chest. The woman's multicolored, flounced skirts stirred in the rising wind, but she stood utterly still. The van was already too far away for Kate to be able to see her face.

"Let's look at your back, kid," Frank said to Sven.

Clare, having paid no attention to Frank's directive to sit down, stood over him. "He's bleeding," she breathed.

Frank gently pushed her aside. "Got you just below the shoulder blade, didn't he?" he said as he examined Sven's back. "Not too deep." He looked at Clare. "It's all right; he's going to heal right up. Remember Ryan's injury?"

"But shouldn't he see a doctor?"

"I have an idea if he needs one, there'll be one handy," Frank said. "Look, why don't you see if there's any fruit juice or water in that hamper and give it to him? Matter of fact, Ryan and I could use something to drink too."

Maggie had the hamper out before Clare could reach under the seat. Together they rifled it and passed around bottles of juice. The wounded and battle-weary drank while the rest of the passengers jubilantly recounted what they'd managed to see of the one-sided battle. Even Marjorie Harrison gave an approving cluck or two.

Kate did not join the excited chatter. She didn't seem to hear the discussion around her, but sat quiet, her face somber as she looked out at the lurid afterglow of the sunset, at clouds that streamed like a crimson lava flow across the sky. Once she looked back at the road behind the van, but she saw only darkness.

☾

The cabin was larger than it had seemed from the outside. A fieldstone and stucco building, it had halls that led off in several directions to warrens of rooms, rather like a hunting lodge that had been added to by several generations without benefit of plans or an architect.

"Imagine finding this just when we'd given up being able to sleep in a bed!" Maggie touched a match to the kindling in the fireplace.

"Yeah, imagine." Frank looked at them all from his vantage point at the front door. "Look, I know everyone's tired, but I think we should set up a watch schedule. I don't think Garcia will bother us; Ryan says he wouldn't bet on that bus going very far without breaking down again, but we should be prepared."

"I sure hope we don't meet up with them again," said Maggie. "The first time we saw those gypsies, they didn't seem so bad; in fact, they were really pretty funny, but back there in the desert—" she shuddered, "it was scary." She glanced at Ryan James, stretched out in an overstuffed chair, eyes closed, his guitar case on the floor beside him. "Anyway, I'll take the first watch, if you like."

Ryan opened an eye. "You shouldn't stand watch by yourself. I'll take it, too."

"Okay, that takes care of the first of three two-and-a half-hour watches," Frank said. "We'll exempt Sven, and I suppose you'll be taking care of him, Clare."

Sven lay on the couch, his head in Clare's lap, his eyes closed. His pallor and the pale lashes against his pale face made him look even more like Clare.

"Any other requests?" asked Frank, looking around.

"You can't expect me to stay up and pretend to be a lookout or guard or some such thing," Marjorie Harrison said.

"Of course not," Frank didn't bother to glance in her direction. "Anybody else?"

"I'm available whenever," Kate offered.

"Me, too. We could take the second shift," said Patrick. Then he looked suddenly conscious. "That is, I mean, if Kate wouldn't mind."

"Of course not," she said.

Frank seemed to hesitate a moment. "Right," he said, "that'll work. I'll take the last watch, and I certainly don't need a partner." He went to the kitchen area at the far end of the open room. "Think I'll put on a pot of coffee, and whoever's on duty can keep it going."

Half an hour later, Maggie threw down the magazine she'd been reading and went to sit on the slatted wood sofa beside Patrick. "I sure wish we had a T.V."

"There's one in my room," said Marjorie Harrison. "I think I'll go watch it."

Maggie stared at her, open-mouthed. "You have a T.V.?"

"Only one station comes through, but that's all right," she said.

"What's the station?" Patrick asked her.

Marjorie was already headed down one of the halls that spread out from the main room. "I don't know what it's called, but it's got the stock market report," she said.

"Why did I know the answer to that before she said it?" Patrick said with a wry grin.

"We'll start the shifts when everyone goes to bed," said Frank, "but it's probably not a bad idea to have someone out on the porch now as a lookout. Even if his bus doesn't break down, Garcia couldn't get here this quickly, but you never know who else might be around."

Kate put aside the book she'd been leafing through and rose from her heavily carved wooden armchair. "Come on, Patrick, why don't we go out and get a feel for this guard-duty business?"

Patrick gave Frank an apologetic glance before he followed her. Outside, Patrick leaned against one of the porch's wooden posts and watched Kate stare up at the star-sprinkled sky.

"Found an interesting book in there?" he asked her.

"One of mine," she said. "I spotted it in the bookcase the moment we walked in the door. I don't know what it means, having it turn up here, but I can tell you it gave me a bit of a charge—make that a rather largish charge. I'm embarrassed to say I was about to mention it, quite casually, of course," she paused, "but suddenly I saw . . . let's say I admitted it would just be asking for admiration. It seemed so petty, pathetic really, asking to be praised for an accomplishment that was simply using a talent I'd been given." She looked at Patrick, who was fidgeting with his shirtsleeve. She gave a little laugh. "What's the matter, Patrick? You're not even listening to my little confession."

Patrick shifted his feet. "I feel like a real jerk, being out here, but I didn't even think when I asked if we could stand watch together."

"What *are* you talking about?" Kate said, amused.

"I should have given Frank the chance to be your partner," he blurted out. "It's obvious he wanted to."

"*What?*"

"Oh, come on, Kate. You must know Frank's interested in you."

"*Frank?*"

"You've got to have noticed." Patrick looked at her. "Frank, y'know? Large guy, broad shoulders, gray hair—"

"Yes, I know," Kate laughed helplessly, "but *Frank?*"

"I swear." Patrick raised his right hand in the darkness.

"Oh, no." Kate covered her mouth. "Oh dear, oh dear."

Patrick gave something that could have been a snort. "I guess most people would think it's an endearing quality of yours, this not realizing how you affect men—Frank in particular—but I happen to like the guy, so I'm afraid I just think it's annoying. I don't enjoy the prospect of seeing our ex-cop get his heart broken."

Kate didn't seem to hear. She stood looking out over the chaparral for several long moments. Then she turned abruptly. "There's something I have to do," she said. "Stay here until Ryan and Maggie come to take their watch, will you?"

Patrick watched her go inside. "Oh, boy, Patrick, did you ever call that wrong," he said softly. Then he added, "Sorry, Frank, you poor jerk, you."

(

Kate poured a cup of coffee and took a sip. "Frank, I have to talk to you," she said, lowering her voice so the others couldn't hear her.

"You sure you want to drink that?" Frank asked her. "You've got the middle watch, you know."

"I know." Kate looked into her cup and took another sip.

Frank shrugged and nodded at the wing to the right of the large, central room. He put out a hand, inviting Kate to come. "There's a place down the hall."

Kate followed him silently. Frank switched on the lights of a small sitting room, and Kate took a seat on the padded wooden bench before a miniature fireplace. Frank remained standing, his back against the rough-hewn mantel, a questioning smile on his broad face.

"Frank, I'm married," Kate said. "My husband, Howard, hasn't been well for a long time, but he ... he has been the most important person in my life for the past eighteen years." She faltered, then quickly recovered. "I've seen him, you know. I mean, when I think of him, when I really need him—suddenly he's there. And he feels that I'm with him. I know it. We had ... we *have* a good marriage. It's the best part of me." She flushed. "I feel like an absolute idiot saying all this, but—" she let the word trail off to nothingness.

Frank Chambers had remained immobile while she talked, staring at the intricate patterns in the woven rug at his feet. Now, with what seemed to be an enormous effort, he looked at Kate. "Thank you," he said. "You don't have to say anything more."

"Frank, I really like you. I like you so very much." Kate stopped, realizing the futility of going on. She stood and reaching up, kissed Frank Chambers lightly on the cheek. Then she turned and walked quickly from the room.

((

When they gathered for breakfast the next morning, none of the watches had anything to report. If Frank was more silent than usual, no one but Kate and Patrick noticed it. Marjorie appeared in her bathrobe, a towel wrapped about her patrician head, showing up just long enough to request that a tray be brought to her room. Clare roused herself enough to offer to deliver it along with the one she'd prepared for Sven. Maggie found a bag of oranges in the refrigerator and made orange juice, while Kate and Patrick cooked pancakes.

Ryan, who had gone for a walk, returned just as everyone sat down at the long, planked table. Brilliant sunshine spilled into the room as the door swung open. "There are mountains to the north, and it looks like high desert outside," Ryan said as he took his place. "We must have climbed quite a way from the desert floor when we traveled last night."

"How do you know what's north?" Patrick asked him.

Ryan looked at him in surprise. "It was clear last night. The north star was right there at the end of the Little Dipper, plain as anything."

Kate stared at him. "I didn't see the Little Dipper, or the big one either. The stars were brighter than any I've seen, but the constellations unfamiliar; I didn't recognize any of them." Kate put another platter of pancakes on the table. "Did anyone else see familiar constellations?" The others shook their heads.

Clare, still looking tired and worn, had come back to get Sven another round of pancakes and juice. "I couldn't sleep," she said. "I came out on the porch during Frank's watch, and we talked about how beautiful the stars were, but how different the constellations looked."

Frank smiled at her. "You said you thought maybe they were angels."

Clare blushed but stuck out her chin. "Not just one angel, I wondered whether each star might be a bunch of them."

"So how come I saw the same stars I see every time I camp out in the Wisconsin woods?" Ryan asked, frowning.

"I wouldn't worry about it." Frank got up and lumbered to the sink with his plate. "Everyone seems to have his own particular points of reference here. For instance, I'm the only one who still has a watch." He gave a slight smile as they looked at their wrists, several with consternation. "Apparently, I need it. I think I know why, but I'm not sure. Only thing I know for certain is that there's a reason for the things that happen here."

"You have any ideas about why we keep running into Garcia and his goons?" Ryan asked.

Frank shrugged. "Maybe it's to show us what the consequences can be for people who choose to prey on others? Or what happens to people who are completely selfish? The fact that Garcia, who couldn't have been anybody's fool in his life as a Chicago stockbroker, seems to be becoming more and more of an incompetent bumbler has to tell you something."

"Which is?" Ryan cocked an eyebrow.

Frank Chambers shrugged. "If you can't figure it out, maybe you need to do some more thinking, the kind most of us seem to be doing." He looked around. "Okay, let's get the show on the road."

"We'd better clean up first, don't you think?" Kate asked.

"Do we have to?" Maggie asked. "Don't you think maybe the place will be cleaned all by itself when we leave?"

"Perhaps, but I wouldn't want to take the chance that it won't be ready for other travelers who might turn up, would you?"

"Wouldn't bother me," Maggie mumbled. But at Kate's look, she hastily picked up an armload of bed linen and towels and carried them to the clothes washer. Within a surprisingly short time, the group had the dishes washed, the laundry done, and the cabin presentable.

"There, that's better," Kate said as she brought her suitcase into the central room.

"Would someone get my luggage?" To everyone's surprise, Marjorie Harrison made the request quite pleasantly.

"I will," Ryan offered. He stopped, looking at the older woman more closely. "My, you look absolutely ravishing, Mrs. Harrison."

Marjorie flushed with pleasure. She did, in fact, look quite attractive, and she knew it. Her face was smooth and unlined, and the gray hair that days before had been carefully combed over a rather sparse spot on the top of her head was now a gleaming chestnut that she'd brushed into a thick French roll. Even more startling was her neck. Instead of the thin, corded neck with wattled, sagging skin that she'd seen in the mirror every day for the past years, the slender neck that rose from her robe was smooth and straight.

"It must be the new skin cream and hair coloring I got in Bucknall," she said, stroking her neck with a long-fingered hand. "The woman said they would do marvels, and I must admit that for once the results were better than promised."

"We should see if you and I could patent that stuff. We'd make a million." Ryan left to collect Mrs. Harrison's bags.

((

The van took off with Ryan at the wheel once again. The road they'd traveled the night before could be seen behind them, winding downward in a series of gentle loops to the desert floor where it snaked through the vast, dusty reddish expanse dotted with occasional shrubs and cacti until it disappeared at the horizon. There was no sign of Garcia's bus or his gypsies.

The van traveled higher, entering the shade of a pine forest, and the van's passengers stretched to breathe the pure air that wafted in the open windows.

"How about trying an experiment?" said Patrick. "I know the radio hasn't worked since we left the Guesthaus, but now that we're out of the desert and not back in the mountains yet, turn the old dial to 98.7 and see what happens."

Ryan reached out and flicked the radio on without answering. As he adjusted the dial, the sound of violins permeated the air.

"Vivaldi." Patrick took a deep breath, inhaling the music much as the others had the fresh mountain air. "Wish I'd asked you to try it before this."

The road leveled off, and the macadam ended. Ryan slowed the van as the road became little more than a sandy track. "I suppose it's too much to ask if that map shows where we are?" he said.

Kate studied it. "There should be a large body of water nearby, but it doesn't show any town around here." She looked out at the woods, at ground covered with masses of violets and dutchman's breeches, with spring beauties, yellow liverwort and white and scarlet trillium. "Wherever we are, it's lovely."

Maggie sat transfixed, taking in the tangle of sassafras and linden and cherry near the road, the maple and birch trees in the valley beyond it. She leaned forward. "This is Wind Haven," she said with a catch in her voice. "We're coming into Wind Haven!"

14

"And what or where is Wind Haven, may I ask?" said Patrick.

Maggie took a moment to reply. When she answered, her voice was so low that Patrick had to lean forward to catch the words.

"When I was little, before my dad left, before we went to live at Coach's, I used to spend two weeks every summer with Grandma and Grandpa at Wind Haven," she said. "Their cottage was right on top of a bluff that looked out over Lake Michigan."

"And this place looks like Wind Haven?" Patrick asked.

Maggie looked at him. "This *is* Wind Haven."

Frank broke the silence that met Maggie's statement. "Looks like the road branches off up ahead. Since it seems familiar to you, Maggie, why don't you direct Ryan?"

Maggie cleared her throat. "Take the left fork down the hill, then go right by that big, bent tree, and up over the next hill and you'll find a parking lot. The lake's just beyond it."

"Lake Michigan."

"Yes." It was a whisper.

Maggie stared out her window as the van negotiated the second hill and came to the parking lot she'd predicted. The parking area was simply a line of slanting, narrow spaces scooped out along one side of the sandy road, the other side of which was a steep, over-grown dune. An upright length of thick branch with a name plate affixed indicated each parking space.

"There." Maggie pointed to a sign that said "Favio" in neat black-painted letters. "That's Grandpa and Grandma's." Her eyes widened as she saw a man and woman emerge from one of the cabins and come down the steps.

"There they are! There's Grandma Inez!" Maggie was at the door even before Ryan had stopped the van. She jumped out, raced to the bottom of the hill and flew toward the stairs, her feet barely touching the cement path.

"Do you suppose—" Patrick stopped.

"That her grandparents died some time ago?" Frank finished for him. "I'd bet on it."

"Welcome." The man left Maggie in the woman's embrace and came toward them, his hand outstretched. Frank took in the unlined face, the neatly trimmed beard and thick head of hair, both almost as blond as Sven's. The man certainly didn't look like anyone's grandfather.

"I'm Neil," he said, shaking Frank's hand. He gestured to the rest. "Good to see you folks. Come on out and stretch yourselves a spell. You can park your transport in the guests's parking space over there."

As the group trooped across the sandy parking lot, Maggie danced back down the stairs, her eyes shining. She pulled a smiling, plumpish woman after her. "This is my Grandma Inez," she said. "She says we can stay for lunch and go swimming after. I've never gone swimming this early in spring, but Grandma says the water's plenty warm enough."

Kate, Patrick, and Frank exchanged glances.

"It's all right," Inez said. "You wouldn't have come here unless this was meant to be a way station in your journey."

"You can't be Maggie's grandmother," said Clare. She flushed. "I mean you look so young." And indeed, but for the ageless wisdom that shown in her eyes, the woman could have been in her mid-twenties.

Grandma Inez's laugh was so infectious the rest found themselves smiling too. "Yes, I'm Maggie's Grandma."

"Is . . . is this heaven?" Clare asked her.

"No, this is a temporary place. But then we always used to say Wind Haven was about as close to heaven as you could get, didn't we, Maggie?"

Neil smiled at Maggie, who had attached herself to her grandmother like a limpet, her arm entwined with Inez's. "I guess some people still think so, don't they?" He escorted them up the stairs to the cottage, talking all the while. "Now you people come on in and have a bite to eat and then you can walk on the beach or go for a swim, if that's your pleasure, or some of you might even like to take a nap."

"You're sure we're not inconveniencing you, Mr. Favio?" said Frank.

"Not so's you'd notice," he said. "But it's not Mr. Favio. That's what you saw on the sign 'cause that's what Maggie remembered. You can call me—" he stopped and looked at his wife, "you can call me Grandpa," he finished, his eyes glinting with mischief.

Inez's look tried to be reproving but failed. "I guess that means you all get to call me Grandma," she said. "Come on in, folks. I just took two loaves of bread out of the oven."

"Did you see that?" Patrick whispered to Frank as they followed Inez up the steps.

"See what?"

"That flash—a sort of a light that went between them when they looked at each other?"

Frank looked at them, his eyes thoughtful. "Yes," he said, "Yes, I did."

The wanderers took chairs on a deck that ran the entire width of the cottage and overlooked the lake. In a surprisingly short time, Inez and Neil served them a lunch of fresh bread and bowls of home-made soup that made the gourmet menus of Bucknall seem precious and over-prepared.

Maggie remained at Grandma Inez's side, unwilling to let her grandmother out of her sight. She jumped up to help slice bread, ran to the kitchen to bring second servings of soup to the table, appearing totally unfazed by the fact that Inez looked as though she could have been Maggie's older sister.

After his initial welcome, Grandpa Neil sat in an armchair at one end of the large living room, his eyes compassionate as he watched the girl follow his wife about. One by one, the guests finished lunch and wandered off, Marjorie Harrison to her room for what she termed her "beauty rest," Clare to the bluff overlooking the lake where she ensconced the recovering Sven in a hammock that swung beneath a huge beech tree, and Patrick to an old upright piano in the room overlooking the valley. He stroked the keys, at first softly executing scales, then playing a Chopin sonata. Ryan James appeared from one of the basement rooms in swimming trunks and invited Maggie to come with him for a swim. At first Maggie demurred, but Grandma Inez shooed her away, claiming she had things to do in the kitchen. Frank Chambers walked aimlessly about the living room, checking out the books on the shelves that lined the walls, and when the Chopin ended, announced he was going to the beach for a walk. His tone did not encourage anyone to join him.

"Seems like everyone's got something that interests them 'cept you 'n me, Dr. Douglas," Neil said to Kate, who had claimed one of the porch's rockers. "There anything you'd like to do?"

Kate leaned back and let the rocker swing into a gentle forward motion. She watched a ring-necked sea gull soar lazily on a current of air above them. "You and Inez are angels, of course," she said quietly.

"Yes ma'am," he said.

"Then, yes, I'd like to talk to you."

Neil sat down on the wooden bench that edged one side of the deck. "Shoot."

Kate considered what she wanted to ask first. There were so many things. "Did this place appear because Maggie needed to be someplace secure and comforting?"

He nodded. "That and 'cause her grandma was a special person for her. People get to see the ones they love—most often it's when they wake up, but I guess Maggie's way of coming here, her injury and all, had something to do with it takin' a while to get together here with Inez. Reckon the time she spent in Wind Haven was about the best of Maggie's young life. This was a place where she could store good feelings, those moments folks keep deep inside that help them out when times are bad. Things weren't easy for Maggie when she was a kid. Even before her dad left, it wasn't good at home; the girl never did have much except for gymnastics."

"You know so much." Kate hesitated. "Do you know about Clare?"

He looked at her intently, as unfazed by the abrupt change of subject as he'd been by her first comment. After a moment, sadness crossed his face like a deepening shadow. "Yes," he said. "I do now."

"A while ago it was all I could do to stop myself from physically attacking the girl," Kate said. "I can't remember ever being that angry. It makes me sick to remember my rage."

"That was from hell, Kate. Spirits from hell wanted you to feel that anger."

A shudder swept Kate. "You mean they made me feel the way I did, think the things I thought?"

"They came; you let them stay." It was a statement of fact, said without judgment. "If you'd gone and told Sven what Clare had done, like you wanted to, well, it would've given them a real toehold. But you didn't."

"You know I wanted to tell Sven?" she said startled.

He held up a hand. "You're thinking about what happened right now. And since you're not trying to hide anything, it's like you're tellin' me the whole story."

"Is . . . is the baby all right?"

"Can't tell you about that," he said. "There's no reason for me to know about it."

There was a small silence. "Do you know how—" Kate said, and then stopped. She cleared her throat and tried again. "Can you tell me, what does a person have to do to get to heaven?"

"It's not what you do *here*. It's the choices you made while you were in the natural world," Neil said. He stretched out his long legs, crossed his feet; when Kate remained silent, he continued gently, "Now, I'm sure you made a lot of choices, good and bad, like everyone else who ever lived. But as you lived your particular life and chose what kind of things you wanted, or how we'd say it is—the things you loved—you began to love doing certain things and being certain ways more than anything else. And that's what you're here to find out—just what it is you love, what makes you you."

"I love Howard." Kate said it softly, as though to herself.

"Yes, you do." Neil smiled at her. "But we're talkin' about more'n just lovin' Howard."

"How do you know about Howard?"

"You told me just now."

"Of course. I forgot. And you know about love; you love Mrs. Favio."

"Yes, I do. But she's not Mrs. Favio, remember?"

"Oh, yes, you said the sign in the parking lot said Favio because that's what Maggie remembers."

Neil nodded. "Because this is Wind Haven as she knows it."

"Then you aren't really Maggie's grandparents?"

"Inez is her grandma, all right, but I'm not the grandpa she remembers. Inez and he came to the spiritual world within months of each other, but they didn't end up in the same place."

Kate's gut constricted. "What happened?" she breathed.

"Well, Max pretty much loved just one thing all his life—and that was Max Favio. Nothing and no one really mattered if it didn't concern ol' Max. Did a good job of hiding it from most everyone, except for Inez, of course; she knew. Naturally, once he was here, his real self came out. A shame, but there it is."

"Couldn't he . . . didn't he want to change when he realized where he was?"

"You don't change here; you don't *want* to change." Neil explained patiently. "That's what I meant when I said your choices are made in the natural world. Here you just become more and more like the person you worked on becoming during your life on earth. You keep on getting better if that's the direction you were going in the natural world, but if you used your life to work on becoming something pretty nasty—" He fell silent.

Kate tried to conceal the shock that jolted her. Neil's calm statement opened up a black hole of terrifying possibilities she found she didn't want to examine closely. "But Maggie doesn't seem to realize you're not her grandfather," she said. "And hasn't she heard Grandma Inez call you Neil?"

"She's payin' attention to what she wants to see and hearin' what she wants to hear. Anyway, the person she's mostly concentrating on is Inez. Like I said, Maggie's always been real close to her grandma."

Kate watched the ring-necked gull loop over the cottonwood saplings and back again. "I guess there's never been anyone I've been particularly close to who has die . . . I mean, come here. I hardly remember my mother; I was only a baby, when she got sick and Dad is a hale ninety-five. He doesn't believe in anything he can't put under a microscope, let alone the concept of life after death." Kate's mouth twisted. "I wonder what he'll think when he comes here."

The ring-necked gull headed out over the lake, and Neil got up and stretched. "Looks like I'd better go help out in the kitchen before I get hollered at."

Kate stilled her rocker and sat, hands clasped in her lap. "Can I ask one more question?" Neil paused, watching intently as the gull drifted back to shore and once again coasted on the currents above them. He nodded. "Go ahead."

"What happens if a person is pretty much a mixed bag of good and bad? Can that person go to heaven?"

He chuckled. "For a professor you sure don't listen real good," he said, his tone taking the sting from his words. "Every last human being is a mixture of good and bad. Generally though, what a person really loves deep down is something that points her mostly toward good or not. Sometimes the thing that a person feels most comfortable with is headin' in the opposite direction, toward downright evil. If a person has at least started to go in the direction of doing good, if she has tried to stop doing what she knows is wrong, she's gonna end up in heaven. If a person really loves what's bad and would do it if she thought she had half a chance of no one findin' out, she's gonna end up in hell. Simple as that. Now, most people don't just waltz into heaven, though I've seen some who did. Mostly, there's a bunch of things you have to learn before you go there and places you go to learn 'em."

"The Res-Medio school," Kate said.

He cocked an eyebrow. "Never heard of it."

"A young woman in Bucknall said she was on some sort of study-work program at a school called Res-Medio."

"Sounds like it could be one of 'em. Likely she was what we call a 'good spirit.' Lot of those around here. You've seen them helping around the towns, in hotels and restaurants. A lot of folks who eventually find their home in our heaven spend some time working in the hotels and resorts hereabouts." He stopped and looked up. The gull had flown off. Neil gave a little shake of his head and grinned. "I do carry on, don't I? I'd best get back to Inez and let you enjoy Wind Haven. Why don't you go for a nice walk?"

Kate got up. "Thank you, I will. Can I ask you just one more thing though?"

"No, you can't," he shushed her. "Reckon you got enough to chew over for the time being."

"But there's a woman named Bella," Kate began. Then she stopped, halted by the gentle but firm shake of his head. Kate attempted a smile as she watched Neil leave. Then she turned and looked out at the lake. She grasped the deck railing and tried to tell herself she wasn't frightened. She tried not to think of Maggie's real grandfather, or of Bella standing on the red sand of the desert watching the van disappear, tried not to wonder what it was that Kate Douglas had grown to love most of all.

(

The notes of the *Brandenburg Concerto* Patrick was playing filtered through the cottage to the deck where Kate stood, reached further to the bluff where Sven was now stretched out on a beach towel, Clare kneeling beside him, applying ointment Inez had given her to his back. The music did not, however, reach the beach far below at the bottom of the steeply angled dune where Ryan watched Maggie finish a series of cartwheels and back flips, and certainly not to where, far in the distance, the tiny figure of Frank Chambers walked alone.

"I don't think I need a spotter, but stand there just in case I don't judge this sand right, okay?" Maggie said to Ryan. She rose on her toes, arched her back, swung her arms and ran into a handspring that propelled her high into the air. Maggie's tightly tucked body turned over twice before landing perfectly, her heels digging into the sand, her arms triumphantly over her head.

Ryan applauded. "So what was that?"

"A double back flip." Maggie paused a moment and then ran a few paces, flung herself forward into a cartwheel in the air, hands outstretched, and ended with a back hand-spring. "An aerial cartwheel/back handspring," she commented as she stood, catching her breath. "Never one of my best moves, but I think I nailed that one."

Ryan held one hand straight up and made a circle with the other. "I give it a ten," he intoned. Then he grinned and said, "I'm getting an inferiority complex; why don't we try something I can do too?"

Maggie brushed the sand off her hands. "Know how to skip stones? My cousins and I used to have contests all summer long."

"You're on," he said.

Maggie sprinted to the water's edge and leaned over, searching for stones. "The flat, brown ones are best," she said. She picked up one and sent it skimming over the gently lapping waves. "Six skips," she said complacently.

"Not bad." Ryan had already picked up three or four of his own flat stones. He pitched one over the water. "Three." He threw another. "Four." He grimaced and pulled off the band that held his hair in a pony tail, shaking his head to let the hair fall over his muscular back. "That was practice; now let's get serious."

Maggie looked at Ryan's shoulder, the smooth skin bearing not the slightest indication of a scar. "I can't get over how your shoulder's all healed," she said. "Do you suppose Sven's back will heal as quickly?"

"Don't see why not. Of course, maybe I healed so quick because I'm special—about time someone realized it." Ryan grinned. He selected a stone and sent it flying. "Ten," he said. "How about you?"

"Say what?"

"I heard you were pretty beat up when you came to the hospital. Did the stuff you did just now trigger any of the old aches or pains?"

"Not a twinge. Not even when I landed hard on my heels." Maggie balanced on one foot, rotating the other in a circle. "See that? It's been ages since I could do that without it hurting."

"What was wrong with it?"

"Hairline fracture that never really had a chance to heal." She made a face. "And that's just one of a whole lot of old injuries. Let's face it—I was too old to try for a comeback."

"Why did you?"

Maggie skipped a stone as she considered the question. "Seven." Then she turned to face Ryan. "To show Coach I could do it without him, I suppose. And to show Mom." She bit her lip. "Mainly to show Mom."

Ryan sent a stone flying over the shining water. It hit in a myriad of tiny skips he did not bother to count. "She didn't want you to compete?"

Maggie gave a short laugh. She squatted on the sand and picked up a handful, letting the golden grains sift through her fingers. "That's all she ever did want me to do, from the time I was a little kid. She ruined her life and nearly ruined mine just so she could sit in the audience and see me try for a gold medal."

Ryan looked away for a moment. "I know something about what parents can do to kids." He said it as though to himself, but when he turned back and saw Maggie's questioning look, he gave her another quick smile. "Mine were really into their kind of religion, none of the brotherly love stuff, just your straight fire and damnation. And church! Man, they went enough to make the folks in Presbe look like pikers. If I'm never in another church building, it'll be too soon for me."

He reached for her hand and pulled her up. "Sorry, I don't know why I brought that up. Look, forget your coach, forget your mom, just kick back and be happy—the way you've been ever since we came to Wind Haven." He ran into the water. "Come on; let's swim."

Maggie leapt over the wavelets with him, squealing as the water splashed her. Then she twisted her hand from his and dove into the cold water, coming up a moment later gasping with delight. She waited for Ryan's dark head to break the water, and when he surfaced, scooped water with both hands and sent it flying at him in a furious barrage. "Water fight," she yelled.

For an instant, Ryan's eyes widened at the surprise attack. Then squinting, he set up a cannonade of his own and deluged Maggie with a Niagara of water that had her covering her head and shouting surrender.

Ryan scooped one last salvo as Maggie stood waist deep in the water, laughing and shaking droplets from her eyes. Then he reached out, brushed the wet hair back from her forehead, and took her face between his hands. "What I wouldn't give to be somewhere off by ourselves, away from all those people," he said.

They were standing so close Maggie felt the velvety reverberations of his voice in the pit of her stomach. She shivered and closed her eyes. He kissed her then, and Maggie flung her arms tight about him and returned his kiss.

(

Frank rounded the stretch of pebble-strewn beach that jutted out into the lake. He could no longer see the cottage on the high bluff behind him, and ahead lay what seemed to be miles of untouched beach and dunes and marram grass. Some of the dunes were bare, their sandy inclines untracked, while on others stands of dark pines, oak, and wild cherry marched down to meet thatches of grass at beach level. He carried a sturdy stick and thrust it into the wet sand as he walked. Occasionally, he stopped to pick up a smooth stone and thwack it with the stick, sending the stone spinning out over the calm water. Shading his eyes, Frank made out an inlet far ahead where a wide stream wandered across the beach out into the lake.

Gulls and sandpipers and swifts and an occasional heron gazed at him incuriously, waiting until he was almost beside them before rising to glide out of his way. Completely unafraid, they flew a short distance out over the lake or settled a few yards further down the beach, or in the case of the swifts, soared up the face of the bluff.

It was all as real as anything he'd ever experienced, Frank thought. Could it be that he really was walking along Lake Michigan's shores, that he was back in Illinois, or maybe somewhere in Wisconsin or Michigan? Had the last few days been illusion? Frank stopped and looked out over the sparkling water. No, he had to face facts. The reality was that he was here and "here" wasn't Michigan or Illinois or Wisconsin, much as it might look like it. He was "here," traveling around in a van with Kate Douglas, a woman who loved, and apparently would always love, a husband who was still "there." *Well, good for her!* Frank swung at a rock and sent it flying over the water, startling a swimming duck.

He wouldn't think about Kate. There were other things he had to sort through. He'd been doing a lot of that lately and not all of it had been unpleasant. It felt good to remember his days on the force before he'd gotten sick, the years of working among men and women he knew he could count on. Not that those days hadn't had their frustrations. How many perps had they taken in who worked the system and walked? Walked right out to continue whatever they'd been doing when interrupted. Even some who made you sick to think about what they'd done, what they'd do again—like the ones who molested kids. Frank felt his fists clench and consciously made himself loosen them. Not all of those guys walked. Some he and his buddies had managed to put away, system or no system. Frank shook himself like a dog coming out of water. *Don't go there.* Instead, think of the things he'd enjoyed while he was on the force; for the most part, it had been a deeply satisfying life.

For me, but not for Marge. The thought came out of nowhere, and with it the unwilling acknowledgement that all those years he had put his work first and ignored his home and his marriage. But then their lives, his and Marge's, had already pretty much fallen apart when Ben—

Frank stooped to pick up another stone. He flailed at it with his stick and missed. *Ben.* What joy he'd felt at his son's birth. But remembering that first, incredible joy only made the memory of their growing concern and dismay, their ensuing anguish, the more excruciating. They'd been told acceptance would come, but it hadn't for Frank. He had never learned to accept the affliction that kept his beautiful dark-haired son imprisoned somewhere far from them. But, oh, he loved that beautiful little boy, the four-year-old who had somehow managed to unlock the front gate and run down the street to the corner of Pulaski. The busy corner. From all accounts, Ben had darted out onto the intersection right into the path of the container truck. Frank felt once again the sharp, stabbing grief that had filled him during the weeks that followed, felt the secret relief that echoed behind the grief. Had Marge felt it? The relief? Probably not—she was too busy blaming herself.

I blamed her, too. Again, the thought came to him unbidden.

A tremor shook Frank Chambers's broad shoulders. No, he'd never blamed Marge; it wasn't her fault. He knew how impossible it was to keep an eye on their quicksilver child. But a clear little voice in his head said, "You did blame her, Frank." And he knew it was true. Frank's jaw tightened. What kind of man was he? How could he have blamed Marge when there was so much to blame himself for? Frank swung the stick in a wide arc and flung it up into the marram grass. *Ben.* The child he'd held and loved. He'd grieved more for Ben while the little boy was living than when he'd died.

Frank had almost reached the inlet when he became aware of a figure in the distance, a man in shorts and a singlet jogging along the shoreline toward him. The man splashed across the shallow stream of the inlet, his bare feet kicking up crystal sprays that shone like tiny diamonds in the sunlight. His pace slowed, and when he reached Frank, he came to a full stop.

"Great day for a run, isn't it?" the runner said to Frank. He was about the same age as Sven, but instead of straight blond hair, he had a shock of black curls that he tried to brush back flat as he wiped the sweat from his even-planed face with the corner of his soaked shirt.

"Don't know about a run, but it's a great day for a walk," said Frank, holding out his hand. "Frank Chambers."

The young man extended his own hand. "Ben," he said, smiling.

15

Frank Chambers recoiled. He yanked back his hand as though the young man's touch had scalded it.

"My God," he breathed. His eyes searched those of the person before him. This man was too old to be the little boy who'd died only ten years before. This couldn't be the child who sat for hours, rocking and gazing at something no one could see. But in the end, it was the eyes that convinced Frank, the startlingly blue eyes. They were the same bright blue, but instead of the empty gaze Frank remembered, there was an electric intelligence, an openness, and with it a calm sympathy that quieted Frank's erratically beating heart.

"Ben?" Frank's voice cracked. "Son?"

The young man's reply was another smile. It was as though he was not quite willing to agree with Frank's question, but did not want to respond with a negative.

Frank forced himself to breathe evenly, to focus on the sand, the pebbles, the lapping water. Sort this out. Take one thing at a time. "You live here?"

"No, I live far from here. I'm an usher."

"An usher. I don't understand."

Ben's blue eyes were guileless. "I and the others of our community are guides. We conduct people from one state to another."

"I guess we're not talking California or Nevada."

Ben gave a chuckle. "No, it's 'state' as in contemplative or peaceful or joyful."

"Feelings."

Ben made a small movement that could have indicated denial, but again he didn't contradict Frank.

"You mentioned only pleasant emotions," Frank wanted to stop this impossible conversation, but knew that you didn't stop an interrogation just because it wasn't going as planned. "What about unpleasant ones? Depression, despair, hopelessness?"

Ben nodded approvingly. "Right. It's the whole thing. It's our job to assist in helping people move from the kind of feelings you've just named to other, better states."

Frank noted but did not comment on Ben's avoidance of naming those other states. "Just men do this?"

Ben's lips quirked. "It's about fifty/fifty. My wife is an usher."

Frank shook his head, trying to clear it. "Wait a minute! You're *married*? I was at the hospital when you were born. Fourteen years ago."

Ben shrugged. "I don't know what you mean by 'years.' I guess you still think from what you newcomers call 'time.' Things will be simpler when you get past that."

Frank felt his knees give. He sat abruptly on the warm sand rather than suffer the indignity of collapsing onto it. Ben squatted companionably beside him.

Frank looked at the watch on his wrist. "You're right. I'm having some difficulty with the time thing."

"It'll come. And the idea of space, too. I've noticed that's a concept some of you newcomers find some difficulty with."

"We do, huh?" Frank studied him. "If there's no space here, why did you speak of the place where you live as being 'far' from here?"

"Because you understand those words. And because the 'state' of people in my community is far away in the sense of being very different from that of the people here."

"Because you're in heaven."

Ben nodded. "We live in a heaven."

Frank caught the word. "There's more than one?"

"Oh, yes," Ben said.

Frank could feel himself sweating. He was certain Ben would answer anything he asked but wasn't sure he wanted to hear any more right now. Matter of fact, he was sure he didn't want to pursue the subject. When he'd glanced at his watch a moment ago, he'd had a glimmer of something, too vague to call a speculation, concerning the whereabouts of its original owner. Frank's mind shied away from the half-formed idea just as he was skirting this one. *Enough! Keep to safe subjects.* "Do you remember anything of your time, that is, your stay with us?" he asked.

Ben's eyes searched Frank's. "I remember your love. And hers."

"You used to get stiff as a board when anyone held you. We wondered sometimes if anything was getting through."

"Since your thoughts are still geared to earthly terms," Ben smiled apologetically as he said this, "it's hard for me to explain how it was, but my world then existed in a kind of—" he paused and chose the words carefully, "a kind of silent tumult. But that tumult was pierced by what I can only describe as shafts of love. These shafts, your love and Marge's and the love that came from the angels around me, entered my silver silences. Even though there were many things my brain couldn't process, both kinds of love nourished me, and though sensory impressions came through imperfectly, they formed a basis I could build on when I came here."

"What happened when you ... came here?"

"I grew up. Faster than you think I should have." Ben's smile broadened. He considered Frank intently. "The woman who became my angel mother looked a lot like Marge, and come to think of it, her husband was a lot like you, Frank."

It seemed strange to hear his son call him by his first name, to hear him call his mother 'Marge,' but what gave Frank an unacknowledged fillip of pleasure was the implication of Ben's wording.

"You mentioned your angel mother having a husband," Frank said, "but you didn't consider him your father?"

"He was my teacher, not my father." As Ben looked out over the water, the glinting sun's reflection bathed his face in radiant light. "I have only one Father."

Frank knew that Ben was not talking about Frank Chambers. "Right." Frank put his chin on the crossed arms that rested on his knees. A light breeze fingered Frank's damp hair, cooled his sweat-soaked shirt. Okay. It was all right. He might not be Ben's father any more, but for a period of time (there it was, time again), he'd been given a charge he'd carried out as well as he'd been able, the charge of caring for this being sitting beside him. Or rather the child who had become this being. This angel. And with the thought came a flood of feelings Frank could hardly distinguish. Awe, satisfaction, a quiet pride, and, yes, a deep sense of humility. Beneath it all, echoed the implications of Ben's statement. He, Frank Chambers, also had one Father.

"I'm glad you thought of me." Ben rose in one easy motion. "But I must leave now. I have things I must do."

Frank got up slowly and dusted the sand from his pants. Although Ben was leaner than Frank, they were, Frank realized, of an equal height. He cleared his throat. "I hope one day I'll be able to see your home, Ben," he said. "Meet your wife."

"I'd like that," Ben said simply. And before Frank could register what Ben intended, the young man stepped forward and enclosed Frank in a bear hug that left him gasping for breath.

Ben released him. "Take care," he said.

"Sure thing," Frank replied, trying to keep his voice level. He found to his surprise that he couldn't see properly. He turned away to blink back the tears, and when he looked around again, Ben was gone. Frank stood staring at the depression in the sand a few feet away, a scooped-out area where Ben had absently dug his feet into the warm sand. Frank stooped to touch it.

((

The frenzied roar of motors split the quiet afternoon, obliterating the locusts's droning buzz and the plaintive call of mourning doves. A moment later five gleaming motorcycles swarmed down the macadam road into the parking lot. On reaching the flat, sandy bottom area, the cycles snaked in a series of tight figure-eights that flung sand into the air as they spun out of their turns.

Neil ran to the back screened porch. "Where are all our folks?" he called out to Inez.

Inez appeared in the kitchen doorway. "The two kids are on the bluff, Kate went for a walk in the woods, and somebody, probably the lady with all the rings, is taking a shower."

"Maggie and the boy are still on the beach and so's the detective," Neil said quickly. "Kate's the only one who might get in their way. I'd better go make sure they don't run into her while they're playin' their games." He gave Inez an exasperated wave and loped down the stairs toward the parking lot.

A bearded man wearing a bandana, clearly the leader of the group, reared his great black machine in the air, its rear wheel clearing the sand like a monstrous metal horse doing airs above the ground. The man on the Harley behind tried to follow suit and barely escaped clipping the leader's engine as he careened by it. Both men were so intent on regaining their balance that neither saw Neil at the bottom of the stairs. They did not, in fact, see him calmly hold up a hand above his head, palm out, until they were within a few feet of him.

"Abort, Mac!" the helmeted third rider yelled. "It's an abort!"

The leader's hairy head snapped back at the sight of Neil. He gripped the brakes and brought his cycle to a skidding halt, barely keeping his balance as his cycle spun around. Within seconds, the five riders formed a semi-circle facing Neil and killed their engines. The leader sat astride his cycle in the middle, breathing heavily. Reddish-brown hair covered most of the man's face, from bushy eyebrows that sprang from beneath the tightly tied bandana to his hair-covered cheeks. His luxuriant beard reached to a barrel stomach that strained against the man's black leather jacket. He reached beneath the beard and scratched his chest.

"We came 'cause we were called," he said to Neil. The nasal, high-pitched whine seemed incongruous coming from the massive frame.

"Not sayin' you weren't, but our group here's a mixture," Neil said sternly. "Don't want any innocents hurt while they get themselves sorted out."

"We wouldn't do that," the leader tried to look reproachful. "But we're allowed to come when we hear a call. And we heard one. Or maybe two," he added. "It's hard to tell in these hills."

Neil frowned. "Two? You're sure?"

"The rest heard one; I heard two." The third rider took off her helmet and shook out a mane of red-gold hair. "One was the usual garden-variety stuff, but the other was . . . ," she paused, "real dark. Dark and sort of muffled."

"Tanya hears things the rest of us don't," said the grinning man on the second Harley. "Sometimes I think she's just havin' fun with us."

"Leave the thinking to me," the leader snarled at him.

"That's enough," Neil said quietly. "I think you all better git. These folks are leaving soon, so there won't be any more calls, not from here at least."

It was obvious the hairy one didn't like the order, but he gave a perfunctory nod and jerked his head at his followers. He started his engine, took the huge bike in a semi-circle, and roared up the steep road without a backward glance, the four cycles close behind him. The acrid smell of exhaust lingered in the parking lot long after the buzzing of the motorcycles faded to silence. Neil turned and walked up the cement steps to the cabin, his face thoughtful.

"Sven here got a look at those machines, and it was all I could do to persuade him not to rush down to the parking lot and beg for a ride," Inez said as Neil walked in the kitchen. She paused, her gaze becoming instantly alert. "You're concerned. Surely it's not about those poor things?" She nodded in the direction of the departed cyclists.

Neil gave the briefest of negative gestures. Inez studied his face a moment and then nodded an abrupt agreement with whatever it was she saw.

"There," she said, "the shower just went off. I'll just make sure the lady has found the towels." She smiled at Clare and Sven. "Suppose you two go on down to the beach and call Maggie and that young man she's with. Tell them I've got fresh-made cinnamon buns and lemonade waiting for them. And if you see Mr. Chambers, tell him too." She watched as Sven and Clare went off obediently, hand in hand. "You're going to find Kate and bring her in?" she said to her husband, more a comment than a question.

"I reckon we'd best gather everyone. It's time they left."

Inez's forehead creased in a small frown. "Even Maggie?"

"Especially Maggie. I'd say it's pretty obvious she was sent here so she can tap into all the good things given her when she was a kid in Wind Haven. More'n likely she's gonna need 'em down the road." Neil placed his hands on his wife's shoulders and kissed her. "Honey pie, you know there's no need to worry," he said softly.

"I know it. I just don't always get my heart to see what my head does." Inez's lips quirked in a slightly shamefaced smile. "You go on and get Professor Kate, and I'll rustle up the rest."

The reactions to Neil's placid observation over lemonade and sticky buns that, while he and Inez had enjoyed their company, he figured the group was ready to move on, ranged from surprise to shock to anger.

"You can't mean we have to leave! We just got here!" Maggie stared at her grandmother in disbelief.

"You're wanderers, darling," Grandma Inez said. "You and the rest of these folks have places to go and things to learn." She brushed the curls from Maggie's forehead. "You've had a right nice afternoon at Wind Haven; now it's time to move on."

"I have no intention of getting back on that van," Marjorie Harrison announced from the couch where she was reading a magazine that looked like *Forbes* or *Fortune*. "This is a pleasant spot, and I intend to stay until I'm ready to leave—" she looked at them, arching carefully plucked eyebrows, "which I doubt will be any time in the near future. As a matter of fact, I'm looking forward to more of this good woman's excellent cooking for dinner." She smiled graciously at Inez.

"'Fraid we'll be leaving, too," Inez said apologetically. "Not that I wouldn't enjoy cooking for you all. Truth to tell, that's what I do at home."

"You're a cook?" Maggie said, momentarily diverted.

"I'm the one who arranges for all the meals in our community at home. Remember how I loved to feed you and your cousins? Well, now I get to do it every day. Manage everything from the regular council luncheons to planning special banquets for the holidays. I have a ball."

Neil beamed at her. "The mayor says you can always tell when Inez has had a hand in things. They have that extra zing."

Kate moved from her position by the sliding glass doors leading to the porch. "You said we have places to go and things to learn," she said to Inez. "Is that why we're traveling around like this? Is there some special itinerary we're following? And if so, what are we supposed to be learning, and why were we given a map in the first place?"

"Especially one that changes every time you look at it," Patrick added.

Inez smiled. "Wish I could tell you, but that's not my bailiwick. I wouldn't get too fussed about it, though. Of course, there's a plan, there's always a plan, and you'll find out about it in good time. And as for what you're supposed to learn, I'm surprised a smart person like you hasn't figured it out yet, Dr. Kate. Like Neil told you a bit ago, you people are supposed to be figuring out just who you are inside." Most of the people sitting about the large living room moved uneasily as Inez swept them all with her kindly smile. "Now, Sven, you go get that picnic hamper from the van, so I can pack it," Inez said, heading for the kitchen. "Next time you folks get hungry, you'll find things in that hamper that'll make your tummy sit up and take notice. I guarantee."

(

Marjorie Harrison's querulous complaints continued long after the van had climbed the hill out of the parking lot and they'd left Wind Haven behind.

"I don't see why we had to leave," she sniffed. "I thought I made it clear I was willing to rent your grandparents's cabin, Maggie. It would have been a simple matter to arrange to have, if not your grandmother, someone like her, come in to clean and cook. It would have been perfect." She inspected her manicured hands and twisted her rings. "I don't want to keep gallivanting around like this; I need my rest. I'm convinced having proper rest is why I feel so good these days."

Patrick let out a gusty sigh. "Mrs. Harrison, I think everyone here is beginning to realize there's nothing we can do about traveling around in this van until we get to wherever it is we're supposed to be going, so we might as well make the best of it. Everyone except you, that is. Don't you think you could make an effort? Process what's been happening, all the things that don't fit in with the world as you know it, and come up with some idea about where you are?"

Everyone but Ryan, who was at the wheel, looked at Marjorie as though willing her to make the step from denial to acceptance.

She stared back at them, her jaw tight. "I am *not* dead." The words emerged from between clenched teeth. "I think you're all quite daft." Her jaw unlocked, and she looked suddenly brighter. "That's it! Ever since we left the hospital, I've had the impression that you people, at least some of you, are, well, a little unbalanced."

"Marjorie, Marjorie," Kate said in wondering admiration. "Never let it be said that imagination grows weaker with age. Yours is as fertile as any I've come across."

"I don't know what you're talking about," Marjorie snapped. But she lapsed into silence; and as the van traveled along sandy, tree-spanned roads, she frowned and looked out the window at the verdant countryside with unseeing eyes.

Could it be true? Could the terrible thing she'd feared and spent so much energy pushing to the back of her mind have happened? And without any apocalyptic convulsion? Good gracious, if it had indeed happened, it had been without even a seismic tremor. Of course, she should have noticed—things *were* different here. Marjorie looked at her hands again. She never tired of looking at her hands these days. So smooth and unlined. She wished she had more than the little make-up mirror in her purse so that she could take another look at her face and neck. These past few years, except for applying make-up and checking her dress before going out, she'd avoided mirrors. But now that she'd begun looking so very much younger—Marjorie took a deep breath and allowed herself to think that perhaps there was just a chance these people weren't crazy. Maybe she was . . . well . . . no longer living.

But she most assuredly *was* living! And if not on earth, then where? In a world much like the one she'd left. Marjorie clasped her long-fingered hands together. Then there was a life after death. She'd always put off thinking about it. Certainly she was a churchgoer, had been ever since Edwin and she had taken their place in society as a young, married couple. They had always been among the first to contribute to any church need, and when they'd divorced—and my, hadn't that been a messy time!—she'd continued to support St. Basil's. Generously. With monthly contributions and all those everlasting donations in response to pleas for special needs funds. And when the church council dithered on for weeks about funding a new sprinkling system, it had been she who'd sent a check for $25,000, along with a note suggesting they use their meetings to discuss more important things. Yes, St. Basil's would not be the church it was today if not for Marjorie Harrison.

Marjorie shifted, trying to find a more comfortable position. Even after forty years of churchgoing, however, she'd never been at all certain about what lay ahead. And despite having attended numerous funerals where vague words of comfort were addressed to the deceased's relatives, she wasn't at all sure the various ministers who had graced St. Basil's pulpit knew either. It really wasn't the sort of thing one spent much time thinking about, not if one were as busy and involved as she.

But apparently there was indeed an afterlife. How remarkable.

Marjorie gave a tiny sigh and closed her eyes. She wouldn't give these people the satisfaction of seeing that she'd accepted the possibility that they might be right. As she'd learned to do over years of committee meetings, she would keep her counsel and see what happened. And if there *was* a heaven somewhere nearby, she would go there. She would be gracious and pleasant, even be humble if need be. Marjorie felt a whisper of something like uneasiness, but quickly suppressed it. Surely those in charge would welcome her. *Of course, they would.* It was hard to remember a time when someone hadn't been pleased to welcome Marjorie Harrison.

((

Clare dozed within the protective circle of Sven's arm, her face warmed by the late afternoon sun. The van hit a pothole, and her eyes opened. She smiled sleepily, not fully awake. "Is it hurting your back, me leaning against you like this?" she asked.

Sven shook his head. His gaze slid from Clare's soft face to the relaxed fingers resting on his arm. "I got to ask you, Clare. What did you see when the van stopped at that village, when you went with that man, Raphael?"

Clare sat upright. "You said we weren't going to talk about it."

"*You* said it, babe. I didn't."

Clare darted a glance at him. Her lips trembled, and she raised a hand to her cheek. "I don't want to talk about it," she mumbled.

"This is all about Essie isn't it? What is it? Did you see her?"

Deep red stained Clare's cheeks. She hung her head, and the silken fringe of corn yellow hair fell forward, shielding her face.

"Tell me." Sven's tone was softly insistent. "Tell me what you saw, babe."

Clare's chubby hand flung back the heavy curtain of her hair. Her blue eyes brimmed with glistening tears that overflowed and coursed down her cheeks. This time, however, Sven did not reach out to comfort her. He sat quiet, waiting for her reply.

"She was lying in a crib," Clare said, her voice so low Sven had to lean close to hear. "She was thin, real, real thin. She cried and cried."

The anguish in Clare's voice tore at Sven but he did not move. "Is that all?"

"No one came." It was an agonized whisper.

Sven swallowed. "Where was she? Wasn't she at your mom's?"

Clare shook her head, heedless of tears that spilled to her chest, making great wet blotches on her pink cotton shirt. "I never saw the room before. It was messy, dirty."

"Maybe you were seeing what happened the day we left; maybe it was before Frau Blore called your mom."

Clare shook her head dumbly, unable to make herself speak.

"What is it?" Sven's voice took on a rougher edge. "What haven't you told me?"

Clare looked away. At first it seemed she was going to dissolve into tears again, rather than speak. But then she took a shuddering breath and said softly, "I was going to call Frau Blore the first place we stopped. I was going to give her mom's phone number."

"But you did give her the number ... before we left, remember?" Sven said. "When you asked Frau Blore to come upstairs and get Essie when she came on duty; you told her your mom's number to call."

With what seemed enormous effort, Clare met his eyes. "When I asked Frau Blore, she said she couldn't do it. I tried to tell her Mom would give her money, but she said she was too busy to take care of a baby, even for a couple of days. She . . . she walked away and wouldn't let me finish, wouldn't write down Mom's number." Clare put her head in her hands. Her shoulders shook.

The others in the van could only hear brief snippets of the whispered conversation, but it wasn't necessary to hear the words to see Clare's anguish. Frank turned in his seat. "Anything I can do?" he asked Sven quietly.

Sven looked at Frank as though he'd never seen him before. Slowly his eyes focused, and he shook his head. Chambers turned back again and began a quiet conversation with the others that gave a modicum of privacy to the young couple.

Sven put a hand beneath Clare's chin, forcing her to raise her head. "You mean we just left Essie on that bed to be by herself all night?"

Clare's eyes were bleak. "I thought it would be just a couple of hours at the most. I was sure I could phone from first place we stopped and tell Frau Blore she *had* to go get Essie, tell her to give Essie the bottle I left in the diaper bag and to phone Mom in the morning."

Sven stared at her.

"We put pillows around her so she wouldn't fall off," Clare whimpered. "And if she cried, really cried, Frau Blore must have heard, don't you think?"

"What if she didn't?" Sven's voice was hoarse. "What if Frau Blore didn't come in to make up the room the next morning?" His mouth fell open, his jaw slack. "Wait a minute! Are you telling me that, even if Frau Blore did find Essie, she wouldn't have any idea who to call?"

Clare simply looked at him, her eyes huge.

Sven's hand slipped from Clare's face and dropped to the cushion beside him where it lay, palm up, fingers curled. His head drooped to his chest, and he stared dully at the floor.

"I wouldn't blame you if you don't love me any more," Clare said, tiredly. She pulled her shirt from her jeans and blotted her eyes with the hemmed edge. "When I realized what had happened, that I wouldn't . . . couldn't ever be able to make the phone call to Frau Blore, I felt—I wanted to die." The chubby, blond girl gave not the slightest indication that she realized the absurdity of her words. "When I was with Raphael and saw Essie, I was sure there wasn't anything that could make me feel worse—and there wasn't, until now—when I realized I had to tell you what I did." Her hands fluttered to her chest as she attempted to explain. "I figured we couldn't take her with us, not out into that storm, and I knew we had to leave or they'd find us and take you back to the brig."

Sven muttered something unintelligible.

"What?" Clare said timidly.

Sven shook his head and cleared his throat. "I gotta think." He didn't look at her. "I just gotta think." He edged a few inches farther from Clare and turning to the window, stared at the blur of pine trunks in the dark forest outside.

16

Kate's heart constricted at Sven's instinctive move away from Clare. Not that she blamed him. Kate had seen enough of the couple's body language to realize the implications of the whispered conversation, and her own earlier reaction to Clare's confession had been far more violent than Sven's. But the desolation she'd glimpsed in the girl's face tore at Kate's heart. Kate turned, about to utter some commonplace that might break the tension, but closed her mouth without saying anything. It was obvious that Clare and Sven were oblivious of their surroundings. Clare seemed to have exhausted her never-ending supply of tears. The girl sat upright, her feet not quite touching the van's floor, and stared straight ahead. The expression on her blotched face was accepting, almost calm, although her composure threatened to crack the one time she ventured to steal a look at her companion's rigid profile.

Frank leaned forward and made an infinitesimal gesture to the rear of the van. "You know what's going on there?" he murmured to Kate.

It was the first time Frank had spoken directly to her since the episode in the cabin, and Kate found herself absurdly grateful that he'd decided to remain on friendly terms. "Clare's just told Sven something that's pretty much knocked him for a loop," she said.

Frank cocked an ironic eyebrow at her. "That much I could tell."

Kate glanced at Patrick, who was listening with unfeigned interest. "Clare talked to me about it, but I don't think it's right for me to say anything."

Chambers nodded. "Right. Glad you were around for her. Well, if you think I can be of any help, let me know."

"I wish," Kate lowered her voice, "I wish she'd talked to someone else."

"Must be some reason you were the one," said Chambers. "Like we keep on seeing, things don't happen around here without a reason. It's pretty obvious that our traveling like this is a process of some sort. It doesn't take a mental giant to figure out that we were put in this van together to help each other."

His words hit Kate like a jab to the gut. "I didn't help Clare," she said, her face bleak. "Just the opposite."

Frank Chambers studied her. "Learn something about yourself in the process?"

Kate looked at him in surprise. "Actually, I suppose I did."

"There you go." Frank settled back, his point made.

"Frank, what happened back there at Wind Haven?" Patrick asked. "Ever since you went on that walk, it's been like you're totally spaced out." Then he corrected himself. "Not spaced out, but it's like you've become some kind of guru. I mean some of the stuff you're saying sounds more like some preacher than an ex-Chicago cop."

Frank Chambers's reaction to this was something that could have been a snort. He eyed his seatmate. "You have a great sense of humor."

"You should have seen the look on your face when you came back from that walk," Patrick insisted. "Like you'd been listening to Brahms conducting the *German Requiem*."

"Never heard of 'em." Then the big man sobered. "But you're right; I did meet someone pretty important. And I've been doing some heavy-duty thinking ever since. But it's not anything the rest of you probably haven't already thought out for yourselves."

"Don't be too sure," Patrick said. He looked back at the picnic basket wedged beneath the rear seat. "I find I'm feeling like it should be about dinner time. Anyone else want to see what Grandma Inez has packed?"

Since leaving Wind Haven, Maggie had been sitting quietly, her demeanor inviting no conversation. At the mention of the food her grandmother had prepared, however, her face brightened. "Yes, let's."

"Why don't we save Grandma Inez's goodies," Ryan James said from his place behind the wheel. "They won't spoil, and I've had enough picnics for a while. I vote we stop at a decent restaurant for dinner."

"And where are you going to find this restaurant?" Marjorie asked.

Ryan grinned at her. "I have this feeling that if we're hungry and are talking about restaurants, we'll come to—yeah, look over there!" He pointed to a discreetly lit sign that had appeared as the van rounded the bend. Marjorie was the only one who expressed surprise that it announced "Shelley's Roadside Restaurant/Bed and Breakfast."

"Get out your wanderers's cards folks," said Ryan. "We've hit pay dirt again."

Despite the restaurant's name, the dinner was hearty and German. Marjorie took one look at the menu and declined to order, announcing that her delicate stomach would rebel at any of the food offered. But after conferring with a waiter who volunteered to see personally that the kitchen prepared something suitable, the problem was solved by her ordering a cheese omelet. Maggie, still silent and thoughtful, sat beside Ryan James at the other end of the table and ate little; Clare, sitting just as silent next to Sven, ate even less. By the time the waiter came with the bill, conversation languished, and everyone seemed more than ready to go to his or her room.

The waiter returned with their wanderers's cards. "Now, if you've decided amongst yourselves who is going to entertain, I'll tell the manager," he said as he handed them around.

"What do you mean, 'entertain'?" Frank's eyes narrowed.

"Just that, sir. Our guests are expected to do something for the entertainment of the rest of the establishment's diners."

"Why didn't anyone mention this when we registered?"

"I wouldn't know about that, sir." The waiter twisted his striped apron, distressed. "Why don't I call the owner?" he said, brightening. And he rushed off before anyone could make more objections.

A moment later he returned with a slight young man dressed in what looked like slim brown plus-fours. A large, crumpled neck cloth swathed the top of his ill-fitting brown velvet jacket. He blinked at them benignly, as though he'd just awakened from a comfortable nap. "No one told you about our entertainment policy, eh?" he said. "No problem, it's just that we insist that our customers, along with paying for their supper in the ordinary way, also help us with the evening's entertainment. You'll find it's jolly good fun, makes things rather like a family outing." He looked at their blank faces. "I say, doesn't one of you sing? Or play an instrument, perhaps?"

"I play several instruments, but I generally get paid for it," Patrick offered.

Marjorie Harrison drew back her head and peered down her nose at the young man. "I used to sing when I was younger, but I never did and do not now perform for strangers."

Frank cocked an eyebrow. "I have no talent whatsoever," he said firmly.

Ryan, who had left his guitar in the van, made no offer to get it, and the rest of the group simply shook their heads.

Kate surveyed their host. "You're the owner, I presume?"

The young man bowed.

"Shelley?"

"Why, yes, but you have the advantage of me, ma'am."

"Kate Douglas." The beginnings of a smile tugged at her mouth. "I don't sing or play, but I write a pretty mean essay."

He bowed again. "Perhaps you could give us a short sample of your work after you've finished your dessert. Please, ladies and gentlemen," he said to the rest, "it's only fair that you offer us some diversion." His tone became cajoling. "After all, is it too much to ask that we entertain each other for an evening? I, for one, would be happy to participate."

"So you'll be part of the entertainment," Kate murmured. "I was wondering about that."

"About what, pray tell?" The young man turned to Kate. "I take it you think you know me?"

"We haven't met, but I've taught you from time to time."

His smile vanished at the amusement in Kate's voice. "From time to time? And what am I to assume you mean by that?"

"Only that the students today are apt to find you, well, irrelevant. They tend to dislike your emphasis on death and grief and gloom. Then, too, your classical allusions are mostly lost on them. Not that I'm defending my students, mind you, but—" Kate closed her eyes and then quoted:

'To Phoebus was not Hyacinth so dear
Nor to himself Narcissus, as to both
Thou, Adonais: wan they stand and sere'

Kate opened her eyes. "Then there's the one that goes:

'The wandering airs they faint
On the dark, the silent stream—
The Champak odors fail
Sweet thoughts as in a dream'

It does seem a bit much, don't you think?" The young man's face flushed. "No, I *don't*; I think it's *beautiful*. I know what it is you don't like, you and the kind who call themselves poets these days. It isn't the classical allusions or the subject matter. You just can't stand a properly scanned line, let alone one that rhymes." He drew himself up to his inconsiderable height and beckoned to the waiter. "Geoffrey, since these people don't wish to help with the entertainment, I certainly don't wish to share my gift with them," he said. "Mark their bill paid and have done with it. As we've already accepted their wanderers's cards, they may sleep here, but tomorrow morning they're to be out of here as soon as they're up." He glowered at the unfortunate waiter. "And after this, check out the crowd for academics before you call me in." He turned and marched from the room without a backward glance.

Patrick eyed Kate with wonder. "Do I read this right? Did you just give Percy Bysshe Shelley the brush off?"

"Don't you believe it," Kate said. "A look-alike, certainly, a wanna-be, probably, but the real McCoy? I seriously doubt it."

"How can you tell?"

"I misquoted a line, a change that made no sense. It should have been 'The Champak odors fail *like* sweet thoughts in a dream'. No poet would have been able to listen to someone mangle his poem and not correct him."

"So what's the deal with this guy and his amateur hour?"

"He wasn't really interested in having us sing for our supper; I bet all he really wants is an audience for his poetry," Kate said. "I think we would have been treated to an ode or two or five our host has just completed and happens to have with him."

Patrick grinned. "That cracks me up."

"Am I following this?" Frank asked. "You're telling us our host thinks he's the poet Shelley?"

"Right."

"The guy who lived a couple of hundred years ago," Frank said.

"Right."

"But he's just playacting?"

"'Fraid so. Though I'd bet by now he's convinced himself he's really Shelley."

Marjorie Harrison rose from the table. "I haven't the slightest idea or interest who that unfortunate young man thinks he is," she sniffed. "This dinner's dragged on quite long enough. I'm going to bed."

"So say we all," Kate said with a sigh.

((

The wanderers climbed the carved wooden staircase to their separate rooms, and soon quiet settled over the little inn. Only a covered bulb on the landing lit the hallway when Patrick tiptoed down the stairs to the deserted sitting room. Bright moonlight poured through the tall windows, making artificial light unnecessary. Yes, there it was. The grand piano sat in one corner of the room, a shawl draped over its gleaming lid partially obscuring a moonbeam path across it. Patrick seated himself on the bench and fingered the keys noiselessly. It had been marvelous playing the old upright at Wind Haven. Despite its age, it had had a wonderful tone. What might this instrument be like? Patrick caressed a black key, slid to the ivory keys, up again to the black.

Frank said he thought their job here was to find out what they'd grown to love during their lives on earth. What did he, Patrick, love?

The ability to bring music from an instrument like this. Others's music certainly, but most especially his own, the songs that came from his head, from his heart, from deep in his gut. Patrick's fingers chased the silent notes. He could hear the thunderous peals, feel the vibrations of the great organ at St. David's when he'd worked on his last composition. And had that been, was it to be the last of his music? The thought was a sharp, visceral pain. Patrick closed his eyes. *Please, God. Please. Music was my life.*

What had he truly loved beside his music? Had he loved Brian? He'd loved Brian's wit, his decisiveness. Loved him enough to feel more sadness than betrayal at Brian's desertion in the days after they'd heard the diagnosis. Patrick rose from the bench and went to the window. He pushed the heavy curtains further aside and stood looking out at the garden's lawn, at shrubs and bushes made into a silver landscape by the bright moon's light. What did he love? What did he want right now? Maybe that was a bad question. Perhaps it should be, what was wanted of him?

To do justly, to love mercy, and to walk humbly with your God. The words came to him without his volition. Not surprising. He'd probably heard more Scripture quoted than anyone outside of a seminary. Or Presbe. But what did it mean? Patrick moved restlessly about the room. He came back to the moonlit window. Surely, loving mercy meant seeing the best in people and doing what you could for those in trouble. He'd tried to do that. How did you "do" justice, though? And what about the "walk-humbly-with-your-God" part? Had he walked with God at all, humbly or otherwise? He'd made it a part of all those Sundays he'd spent in organ lofts waiting for the priest, minister, or the occasional layman to finish the day's sermon to think about his week, to sort out those things he'd done that he wished he hadn't, the things he should have done but hadn't. Those wonderful lines from the Anglican Confession often came to mind as he sat on the hard wooden organ bench. "We have left undone those things which we ought to have done, and we have done those things which we ought not to have done." But the resolve to do better that followed these weekly catalogues met with discouragingly limited success.

And sure, he had prayed, especially when life had taken potshots at him. He'd never been too sure that God was listening, though. Patrick stuck his hands in the back pockets of his jeans. *Are you listening now?* he asked silently. *If you are, if there's enough worth saving in me, let me be part of your kingdom. You gave me the ability to make music. Let me continue to use that ability and perfect it. To praise you.* That last thought came unbidden—and was immediately followed by a hot flush of shame. Who was he to think God would have any interest in his praise? Patrick bowed his head and covered his face with his hands. *Jesus, Lord who made me, forgive me, save me.*

Patrick stood motionless a long while. Then he made his way though the moonlit room to the hallway and slowly climbed the stairs.

☾

Frank Chambers stopped at the tiny office/alcove off the entrance hall. "What do we do about breakfast?" he asked the woman sitting at the cluttered desk. "Your Mr. Shelley was a little upset with us last night—claimed he wanted us out as soon as we got up."

The woman smiled; it wasn't an especially nice smile. "Oh, Shelley knows we must give you breakfast if you wish it. Shelley's forever trying his little ploy of wheedling people into becoming his captive audience, but your group seems to have been one step ahead of him." She didn't seem at all displeased at this.

"Well, fine then. If it's really okay for us to go have breakfast before we head out, I'll tell the group." Frank waited for some affirmation, but the woman was already immersed in her books. "If it's too much trouble, I'm sure we can find a place down the road," Frank said at last.

The woman's head snapped up. "Did I say anything about trouble?" she shrilled. "Did I so much as blink when you asked about breakfast?"

Frank merely looked at her with interest.

The woman tried an unconvincing glower. "Now I suppose you'll make it seem as though we've tried to shortchange you, and then we'll have the authorities down on us," she said.

"It hadn't crossed my mind," Frank said mildly, "but now that you mention it, I'd say it might be a real possibility."

"Oh, please, don't call them!" Any fire was gone from the woman's voice. "Shelley's got the authorities panting down our necks every time I turn around. Last time they said if they were called again, we couldn't stay."

Frank looked at her sharply. "These authorities, do they ride motorcycles?" he asked.

"Of course not. Sometimes they come in a police car. Mostly they just appear at the door. Why would you imagine they rode motorcycles?"

"Just a thought." Frank Chambers nodded and went to herd his little band into the breakfast room where he urged them to order promptly so that they might be on their way.

Half an hour later Ryan maneuvered the van out of the inn's parking lot and onto the road. Frank leaned across to Kate and said above the noise of the motor, "That incident last night and something that happened this morning make me think we've come to an area where we're going to have to watch out for ourselves. I think it may be dangerous."

Kate raised an eyebrow. "What about last night? Even if Shelley had succeeded in capturing us as an audience, I don't see how listening to some bad poetry could be considered dangerous."

"I don't think we had anything to fear from Shelley, or the rest of them for that matter. But the people at the inn are living on the edge of the law. And that tells me we've entered territory where we'd better be alert."

As though it had been brought by his words, a swirling wind came out of nowhere, buffeting the van and for a moment it rocked crazily. Ryan swore and gripped the wheel. "Storm coming. Look at those clouds!" he yelled.

The helpless occupants of the van watched flotsam whip past them through the suddenly darkened air. The storm hit with a roaring gust that slammed into the van and pushed it sideways. Sheets of rain made the frantic windshield wipers that Ryan switched on irrelevant.

"What *is* this?" Maggie shouted, her voice barely audible against the wind and savage rain beating the van's roof.

Ryan peered out through the curtains of rain, trying to see a road that was awash with torrents of water. His lips set in a thin line. "If it doesn't stop, we're going to be washed off the road," he yelled. "It's all I can do to keep this baby going."

But the rain stopped as suddenly as it had started. The wind died. Sun sparkled on the wet fields of grass. A few yards farther and the grass was dry. Sven twisted about to look out the rear window at the dark, glowering sky. "It's still raining back there," he said. "You can't see the inn, it's raining so hard."

"What was *that* all about?" Patrick said, shaken.

"I'm not sure I want to know," Frank said grimly. He glanced at Kate. "Do you still have the map?"

"Right here," she said, taking it from her pocket. "But I haven't looked at it lately. There didn't seem much point."

"I'd like to see if any pertinent changes have appeared."

"Here we are. Here's the inn, and this must be the lake, but that's funny—I don't see Wind Haven, and you'd think it would be somewhere near the inn since it was the last place we visited before the Inn."

"What about Eastlight?" Patrick asked.

Kate went back to the map. She looked up, her eyes serious. "It's not here. Eastlight isn't on the map anymore."

((

For the rest of the morning the van passed mile after mile of wooded land. No one commented on the micro-storm, and after the initial startled reaction to the disappearance of Eastlight from the map, no one spoke of this either. Although it was obvious that everyone felt a certain measure of uneasiness, no one seemed willing to speculate on why it suddenly seemed so important that the location of the city remain on the map, a city none of them knew anything about.

Even when they stopped mid-morning to let Ryan relax and the rest stretch their legs, there was little mingling or conversation. Sven slouched away from the rest to the edge of the small clearing where he stood staring into the sun-dappled woods. Clare looked after him, but did not attempt to follow. Marjorie made two rapid circuits around the clearing and then got on the van again, impatient to be gone. Maggie and Ryan, who walked a short way up the road, deep in conversation, seemed the only ones of the group who had anything to say to each other. After a brief saunter into the woods, Frank returned to stand beside Kate, who was inspecting a clump of purple hepatica nestled in the mossy ground of the rocky hillside. "You said there's another body of water ahead?" he asked.

She slipped the map from her pocket and studied it. "Looks like it. Not as large as the last one though."

"If our past experience is anything to go by, there should be some picnic areas around it. Think we'll be able to make it by lunch?"

"I should think so. If we want to."

"Of course."

And to neither Kate's nor Frank's surprise, shortly after they'd resumed their travels, a lake appeared on the horizon. The landscape had changed to a vista of bleak plains, with only a few trees dotting the panoramic view. In the foreground, tall grasses covered the fields on one side of the road, while on the other, the same grasses grew far out into the broad expanse of shallow brown water. Beside a patch of open water just ahead was a mowed area, and within the mowed circle were two dilapidated picnic tables with rotting wooden benches.

"This is not my idea of a picnic place," Mrs. Harrison said. But then she continued hastily, "However, as it's lunch time, we might as well stop."

"Okay, everybody out who wants some more of Grandma Inez's goodies," said Ryan.

Sven hauled the picnic basket to one of the wooden tables, purposefully ignoring Clare. She began to follow him but then halted and went to stand by the door of the van, twisting her hands. Maggie hesitated as she passed the stone-faced girl, but then, uncertain what to say, she simply went to the picnic table and opened the basket, taking the layer of linen from the top. Kate did stop beside Clare when she got out of the van, though she too seemed uncharacteristically unsure of herself. Whatever she was going to say remained unspoken however; both she and Clare froze, startled by a high, piercing scream.

They ran to where Maggie stood staring into the huge basket on the table. The petite gymnast held her hands to her chest just below her throat, palms out, fingers curled, looking like an absurdly begging puppy. Sven and Ryan rushed to her side, Frank close behind, and she stepped back, mutely making a tiny gesture toward the basket. Ryan leaned over and let out a low whistle. The muscles in his face twitched, and his hands clenched into involuntary fists. He moved aside, motioning to Sven and Frank.

The two men cautiously peered in the basket. "Snakes," Sven announced, drawing out the word. "Snakes all over the bottom. Must be twenty of 'em. Small and black and shiny and they're all twisted together in a ball like a bunch of licorice sticks."

Patrick, who had stayed a safe distance away, made a barely audible noise and covered his mouth.

"And look in that pink container," Maggie said, her voice shaking. "There's something moving inside."

Frank reached for a knife and poked inside the basket. "You're right. There's something in there." He took a fork from the pile of cutlery and using it and the knife, lifted a clear, pink plastic container from the basket and set it on the table. "Scorpions." He looked slightly green. "Can't say that I've ever liked snakes or scorpions."

Ryan squatted to bring the round container to eye-level. He did not, however, pick it up. "Yup, scorpions," he said. "Quite a few of them."

For once it wasn't Frank Chambers who took charge of the situation. By common consent, Sven and Ryan worked together to empty the basket, carefully fishing out the rest of the containers and placing them on the table. That done, they simply upended the basket and tossed the squirming mass of vipers far out into the tall weeds. The rest watched in horror as the ball of glistening snakes separated mid-air and slithered into the brackish water.

"No bikers or gypsies around to blame it on this time," Frank murmured. He scanned the empty horizon. "Just us."

"I hope you're not insinuating one of us substituted those snakes for Inez's food?" Marjorie Harrison demanded. "It's obviously the work of someone at the inn."

"I didn't mean one of us actually put them in the basket, only that perhaps they appeared *because* of us."

"Because they represent something inside us," Kate said slowly. Her hand went involuntarily to her stomach.

"Ridiculous," Marjorie snapped. "I wish both of you would stop talking that way and do something about the problem at hand." Seeing she had their surprised attention, she said, "Someone has to get rid of those scorpions, and then I'd advise taking a good look at what's in the rest of the boxes."

"Makes sense." Chambers squared his shoulders and approached the table. He leaned over stiffly, hands on his knees, and peered at the row of plastic containers.

"Hey Frank, if you don't like being around these little critters, don't feel you have to deal with them just because you're a cop," Ryan said easily. "How about you and me checking out the rest of these containers, Patrick?"

"No way—not me. Those kinds of things make me puke." Patrick's face was pale. He took another step away.

"Right." Ryan made no attempt to hide the scorn in his voice.

"Oh, come on, Ryan, let's not make a big deal of it." Frank made a move to pick up a large, square container. "They're just big insects."

"I'll help." Clare said softly. She took the container from him and holding it out as far as she could, carefully lifted the lid's corner. "There's sandwiches in this one." She took off the top of the container and laid it aside. "Yuk," she said, "there're ants in the sandwiches." She opened the next container on the table and then the next. "There're ants in all of them."

Kate came forward to look over Clare's shoulder. "I'll take ants over scorpions any day, but it looks like we'll have to go elsewhere for lunch."

"I don't think I'll ever want to eat again." Maggie shuddered. "I don't want to stay here. I really, *really* don't want to stay here."

"I don't think any of us does," Frank said. "Look around. This place looks like something out of an environmentalist's nightmare."

"And it smells." Marjorie pinched her aquiline nose. "It didn't when we first got here, but it does now. Like sewage."

"Frank's right," Kate said. "I think we should leave. *Now.* Before something else happens."

Chambers cleared his throat. "Okay, let's see if there's a restaurant down the road. It's always worked before. Ryan, if you want help with the driving, I'd be glad to take a turn."

Ryan refused the offer with a quick shake of his head.

"What about the picnic basket?" Maggie asked. "Aren't we going to take it?"

"No." Patrick said it before anyone else could speak. "That thing doesn't go in the van with us. We leave it here."

A small silence met this. Although no one voiced agreement with Patrick, it was apparent nobody was anxious to have the basket travel along. Except for Maggie.

"We can't just leave it," she protested. It's awful how those things got in it, but how do we know it will happen again? Every time I see that basket I remember Grandma Inez packing it. It makes me feel close to her."

"Take a picture." Patrick headed for the van. "You can haul it out and look at it any time you want."

"Patrick's right, you know," Kate said to Maggie. "I wouldn't feel too happy having that basket under the back seat. And would you like to be the one who opened it next time we stop for a snack?"

Maggie gave Ryan James a quick look, but Ryan merely shrugged and held out his hand to her. After a second, Maggie took it and followed him to the van.

"What do we do with all this stuff?" Sven indicated the containers on the table.

The muscle in Frank's cheek twitched almost imperceptibly, but he went to the table and gingerly replaced the containers in the picnic basket. "Anyone got a pen and some paper?" he said.

"Here's a pen," said Kate, fishing in her pocket, "but I don't know about paper." She thought for a moment and then took out the map and looked at Frank in question. At his nod, she carefully tore off a corner piece.

He quickly penned a note and tucked it securely into the basket's woven top. "Danger! Scorpions!" Kate read. "You didn't say anything about the ants?"

"I thought 'Danger! Scorpions and Ants!' might lose something of the desired effect." He moved toward the van.

Kate fell into step with him. She looked over and gave him a tentative smile. "Frank, I've been thinking about what I said to you back there at the cabin. It needed to be said, but I realize I must have sounded pretty insensitive. Thanks for being willing to overlook my heavy-handedness. Things have been a little difficult for me lately and I . . . I value your friendship."

"Difficult?"

"It has to do with, well, with Clare and what she's going through. I really shouldn't say any more, but thanks for just being there." She grabbed the door handle and stepped into the van.

"No problem." Frank looked after her and his jaw tightened; but after a moment, he took a deep breath, got on the van, and took the seat next to Patrick. "You don't like snakes and scorpions either, hey?" he said companionably.

"Not particularly."

Frank studied his seatmate. Patrick's hands were clenched in tight fists and a thin line of perspiration beaded his upper lip. Frank responded to these rather than to Patrick's offhand tone. "Hey, lighten up. We left all those wiggling beasties behind, right?"

Patrick did not answer and for the next few miles became engrossed in the passing scenery. Frank left him to his thoughts until the younger man turned from the window and sank back in his seat. "Want to talk about it?" he said.

"Not particularly," Patrick said again.

Frank nodded. "Okay, but if you do decide you'd like to talk, I'm available. Not that I'm some kind of shrink or anything, but I've listened to a lot of stories."

Patrick didn't avail himself of Frank's offer, but he did unclench his fists and gradually his stiff posture relaxed. Finally, he leaned back against the seat and let out a deep sigh. Frank took all this in silently. Why was Patrick so unwilling to discuss his fears? Because he had some private knowledge of how those varmints had gotten into the basket? No, Frank decided—not Patrick. Then who? Or had all this morning's events—the storm, the disappearance of Eastlight from the map, and now the basketful of snakes and scorpions— simply been meant to warn them?

Of what? That they were heading in the wrong direction? That they were in danger? Frank looked at the silent faces about him. Or that one of *them* was the danger?

17

To no one's surprise, they soon entered a small village. Some but not all of the wooden houses lining the main street were painted, although judging from the condition of the peeling colors, any painting had been done long ago. Smoke wafted from a few chimneys, and a chill wind blew pieces of trash about barren yards. Those by open windows hurriedly closed them against the sudden drop in temperature.

"There's a restaurant," said Patrick pointing to a log cabin with the sign " _OOD AND _ _INKS" above the entryway. "But I'm not sure we should stop."

"You folks stay here." Frank stood, his head brushing against the van's ceiling. "I'll take orders for sandwiches and bring them onboard."

There was a beat of silence.

"Make mine egg salad, if they have it," Kate said.

"Lettuce and tomato, hold the mayo," Maggie piped up.

《

Frank's errand successfully carried out, the van's passengers munched thoughtfully as they journeyed on, through sere, stubbled fields, into a wild, rocky plain. At last Marjorie said, "It's high time we stopped. I need to get out and walk."

No one objected when Ryan pulled off the road and parked near a cairn of rocks.

"We could all use a little exercise," Frank said, climbing stiffly out of the van. "Just don't anybody go too far. Stay within sight of the van."

Kate moved into the shade of a rocky outcropping and, leaning against the rough stone, undid the top button of her shirt and fanned herself. "We're not out of the wilderness yet, are we?" she asked the big man beside her.

"Nope." Frank eyed her soberly, then looked out over the bare landscape that had replaced the tall grass prairies. "Sure doesn't look like it."

"It's rather what I remember the Badlands looking like." Kate sucked in a quick breath and looked away, catching her upper lip between her teeth.

"What is it, Kate?"

"I was thinking about the places we've been lately. Ever since Wind Haven, they've been getting steadily worse. Why? Have we been judged and found wanting? Have *I* been judged?"

"Look, from what I've seen so far, I don't think we're judged," Frank said. "I think God allows us to judge ourselves. We've seen how folks in Presbe and Bucknall learn about themselves. It's pretty obvious we've been sent on this trip so we can do the same."

"If you're trying to make me feel better, you're not succeeding."

"Hey, Professor, lighten up. One thing I learned in twenty-five years on the force is no one's a hundred percent good or bad. We all make mistakes. I've seen some basically decent people make some pretty lousy choices. Since we came here, I've been thinking a lot about mine. I just hope the times I tried to do what I thought was right will be enough to make up for the times I screwed up." He frowned, looking as though as though he'd just remembered something.

Kate eyed him. "You're saying if we did enough good things, they'll balance out the rotten ones?"

Frank shook his head. "I don't think it's *what* we did so much as *why* we did it, the, I don't know, the patterns we formed in our lives." His eyes darkened. "It's some of the 'whys' in my life that have been bothering me."

"Sounds like a particular 'why.'"

Chambers studied his shoes. Did he want to tell her about the thing that had been flicking at the edge of his mind ever since

Presbe? That there had been the reoccurring image of that whimpering perv Cal and he had interrogated? Why should that particular interrogation bother him? After all, they knew the guy had done
it. And he'd confessed. Took some doing, but he confessed. Not that
Frank felt good about what happened later, but at least one scumbag
was off the streets. Then there were other recollections that had
claimed his attention as he'd watched the passing landscape, fester-
ing memories he hadn't thought of in years.

Frank let out a breath. "Okay, there are some things I can't seem
to get out of my mind. They keep popping back. One time in particular back when I was a rookie cop. It was during a St. Patrick's Day
parade, and I spotted this kid who looked like he was stalking somebody. Turned out he was planning to kill his high-school principal,
and I was the guy who stopped him. Got a medal for it. But . . . you
see . . . I didn't know the kid was planning to kill anyone. All I knew
was he was dodging in and out of the ranks, lookin' for someone and
disrupting the parade. I went to collar him and he gives me the usual
lip and I give him the 'you're-outta-here' wave. Then, before I know
what's happening, the kid turns and hits me, in the gut—" he
glanced at Kate, "actually not in the gut—lower. Nearly flattened
me. Well, I was almost as big as I am now, and I went crazy. Hit him
with everything I had. He went down. And when he started to get
up, I hit him again. I was really pounding that kid, didn't care if
anyone saw me, didn't care if I made the six o'clock news along with
the mayor. That's when he pulled the gun. We struggled, and the kid
ends up dead. Lucky for me he's got a note on him, says how he's
gonna blow away his principal, a couple of teachers, then kill
himself. Everyone thought I'd seen the gun before I tackled him, and
I wasn't about to tell them any different. So I end up bein' a hero, but
I knew damn well I wasn't." Frank rubbed his chin.

"It bothered you, didn't it?" she said softly. "A lot?"

"It was years before I could even watch a St. Patrick's Day
parade," he admitted. "Always asked to be excused from duty." He
dropped to one knee and pulled at a piece of yellowed grass. "Never
beat on a guy like that again."

"So you learned." Kate said it quietly. "And that's what you were
talking about just now, right? If you hadn't learned, if you'd denied
what you'd done and made excuses, the violence and ugliness of that
act would have become a part of your 'pattern.'"

"Yeah, well." Chambers tossed the grass aside. "Y'know I loved my job—most of the time. Liked bein' a cop. But there was another side of it I hated. I realize now how angry I was a lot of the time—mad at the courts for lettin' the perps walk after we'd spent months and sometimes lost good men bringing them in, mad at how the laws made it easy for the bad guys to buy guns that made our bullet-proof vests a joke, and disgusted with the lowlifes that got away with murder, especially the ones who preyed on kids—" Frank shook his head and rubbed his eyes. "I never admitted it 'til now, but Marge had to put up with a lot. It wasn't so much the times I was so dead tired I didn't do anything but bolt down dinner and watch T.V.; it was all the nights I came home choking on my rage, ready to find fault with anything and everything around me—and the closest thing too often turned out to be her. No wonder she decided the dentist was a better bet."

"Oh, Frank," Kate said softly, then stopped as she saw Patrick coming toward them.

"Anybody seen Ryan?" Patrick said as he approached. He wiped his face with a handkerchief and stuffed it in back his pocket. "I say this pit stop has gone on long enough; we'd better get a move on if we're going to find a place to stay tonight."

"You're right." Frank rose and brushed the dust from his chinos. "I'll see if I can find him. Why don't you two round up the rest?"

"Frank and you were deciding the fate of mankind?" Patrick asked as Frank strode off.

"We looked that serious?"

"I wasn't sure who was going to break down and bawl first. Figured Frank had the edge. Everyone knows teachers are tougher than cops."

"Patrick, you're absurd. But then you already know that." Kate reached out and touched his sleeve. "You may be absurd, but you're a very nice person, by the way."

Patrick colored. Before he could say anything a shout rang out, and both Kate and Patrick spun toward the sound.

"That's Frank!" Patrick sprinted in the direction of the cry. Kate ran after him, joined by Sven, whose long-legged strides quickly took him ahead of her.

They found Frank behind a pillared formation that rose like a fossilized sand tower against the blue sky. The big man knelt astride a crumpled Ryan James who lay sprawled on a huge, flat rock. Frank held Ryan's ponytail in a brutal grip that twisted the younger man's head to one side. It looked as though it would take very little added pressure to snap Ryan's neck.

"Frank!" Kate gasped, "Don't!"

Chambers didn't loosen his grip or take his eyes off Ryan James. "Maggie's over there," he growled. "You better help Clare take care of her."

It was only then that Kate saw Maggie slumped against a stalagmite-like rock formation. Her arms were tight about the hard stone, as though clutching a stuffed toy. Clare knelt beside her.

"I was just back there when I heard someone cry out," the blond girl said to Kate. "Mr. Chambers and I got here together." She leaned over Maggie again. "Can you help me untie these knots?" she asked, "I don't have any fingernails and—" She stopped, staring at the perfectly shaped nails on her fingers, then gave her shoulders a little shake, and moved to attack the knots that bound Maggie's wrists to the narrow column of layered rock. The knots loosened, Maggie fell into Kate's outstretched arms like a marionette released from its strings. Blood from a scrape on her chin trickled down her neck and disappeared into the top of her t-shirt. Her eyelids fluttered but did not open.

Kate rounded on Ryan James, eyes blazing. "What did you do to her?"

Ryan lay motionless, his head twisted back, mouth open, straining against Frank's implacable grasp. A faint twitch of one shoulder was the only indication that he'd heard her question.

Clare took Maggie from Kate and gently placed her on the ground. "She's breathing okay. Maybe she just fainted."

Distracted as she was, Kate gave the blond girl a brief, assessing glance. What had happened to their perpetually weeping teenager?

"I think this creep hit her when she cried out," Frank said.

"Didn't hit her," Ryan gasped. "I was just trying to quiet her, and she fell into the rock and knocked her chin."

Although Frank did not release him, he eased his grip and let Ryan move to a slightly more comfortable position. "Okay, let's hear your version," he said grimly.

Ryan James grunted and tried to turn on his back. He managed a half-turn before Frank jerked him short. "We were just kidding around," Ryan muttered. "I was showing her how I could lasso," his eyes flicked to the rope on the ground. "We were playing like she was the calf and I was the cowboy, just fooling around, and one thing led to another and all of a sudden there she was—lassoed and tied up and I . . . I guess I couldn't resist, well, taking advantage, sort of. So she gets panicky and starts yelling. That's all. That's all there was to it." He took a cautious breath. "Look, let me up, will you?" he said. "I'm not going anywhere."

Except that he was having trouble breathing because of the angle of his neck, Ryan might have been speaking about a problem with the van's motor. He sounded so ordinary, so guilt-free, that if it hadn't been for Maggie, whose groggy movements showed she was beginning to regain consciousness, his listeners might have believed him.

Maggie moaned, opened her eyes and looked about, her gaze unfocused. Then she saw Ryan and sat up. "You jerk!" she spat. She rubbed her chin and winced.

"Calm down. I might have been a little rough, but you were enjoying it—at least for a while there," said Ryan. "Don't try to say any different."

"Maybe I did—until you wouldn't stop," Maggie snapped. "When I realized you had no intention of stopping and yelled for help, you smacked me so hard I hit the rock and saw stars."

"An accident."

"On purpose!" Maggie glowered at him in fury.

"Hold it! Hold it!" Frank shifted his grasp slightly. "Has this guy tried anything before?" he asked Maggie.

"Not like this, not really—well, sure when you guys weren't around, we kissed and he grabbed me and stuff. He's a guy after all. But nothing like this." Her eyes filled with tears. "This time it was like he was some kind of animal, like he didn't care what I said or did. I . . . I was really frightened."

"Uh huh," Frank Chambers drew the syllables out thoughtfully.

"What do you mean 'uh huh'?" Kate said.

"I've been expecting something to happen since the incident with the picnic basket. Those scorpions and snakes were a warning that some of us were dealing with some pretty bad stuff."

"Say you're right and he's the reason for those scorpions," said Patrick. "Why would he try something like this with everybody around? He had to know he couldn't get away with it."

Chambers looked at Kate and then at the others. "It's not just getting harder to say one thing and mean another. I think it's getting harder to keep from acting out what's in our minds and hearts. It's getting way harder to control our actions."

"Makes sense." Patrick eyed Ryan's sprawled figure. "He's been fighting to stay in character, and for some time it hasn't been easy. Like I've known since Presbe that he's the one who trashed my stuff and tossed it out."

The rest stared at him. "How do you know that?" Kate asked.

Patrick shrugged. "Wasn't hard to figure out. He's been on my case since the beginning, partly because of who I am, partly because of who he isn't."

"Who he isn't?" Sven repeated.

"The guitar's for show. Sure, he strummed a few bars back at the hospital, but has anyone seen him take it from the case since then, since he learned I'm a musician? I haven't. The guitar is part of the persona he cultivates. I think there's a whole different person behind the good-time-Charlie with the ponytail. Frankly, my guess is the guy lies like a rug—about any and everything."

"Why?"

Patrick shrugged again. "How should I know? Maybe he wasn't paying attention in Sunday School."

"Sunday sch—" Maggie stared at Ryan. "He told me his parents were like those people in Presbe," she murmured, "but worse—that they went to church even more and—"

"Spare me the psychology, please!" Despite the fact that Frank Chambers still maintained a firm hold on his hair, Ryan managed a mocking glance in Maggie's direction. "Let's get back to the here and now. What are you going to do, pretty girl, bring charges? Better get a damned good attorney; after all, you allowed yourself to be tied up. And then I didn't actually do anything."

"Only because Frank decked you."

"I wonder if it's possible to access records here?" Frank said, musing. "Police records," he explained to Kate's questioning look. "Mr. James is a little too familiar with the idea of charges being brought. I'd be willing to bet he has tried something like this before."

"Oh, he has, he has." The nasal Eastern twang came from behind the pillared rock opposite them. A generously made-up woman with long blond hair stepped out from the shadowy rocks and walked past Sven. She wore impossibly high-heeled shoes and care-fully avoided the loose stones that littered the ground, stopping a prudent six feet from Ryan's recumbent form.

Ryan craned his neck as far as he could in an awkward attempt to look in her direction. "Darlene?"

"You got it." When she saw that Frank Chambers still held Ryan securely, Darlene took a few cautious steps closer. She twisted a strand of blond hair about her finger and examined the captive man. Her bravado collapsed, and her lips quivered. "You shouldn't oughta have done that to me, Ryan."

Ryan tried to twist away, but Frank tightened his grip so that the younger man remained facing the woman. "I don't know what you're talking about," he said sulkily.

"I shoulda known when I got back from the john that you'd slipped that stuff in my drink. It tasted so funny. But who knew you were that kinda guy? When I woke up and realized what had hap-pened, I couldn't get anyone to take me seriously—not 'til I took myself to the hospital and they called the police. By the time the cops finally found you and hauled you off to jail, I'd moved out of state to stay at my sister's. I was on my way back to testify at your trial, but I never made it, did I?" Darlene gave the assembled group a lopsided grin. "How was I to know the car I rented was going to meet up with a semi and make it a permanent relocation? So, of course, this guy gets out on accounta now there's no case, and the way I hear it, it wasn't long before he tried the pill-in-the-drink routine again." She turned back to Ryan James. "You figured this time you better get out of town before anyone started looking for you, so you skipped off to Europe, right? And here you are at it again, even without any pills to help out."

Maggie put her hand to her stomach. She looked as though she might be sick.

"Don't feel bad, honey," Darlene said quickly. "He's played his little game for the last time." She turned to back to Ryan. "I gotta leave now 'cause there's someone else who needs to see you. But before I do, I got news for you, lover. Look around. You think this place is crappy? It's Disney World compared to where you're going." She gave him a last, hard look and headed for the rocky outcropping where she'd first appeared. The clatter of her high heels sounded on the stony ground until she rounded the boulder.

"So that's the way it is?" Disgust tinged Frank's comment. "You'd best sit up, friend." He hauled Ryan to his knees and unfastened Ryan's belt. Then, drawing the belt from the loops, Frank methodically bound Ryan's hands behind him.

"Didn't she say something about someone else coming to see him?" Patrick said uneasily.

He had no sooner said the words than a buzzing sound, like a swarm of angry bees, came from out across the desert. The noise increased until it became the roar of engines. The little group exchanged uneasy glances as five motorcycles, one with a side-car, zoomed across the stony plain toward them.

"Those are the cycles that passed us on the road a few days ago," Frank said as they approached.

"Yeah, they were in the parking lot at Wind Haven, too." Sven peered at them. "'Cept for the Electra-Glide with the side car. That's new." The machines peeled off and came to a noisy stop just outside the pillared formations. Sven walked toward them, eyeing the leader's Harley covetously. "That baby's an Old Boy, am I right? A Heritage Springer?"

"Hell, no, kid, this is the real thing. 1948." The hirsute leader transferred his attention to Ryan James. "We've been having a real hard time tracking you, sonny. Put us to a whole lot of trouble this past while. Not very polite, seeing as we're your welcoming party, so to speak."

"You're the police?" Frank asked him.

The leader flicked a glance at Frank and shifted his weight in the seat. "Not exactly." He examined the leather gauntlet that covered his hairy forearm. "They won't let us have side arms like we wanted, not even uniforms like the real police." Then he regained his bluster. "But they let us be in charge of the folks hereabouts who're headed our way, and if those folks try to hurt anyone, well, we're the ones who take 'em in and haul 'em off."

Though he remained kneeling, Ryan cautiously edged closer to Frank. "You're not hauling me anywhere, jackass," he hissed.

The man on the motorcycle didn't seem to take offense. "Seeing's you'll be with us a while, you'd best keep that mouth shut," he growled. "Now how's about comin' along with us. Or would you like to give us an excuse to play hardball?"

Ryan James struggled to his feet, his dark eyes darting from one cyclist to the other. "I don't have to go with you or anyone else," he said. "We're wanderers." But the low vibrato in his voice was gone; the words came out frightened, high pitched. He felt for his back pocket with his bound hands. "I have a card that says I'm allowed to travel wherever I want."

Frank had been watching the leader with quiet interest. Now, without a word, he unbuckled the belt that bound Ryan James's wrists.

Ryan rubbed his wrists and took a wallet from his pocket. He flipped through the cards, frowned, and searched through them again.

"Guess it's gone," one of the cyclists said. "Guess you're not a wanderer anymore; looks like you're going to have to get used to being just plain folks like us."

"Oh, he's not plain folks," the leader said genially. "This guy's someone special. We're gonna have to get a pass of our own just to take him where he's going. No one's allowed in his sector but the locals."

A look of panic swept Ryan's face. "Look, let's see if we can talk about this," he said. "Maybe we can figure out a way—" He moved with astonishing rapidity. Feinting one way, then spinning about, Ryan darted though the little group and dashed toward the van.

Before any of the wanderers could react, the cyclists's leader leapt off his cycle, and taking a dart-like device from his backpack, sighted his quarry, and threw it. The dart hit Ryan between the shoulders and spread at impact to send out a cluster of slender filaments that wrapped themselves about his body from chest to knee. Ryan cried out and stumbled; but before he could fall to the ground, the leader jerked on the rope, and Ryan was rocked back to his feet, a pupa enclosed in an upright cocoon of silvery wires.

"He's yours, Jake," said the leader. Jake took the rope and proceeded to haul in a stunned, protesting Ryan who had to take hasty baby steps to keep from falling.

The leader turned back to his awe-struck audience and scratched his paunch. "We'll just take him off your hands and be on our way," he said. "That is if Jake can get a move on," he added, watching Jake's struggle to angle a wild-eyed Ryan James into the small sidecar.

"He's in, boss," Jake panted.

"Maybe we'll see some of you later." The leader gave a rough salute, climbed astride his Harley and roared off, followed by his four subordinates and Ryan James, whose trussed body bounced up and down in the sidecar as Jake's cycle zigzagged over the rocky ground.

Maggie expelled a breath that came out as a moan.

Kate put an arm about the girl. "It's over," she said. "He's gone."

"What an idiot I was," Maggie gazed at the disappearing caravan. "What a stupid, naive idiot."

"How could you know?" Frank said. "I'm the one who should have known. I should have paid attention to the signs." He stretched out his arm and looked at the bare wrist beneath his shirtsleeve. He said nothing more, but Kate saw his jaw tighten, saw the bleak look that came into his eyes.

"What should you have known?" Patrick asked.

"I should have figured it out in Presbe. You did, at least partially. At the time, I couldn't understand why Ryan would want to go out to the alley. Of course, he had to make sure he hadn't left any evidence that might point to him. He hadn't counted on his presence drawing those pseudo-cops who proceeded to beat the crap out of him."

"But why would he try something like he did just now when his chances of getting away with it were slim to none?" Patrick persisted.

"My guess is that he'd gotten to the point where he didn't even think about being caught. He wanted to play his games with Maggie, so he just went ahead and did it. Couldn't help himself. Those robocops probably came to Wind Haven because he was already thinking about it then."

"I don't want to stay here." Maggie shuddered. "I want to leave. Now."

Frank looked at her. "How bad is that cut?" he said, his voice gentle. "Still hurt?"

Maggie felt her chin. "No," she said, surprised. "The pain's almost gone." She brushed back the hair from her forehead. "Matter of fact, I've competed with a heck of a lot more pain than this." Her effort to smile was only partially successful. She sniffled and wiped her sleeve across her face. "Sorry I'm being such a dork."

"You're entitled." Frank said gruffly. He turned to the rest. "Come on, folks; let's see if we can get out of here and travel to a more user-friendly place." He offered an arm to Maggie, but she shrugged it off. She trudged toward the van, eyes bleak, her lips set. She moved as though weights were attached to her feet. Frank watched her and gave a slight shake of his head.

"She'll be all right," Kate said quietly. "She just needs to get through this by herself."

Clare darted a glance at Sven, waited a moment, and when he didn't appear to notice her, lowered her blond head and docilely followed Maggie.

"Aren't we an amazing group of misfits?" Patrick said. "Speaking of which, where's Mrs. Harrison? Anyone seen her?"

They looked at each other and scattered. Frank and Patrick clambered onto the large rocks to survey the plain, Sven ran to check the van, and Kate headed for the grassy plain where she and Frank had been earlier. Before she had gotten more than a few steps, however, a shout from the van rang out.

"She's here!"

They scrambled to the van where Clare and Maggie were leaning over a huddled Marjorie Harrison in the back seat. Marjorie raised her head and looked at the group, then ducked back, covering her head with her arm. "I saw those brutes with Ryan. Don't let them take me!" she quavered. "Don't let them take me away!"

"They came for him, not you, Mrs. Harrison." Clare patted Marjorie's arm.

"I don't want to stay here. I want to go— "Marjorie took a hiccuping breath, "I want to go to heaven."

"Praise be and hallelujah. The lady's decided she's not in Peoria."

"Shut up, Patrick." Kate took a seat beside her. "We'd all like that, Marjorie. At least, I think that's where most of us hope we're headed. Look here; let's see what we can find ahead." She took the map out of her pocket and unfolded it.

"Let's not even go there," Patrick muttered. He looked at the keys dangling from the ignition. "Since we seem to have lost our main driver, who's going to take over?"

"I will," Sven said. He did not look at Clare.

"No, I will," Maggie announced. "I'm a good driver, and I want to do something. I really don't care to just sit here and think." And without waiting for further discussion, she slid into the driver's seat and started the motor.

Frank's lips twitched. "Now that's settled, let's see if the map says where we should go." He looked at Kate, who was staring at the paper in her hands. "What's the matter, Kate?"

She looked at him. "Oh, my," she said.

"What?"

"Eastlight. It's back on the map, and it looks as though we're nearly there."

18

"Maggie's a pretty good driver," Frank said mildly.

"What did you expect," Kate asked, "an interval of bumper-car driving until one of you men took over?"

"My, we are testy."

"Sorry, I'm not in the best of moods." Kate pressed a knuckle against her lips. "I can't get Ryan out of my head. He's a horrible person who did some terrible things when he lived on earth, but still— to see him hauled away like that—" She shivered. Then she took away her hand and revealed a half-smile curving her lips. "And I have to confess, there's something else. I've about had it with our resident would-be angel."

"Marjorie's still going on about heaven?"

"Our Marjorie cornered me last time we stopped to stretch our legs. She doesn't want to head for Eastlight, she doesn't want to pass 'Go' or collect two hundred dollars, she doesn't want anything but to march straight through those pearly gates. Right now."

"How does she think she's going to arrange that?"

"Same way she has arranged things all her life. By ordering and complaining. Marjorie thinks if she whines loud enough and long enough, the angels will get so tired of it, they'll take her into heaven just to stop it."

"She may have something there. I would. But doesn't God come into this? I thought he made that kind of decision."

Kate's smile abruptly disappeared. "I've just become used to the idea of having angels around. The concept of God being nearby scares me silly."

"Interesting that you think he's nearer now than he was when we were on earth."

"Don't you think he'd have to be?"

"Maybe. I only know there were times in my life when I felt his presence in a way I haven't here—at least, not yet."

Kate glanced at him and then at her clasped hands. "May I ask when that was? When you felt God near you, I mean? I ask because, even though I've certainly read enough and thought enough about the world's religions to believe there must be some Supreme Being in charge of things, I've always had trouble with *my* idea of God. I've never felt a personal connection." She did not look up. "I guess the closest I've come is when I read what Jesus taught in the New Testament."

"Once I prayed for my son to live, prayed as hard as I could," Frank said into the ensuing silence. "But he died. Then I prayed again, gave Ben into God's hands, and asked God to care for him the way I hadn't been able to. I felt his presence then. I knew Ben was safe.

"And there were other times. One summer morning on a small lake in northern Wisconsin when I sat in a fishing boat and watched the sun come up. I was thinking about how beautiful it was and how grateful I was to be part of it all and suddenly I felt, I dunno, like I was sitting in the middle of a prayer, talking to God."

Kate's jaw tightened. "My life could have done with more praying," she said. She'd meant it to sound sophisticated and slightly ironic, but the words came out wistful, tinged with remorse. "As I said, it's not that I haven't thought about God, about morality and mortality," she said after a moment, "it's just that the Maker of the universe always seemed so 'out there,' so unapproachable that it made prayer rather difficult. I did pray, but I've never felt any, well, any response."

"You said the closest you've felt to having an answer was when you read the New Testament," Frank said. "There must be some reason for that, so how about talking to Jesus? The man who walked on earth and said those words." Frank gave a short laugh. "Sorry, didn't mean to preach. Maybe that's what I ought to be doing. Really praying, not just sitting here thinking about what I did and didn't do during my life."

They sat in silence. Kate thought of the beach at Bucknall, the warmth she'd felt when she'd crouched sobbing on the sandy beach. She'd felt enfolded by complete, unconditional love. Had it been God's presence she'd sensed? And immediately afterward she'd been given the gift of seeing Howard. She'd accepted the comfort and promise of that gift with a hasty "Thank you" and gone on with her journey. Instead of examining the experience, she'd pushed it to the back of her mind to think about later. She, who had always prided herself on her ability to face whatever needed to be faced. Talk about avoidance.

"What is it, Kate?"

"Maybe I *have* felt something like the experience you're talking about," she said, musing. "I'm going to have to think about it." Kate eyed him. "By the way, I've been waiting to ask about what happened back there—you know, when those people you called the 'pseudo-cops' rode off. You looked as though you were in shock."

"After that scene with Ryan, we all were in shock," Frank said evasively.

Kate caught her lower lip. "Sorry. I don't know why I'm asking all these personal questions. It's not my usual style."

Frank sat silent for a moment. "I guess you're asking them because you need to know," he said. "You know that watch of mine that keeps on appearing and disappearing?" His voice was husky with emotion. "It was my dad's. I took it after the doc in ER pronounced him dead." Frank looked out the van's window. "I used to see that watch coming at me just before I caught one of Dad's backhand clouts. Saw it the times he unbuckled his belt to give me a beating—sometimes the beating was because I'd gotten into trouble, sometimes it was just because he could." He paused. "I wasn't as big as he was then." He gave Kate a wry smile. "So when he died—I was sixteen—I slipped it off his wrist and onto my own. Partly to remind me that he couldn't hurt me any more . . . but mostly to remind me not to pick on anyone smaller or weaker."

Kate took a quick breath and touched his arm. "You don't need to wear it, Frank. You definitely don't need that watch anymore."

"Maybe. But I saw it just now."

Kate looked puzzled.

"On the wrist of that head motorcycle honcho." Frank gave Kate a quick glance and looked away. "Yup, that was Dad. Best sergeant the Chatham Branch ever had—and the worst husband and father on the block."

"Did he recognize you?"

"Hard to tell. I don't think so. Look, let's drop it."

"I'm so sorry," Kate whispered.

Frank dredged up a brief smile. "'S okay." He turned to look at the rear of the van where Sven and Clare were sitting, facing away from each other, each looking out the nearest window. "I thought things were looking up, but they haven't patched it up yet, have they?"

"No," Kate said. "I wonder if Sven realizes he has to take some of the responsibility for what happened, that he can't just shove it all off on that girl." She caught herself. "Getting to be a regular expert on judging others, aren't I?"

"Don't knock it. I find I prefer judging other people to judging myself," Frank said. Then he whistled. "Hey, looky there."

Kate looked out his window. "We're out of the Badlands and into a valley, if that's what you mean. Looks like orchards over there in the distance."

"Uh huh, but look up."

"Hey, look what's up there!" Maggie said at the same moment.

The breath caught in Kate's throat. "Do you think it's Eastlight?"

Maggie slowed the van. Everyone craned to see the mountain that rose high above them. A city gleamed atop the mountain's peaks, its slender towers glistening pink and orange and mauve in the sunlight.

"The road divides up ahead," Maggie said. "Should we take the fork that goes up the mountain or the one that continues along the valley?"

"The one up the mountain. It goes to heaven," said Marjorie Harrison.

The rest stared at her.

"Care to tell us why you're so sure?" Patrick asked her.

"I just know it. And I want to go there."

"Looks like you'll have to talk your way past a sentry." Frank indicated the man standing in front of a small guardhouse by the side of the road that led to the foothills. The guard wore a khaki uniform like Rafael, the angel who had spoken to Clare. This man was a lot larger than Patrick, larger even than Sven, though not quite Frank's size. The guard waited until Maggie brought the van to a stop, then opened the door, saluted politely, and stepped inside.

"You folks lost?" Then he looked into their faces and said, "Oh, you're wanderers. Any particular reason you're sightseeing here-abouts?"

"Is the city up there Eastlight?" Frank asked.

The guard suppressed a grin. "Not hardly. If you turn around and take the valley road to the left, you'll find a pass in the third mountain on the second ridge over on the other side of the valley. It leads to Eastlight."

"But the city up there," Marjorie said, "it's heaven, isn't it?"

The guard looked at her. "Yes, it's a heaven."

"I want to go there," Marjorie announced. Then she added quickly, "I'm sure it will be all right. If you'll just tell them Marjorie Harrison wants—" she stopped, uncharacteristically flustered, "if you'll tell them Marjorie Harrison would very much appreciate being able to come visit, I'm sure they'll say yes." She gave him her most winning smile.

The guard took a phone from his belt and punched in a number. The group in the van couldn't hear his murmured conversation; but when he snapped the phone shut and rehooked it to his belt, he inclined his head toward Marjorie and motioned her forward. "If you'll come ahead ma'am, a car is being sent."

Marjorie was out of her seat in an instant. She charged from the van onto the road, forcing the guard to take a quick step backward to avoid a collision.

Frank cleared his throat. "What about the rest of us? Can we come, too?"

The sentry regarded him. "I think it's best you didn't."

"You're not even going to call and ask about it?"

The guard's scrutiny of Frank intensified. "Is that what you want?" He examined the faces of the others. "And the rest of you?"

Kate stirred uneasily. "Frank, I don't know—"

"No!" Patrick wiped his hands on his pant legs and clasped them together. "I'm going to stay here."

Frank frowned. "I guess we won't go," he said slowly. "I guess we'll wait until we're invited."

"Good idea," the guard said. He jumped off the van. "Looks like your car's here, Mrs. Harrison."

The group watched the sentry hand Marjorie Harrison into a long black sedan, watched the car disappear into the trees that hid the road winding up the green mountain.

"Doesn't anybody have a Ford or Chevy here?" asked Patrick. Although his tone was easy, his hands were still clenched. A bead of sweat trickled from his hairline down his cheek.

"I'd like to know why she gets to go up there and not us," said Maggie. She was about to expound on this, but at that moment the sentry poked his head into the van again.

"You're welcome to come out and stretch your legs," he said. "You might like some water or juice or a piece of fruit before you head out."

"You're sure it's okay?" Frank asked cautiously.

"Sure. I'm about to have a snack; join me if you'd like." The guard strolled into the guardhouse, leaving the door open behind him.

"It's all right," Clare said quietly. "He's just like Raphael. If he says it's okay, it is." She looked down, refusing to meet the others's startled looks.

The group trooped inside what seemed more like a comfortably furnished hunting lodge than a guard house and looked about. A chintz-covered couch sat against one wall, a matching overstuffed chair with a small table and reading lamp perpendicular to it; in the middle of the room stood a sturdy pine table and six blond wooden chairs.

"Help yourselves." The sentry set a tray of glasses and a crystal pitcher of clear water on the table next to a basket filled with apples, pears, bananas, and peaches.

"I'd give a lot to know what's happening with Marjorie," Frank said, taking a pear and slicing it with his pocket knife.

"You'd like to see how your friend's visit to our heaven is going?" the sentry asked.

Frank looked up, surprised. "Sure would. I think we all would."

The guard nodded. He clicked a button and the opposite wall of the guardhouse became a screen on which was a picture of a sunlit scene. Marjorie Harrison stepped from the sedan. Over her shoulder the viewers could see gardens in the background formed in shapes of circles and squares and rectangles. Each garden was bordered by boxwood and planted with flowers that were shades of a particular color, one all white, one lavender shading to blues, others red shading to rose and pink, another yellows. The gardens spread out into the distance as far as they could see. The images on the screen were sharp and clear, the colors vibrant, and Marjorie's newly firmed, unwrinkled face, ecstatic. She walked briskly to the broad stone stairs that led to what looked like a French chateau.

"This is a villa on the outskirts of our city," the guard said as a woman in country tweeds came out of the mansion and walked down the steps toward Marjorie. "When Mrs. Harrison saw it, she told the driver she wanted to stop."

"Why?" Maggie asked.

"She said it looked like a chateau on the Loire she'd always wanted to visit. Claimed she was sure the owners would be her kind of people."

Maggie snorted.

The tweed-clad woman came down the stairs to greet Marjorie, a pleasant, enquiring smile on her lovely face. The smile wavered and vanished, however, as she looked into her guest's face. "Marjorie? Marjorie Harrison?" she said.

"Why, yes." A pleased smile wreathed Marjorie's face. "Have we met?"

"Yes, we have." The woman was silent a moment. "My name was Linda Lopotski."

Marjorie's eyes widened. "You can't be! Linda was a dumpy little—" she caught herself. "You really don't look anything like Linda. You can't be she."

"I suppose you could say I'm someone quite different now," the woman agreed. "But once I was the Linda who lived next door to you."

"Oh." Marjorie's confident smile became rigid. Then she lifted her chin defiantly. "You didn't need to take the children and run away, you know. It simply made what was admittedly a bad situation worse—because, of course, then it all came out. When Edwin discovered Ted and I were ... ah ... involved, he might have been content to let it go if the whole thing hadn't become common gossip. As it was, the silly man felt he had to ask for a divorce."

The woman on the stairs above her searched Marjorie's face. "Is that all it meant to you? Had you no grief for the devastation you caused? The two marriages you destroyed?"

"But that's my point! They didn't have to 'be destroyed,' as you so dramatically put it." Marjorie put an arm across her chest as though she felt a sudden pain. Then she changed the motion, flattening her hand to smooth the material of her well-cut jacket. "Really, Linda, it was all so long ago." She gave an abrupt little laugh. "I can tell you I was quite sorry about the whole thing—it was such a mess."

"You truly felt sorrow?" the woman asked, interested.

"For the mess, yes, not for having what was essentially a harmless little affair," Marjorie said, her tone straightforward. "If only you hadn't made such a fuss, it would have been over and done with in a civilized manner. Actually, I didn't mind giving Edwin a divorce; we weren't all that well suited anyway. But you should have stayed. You could have had Ted back, you know. It wasn't as though I wanted him. I valued my independence far too much to keep him around longer than necessary." Marjorie colored slightly, her mouth snapped shut. "I . . . I can't imagine why I'm going on like this," she stuttered. "The whole thing is long since past, and like you, I'm really a totally different person." She hesitated. "I . . . don't suppose you're going to let me in?" Coming from anyone else it would have been a plea.

"It's not for me to let you in or keep you out," Linda said mildly. "Anyone who feels comfortable here is welcome." She stepped aside, and Marjorie quickly mounted the stairs. Linda's nostrils twitched as she passed, as if she'd suddenly caught a whiff of something sour. "Perhaps you'd better not—" she said.

Marjorie did not slow her charge. The group in the guardhouse watched Marjorie finally hesitate as she reached the top step, then march up to the great carved door. They saw the flash of light as she reached to touch the golden knob, heard Marjorie's shriek, saw the round "O" of her mouth, saw her jerk her hand away and hold it to her chest, smelled the odor of burned flesh. The woman who had been Linda ran up the stairs to Marjorie. Reaching out, she lightly touched the injured hand, and immediately a look of astonished relief replaced the contorted pain on Marjorie's face. She blinked, gave her head a slight, puzzled shake, and seemed about to try to open the door again.

"Oh, no, Marjorie, don't!" Kate said, wincing.

But Linda had quietly slipped between Marjorie and the door. She held up her hand with a gesture that was almost supplicating.

Marjorie, however, persisted in her advance. The group in the guard house watched Marjorie push past the woman and, without touching the knob, elbow open the door. A brilliant light shone from the building's interior. As it flowed over and about both women, the group below saw Linda's face reflect the translucent glow. The skin on Marjorie's face, however, sagged, her nose became hawk-like; she clutched her throat, gasping. She clawed the air.

Distress washed over Linda's beautiful features as Marjorie coughed and struggled to breathe, but she made no move to stop the older woman as Marjorie stumbled down the stairs to the driveway. Marjorie gave a gasping sob and tottered down the drive; it seemed that she breathed more easily with each step.

Marjorie stopped to straighten her suit with a shaky hand. "You . . . you nonentity," she spat at the woman above her. "You always were an insignificant little mouse, a poor, squeaking thing who couldn't satisfy her husband and did nothing but mewl when someone else did. Oh!" Marjorie jumped like a scalded cat. She brushed angrily at the skirt of her suit. A wisp of smoke rose from the material and the hem curled, singed. Marjorie beat at the material and then frantically unbuttoned the skirt and ripped the smoldering fabric from her body. Still backing away, now clad only in a jacket and torn half-slip, she cast a look of pure hatred at the woman on the stairs. But she uttered no more maledictions, not even when the woman who had been Linda was joined by a tall, red-headed man who came through the open door and clasped his arm about her. Pausing only long enough to scuff off her high-heeled shoes, Marjorie turned and ran down the mountain road into the trees.

There was silence in the guardhouse. The group stared at the screen. The image of the man and woman on the steps flickered and dimmed. The screen went blank.

"Will she find her way back down here?" Maggie asked, the words almost inaudible.

"I don't think so," said the guard.

"We have to go find her," Clare whispered.

"I wouldn't try it," the guard said firmly. "I doubt that she'd like you to do that—coming back to you people is the last thing she wants. If I were you, I'd get on with your journey to Eastlight."

"We can't just leave her—" Kate swallowed.

"She has left you. Evidently your paths lie in different directions."

"Won't we see her again?" Clare asked.

"No." The guard hesitated and added, "That is, unless one of you loves the same things she does, unless you choose to live where she does."

"Is it—will it be a terrible place?" asked Clare.

"Not to Mrs. Harrison." The sentry smiled at her. "It's time you people continued your journey. Why don't you let me give you a thermos of water and some fruit to take along." He handed Frank a neatly wrapped package and nodded a cheery goodbye.

The group silently trooped back to the van. Maggie shoved the keys at Frank and crept to one of the middle seats. She clasped her arms about her chest as though to hold herself together.

"Any more drop offs, and we won't need a van; we'll be able to make do with a Volkswagen," said Patrick, taking the seat beside her.

Maggie inched closer to the window.

"Just a little attempt at humor there," he said, getting up. "Apparently, it works about as well as Marjorie's gate-crashing."

"No, don't—" Maggie raised an outstretched hand to him. "I didn't mean . . . it's just . . . it's just that I'm so scared."

"Join the crowd." He came back and sat down.

She didn't speak as Frank put the van in gear and carefully navigated the road back to the valley. A tear trickled down her cheek. She brushed it away. "It's no fair," she said at last. "Maybe I haven't been a real good person. Maybe I should have gone to church and stuff like that, but I never did anything really bad." She looked at Patrick, her eyes wide. "I don't want to end up like Mrs. Harrison, and I sure don't want to be dragged off like, like—" She stopped, unable or unwilling to say Ryan's name. "It's funny when you think about it, y'know? I shouldn't be scared; I should be ticked off. I'm the one who has been royally screwed all my life. Every single person I've ever trusted has let me down."

Patrick regarded her a moment. "Grandma Inez?" he said.

Maggie's aggrieved look softened. "No, not her."

"Hold that thought," Patrick said quietly.

"What d'you mean?"

"Think about Grandma Inez and your summers at Wind Haven, and you won't be as frightened about what will happen."

Maggie was silent. Then she said, "It works. How'd you know?"

"It's always worked for me. I think about music. I hear Reger's *Benedictus* or maybe Liszt's *Prelude* and *Fugue*. When we were in the middle of that thunderstorm back at the diner, I closed my eyes and heard '*Wie lieblich sind deine Wohnungen*.'"

"'Scuse me?"

"'How lovely is Thy dwelling place'—from Brahms's *German Requiem*." Patrick cleared his throat. "I hope…that is, I had hoped—" he did not finish but said instead, "Keep this up and we'll both be in tears."

Maggie managed a wan smile. "What did you mean when you said it's always worked for you? Like when?"

"When I was a kid, the guys in the neighborhood didn't really know what to do with someone like me. So they tortured me." Patrick looked at the hands clenched tight on his knees. "Oh, not really tortured, but it was bad enough that a nine-year-old thought it was torture. The music didn't work during those sessions. Not when they tossed a snake into the tool shed and then me in with it, not when my cousins put me in the root cellar and I squatted in the dark and felt spiders crawling over me. But after they let me out and I ran to hide in the attic, that's when I'd play the music in my head. And after a while I'd stop shaking."

"Oh, Patrick!" Maggie said. She took his hand in hers. He hesitated, then clasped hers and held it tight.

⟨

They were traveling toward what looked like the opening of an arroyo. While not as verdant as the rest of the valley, it was not arid. Groves of trees grew beside a bubbling stream that wound along the bottom and disappeared into a cave at the far end of the canyon. Frank slowed the van at the beginning of a dirt track that led into the canyon.

"That cave is huge," Maggie said, craning to see. She caught her breath, suddenly alert. "Hey, was that someone going into it?"

"I saw a flash of something, but it's too far away to see what it was," said Frank.

"Don't go down that road, Frank!" Patrick said, his voice shrill.

"I don't intend to." Frank increased his pressure on the gas pedal and steered the van past the entrance. "We're not into investigating caves; we're headed for Eastlight."

"What was it?" Maggie whispered to Patrick.

He shrugged and did not answer.

"You saw who was going into the cave, didn't you?" she persisted.

For a moment, it seemed as though Patrick wouldn't speak, but then he gave her a strange look. "I think so. It looked like . . . Marjorie."

Maggie's eyes widened. "How could that have been Mrs. Harrison? Whoever we saw was high tailing it across the rocks like a gazelle."

Patrick shrugged again. "She wasn't wearing shoes, remember? And now she's got on some kind of dress, but I'm sure it was Marjorie." He obviously didn't want to say more, and after a look at his face, Maggie didn't press him.

No one attempted further conversation as they drove through the valley, past woods and orchards, until at last they came to the foothills. Maggie and Patrick saw the sign at the same time, a sign with the word "Eastlight" carved on it. "Hey look!" said Maggie, "it's pointing toward the mountains."

Kate was the first to notice a woman standing not far from the sign. "Stop, Frank!" she called out. "Stop!"

Frank stepped on the brakes and pulled back on the wheel as if bringing in a 747. Kate already had the door of the van open before the tires stopped spinning on gravel.

"Bella!" She ran to the woman, her hands out. "You did it! You left him!"

19

Bella had shed some of her gypsy skirts. The remaining ones were even more ragged and torn than when they had last seen her, but the little that was left of the gaily striped over-skirt was damp and clean. So was Bella.

Bella's eyes, dark-ringed and hollow with fatigue, followed Kate's glance to her clothes. "I'm still wet. Washed my stuff in the stream over there. First I was using sticks to try to bash the dirt out, but I found the sticks had a sap that made a kind of soapy goop that made as good suds as anything I ever got at the store." She raised her hand and sniffed the skin of her forearm. "Even smells good."

Kate ignored Bella's scientific discoveries. "Did Garcia—was he very angry with you for letting me go?"

"Oh, that. Yeah, he was angry." Bella gingerly pressed a hand to her ribs.

Kate bit her lip. "How did you get away?"

Bella looked at the ground. "I prayed, like you said to. Finally, I prayed."

Kate, suddenly aware of the faces staring at them from the van's windows, led Bella a few steps farther from the open door. "What happened?" she said quietly.

"In the end, I was just out of there. Like, one minute I was there, the next, I wasn't. Didn't know it would be so easy." Bella's mouth tightened. "Didn't know it would hurt so much either."

"You still love him?" Kate said, her tone incredulous.

"I don't know. I only know that it hurts not to be with him."

Frank stepped out of the van. "Good to see you, Bella. Coming with us?"

"You think they'll let me?" Bella said hesitantly. "I don't have a wanderer's card."

"Won't know until we give it a try, will we?" Frank said. "Come on, climb aboard and let's see what happens."

Bella gave him a dubious look, but gathered her damp skirts and climbed into the van. "Thanks, folks, I appreciate the ride." She looked around. "Where's the guy with the pony tail?"

Kate gave her a gentle push. "Sit down; I'll fill you in."

"I felt something was wrong with that one," Bella said after listening to Kate's recital. "And as for the Harrison woman, I can tell you where she is."

They all stared at her. Even Frank slowed the van to look back at Bella.

"Y'know the cave in the canyon back there? You must have passed it—it's back there in the direction you just came from. Well, that's where we've been camping. Ollie noticed it and decided what's left of our tribe should go in and explore. So we went down one passage after another and finally came to an opening where there's a kind of daylight, not sunshine exactly, but enough to see by, like on a real overcast day." Bella's eyes darkened at the memory. "Ollie seemed to be able to see a lot better than the rest of us, and he says how great it is and what a good hiding place it will be, but all I can see is this marshy swamp with some huts in the middle. And I don't want to stay. I get so nervous that I convince Ollie we should come back and camp in the central cave. Well, we do, and that's where your Mrs. Harrison comes in." She paused and looked at the others. "Hope none of you guys is a special friend of hers, 'cause that broad is just not one of my favorite people."

"I don't think anyone here is a member of her fan club," Frank Chambers said. "Go on."

"Well, we're out in the valley, the women are tryin' to scrape up some food for dinner, and all of a sudden one of the men comes back dragging this Harrison woman. Says he found her wandering around the cave. And when she sees us and recognizes Ollie, she starts acting real coy and says she was just lookin' for him to ask him about her stocks and bonds. 'I really didn't care to stay with those other people; I'd rather be with you,' she says. I'm telling you, the woman went on like a cat in heat."

"Marjorie?" Kate said, astonished.

"Oh, yeah, Marjorie. She's not such an old woman any more, y'know, not by a long shot. Anyway, after supper, Ollie gets out his briefcase—and I haven't seen his briefcase since we came here—and tells her to come with him farther in the cave so they can go over her portfolio. He takes a torch and goes off, and I stand there and watch them and realize I've been lettin' him hurt me and drag me down with him ever since we've been here. And I wonder why I let him do it. I wonder what's gonna happen if I keep on bein' with him, if he's going to make me go back to that dark place beyond the cave. That's when I prayed." Bella smoothed her drying skirts, pressing out the wrinkles with nervous fingers. "Hard as I could. Eyes squeezed tight shut like a kid."

"And?"

"When I opened my eyes, I was on the other side of the clearing. I started running and ran as long as I could and then walked until it started to get dark. Found some branches and made a bed on the ground, and come morning I walked some more, 'til I saw the sign to Eastlight. I remembered you said that's where you were going, so I decided to wash up and hang around. Hoped you'd come this way, that I hadn't already missed you."

"I'm glad we didn't."

Bella looked at her. "You really are, aren't you?"

"I couldn't get that picture of you out of my mind," Kate said. "Seeing you standing there in the road as the van left. Oh, Bella, I felt awful."

Bella's mouth was grim. "Let me tell you, watching you guys drive off wasn't exactly the highlight of my day either."

They had crossed the mountain pass to the other side. Frank gripped the wheel. "Look!" he said. He drove off the road onto a widened space at the edge of a steep escarpment, and the van's passengers scrambled out to look at the city spread on the plain below. They could clearly make out skyscrapers, towers, and busy thoroughfares passing though broad, green parklands. Suburbs of houses and low buildings and tree-lined streets ringed the city like a necklace.

"Gee, Dorothy, is this Emerald City?" Patrick murmured to Maggie.

Maggie swallowed. "You think it's one of those places that looks like heaven but really isn't?"

"That's something we won't know until we get down there," he said cryptically.

Frank tossed the van keys from one hand to the other. "I guess we should go find out."

Bella stood very still and looked down on the scene. She did not ask for an explanation of Maggie's statement or comment on Frank's.

((

Signs led them from the outskirts to the city's hub and a large, busy parking lot in front of a two-story Visitors' Center. The center's great hall, filled with travelers, buzzed with conversation. Exhibits and information counters and kiosks containing pamphlets that described Eastlight's attractions stretched around three of the walls. The fourth wall was a series of glass doors that stood open to the sunlight. People crowded about the information counters asking questions of the attendants behind them.

Frank Chambers approached the nearest counter and spoke to the plump, red-haired young woman behind it. When questioned, she eyed him intently and pointed to the other end of the great hall. "You'll be wanting the information for wanderers, sir," she said.

The little group followed Frank like obedient ducklings. First Maggie and Clare, then Sven and Patrick, and finally Kate trailed by Bella, who nervously tucked her blouse into her skirt.

"You're fine," Kate whispered to her. "Look at your skirts."

Bella looked down and took a startled breath. "They're mended!" She brushed the brightly colored material with a tentative hand. "No, not mended," she said. "They're ... they're like new."

They had reached the counter whose sign announced "Wanderers' Information," and Frank took his place in line. The man behind the counter finished answering a young couple's questions, produced several pamphlets for the next two people in line, and it was Frank's turn.

"Good morning, my name is Donald," the agent said as he took Frank's wanderer's card. He drew a ledger from beneath the desk, checked it. "You dropped off some of your friends on the way?"

For an uneasy moment, Frank did not answer.

"It happens," the young man said, quickly. "Not many bands of wanderers get as far as Eastlight without losing a few members. Now, let's see what we can do for you." He pulled out another drawer in the counter.

While he was rummaging about, a woman wearing a business suit approached the group and, ignoring the rest, spoke directly to Bella. "May I help you?" she said.

Bella moved closer to Kate. "No, thank you."

"But, my dear, this information counter is for wanderers."

Bella inched away until she was behind Kate and opposite the woman.

"She's with us," Kate said firmly.

For the first time the woman looked at Kate. "No, she's not." It was a reproof, but gently said.

Kate felt a flush of embarrassment that quickly turned to irritation. Why was this woman addressing her as though Kate were some unruly student? Professor Kate Douglas gave reprimands; she didn't receive them.

But the woman had already returned her attention to Bella. "I know you're grateful to these people, but you need help, help that you can only receive from us," she said. "Won't you come with me?"

Frank had turned away from the man at the counter and joined them. He cleared his throat, "I'm not sure we ought—"

Kate took a step forward. "She's not leaving us unless she wants to."

"Of course not." The woman did not shift her gaze from Bella. "Would you like to come with me, Bella?" she said again, the kindness in her voice dispelling any sense of threat.

Bella looked into the woman's eyes a long moment. Then she sighed like a tired child. "Yes," she said. "Yes, I would."

"Come along then." The woman put an arm about Bella's shoulders and led her away though the crowds of visitors to one of the great glass doors at the front of the building where they went out onto the sunny terrace. Bella did not look back.

"Bummer, Kate. You ride to the rescue, and someone comes along with a whiter steed. Or tosses a bigger life preserver. Or whatever."

"Thank you, Patrick, but I don't care if Bella gets rescued by the French Foreign Legion. I just want to be sure she's all right."

"She will be." The man named Donald gave them an amused glance. "You don't have to worry," he said to Kate. "Your friend will be with people who can help her recover."

"How do you know Bella needs to recover from anything?"

"It's pretty obvious your friend is one of the injured. And then, the woman who came to help her is clearly an assistant." He saw Kate's puzzled look. "An assistant is—let's see, I guess the best description for you would be a kind of psychiatric nurse. Her job is to help anyone who has experienced psychic damage." Donald smiled reassuringly. "As I said, you needn't worry; they're good at what they do. Now maybe we'd better get along with your plans. We offer some things I think you'll find unique." He handed Frank a handful of pamphlets, "Here are some events that might interest your group," then held out a sheet of paper to Maggie, "and there's something at the Sports Dome tomorrow that you might enjoy."

"Gymnastics?" Maggie said. Her obvious pleasure lessened as she read the notice. "Oh, a tennis match," she said. Then she gave a little yelp. "Hey, Val's playing!"

"Val?" Patrick asked.

"Val Shellenberg. The girl who welcomed me at the Guesthaus." Maggie turned to Frank. "Can we go?"

"I don't see why not." Frank turned back to the young man behind the counter. "I not sure if there are other questions we should be asking. Like, as wanderers, is there anything we should know? Anything besides what's in this material you've given us?"

"You mean is Eastlight an imaginary heaven, and do you need to be careful not to sign up for anything without reading the fine print?" Donald laughed. "No and no. You don't even need your wanderers's cards here." He hesitated. "But I'd hang onto them, just in case one of you decides to do more trekking around the countryside." He motioned to a group of sunburnt men and women standing behind Frank. "If you could step to up the counter, I think these people are taken care of," he said to them. "My name is Donald. May I help you?"

⟨

Kate took a chair next to Frank at a small table on the patio outside the hotel's restaurant. "Maggie tells me Sven and Clare were given separate rooms, and there was the usual brouhaha, which rather surprised me because Sven and Clare haven't been . . . together lately."

Frank speared a piece of pineapple from the tray of fruit in the middle of the table. "Just what problems have those kids been having? You seem to know more about it than the rest of us."

Kate picked up a spoon, twiddled with it, then looked at him with sudden decision. "You know the baby Clare's been so desperate about? They left her behind at the rooming house, at their last stop the night of the accident—before they came here."

"What? You can't mean they just left her?" Frank shook his head and sighed. "Don't know why it should surprise me. I've seen enough kids treat their babies that way, like some toy they couldn't be bothered to cart along with them."

Kate closed her eyes. *Don't judge the kids*, she told herself. *Don't enjoy hearing Frank judge them.* "Sven thought Clare had arranged things with the woman who ran the place, that she'd agreed to take care of the baby until Clare's mother came." Kate's voice grew husky. "But the woman refused, and Clare felt she had no choice but to leave her baby in the room anyway. She says she intended to call at their first stop to alert the woman to get the baby; but, of course, it didn't happen—a slick section of pavement on the Autobahn took care of that."

Frank gave a low grunt.

"Right." Kate brushed at her cheeks, found them wet.

"How did Sven find out about it? And what happened to the baby? Does Clare know?"

Kate half-smiled at this quick switch to interrogation mode. "Sven knows because Clare told him. I'm not sure how much Clare knows about what happened to Essie, but she was shown something by the angel who stopped our van outside that little village. Whatever she saw made her even more sick with grief and remorse."

"That was obvious."

"But she's stopped crying. I think Clare has done some growing up."

"Poor kid," Frank said. "Poor kids. All three of them."

"So . . . do you think the people here at the hotel know all about this?"

"Maybe, maybe not, but they wouldn't put unmarried couples together anyway. Not here."

Kate looked at him, startled. "Who told you that?"

"I came by when Sven was about to take the place apart and heard the manager give him a short course on the way they do things in Eastlight. You're married, or you have separate rooms."

"So Sven agreed to bunk by himself?"

"In case you hadn't noticed, our Sven doesn't take no for an answer. I suspect it's a matter of what I'll laughingly call 'principle' with him. From the way he and Clare were looking— or rather *not* looking at each other—I don't think they would use the room for anything other than staring at the walls."

"So what happened?"

The manager finally said she'd contact the authorities and have someone come talk to him, that it would possible to be together if that's what they really wanted." Frank frowned. "The way she said it lit up warning signals in my feeble brain."

"The way it did when the sentry asked us if we were really sure we wanted to visit the heaven he was guarding?"

"Yup."

"Oh, my." Kate bit her lip. "What do you think we should do about it?"

"I'm not sure we should do anything. Eastlight isn't like the other places we've seen; it may not be heaven, but everything seems pretty much under control here. After all, if Sven talks to the guy he has demanded to see and, as I suspect, finds out he has to leave Eastlight to get his way about the room, it's his decision."

"And what Sven wants will happen to Clare too, no matter whether they're speaking or not." Kate got up. "You must think I'm an incorrigible busybody, but I can't sit here and let Sven get her into any more trouble than she's already in. I haven't told you the whole story about that little interview I had with her, but I, well, I feel somewhat responsible for her." She got up, not meeting his eyes. "Go ahead—tell me I shouldn't interfere."

"I wouldn't presume to tell you anything, Kate. Just be careful."

((

Kate asked for and received Sven's room number. "But he's not there," the desk clerk said. "He's in the West Conference Room with the non-resident manager." Both the clerk's tone and her eyebrows went up as she announced the presence of this personage.

"Where's the conference room?" Kate asked briskly. "I'd like to see the non-resident manager, too."

Kate could hear shouts and tearful pleading before she was half-way down the hall.

"She's not going anywhere, and I'm not either."

"Please, Sven, you're making it worse," Clare's thin counterpart rang against Sven's snarl.

Kate paused outside the heavy oak door and took a breath. She needn't have steeled herself, however, for aside from an incurious glance from the man in a blue suit sitting at the head of the gleaming conference table, no one in the room paid the slightest attention to her.

"At this time, it isn't appropriate for you to be together," the man was saying to Sven. "You can, if you choose, surrender your wanderer's card and leave Eastlight, but I assure you the better choice would be to do as I've suggested, enter the program I told you about and let Clare go where she has been enrolled."

Sven looked at the girl beside him. He stood silent a long moment, then reached out his hand to her. Kate's stomach tightened at the explosion of joy that lit Clare's face as Sven took her hand in his.

"If she's going anywhere, I go too."

"I don't think so," the man at the head of the table said mildly. "You're not invited to the place she'll be entering."

Sven's jaw jutted out. "We're not gonna be separated."

"It's not up to you. Actually, not much of anything is up to you. Since you've decided not to follow Eastlight's policies, Clare and you must go where there are rules rather than suggestions." He paused and looked at Clare, who had half-raised her free hand, like a second-grader asking permission to speak. "Yes?"

"Am I...going to hell?" she asked quietly. "Because of what I did to Essie?"

"No, child, you are not. But there are and will continue to be consequences of that act—for you and for Essie." Clare pulled her hand from Sven's and stood straight and silent, her head bowed. Sven made an attempt to recapture her hand, but then thought better of it and placed his arm about her shoulders. The non-resident manager came around the table and touched a handkerchief to the tears that trickled down Clare's cheeks, then tucked the linen into her hand. "There are things you both must learn," he said as he went back to his position at the head of the table. "Of course, if you really don't want to learn what we have to teach, you are free to go elsewhere, Sven." His eyes softened as he looked at the girl's drooping head. "Clare, however, will not go with you."

At these last words, Sven started as though he'd received an electric shock. A look of pure anger replaced his look of despair. He took the distance between himself and the man at the head of the table in two long strides and looked down on the slim man in the blue suit, his arms half bent, his hands fisted. "You're not sending her anywhere," Sven growled. "She stays with me."

The man surveyed Sven quietly. "No, she does not."

Sven lunged. The non-resident manager hesitated longer than Kate thought possible, then at the last possible moment turned aside and put out a hand to break the force of Sven's fall. Clare uttered a shrill cry, but Sven was up before Clare reached him. He grunted with pain, rubbed his stomach where he'd hit a chair, and charged again. This time his hands almost caught the non-resident manager's shoulders, but the man gave a quick twist and Sven's grip slid off as though the man's body had an inviolable sphere shielding it. Sven staggered and slammed against the wall. He stood, shaking his head groggily, as if considering the advisability of another attack.

"Enough." The slim man held up a hand and stopped Sven short.

Clare flew to Sven and threw her arms about him. "Please, don't hurt him," she wept. "Please, can't you just . . . just leave us alone?" She smoothed Sven's bleeding face. "Can't we just be together?"

The non-resident manager looked at them a long moment. "You really do love each other, don't you?"

Clare looked up, her eyes alight with hope. "You'll let us stay together?"

"It's not up to me, my dear. As I said, arrangements have been made for you. You really need to learn the things you'll be taught where you're going, you know. You prayed about it Clare, remember?"

"You mean just before we got to Eastlight? When I prayed there was some way I could make up for—" Clare choked, unable to finish.

"Sven has things to learn, too," the man continued. "There are several programs that will to teach him what he needs to know." Then he smiled. "And since you love each other as you do, there's a good chance you'll end up together. Matter of fact, I wouldn't want to bet against it. Now, young man, will you kiss your betrothed goodbye and come with me? Or are you going to try for three out of three falls?"

Sven blinked and looked from Clare to the man at the head of the table. Clare reached up and wiped a trickle of blood from the corner of his mouth with her shirtsleeve. She kissed him. "Go with him," she whispered. "He figures we'll be together, and he knows about these things."

"How does he know?" Sven growled, unconvinced.

"He's an angel."

Sven put his arms around Clare and held her to him. He looked over her head at the non-resident manager and swallowed. His shoulders slumped. "Okay," he said, his voice a rasping whisper. He leaned down to kiss Clare's forehead, her mouth, then released her. "Okay." The non-resident manager reached out to touch Sven's shoulder. He looked at Kate, for the first time since she'd entered the room acknowledging her presence. "Take Clare to the front desk," he said. "Sylvia is waiting for her." He turned both Sven and himself about so their backs were to the two women, and they were gone. In their place was only a dim, shimmering light that quickly faded.

Kate reached out to Clare, not trusting herself to speak.

Clare took Kate's hand. "We *will* be together. I know it," she said, her eyes pleading.

"An angel told you he thinks there's a good chance of it; you can't ask for better odds than that."

But Clare's hopeful look became anxious. "Kate, do you think this place I'm supposed to go to—do you think they'll be able to tell me how to help Essie?"

Kate began to speak, but stopped before uttering the easy words of comfort she'd intended to say. "I don't know, Clare," she said. "I just don't know."

⟨

The brown-haired woman who stood chatting with the desk clerk turned out to be Sylvia. She looked no more than twenty-five; but when she came forward to greet them, Kate saw that, like Grandma Inez, the wisdom and compassion in her dark eyes did not belong to anyone in her mid-twenties.

"We're looking forward to having you with us, Clare," she said to the girl. "My car is outside at the curb. Why don't you get in it, and I'll have your things brought out."

Clare gave Kate an anguished look but trudged out obediently.

"She'll be all right," Sylvia said to Kate.

"The non-resident manager said . . . he practically promised Clare and Sven, the boy she's with, that they would be together."

"Did he?" The woman smiled. "Boris is such a softie. He probably shouldn't have said that, but I can see why he did." She signed a form, handed it to the desk clerk and turned back to Kate. "There's a lot Sven and Clare must learn separately before they can begin learning together. Both those children have to face up to what they failed to do for Essie, but by no means are all their lessons sad ones. It will be an exciting time during which they'll be given the tools to live a joyful, useful life. And, yes, they probably will be together as husband and wife." She signaled to the bellman who had appeared with Clare's suitcase. "Once they've learned more about themselves and the life of heaven, it will be their choice." She held out a hand to Kate. "Have a pleasant stay in Eastlight."

(

Maggie joined in the applause of the crowd below and then slouched back in the hard stadium seat. "So Sven and Clare are gone too."

"That leaves the four of us." Patrick didn't sound happy about it.

"Look at it this way," Frank's head followed the back-and-forth flight of the tennis ball, "according to Kate, at least Sven and Clare are going to make it. For a while there, the odds of members of our group getting to go somewhere pleasant sure didn't seem too good." He cheered as Val sprinted to the net to retrieve a drop shot. "Y'know, I've never been particularly into tennis, but this doesn't look exactly like the game I remember. It's sort of like Val and her opponent are seeing how many times they can rally, like they're using as many different shots as they can each time they hit it."

"I think you're right," said Kate. "They keep hitting one impossible shot after another, but as far as I can tell neither is really trying to put it away."

"Maybe winning isn't what this is all about," Frank said.

But apparently there had been a game or some games, because the two players took seats beneath the umpire, toweled their sweating faces and helped themselves to drinks. The crowd relaxed during this intermission, and there was a murmur of conversation, but none of the spectators left the stadium.

"Guess it's not ended," said Patrick. "There's a vendor; let's ask him what the game's all about." He waved at the man coming down the steps, a box of assorted candies and fruits slung about his neck.

"Milk Duds! I haven't seen those in years!" Kate patted her pockets, looking distressed.

"No payment needed. Compliments of the house." The vendor smiled and handed her a small box. He squatted on the cement step and said companionably, "You people are curious about the tennis? It's a little different, but essentially the same game. We call it a tennis competition."

Kate helped herself to a Milk Dud. "Didn't look like a particularly fierce competition. Not in the proper sense of the word."

The vendor looked at her, engaged. "You're interested in language? Then you may know that 'competition' is from the Latin 'competere,' which means 'to strive together.' That's what they're doing down there, striving together. Each player respects her opponent and honors her with the very best game she can give. There will be a winner, but that's secondary to the game itself." He rose, gave them a friendly nod and went back up the stairs.

"Well." Kate gave a little laugh. "Do I feel put in my place, or what?"

"Have another Milk Dud," Frank said kindly. "Let me guess. They're your favorite comfort food, right?" He took one from the box she offered. "Next question. Why do you need comfort food?"

"Same reason you're sitting there cracking your knuckles, I suppose. I'm wondering if the fact that we've made it to Eastlight means we're all going to heaven, or whether we're going to lose someone else. And, of course, the big one—when will it be my turn to find out?"

"Can I have one of those?" Maggie said. The game had resumed, and Maggie held out her hand to Kate without taking her eyes from the action on court.

Kate handed her the box. "I don't know why you're worried, Maggie; you're the person who has her very own welcomer here in Eastlight. By the way, what did Val say when you called?"

"She said I could come visit her in the players's area after the match." Maggie said, her face glum. She scooped a Milk Dud from the box and bit into it.

Kate joined a round of applause. "That's a problem?"

"At first Val sounded glad I called, but actually I had to sort of invite myself. She's not a greeter anymore, you see. She has a new job and just came here from her community for the tennis tournament. She said she'd be happy to see me, but then she had to check and see whether it would be all right. It's like she wasn't sure if she was supposed to be with me." Maggie poked a searching finger into the Milk Dud box. "Or like maybe I wasn't supposed to be with her." She looked into the box, then up at Kate, her face pale. "Oh, no! I've eaten all your candy! Kate, I'm so sorry."

"Don't be a goose," said Kate. "We've all been chomping away at it."

But Maggie looked stricken. She covered her mouth, her hand pressed against her lips. She glanced toward the aisle and for a moment seemed about to head for the inner hallways of the stadium. Then she lowered her hand to her lap where it clasped the other, fingers laced together, and sank back in her seat.

"Better get to your friend if you want to see her," Frank said a moment later over the crowd's applause. "They're shaking hands down there. Looks like the game's over."

Maggie hesitated, then ran down the stadium stairs toward the players.

Kate bit her lip. "I don't know what I was thinking of, handing her that whole box of candy." She rose and began picking her way along the crowded aisle.

Frank shrugged into his jacket and followed her. "Yeah, the bulimia's seemed pretty much under control."

"You've noticed."

"Of course." Frank patted his pocket and pulled out three pamphlets. "By the way, I left most of these back at the hotel; the ones containing general information about Eastlight I thought we could share when we're together at dinner. But I brought along some for you guys to take a look at. Here, see what you think," he said, handing them to Kate.

"They gave you these at the Visitors' Center?" She looked at the top one and then the second. "Who's the joker? They're blank."

"All of them?"

"No wait, this one has printing on it." Kate read it silently. When she raised her head a bright spot of red stained each cheek. "Have you read this?"

Frank held out his hand, and Kate gave it to him reluctantly. He glanced at it. "It's a folder of blank paper to me," he said. He handed it to Patrick. "What do you make of it?"

Patrick examined it. "Nothing," he said. "Okay, what's up?"

"Last night when I was going over these pamphlets I found one I was sure was meant for me," Frank said. "It was an announcement of a meeting covering a subject I don't particularly want to share with any of you at the moment." The memory of the shattering vision that came when he'd read the pamphlet stopped him momentarily. Frank's head lowered.

Who would have thought the rat-like little man was innocent? Who would have thought anyone would confess to such a disgusting crime if he hadn't done it? Harvey Sable, that's who. *Harvey Sable.* At last he'd been able to put a name to the pale, stooped waiter he'd seen at the mountain restaurant early in their travels. Last evening he had learned what he should have known as an experienced cop, what he would have realized years ago in that interrogation room if he hadn't been so certain he was right. That if a person was vulnerable enough, and without the intellectual and physical resources to withstand it, days and nights of unrelenting questioning by a couple of determined cops could make him confess to just about anything. Even when Harvey had committed suicide before the trial, Frank hadn't given it all that much thought. One rat less. But the wan little man who had appeared in his hotel room last night had been innocent. At least of the crime Frank had been so sure he'd committed.

"*I'm Harvey Sable.*" The little man had looked at Frank reproachfully. "*Why'd you treat me like that, Frank? Why did you and your partner lean on me like you did? I didn't do it, you know. I told you and told you, but you didn't believe me.*"

Frank had seen nothing but baleful truth in the pale eyes. His hand reached to ease the darting pain in his chest. He'd been so sure. What could he say to this man he'd wronged, whom he'd pushed to his pitiful limit and beyond? "We . . . I shouldn't have done that," he mumbled at last. "I'm sorry."

Harvey cracked his knuckles. "*You should be,*" he said. "*You sure should be.*"

And before Frank could ask if there was anything he could possibly do to make up for the damage he'd done so long ago, Harvey turned and simply vanished. Frank stared at the space Harvey had occupied. Was Harvey Sable a rat? Maybe. But apparently he had not committed the grisly crime of which Frank had personally convicted him. Frank had spent a long, sleepless night thinking about it.

Now Frank gave his head an abrupt shake. "Looks as though there's one of these pamphlets directed to each of us and only the person involved can read it. I don't know about yours, but mine had a list of places and times, and suggested an early sign-up."

Kate flicked her folder from Patrick's hands and studied it. "Mine's a symposium, and it says here the hotel concierge will arrange to sign up participants." Kate smacked the paper against her skirt. "I thought the idea was to stick together. Do we really want to participate in separate events?"

Patrick didn't answer. He had been reading one of the two remaining pamphlets, his shoulders hunched. He handed the last pamphlet back to Frank, his face grim. "This must be Maggie's," he said. "See you later. I'm going back to the hotel."

Frank and Kate glanced at each other as Patrick darted down the steep steps and disappeared into the crowds leaving the stadium. "I only hope the people who put together these meetings have some idea of what a genuinely nice guy Patrick is," Kate said. "Oops." She covered her mouth with her hand. "How quickly we forget where we are and why."

"Care to translate?"

"Not really. Let's go get Maggie."

((

The vision came to Kate as unexpectedly as an afternoon shower on a sunny day. One moment Frank and she were edging their way past chatting tennis fans and the next she saw Howard sitting at his desk in the study of their Wisconsin home. His chair was half-turned from his desk as he read from the top of a stack of papers spewing from the printer. A satisfied twitch at the corners of his mouth was all he allowed himself, but Kate felt his pride and sense of accomplishment, his relief at having finished this task. It was as if his feelings were her own.

"You did it, darling!" she said. "I knew you could."

"Done at last," Howard murmured to himself. His expression softened. "Thanks to you, my love. Thanks to the pig-headed, no-excuses-taken confidence you've always had in me." He stared into space. "Kate?" he whispered. "You're here. You're here with me, aren't you?"

Kate could not speak. The bond she felt between herself and the man at the desk was so strong, contained such joyous promise, it took her breath away. Sheer happiness flooded every part of her.

Howard's eyes filled with unshed tears, but the smile on his lips deepened, and in that moment Kate knew he was aware of that bond too.

"What's the matter, Kate?"

Kate found herself clutching the railing leading to the stadium stairs. She met Frank's worried gaze and wailed. "Oh, Frank, why did you have to interfere?" She caught herself and gulped. "Oh, dear, I *am* sorry. Truly, truly sorry. I'm really so grateful; I don't mean to be greedy. Look, I'll sign up. I'll sign up, and I'll go to that symposium and learn all I can and—"

"Kate, what are you babbling about?"

The noise that erupted from Kate was something between a chuckle and a sob. She took a steadying breath. "I wasn't talking to you, Frank," she said at last. "I . . . I think I was asking the Lord to forgive me. I think maybe, at last, I was really praying."

"What happened?"

"I saw Howard. I saw my husband."

"Here? Just now?"

Kate nodded.

"That glow in your eyes should have told me," Frank said quietly. "It must have been wonderful. Sorry I interrupted."

"I don't think there is such a thing as an interruption here. I was given a gift. And when it was time for it to end—" Kate stopped and began again, her smile crooked, "when it was time for it to end, instead of being thankful I cuss out the nearest innocent bystander."

Chambers grinned at her. "It's been forty years since anyone's called me innocent." He stretched to see over the heads in front of them. "Hey, look, there's Maggie. Maggie, we're over here!" He waved the remaining brochure at her.

"You're not going to give her that?" Kate said. "It's probably telling her about lectures on eating disorders, and if there's anything Maggie doesn't need right now, it's that." Then she saw his frown and continued more uncertainly, "Don't you think that after the Ryan episode the girl needs some breathing space?"

"Time was I might have agreed with you," Frank said. He looked at the folder in his hand as though surprised to find it there. "But I was given these to hand out. Don't figure it's up to me to decide who gets what when."

Kate didn't agree or disagree. She wasn't listening. Her nose twitched like a bird dog sighting quail. "Who's the man with Maggie?" she asked. "The one who just put his arm around her?"

20

"Hi, I'd like you to meet Tony," Maggie said. She slipped out from Tony's embrace and gave a little skipping step as she approached them. "He says there's a bunch of elite gymnasts here. He's going to introduce me, arrange for me to work out with them."

The man beside her wasn't much taller than Maggie, but his trim, lithe body was smoothly muscled, something made abundantly apparent by a shirt that fit him like a second skin. Deep laugh lines carved the tanned skin around his bright blue eyes. "As if Maggie Stevens would need an introduction to any gymnast. The folks around here have been waiting for her to show up. I'm surprised you've been able to keep the kid away from the gym this long."

Frank nodded a cautious greeting. "We've been traveling a lot since we got here." He shifted his attention to Maggie. "Val introduce you to Tony?" he asked.

"I really didn't have a chance to talk to Val. First I had to wait while she got dressed, and then her coach had to talk to her. In the meantime, Tony and I got to talking and, and—"

"And I just spirited her away," Tony said, laughing.

"Give her the folder, Frank," Kate snapped.

Chambers looked at Kate, eyebrows raised.

"Give it to her."

"For me? Thanks." Maggie stuffed the brochure into her backpack without looking at it. "So . . . I'm glad you guys saw me because I didn't want to have to leave without telling you where I was going, because, you see, Tony has his car outside, and he wants to get away before the parking lot starts filling up with people coming to the next event and—and, hey, where's Patrick?"

"Back at the hotel reading his brochure. We each got one." Kate patted hers. "By the way, you intend to be back by dinner, I hope. Frank and I have something special planned."

Maggie pursed her lips. "I hadn't thought about it, but if you two have gone and arranged something special—" Her face brightened. "How about if Tony comes too?" She turned to him. "Can you?"

"Sure thing. That is, if I'm not butting in."

"Not at all." Kate gave him a thin smile. "Maggie, try to find a minute to take a look at that brochure, will you? And, oh, Tony, is there a way we could reach you in case we have to get hold of you for any reason?"

"Absolutely. Here's the number of my hotel." Tony took a piece of paper from the back pocket of his jeans and scribbled on it. "I'm looking forward to this evening. See you then." He put a hand beneath Maggie's elbow and steered her toward the exit.

"What was all that about?" Frank said.

"You didn't feel it?" Kate hugged her arms about her chest. "Duplicity oozed from every pore. I wouldn't trust that man to take out my garbage. How Maggie could let herself—"

"Hold on. I didn't particularly cotton to the guy, but how come you know he's a sleazebag from a couple of minutes's conversation? And anyway, what's this about us making 'special dinner plans'?"

"I trust you to come up with a restaurant that serves the kind of food you think Maggie would like." She sniffed. "As for Tony, I'm not sure why I feel the way I do about him. Maybe he reminds me of too many BMOC's I've seen who've played havoc with my students. I'm positive Maggie shouldn't trust him. I swear, that girl attracts rotten men the way a ripe peach gathers fruit flies."

Frank frowned, ignoring the exiting and entering spectators who eddied about them. "How come you're so certain about this one and you hadn't a clue about Ryan?"

"None of us had a clue about Ryan; I think maybe it's getting easier to see what's behind facades here."

"Okay, say you're right. We're in Eastlight. Isn't this a pretty safe place?"

"I don't think everyone here is necessarily headed for heaven. Frank, it's not like me to make snap judgments, especially when I've nothing to go by but intangibles, but—and this may sound crazy—there's a kind of aura about him that disgusts me. I know he was perfectly polite, but it was all I could do to speak civilly to him."

"You think you were civil? The guy could have used your words instead of ice cubes in his lemonade." Chambers's voice held amusement, but his eyes were serious. "I have to admit I'm not too happy about him myself, but what can we or should we do? Ever since Marjorie left us, I've had this feeling it's time for each of us to go in the direction the person feels drawn." He guided Kate through the crowd toward the open doors of the stadium. "I'm sure one of the reasons we were put together was so we could help each other, but there's a fine line between helping and interfering."

Kate bit her lip. "I know, I know."

"In this case, I say we trust your feelings about this guy of Maggie's and keep an eye on him—and her."

They didn't speak again until they got to the van.

"You said you don't think everyone here is headed for heaven," Frank said, his voice lowered. "Well, we've watched Marjorie Harrison hightail it to a place neither of us wants to be and seen Ryan James dragged off somewhere I don't even want to think about." He gave her a level look as he opened the van door for her. "Think we have a chance, Kate?"

Kate shook her head. "I don't know. When I saw Howard, I thought so for sure. But—I just don't know."

❨

"You left Maggie a message with the desk clerk?" Frank asked Kate as the maitre d' seated her opposite him.

"And one in plain sight on the pillow of her bed," she said. "You left a note in Patrick's room?"

Frank nodded. "Concierge said he came in and signed up for whatever was scheduled for him, but where he went then is anyone's guess. I figure he wouldn't take off without letting us know, so he ought to get it."

Kate looked around the restaurant. "Whatever made you pick Thai food?" she said.

"I like it. Besides, whaddaya bet everyone will get the kind of meal he likes anyway, Thai restaurant or not."

"I keep forgetting. It's so much the same and yet so different here." She leaned back. "We haven't done anything since we got to Eastlight except watch a tennis match and sightsee, but I'm so dog-gone tired I could fall asleep right here. It feels good to kick back and relax."

"I don't know about you, but a lot of my time seems to be spent going over things I've done and haven't done. And let me tell you, it's not easy." Frank rubbed his chin. "In fact, it's downright exhausting."

Kate gave him a commiserating look. "You, too?" She drummed her fingers on the table. "Why don't they come?"

Frank stood up. "How about that? I was wondering whether thinking about them might hurry up the process. Hey, there Maggie. Where's Tony?"

Maggie slid into the chair Frank held for her. "I told Tony I thought maybe I shouldn't have invited him since this was something special you'd arranged. He didn't like it much, but he said he understood." Maggie sat stiffly, twisting her hands and looking down at the straight, perfect fingers of her right hand, the unmarked palm of her left. "Actually, I didn't much care whether he liked it or not." She picked up the menu and became absorbed in the list of entrees. "I read the folder," she said.

Kate glanced at Frank. She gave an almost imperceptible shrug.

"Going to sign up for the classes?" Frank said.

Maggie looked up. "Who said anything about classes?"

"Your brochure. Didn't it offer lectures or classes?"

"Don't give me that. You know what it offered. It was promoting some kind of support group thing. I can just see you two saying 'Maggie obviously has a problem, but instead of talking to her let's give her this pamphlet and see if she bites.'"

"Wait a minute! We didn't read each other's brochures," Kate said. "We can't. Mine offered a symposium, and I'm sure Frank's told him about something entirely different. We gave that one to you because neither Frank nor Patrick nor I could see any printing on it, just blank paper. Really, Maggie, that's the only reason we knew it must be yours."

Unconvinced, Maggie stared at Kate, her eyes cool. "I read the whole thing while I was waiting for Tony outside the ice cream parlor. We were passing by, and all of a sudden Tony stops the car and says he's going inside to get me a chocolate sundae. I didn't ask him to or anything—he just said he wanted to get it for me. Anyway, I'm sitting in the car, and suddenly I thought about the folder and your saying I should be sure to read it. So I did." Maggie took a breath. "I don't care what they say; it wasn't about me. No way. It was all this stuff about people who want to control other people, how when they feel helpless, they use all sorts of ways to try to get some kind of control." Maggie's lips quivered. "I'm not the one who should be signing up for the workshop. Just about everyone I've ever known would be better candidates. Ever since I was a little girl, everyone—from Coach to Mom to Jerry—had so much say over what I did that sometimes it felt like there was hardly a piece of me left that was really me." She lifted her chin. "I'm not going to sign up for that group thing, but I decided I didn't need that sundae Tony was ordering either. Nobody's going to tell me what I should or shouldn't do. Not Tony nor anyone else. I only came here because you arranged this special dinner thing, and I'm leaving as soon as we're done."

There was a moment's silence. "Sounds good to me," said Kate. "Just one thing and I'll shut up. Rather than rejecting 'the group thing' out of hand, why not ask someone like the concierge at the hotel to tell you more about it?" She saw Maggie's mulish expression. "Okay, cancel the concierge. How about someone else?"

"Who?"

"God."

Maggie looked at Kate, uncomprehending.

"Have you thought of praying?"

"Oh sure, and how's God going to answer? By fax or something?"

"Remember where we are, Maggie," said Frank. "Anything's possible. Now, why don't we deep-six the pamphlet/brochure conversation? Or at least have a cease-fire and talk about something else. Where's Patrick? It's time he showed up so we can—" Frank looked up and waved. "I like the way things work around here," he said as Patrick came through the revolving door, walked up to the maitre d' and was directed to their table.

Chambers motioned Patrick to the remaining seat. "Glad to see you," he said with a grin. "I was going to be seriously irritated if you didn't show." He tapped his water glass. "Folks, this dinner was arranged in honor of a very special occasion. Kate, you might not have had this in mind when you told Maggie about it, but maybe you knew more than you thought." Frank raised his glass. "Been thinking about it, and I'm guessing that tonight may well be the last time we're together."

Kate's mouth opened, then closed again. The color washed from Maggie's face. Only Patrick remained unmoved. He stared at his water glass and then lifted it. "Let's give first prize to the Chicago cop; obviously he's been paying attention. I just asked at the hotel. We're not booked there beyond tomorrow."

Maggie darted a look around the table. "Where are we going?" she whispered.

"I think we'll be staying with whatever group we've signed up with," Kate said slowly. She twisted her fork between her fingers and then put it down, aligning it carefully beside her plate. "My folder gave directions; says the place is a short walk from the hotel."

"So's mine." Frank took a drink of water and held up his glass. "Just in case I'm right—and from what Patrick says it looks like I am—I want to take this opportunity to say that I've enjoyed being with you people. Wish Sven and Clare could be here with us, but from what Kate says, it looks like they're gonna make it, bless 'em." His eyes swept his three companions. "I'll miss you. I'll even miss Marjorie, though I couldn't tell you why." Frank's gaze came to rest on Maggie, who was staring into space. He cleared his throat. "Guess I should stop blathering. Let's order."

Patrick stood up. "Not me. I'm going back. Just came by to let you know what's happening," he said.

"Patrick, no!" Kate said.

"Stay, please." Maggie held out a hand to him.

"Look, I don't want to be a drag, but I can't sit and shmooze." Patrick looked down at them. "I have things to do—one of which is to apologize if I've said anything that hurt any of you. I do that sometimes. Bad habit of mine." The hands at his sides were balled into fists, the knuckles white. "I've come to understand a lot about myself on our trip. I've always wanted to be the best, had to be, and as far as my music, I nearly was. Hugged that feeling to me and told myself it was everyone else who was lacking. I always considered I was a loner because of being 'different,' but I know now it was partly 'cause I liked it. I liked sitting in my organ loft above the rest of the congregation, enjoyed that feeling of being apart and above everyone else." He turned his head, and when he looked back, his eyes were bright with tears. "But enough about that. There's another thing I want to tell you." He paused. "I love you people. I've come to feel a real part of our little group during this trip. It's been wonderful. And I wanted to say thanks." He turned and bolted for the door.

"I think I may cry," said Kate.

"You do and I may have to clip you one," Frank growled. He wiped his eyes with the napkin crushed in his beefy hand. "Waiter, I think we'll order now."

(

Frank took a program from the man at the door and walked into the sloping lecture hall. The room was smaller than the auditorium at the Guesthaus; he estimated it would hold about a hundred people. Although only a quarter full, the hall's seats were being rapidly taken by people who streamed past him, most singly but some in groups. Frank took the folder from his pocket and stared at it. Did he really have a problem with wanting to dominate people? Frank's hand rose to rub the back of his neck where the barest suggestion of a headache niggled. He'd never thought of himself as a control freak, but he'd been considering the possibility ever since he'd read the pamphlet, ever since Maggie had told them about hers. And ever since last night when he'd lain awake remembering Harvey Sable's interrogation. Realizing what a terrible injustice he and his partner had perpetrated—on Harvey, on the whole system they had sworn to uphold.

Was having that kind of power part of why he liked being a cop? Partly. In the beginning he'd enjoyed the opportunity being a cop gave him to make people do what he wanted. But over the years, he'd fought the tendency. Thought he'd pretty much put it behind him. But maybe not. Marge certainly hadn't thought so. And—heaven help him—neither had Harvey Sable.

Frank shoved the folder back in his jacket pocket and looked over the crowd. He already missed having Kate and Patrick around, and, yeah, little Maggie, too. For the first time since he'd gotten over the divorce, he felt lonely. He understood only too well Patrick's declaration that he'd loved the group, loved being part of it.

Frank shifted his position and gave an impatient shrug. Having to stand here and wait for whatever was going to happen to begin was beginning to get to him. Waiting had never been something he did well. Would it help if he thought of Ben? Would Ben appear? What could Frank say to him if he did?

"Frank!"

He whipped about to see Kate's astonished face. "Kate!"

"What are you doing here?" they asked in chorus.

"This is where they've scheduled my program," said Kate.

"You're kidding! Mine, too." Frank took her elbow. "Come on; let's sit here at the back."

"So we'll be able to see Patrick if he comes? Or Maggie?" said Kate. "But Frank, we're all so different. The pamphlets offered such different sessions for each of us. Do you think we'd really be brought to the same place?"

"Exactly what did your folder say, Kate?" He saw the guarded look on Kate's face and said quickly, "Mine told me more than I wanted to know about something called the 'love of dominion.' Talked about people who are workaholics and try to order their world by having things their own way, about people who have to put their stamp on everything."

Kate's chin went up. "Mine talked about teachers who tend to dominate, both in the classroom and out of it. It didn't exactly claim they're all egomaniacs, but—" She gave a short laugh. "Listen to how I keep it all safely in the third person—'they' and 'teachers,' never 'me' or 'I.' Sheesh. The whole thing was a verbal portrait of me."

Frank stared into the distance. "The need to dominate, to control. Remember what Maggie said? I wonder if that's the common denominator?"

"For our group?"

"Marjorie sure fit the bill in spades, wouldn't you say? A major player in the manipulate-and-dominate area. And from what we heard of his history, Ryan's off the scale when it comes to needing to dominate other people. I don't know about the two kids. Maybe theirs is more the potential of some form of wanting to control. And Patrick said last night that he—"

"What about me?"

Patrick stood in the aisle, smiling at them. It wasn't his usual self-conscious grimace, it was a real smile. "Didn't think you'd see me again, did you?" he said, slipping into the seat next to Kate.

For an answer, Kate put an arm around his shoulder. "I don't know when I've been so glad to see anyone." She patted his thin back. "Except Howard, of course. We were just discussing the need to control or dominate. Somehow I never thought you had that kind of problem."

Her bluntness didn't seem to bother Patrick. "So you figured out the connecting thread between us," he said. "I think it's part of the make-up of everyone on the van, each one of us in our different ways. But, thank God, it wasn't what I loved most of all."

Frank looked at Patrick from beneath beetled brows. "You're telling us you *know* what you loved most of all when you were in the world?"

"I'm not absolutely sure, at least not yet, but I'm beginning to see what makes me who I am. There's music, of course. But it's not only music itself; I love being able to give the joy of music to others, my own music and other people's. It's been the central part of my life. I haven't always been kind, and I haven't always done what I knew was right; but most of the time, I did try. And since I tried, a lot of my other aspects can be—what did Shunji say?—can be overlooked or set aside. I'm not too sure about that part yet."

"Who's Shunji?"

Patrick leaned forward eagerly. "I stopped by the concierge last night before I went back to my room," he said. "Said it was an emergency; I had to see someone, tell someone about the things that have been tearing me apart since we got here. So they called, and Shunji was sent to me. We talked all night. It was sort of like a crash course on what this place is all about. He told me it was good that I've been thinking about my faults, but maybe it was time I should cut out the wailing and breast-beating. I guess there weren't all that many times I sat in the organ loft feeling above it all. Shunji said all those times I was thinking about my life during those sermons, the times I realized I'd been petty or mean or really hurt someone and resolved to do something about it and then actually did—or tried to—well, they were more important than I knew. He said God doesn't want me to just concentrate on the lousy parts of my life while I'm here; I should remember the good parts, too." He stared at his hands. "I've been wondering where God is in all this. Turns out he's nearer than we knew, nearer than we have any idea. Y'know the sunlight that's filling this hall?"

"You're telling me it's God?"

"No, but it's a manifestation of his love, his wisdom. Shunji said that sometimes in heaven, God appears in the sun. In the world we came from, the sun gave heat and light; the sun in this one *is* heat because it's his love, and it *is* light because it's his truth or wisdom. Everything we have, everything we are, comes from those two things. Shunji told me—" Patrick spread his hands as though trying to encompass ideas so huge they defied explanation. "He explained all kinds of stuff I've thought about all my life but never understood, never even heard discussed. I still have a lot to learn before I'm ready for the next step, but I understand enough to know the next step is there for me to take if I want it, if I work at it." He examined his long-fingered, musician's hands, then looked up. "Shunji offered to take me to this place his wife and he run. It's real small, a sort of school that's run on a tutorial system. Shunji and his wife don't actually live there, but they'll be there every day for classes, and he has offered to be my tutor."

"Shunji and his wife are . . ." Frank found he had to hesitate before saying the word, "angels?"

"I always said you were quick, Frank." Patrick's grin took the sting from the words.

Frank's disbelief warred with acceptance. Acceptance won. He grinned and feinted a punch in Patrick's direction. "So you're going to school and have an angel for a teacher. Way to go, kid. But if you've got this scholarship or whatever, how come you're here with us?"

Kate shook her head in wry amusement. "I wondered about that, too. Why are you here, since it seems you know where you're going and we're sitting here without a clue?"

"Shunji said I could come by to let you guys know my good news, say goodbye before we leave," Patrick said. He looked around. "I was hoping Maggie would be here too."

Kate sobered. "I'm worried about that girl," she said. "Do you think she understands how important it is to sign up for the support group?"

"She'll do it," Patrick said.

"You know that?"

"Not for certain. But I've gotten to know her pretty well. Maggie's been exposed to a lot of bad stuff in her life, but I don't think she made it a part of her. The kid's kind and generous, and I'm willing to bet the choices she made before she came here reflect that. She'll sign up." He got up. "Look, I really gotta go." Still he hesitated. "I hope we see each other . . . later," he said.

"I sure hope so too." Frank held out a hand, and Patrick gripped it.

Kate rose. She kissed Patrick. "Go. Go find Shunji. If we see Maggie, we'll tell her you came to say goodbye." She pushed him toward the exit of the now nearly filled auditorium.

Patrick hurried off. By the time he reached the door, he was running.

"There's one good kid," Frank said, looking after him. "Even back at the clinic in Switzerland I was impressed by the way he noticed other people, how he cared about what was bothering them, how they were feeling."

"Once you get past the smart-aleck exterior, he's a love," Kate agreed. "And come to think of it, that facade's already changing, sloughing off like an old skin."

There was a rustling among the crowd as a woman walked across the stage. She was a large woman, and as she strode past a small, carved table that stood in the center of the stage, the diaphanous material of her flowing caftan billowed behind her, a flaming cloud of red and orange. She sailed to the podium at the left of the stage, came to rest behind it, and adjusted her voluminous sleeves. "Welcome." The rich music of her voice easily reached the farthest seat in the hall. "We're delighted you have chosen to join us," she continued. "After this first general meeting, some of you will remain with us, and some will be given information about where your instruction will continue."

"Mind if I join you?" The whisper came from beside them. Maggie Stevens scooted into the seat next to Kate that Patrick had vacated.

"Maggie, you came!" Kate leaned over and hugged her. "Bless your little pointed head."

"That lousy pamphlet," Maggie murmured. "I didn't want it to be me it was talking about. But, of course, it was. And I sure as heck didn't want to be in any stupid support group. Still don't, but I know I have to. So here I am. How come you guys are here?"

"Same type of problem as yours but different aspects of it," Kate said, tight-lipped. Surprising how much it hurt to admit it. She cleared her throat. "You know that support group you've been dreading so much?"

Maggie nodded.

"I have a sneaking hunch you're in the middle of your first meeting. Along with Frank and me."

"Really? I'm with you guys?" Maggie frowned. "Where's Patrick? Why isn't he here?"

"Patrick's okay. You don't need to worry about him," said Frank. "He was here a minute ago, said adios and went off to the next step of *his* specifically tailored future." He leaned over and gave Maggie's hand a squeeze. "Glad you decided to make it, kid."

Kate put a finger to her lips. "Listen."

"We like to take note of people who have had great difficulty in making the decision to come to us for instruction," the woman onstage was saying, "because when those for whom it is especially hard to seek help decide to come to us, it's a cause for special joy and celebration. And there are some of you here today for whom the decision was especially difficult," she said, scanning the audience.

Kate could feel Maggie tense beside her. This is definitely not a good idea. Oh, don't go there; please, please don't call attention to Maggie, Kate prayed.

The woman's smile broadened. "I won't call on anyone," she said, "but you know who you are, and I want to give you a special welcome. We're glad to have you take this next step with us. And now I'd like our ushers to pass out the assignments. We do this at the beginning of the program, so that you may take the time during the service to direct your thoughts and your thanks . . . " she paused, "to where it's appropriate."

Uniformed ushers, arms laden with baskets of envelopes, had already begun to deliver them to the first rows. The sound of tearing, rustling paper filled the room as the recipients ripped open their envelopes. The wanderers seated in the back row could see that, while most took what appeared to be a letter from their envelope, some slipped something solid from the packet and studied it.

"You'll note that your envelope is addressed to you alone," the woman's rich voice was saying. "After you've read your assignment to see where you will go next, we'll get on with the program."

An usher finally reached the upper row, handed Maggie an envelope, gave another to Kate. Kate felt her bulky envelope, opened it carefully and slipped a large, green oval from it.

Maggie already had a green oval in her hand. "Pass from East-light to the Academy," she read.

"That's what mine says too," Kate whispered.

The hand Frank reached out to receive his envelope shook with a noticeable tremor. His big fingers fumbled with the envelope and finally ripped it in half. A green oval fell to the floor with a clatter. Frank dove for it and capturing the disk, held it before him, squinting. He gave a huge sigh. "Mine, too," he said.

The woman at the podium tapped the microphone, and the buzz of conversation quieted. "I think we all would like to thank the One who led us through our life on earth and brought us here, the One who has provided for the next stage of your journey in this world." She waved a graceful arm toward the rear of the stage, the sheer material of her sleeve fluttering like an iridescent butterfly wing. "Jasper, would you lead us?"

The man who emerged from the wings wore a navy jacket, white shirt, and gray slacks. He carried a book that he carefully placed in the center of the small table. As he opened the book a flash of light shot from it, and the illumination in the room increased a hundred-fold, as though there had been a sudden surge of power. Jasper stood, his head lowered, then turned to face the expectant audience.

"Each of you has brought with you your particular idea of God," he said. "Some of these ideas are nebulous in the extreme, some are specific, all are informed by what you learned during your life on earth. Whatever your idea of God has been, it will become more clear, indeed, more accurate, as you take up your life here. In a moment, I am going to invite each of you to address the God you know." He turned to face the shining book and stood silent for several heartbeats. "Let us kneel in prayer," he said.

The three in the back row exchanged glances. "I have a feeling," Frank whispered, "the good stuff is about to begin."

· ABOUT THE AUTHOR ·

NAOMI GLADISH SMITH, a former teacher, is the author of *The Arrivals* (2004), which also is a Swedenborgian novel; the mystery *Buried Remembrance* (1977); and numerous essays and short stories that have been published in the annual anthology THE CHRYSALIS READER, *The Christian Science Monitor,* and *Interludes Magazine.* She is also a regular contributor to WBEZ, the National Public Radio station in Chicago, Illinois. Visit her web page at **www.naomigladishsmith.com.**

· ACKNOWLEDGMENTS ·

Anyone who has read the works of Emanuel Swedenborg knows how great a debt I owe to these books. I strongly recommend that those who want to know more about this vision of the afterlife go directly to the source and read one of the many translations of Swedenborg's *Heaven and Hell* that are available. In writing *The Wanderers,* I borrowed freely from the vivid descriptions of the spiritual world that are found in *Heaven and Hell* and in many of Swedenborg's other books. In fact, the whole concept of the imagined world of my story is derived from the writings of this eighteenth-century sage. For this and much more, I am truly grateful.

Thanks also to Mary Lou Bertucci, my able and patient editor, and to all the staff of the Swedenborg Foundation.

1. *The Wanderers* envisions a group traveling through a spiritual world that is neither heaven nor hell. Does a "world of spirits" where the newly arrived must learn about their true nature seem logical? How does the depiction of a self-judgment differ from or agree with judgment in various religious traditions?

2. Many of the characters in this book expand their outlooks on their journey. Which character do you feel becomes the most self-aware?

3. The question of love arises in several situations. Kate Douglas experiences visions of her husband Howard. Because of these, she comes to believe that Howard and she will be reunited after his death. Maggie Stevens's grandmother has a different husband in the afterlife from the man she was married to in her earthly life. The "gypsy" Bella is still in love with the man she loved on earth, the scheming Garcia. What do these stories suggest about the nature of true love?

4. The young lovers Sven and Clare are central to the book. At the end, it seems that they may eventually be united as a couple in heaven. How does the depiction of the two characters fore-shadow their possible redemption?

5. Frank Chambers had to make critical life-and-death choices in his job as a police detective. He undergoes a crisis of conscience when he reviews some of his decisions during his lifetime, in particular, his getting a confession out of an innocent man. Do you think that Frank may be forgiven for this act? Discuss the stresses of his profession that might have led him to make his choices.

6. The issue of bulimia is raised in the character of Maggie Stevens. Maggie's education requires that she face up to her eating disorder and how she used it as a way to control her life. Do you feel that this is a realistic depiction?

7. Two of the young men in the book, Patrick Riley and Ryan James, have had defining sexual encounters in their lives. Of the two, Patrick is the more concerned about being saved because of his sexual orientation, yet it is Ryan who is explicitly damned in the book. Discuss Patrick's character and what you think of his chances for salvation.

8. Frank encounters his son Ben in the afterlife. Ben, an autistic child who died at four years old, is now a grown and married man. How does Ben explain his adult angelic life? What is suggested from this encounter about the experiences of children who have died?

9. *The Wanderers* offers an unusual depiction of an afterlife. Ben tells Frank that there are multiple heavens, where like-minded angels live, while Ryan's captors indicate that some hells are worse than others. Does this idea make sense to you? How do you think it connects to the equally unusual depiction of judgment in the book?

10. Several of the main characters meet people they had known on earth. Maggie visits her grandmother; Frank sees his son Ben; Marjorie Harrison seeks out her stockbroker. What does the person each character meets tell us about his or her earthly life? Why is it necessary for them to meet again?